Momma's Purle

Bridget Davis

Murdock Publishing Company
A Division of Black and White Enterprises

Murdock Publishing Company
A Division of Black and White Enterprises

This is a work of fiction. The characters, incidents, and dialogues are products of the author's imagination and are not to be construed as real. Any resemblance to actual events or persons, living or dead, is entirely coincidental.

ISBN 0-9668865-0-X

Printed in the United States of America

To Linda
It was a pleasure
meeting you...

Enjoy!

Brett D.

ACKNOWLEDGMENTS

--I would like to thank my father Benjamin Davis for giving me life, parenting the best way that he knew how with what he had, and loving me unconditionally. Thank you, daddy, for all of your words of wisdom and positive words of encouragement that allowed me to believe that I could accomplish any goals that I set out to accomplish.

--I thank my children Racquel and Kenneth for being my children, adding the gift of motherhood to my life, and making each day challenging and fulfilling.

--Thank you to my husband, Bernie, my soul mate, for being you and loving me. Thank you for contributing more than your share to our relationship when I fell short.

--I thank all of my sisters Crystal, Cherilyn, Valli, and Fern for all of my experiences with them while growing up in Harlem that helped to mold my character.

--I would like to thank Lilith, Diane, Melissa, and Stephen Pincus for their participation in my life. Thank you, guys, for affording me the opportunity to see another side of life besides poverty at the age of seven.

ACKNOWLEDGMENTS

--Many thanks to my Editor, Beverly Kleinle.

--Thanks to my three best friends Rhonda Sally, Miriam Rodriguez, and Kim Jackson for being there for me when I needed your friendship most. You will truly always remain my home girls.

--To all of my aunts, uncles, and cousins. If I had to pick and choose all of my family members, I would pick all of you. With all of my love to the above mentioned.

--And I thank God for life!

Preface

Momma's Purle is a wonderful realistic story of the struggles of single black females who are left with the common obstacles and challenges of motherhood and relationships. The issues of poverty dealing with the means of substance abuse by our young men and women as an escape to get through such painful dilemmas of life are often consumed by the best of us. Statistically the numbers have gone down on those who are abusing heroin but with a large number of users of crack that is truly indicative of a large audience that reflects a need to know crowd out there. A need to know that any dependent personality leads to the loss of what is most important to us, family or life.

Momma's Purle has a universal appeal. Whether it is enjoyment, knowledge to a class of people who have nothing, or just strength to carry on when you're at your weakest point in life and feel that the odds are against you; we have all been there.

My theory of life is that if you never see or hear then you will never know. I know first hand about the issues that are quite prevalent in the poverty-stricken communities that have buried many of our fine young men and women. After growing up in Harlem in the Drew Hamilton Projects losing many friends to drugs and crime and a victim of crime myself, the pain continues to linger on.

There are many characters such as Sarah James out there who need to see a story similar to theirs and add hope to life. The intent of this story is to trigger a positive reaction and help to motivate a will to live in those who see no way out. After all, each and everyone one of us has a purpose in life, a story to tell. To find that purpose and live it, I believe is a challenge within itself....

Dedication

I dedicate this book to my mother Gloria Harris Davis, the Sarah in my life who devoted every moment in time to raising her daughters in Harlem. Her encouragement, words of strength that embraced the opportunity for me to succeed at whatever profession I chose; I thank her for all of her verbal ingredients bestowed upon me to allow me to wake up each morning and face each day with a humble beginning. To realize my dreams and take it to the reality of my highest potential, I thank you mommy. You are not here with me in the flesh to witness my achievements, but spiritually your presence will linger on within my heart eternally and continue to inspire me to reach the pentacles of success.

"Dr. Crane how long do you think it will be before I am able to go home? I miss my girls something terrible. They have no idea of where I'm at, whether I'm dead or alive. I've been here for three days, and three days seem like a lifetime when there is no contact with the outside world or your family. If I'm not allowed to use the phone again today, I think I'll just die."

Dr. Crane sat in his straight chair with his straight face expressionless. His black piercing eyes totally incapable of relating to my situation as a black female rearing five young girls. I am 32 years old, responsible for five young lives, and I'm afraid. I'm holding on to a distorted perception that my daughters can only accomplish half of their dreams or endeavors when all is called for. My challenge is this, I must guide these five young lives in Harlem to grow up and eventually become productive citizens in society. They must be able to function as productive citizens being independent and not having to rely on any man for financial or emotional solace holding on to the perception of reality that they can only accomplish half of their dreams or endeavors when all is called for because they are black females. I must instill in the girls that they absolutely cannot slip and slide through life doing just enough to get by. Above all, I do not want them to fail.

"Dr. Crane, it is extremely difficult and frightening when I know what I am supposed to do as a parent. What path to lead the girls? The problem is just not knowing how to get there. It is scary. Do you know what I mean?"

Dr. Crane didn't answer; he just looked at me. I continued to talk.

"Actually the real challenge is all of the obstacles that I must contend with while rearing the girls in the heart of Harlem without the financial or emotional support of a positive male role model."

"Dr. Crane all mothers want good fathers for their children. My philosophy is that a mother can only do the job of a mother. A mother cannot take the place of a father."

Dr. Crane looked at me with a blank expression on

his face, an expression that was evident of his lack of knowledge to my concerns. Or maybe he just didn't understand a word that I had said. What was I trying to say? It was obvious that he couldn't relate. Thinking to myself all of the books that Dr. Crane has read in medical school, research conducted on oppression, and psychology symposiums attended, there is no way that he will ever know the true meaning, the sense of survival and the feelings of maternal desperation from my perspective. In other words he can look out of my window, but he won't be able to see the other side.

Almost able to anticipate Dr. Cranes words before spoken after assessing his body language, "Sarah, until you are able to discuss the reason or reasons openly of your actions, the destructive behavior that resulted in your admission here at our psychiatric unit, that is how much longer it is going to take before you get to see your girls again."

Quietly I thought to myself, this man needs psychology experience from my world. I know for a fact that Dr. Crane doesn't give a rat's tail about my girls, myself, or how much they miss me and my need to see them. All I know is that I had better tell this Dr. a good story, true or false, right now before this session is complete and the decision is made to extend my stay here. As I took a deep breath I knew not only did I have the burden of telling this man a good story, but also the story had better be good.

Just from my intuition I know that he is at the stage in his profession where he needs to thrive. The good Dr. Crane began to speak, and I interrupted. Hmm. "Doctor the reason, well my rationale for my actions that landed me at this hospital, was that I was at a desperate point in my life where my judgement was off. I felt a feeling of worthlessness because I have not been able to promise my girls that one day they won't end up like me. When I say end up like me, I mean having nothing to offer another human being in life except a beautiful smile, a co-dependent needing another human being to validate my happiness in life, "not having a profession to rely on to become financially independent."

Because of all of the above neither am I able to

promise the girls that maybe one day they will no longer have to look through the glass of our kitchen window that bears a full view of garbage in the large alley way beneath the window.

"There is no grass out there, Dr. Crane, and we cannot open the kitchen window on a nice summer day. If we do the smell of garbage, and possibly the distinct odor of a decayed body to go along with some icebox soup just may ruin our appetites." Dr Crane, not saying a word, continued to look directly at me.

"Dr. Crane I feel worthless. I gave birth to those five beautiful girls, and I am not able to show them or provide them with a better lifestyle. They should be living in the country with grass and trees. They should be able to wake up to the sound of a rooster's call. And they should be able to smell the fresh air of day and night. I want them to play with small animals and collect lilys and daffodils from a near by field."

"I feel as if I have delivered the girls into a long life of bondage. I am not financially able to show them a better way of living, and it hurts. I feel worthless, inadequate. And these feelings are persistent with every waking moment of the day."

As I began to cry uncontrollably, I could see through my tears, that what I had just said was exactly what the Dr. wanted to hear. I could not believe that I was telling this man who I didn't know the truth. What is the truth? Maybe I haven't lost sight of reality, thinking and believing that I should have more to offer my children here in the ghetto.

I was shining a bright light into my heart for him to see every ache, every pain that I have endured since the moment I realized that I was the person that God had chosen to govern the lives of those precious girls, precious to no one except me.

Continuing to express my feelings to the Dr., hopefully making him understand that I am not crazy, however, just frustrated with my present situation that right now appears to be impossible to change. I continued to explain to the Dr. the reason for my actions that led me to this place. But I knew this was all formality to gain access to a different level of my mental stability. I had no problem with this agenda, especially knowing at the end of this mission I would be discharged. Speaking slowly and clearly, "I became extremely weak, Doc, for a moment. I tried to escape the pain. I know that what I did was stupid, selfish, and a knee jerk reaction that didn't warrant one at the time. If I could take back last Thursday, I would definitely do things differently."

As Dr. Crane looked up at me with his furrowed brows holding his pen and pad in his hands, I could tell that he wanted to hear more. Reaching over to his desk to grab a tissue to wipe the tears from my eyes thinking to my self, "That is it, Mr. I'm not handing over any more juicy emotions from my world." This session had become more painful than I had anticipated. All of a sudden, I felt as if I was lost for words.

Speaking in a monotone voice Dr. Crane said, "Attempting suicide, Sarah, was risky. You talked about missing your daughters. Have you thought about if you had succeeded with your suicide attempt, your girls would probably miss you forever taking into consideration that death is final."

Thinking to myself, where did I get the courage to do this? Was I truly that desperate to relieve the agony that had taken over my ability to think rationally? How could I resort to such drastic measures?

I couldn't feel any worse at this point about slitting my wrist. What in the devil was I thinking about? What a stupid and dangerous thing to do. Silence took over the room as Dr. Crane began writing in his pad. Apparently, his thoughts moved quicker than the ink flowed to the tip of his pen. My mind began to race with thoughts, thoughts of the welfare of my children and who was looking after them. Were they all right? What were they thinking? There are so many questions that I need answers to right now.

I couldn't go any further with this session without knowing the answers to my questions regarding my children. I interrupted the session that I was in with the Dr. to request to use the phone. Dr. Crane had no problem with the short interruption. I called home, and my mother in law answered the telephone. Thank God she was at the house with the kids. I guess my husband, Lee, must still be at work from last week (thinking sarcastically). I am not sure if he is aware that I am in the hospital. I could see that Dr. Crane was listening to my entire conversation as I spoke. His upper body moved toward my direction extending his ear beyond his shoulder. You would think that he would be a little more discreet.

While speaking with my mother in-law, Bootsey, she could not answer any of my questions. The two youngest girls were sitting next to her on the sofa, and the phone cord could not extend into the next room. If I couldn't count on anybody else in the world, I could count on Bootsey. She had come all the way from New Jersey with her bad knees and all. Bootsey did get the chance to tell me that the girls were fine. Exactly what I needed to hear.

As I looked through Dr. Crane's office window around the big room I could feel that surely these people here were all crazy. I knew that I did not belong here. Some of them appeared to be lifeless, their faces without any expressions. All I knew was that I wanted to get out of here right away before I started to look like them. The lord knows that I am far from crazy, or am I?

Finally Dr. Crane was finished writing in his pad. Raising his head, he looked at me with an expression of satisfaction and said "Sarah I do not feel the need to keep you here any longer. You have been able to openly discuss your problems, the pain that you have experienced that led up to the events that took place last Thursday. There is just one more question that I need an answer to."

Oh No! At that point I could feel the heat rising under my skin. For some reason I thought that we had gotten beyond the question and answer point that validated my sanity. I thought that I was home free as far as the question and answer session was concerned. In a high pitched weak voice I said while on the verge of tears due to the frustration that had entered my belly. "What is it that you need to know

Dr. Crane?"

Folding his hands on his desk in front of him, his body language revealing his superiority with a dash of exuberant control as he sat with perfect posture his head upright and chin outward said, "Sarah if you should experience those same feelings of despair in the future how would you handle things differently?"

A feeling of relief came over me; I could feel the heat leaving my body quickly and my skin cooling off. Thinking to myself, this is an easy question.

"I have experienced despair in the past, Dr. Crane, and I have handled it well. I have gotten through each and every obstacle with the help of music, poetry and cooking. These pleasures have been the source of my strength in the past setting me free of the despair and pain that lived in the pit of my gut giving me the instant relief that was needed to get through that day."

I continued to explain to the Dr. that living one day at a time was the key to my longevity. I am here now because I allowed my emotional distress to overcome my perception of reality. Feeling totally confident with this answer now perhaps Dr. Crane will understand that I truly am in control of my life. As human beings we are all subject to clouded thoughts that can distort the reality of our perception allowing us to fall short of perfection as would be expected when life is not going the way one would anticipate. "Dr. Crane, truly I want to live. Right now, I think that is what matters most."

The Dr. stood to his feet, glancing quickly at his watch saying, "Sarah, I am completely satisfied with the outcome of our session. I'll get the papers ready for your discharge along with the appointment dates for your weekly follow-up visits. Sarah, you will be seeing Dr. Stokes for follow-up visits. Dr. Stokes is the director of our psychiatry department here at Harlem Hospital."

Instead of having to look up to Dr. Crane during our conversation because he was standing and I was sitting, I stood to my feet also. I smiled and extended my hand out to shake his hand totally forgetting about my wrist being wrapped with thick white curlex bandage a reminder of my attempted suicide. A feeling of complete embarrassment came over me. I dropped my head no longer able to look at Dr. Crane's face but looking down at the floor without an ounce of self-esteem left in me. He handed me a prescription for medicine that he said would take the edge off of life. Was he being sarcastic or professional?

Walking very fast toward the exit sign, I exited the front entrance of the hospital and threw the prescription in the garbage. I didn't trust this Dr., and I wasn't going to put anything in my mouth called Thorazine. It sounded like a pill that would control your every thought taking away ones' own thoughts and individuality.

CHAPTER TWO
BACK HOME WITH THE GIRLS

After exiting the hospital I looked up, and at that moment my bus pulled up. What perfect timing! Everything would work out fine if the rest of my life fell into place like this. It felt great to be out of that hospital. The bus ride was great. A few familiar faces from the neighborhood sat around on the bus. I got off of the bus at 114th street and 8th avenue. All I could think about was my girls. God I missed them. I knew that I had a great deal of explaining to do, not to the three youngest girls but to the two oldest, Marcey and Purle.

Walking quickly after getting off of the bus I could see my two youngest girls, Olivia and Kim, jumping rope. My, My, My, those sweet girls can jump some double dutch. All the girls in the neighborhood jumped double dutch.

There's not much more to do in the neighborhood besides free lunch in the summer time at the public school, double dutch jump rope, and an annual block party. There are Daisy's boys dancing in the middle of the crowd again. Those boys love to dance. Every time that I see them they're shuffling around with their feet not missing a beat.

Those boys have rhythm like I have never seen before. How in the world could they shuffle around and move so quickly on their feet on such a hot day wiping the sweat away with one-hand and snapping their fingers with the other hand. Those boys have the rhythm that I have never seen in my life. Whenever you hear music, you can bet that you will see Daisy's boys dancing to the sound of it. I guess its better than being strung out on drugs or robbing people in the neighborhood.

With President Nixon calling it quits to the Vietnam War, all you see in the neighborhood is heroin addicts returning home from the war. It is a pathetic sight, a shame to see so many parents broken hearted.

The fact is that their sons are no longer able to deal with waking up each day able to cope with life. Either their sons are returning home in body bags, or returning home with the profound inability to cope with waking up each morning or afternoon to the sounds of explosive devices within the confines of their minds, setting off a reaction of war within their spirit. Often their families become vulnerable as the targets of enemies perpetuated by the bloody aftermath embedded into their memory. Not able to make a true distinction between friend or foe, hostility and anger surfacing with out prediction often leaves the aftermath of severe pain. Therefore, what we have in this community is an overabundance of drug abuse used as a tool to escape the pain of the past allowing an escape into a world of emotional freedom.

As I began to walk closer to the apartment building I could see the same faces from afar that I saw the day that I left. Everyone who I saw the day that I left assumed their same seats on the stoop, and some of the neighbors had on the same clothes. I knew that time hadn't stopped, but it sure feels like it did.

This must be the hottest day of the year. The humidity is brutal, and this long sleeved blouse isn't helping me at all. "Mamma, Mamma," Olivia and Kim were yelling as they spotted me a half a block away running right into me.

"Hey how are my two favorite girls?"

They spoke at the same time, "Fine."

"Mamma, where have you been?" Kim yelled out.

I hesitated responding to Kim's question noticing all of the nosy busy bodies sitting on the stoop neighbors out of hibernation with all of their tentacles out searching for the information, the juicy stuff to pass on to the next bunch that will sit and watch when their shift is up.

"Hush baby. I'll tell you all about where I've been when we get upstairs."

Olivia shoved Kim on the shoulder and said, "Hush Kim. You know that we're not supposed to talk about our family business outside," whispering in Kim's ear," especially in front of Mrs. Noobey."

Thinking to myself my sweet Olivia was right. That is exactly what I have told my girls many times. Never discuss family business in public.

No sooner than the words left Olivia's lips, there sat Mrs. Noobey on the stoop in her usual spot. If there is something that you wanted to find out in the neighborhood, all you had to do was ask Mrs. Noobey. She knew everything. And what she didn't know she made up. No one ever had to walk down the street to the number whole to find out the daily numbers. Mrs. Noobey would put up the amount of fingers to signify the daily numbers to whoever entered the apartment building. I would say about 90 percent of the tenants in the building placed number bets at the neighborhood number whole. The runners were the people who took the bets into the number hole; and when there was a winner, the runner received a percentage of the winnings.

I was happy that I decided to put a long sleeved shirt on before leaving the hospital. If not, the welcome wagon on the stoop would have surely noticed the bandage around my wrist.

"Hey Sarah, where have you been?" Mrs. Noobey asked. "I haven't seen you in about a week."

I responded to Mrs. Noobey's question without hesitation, "Ask me no questions, and I'll tell you no lies." With a half grin on my face I knew that this response would piss her off. She is so nosy, I thought to myself! Her name should be Nosy Noobey.

I could hear Mrs. Noobey whispering to Gladys Fletcher another nosy neighbor as I walked through the entrance of the apartment building "I heard her husband beat her so bad that the ambulance had to carry her out on a stretcher."

I just laughed to myself, shook my head, and winked

my eye at Olivia and Kim because they'd also heard what Mrs. Noobey had said. By the looks on their faces I knew that I didn't have to respond to the nonsense that had uttered from Mrs. Noobey's lips. Olivia and Kim had enough sense to know that Mrs. Noobey didn't have a clue to any insight regarding our family business.

Before I could get into the apartment the girls began to complain. "Mamma, Bootsey was mean to us while you were gone," the girls whined. "She spanked us, and she didn't let our friends come up stairs to play with us."

I said, "Well Kim, Olivia, you know that Bootsey does the very best that she can by you girls. Bootsey came all the way from Hoboken N.J. to look after you girls while mommy was away, everything Bootsey needed to do for herself she saved it for later just to come to take care of you girls."

Kim began to pout, because I didn't see things the same way her little eyes saw things. She began to pout while twisting her braid on the top of her head as she often did when she was distressed.

"She's mean," Olivia said.

"She's not mean, Olivia," I responded as I continued to walk up the stairs, panting and out of breath just at the second level with two more levels to go.

We lived on the fourth floor. No elevators were working as usual. "Bootsey is strict, but she loves you girls dearly"

"No, she don't," Olivia said. "She is mean, and I want her to go home now."

I just smiled at the girls while panting out of breath barely able to make it up the last flight of stairs without gasping for air.

Finally, we were on the fourth floor. Olivia pushed open the door to the apartment yelling, "Marcey, Purle, Madison, Mommy is home."

"Oh Sarah, Sarah," Bootsey cried extending her short arms out to embrace me as I walked into the apartment." Bootsey stood about 5ft tall weighing about 140 to 150 pounds. She had a round face with beautiful straight silver hair that she kept parted on the side outlining her face like a picture frame. Everybody called her Bootsey because she wore short ankle boots different colors and different styles all the year around.

Looking around the apartment I could see that Bootsey kept everything in order while I was gone. My goodness was I happy that she was here. How would the kids have managed without her? It's plain and simple they would not have. Although our furniture is old and worn and the living room drapes don't match in color with the furniture, the apartment was squeaky clean with the fresh smell of pine. This definitely helped the appearance of our worn furniture that seemed to have taken on the personalities of the people living within the same confines thereof. Bootsey couldn't cook, but she could sure clean a house.

"Wo!" I sighed as I flopped down on the sofa loosing my balance half way down. The sofa was down on the floor. Making it known to everyone that I was tired, and hungry and kicking off my sandals, "It feels so good to be home."

"You must be hungry baby doll," Bootsey said. She often called me baby doll. "I was just getting ready to send Marce, and Purle up the street to Sonny's on 7th avenue to get some fish and chips."

Reaching down into my purse, I pulled out a twenty dollar bill and handed it over to Bootsey. At the very second that I was handing Bootsey the twenty dollar bill, she pushed my hand away. "This one is on me," she said. Although I knew Bootsey meant well, she was on such a tight fixed income that I could not allow her to pick up the tab for the fish and chips.

Responding quickly to her generous gesture I said, "Oh, you cannot pay for this. I need change for a twenty-dollar bill. You can pick up the tab next time, Bootsey," I said. What a quick response. Yes, I still had it the witty quick thinking on my feet personality that had gotten me thus far.

"Where are Marcey, Madison and Purle?" I asked.

Bootsey said, "Marcey and Purle are in their room listening to music, and Madison is at the park. Madison had baseball practice, and I told her that she had to be back home no later than 4:30 p.m. With her appetite I'm sure she'll be back at 4:00 p.m."

I was so happy to be home from the hospital. I called out for Marcey and Purle by yelling through the house. They both came running at the sound of my voice. Umm, Ummm, Umm, there they stood with big grins on there faces.

Purle smiling from ear to ear with water filled eyes. "Oh momma its so good to see you," Purle said, giving me the biggest hug that I have ever received in my life.

I began to cry as I hugged Purle in return, whispering into Purle's ear, "Purle, I am so sorry."

"Momma, please don't apologize to me. I love you, and that's all that matters to me right now. You are home and safe." Marcey stood beside Bootsey quietly not saying a word.

"Marcey come here and give your momma some sugar." At that point there was no sign of emotions in Marcey's eyes. The hug that she gave me was cold, shallow and lifeless. I knew that at this point my daughter, Marcey, needed me more now than ever. There was something going on with her something serious that needed to be addressed right away. Those big brown eyes were lifeless. I had never seen her this way before. "Marcey, come sit next to me here, lets talk." Giving me a half smile and nodding her head yes, we sat down to talk.

"Marcey what's the matter," I asked. Knowing that she was fully aware of my suicide attempt I came right out and asked her, "Are you angry with me, honey, for attempting to kill myself?" Marcey nodded her head yes. I almost got the impression that my sweet daughter couldn't talk. Some type of emotional breakdown had hindered her part of the brain that allows us to say what we think. She was speechless.

Exactly at the moment that I thought that Marcey had lost her speech from the stress that she had sustained during the last four days of my absence, she said in a whispering voice, "Momma, how could you do that to us?" I didn't know what to tell Kim and Olivia. The tears began to roll down Marcey's face. "Momma blood was everywhere. When I came home from school and found you lying on the bathroom floor, I thought that someone had broken into our apartment and murdered you. I was never so afraid in my life." When Marcey looked up at me with those big brown eyes filled with tears, I thought that my heart would surely break into a million pieces.

"Momma you know that Daddy don't come home no more. You are all that we have."

Covering my face with both of my hands, overcome by shame, and hurt while trying to compose myself and maintain emotional strength for once in my life, I took Marceys hands holding them in my hands tight, looking her in the eyes, "I am so sorry, I am so sorry. I know that I am not able to change the past, but if you forgive me we can move past this and concentrate on making life better for all of us in the future. I can promise you that I will never do anything like that again."

Life is full of pain and sorrow, but you know it is how you handle the pain and sorrow and what you learn from the experience while getting through it that is what creates a better person. "Marcey, I have learned a great deal about life from this experience. I have learned that what is life without forgiveness, and what is love without a free spirit. I have also learned through this experience that my daughters are more important to me than any bad situation that may arise. I feel confident enough to trust myself and my god given instincts to make the right decisions for this family including myself. Believing in myself and my ability to make sound decisions, hopefully, will one day lead to the success in each of you and will validate my credentials of being a good mom after all."

CHAPTER THREE
TWO YEARS SINCE MOMMA'S
NERVOUS BREAKDOWN

It has been two years since Momma had her nervous breakdown. Marcey thought, wow, how time goes by so quickly. She is now working at a rehabilitation center for ex-heroin addicts. It is convenient for her to get to work, and it gives her a feeling of importance. Momma is good at counseling other people. She just has a hard time counseling herself. She should always have a job dealing with the public in this line of work. She is so good at it. The overpopulation of heroin addicts in the neighborhood since the end of the Vietnam war should keep momma in business counseling for a long time. Momma never graduated from college. However, I think that she holds the highest degree that anyone could achieve in life. That is the degree of survival, commonsense, and the ability to anticipate adversity and handle it with the greatest political expertise.

I often thought does Momma really need Daddy to help her take care of us? That is the one thousand-dollar question. Personally, I think that Momma could do better surviving by herself. The emotional excess baggage I know she could surely do without. Momma is a fine woman; and when I grow up, I want to be able to carry myself and handle situations just like her. I mean the way that she can just figure out everything. The way that she stays to herself being private and not evenpicking up a boyfriend after what daddy did to her.

Daddy came in the middle of the night last year, with his girlfriend waiting for him downstairs in the car. He packed his clothes in a matter of 30 minutes in two big garbage bags, didn't say two words to momma or us, and we haven't heard from him since. I know that deep down inside it is killing Momma, but she's been holding her own ever since he left. Never showing any emotions when Kim and Olivia bring up his name. Maybe it isn't a good idea for her not to talk about it.

Speaking of relationships and love, I am in love with a boy named Marcus. Purle is in love with his brother Tyrone. Marcus and I have been seeing each other for the past six months, and just recently I would say within the last two weeks, the relationship has gotten more serious. Marcus and I went to the Apollo Theater last Friday night. We decided to walk home after the show was over. What a beautiful night for walking! While walking home, we were looking up at the sky trying to count how many stars were up in the sky without any success. There must have been at least fifty million stars just in one city block radius. Marcus is intrigued with the entire solar system. If he had his way, he would observe the stars all night. Purle and Tyrone were supposed to have come along with us to the Apollo, but Purle said that Tyrone had to work at Jimmy's Grocery store and couldn't get the evening off. What a shame! We had to have all of that fun without them.

Marcus is a quiet boy. He is handsome and smart, and he has just received a full scholarship with acceptance to Georgetown University in the fall. Marcus wants to major in Criminal Law/Political Science. I know that he is going to do quite well.

Momma thinks that Marcus is a fine young man. On the other hand, Tyrone is also handsome but loud spoken with a limited amount of social intelligence momma says. Tyrone says that he doesn't wish to attend college. His rationale for this concept is that college is a waste of time for black men. He says that there are no decent paying jobs for them. Momma says that Tyrone is sneaky and cunning. When Momma says these things about Tyrone, Purle gets very upset. It's obvious that she strongly disagrees with Momma's evaluation or should I say opinion of Tyrone.

I just turned 18 years old, and I am the eldest girl in the family. Sometimes it could be quite difficult being the eldest in the family because momma expects me to set good examples for my younger sisters. I feel terrible because I have no desire, either, to attend college. I would prefer to stay with Momma to help care for Olivia and Kim and to make sure that she will be alright. Hopefully, Purle, Madison, Olivia, and Kim will attend college. I know for sure that Madison will attend college. She is the genius in the family.

Madison's teachers at school have already had a conference with Momma regarding her academic achievements. The Board of Education tested Madison and her results, momma said, soared well above average. Momma is so proud of Madison. Momma tells everyone in passing how smart Madison is.

MOMMA ISN'T CRAZY

Everybody in the neighborhood thinks that Momma is crazy. Momma has a different way about her. Momma would wear different hats all year around, winter, spring, summer and fall. When I say different, I mean different the kind of stuff that nobody else in the neighborhood wears. Momma has a head full of hair that she cannot manage. Its dark brown with thick waves covering her entire head. Her hair is not too long, shoulder length.

Momma would approach the building where we lived and would continuously recite under her breath different sayings mostly poetry by Edgar Allen Poe who was momma's favorite poet. Nobody knew what she was saying. Everybody just thought that Momma was talking to herself constantly. I think that this habit of Momma's was a form of escape from the reality of the Ghetto. The graffiti on the walls, the urine that lit up the entire apartment building from top to bottom and most of all was the reality of being associated with the poverty that was so visible, prevalent, and unappealing.

Momma would say to her daughters, "You can live in an environment, but you don't have to be apart of it." How true was this theory of Momma's? Could you truly live right smack-dab in the middle of the ghetto and disassociate yourself from it?

Momma was so special. She knew that people thought that she was crazy, and she didn't care what anybody thought of her. Momma made it crystal clear that she didn't care what people thought of her as evidenced by looking straight through the nosy neighbors as they laughed and whispered as she would enter into the apartment building where we lived.

Momma's taste in music was also very different. She would listen to Opera, "Madam Butterfly," Jazz and Billie Holiday singing the Blues. No one else in the building listened to this type of music. Sarah James was definitely different than everybody else but had a heart of gold. She would give a stranger her last fifty cents, and then hand him over her purse to sell if he asked her for it. Just don't ever try and take anything from Momma without asking first. Then all hell would break loose. I would often ask myself the question, why is Momma so different? How come she is not happy with where she is at as far as her financial status, her environment? It was evident that Momma had Champagne taste with a beer pocketbook. Her spirit was not free. It was confined to the limitations of 114th street and 8th avenue.

Momma is an attractive woman, like I said she has a full head of hair. Fair skin in color and after having five children, her waistline was still visible. Heads would turn when she passed by.

Momma didn't have much family that we knew of. Her mother died when she was only eight years old. Momma had an older sister who was put up for adoption after birth. Momma's mother was only fifteen when she gave birth to Momma's sister who was put up for adoption. Momma said that she had never met her sister. I just cannot imagine having to give your baby away to strangers after carrying the baby for almost a year. Experiencing the bond that is created during those months, it must be the closest thing to loosing your mind.

Momma would tell us a lot of stories about her mother. Most of the stories were interesting and for the most part very sad.

Momma told us that her mother died from a broken heart of not being able to keep her baby whom she named Purle. Momma also said that before her sister was put up for adoption her momma got the chance to give her baby a gift. The gift was rosary beads made out of rare African stones.

Momma never talked about trying to find her sister, Purle, who she never met. When Momma's daughters would ask her why she never tried to find her sister, Momma would say "I don't know her," or "I don't have the desire to meet a total stranger and call her my sister." All we knew was that Momma had a sister who was somewhere out there in the world. We knew that this woman was twelve years older than Momma and that her name was also Purle. Not very much to go by. I guess we have to live with the fact that we'll never know our Auntie Purle.

Momma said that after Grandma died, a neighbor by the name of Josephine Smith took her in and raised her as her own. Momma often spoke about how wonderful Josephine was to her. Josephine had no children of her own. She and her husband, Sid, momma said, tried for years to have children without success. Josephine and Sid provided Momma with everything that she needed in life while growing up. It was evident that when Momma spoke about these two people, who had raised her in Harlem as their own child, the love she felt for them truly radiated. It is unfortunate that Momma's children never got the opportunity to meet these nice people from Momma's past.

Momma said that when she was pregnant with Marcey, Josephine and Sid had gone out to a New Years Eve party on Long Island. Her and daddy had a disagreement, and she had gone home to stay with Josephine and Sid for a few days. After the third day of visiting New Years Eve, Momma said that she was awakened to a loud knock at the door. There stood two police officers at the door asking if that was the residence of Sid and Josephine Smith. After Momma responded yes, the news that followed was devastating. Josephine and Sid were both killed in a car accident, a head on collision accident, a hit and run by a drunk driver. Momma said that she knew at that point that her life would never be the same. Momma was grateful to have had the opportunity to spend the last three days of their lives together.

CHAPTER FOUR
MARCEY'S LIFE'S PLANS

Purle has a job working at a fast food restaurant downtown Manhattan. She loves it always coming home with a new story everyday about a customer adding humor to the family at dinnertime. When Purle gets paid every Friday, she gives Momma $50.00 out of her paycheck. I feel a little jealous because I have no job, and I have no money to offer Momma to help with the bills. I feel that I should be the one contributing financially to the household since I am the oldest daughter. In a sense, I also feel sort of responsible for Momma since I am the oldest girl. There's a lot of pressure being the oldest in the family.

This is my last year in High School, and I will be graduating in June. After graduation I know for sure that I will find a job. The plan that I have in mind is, when Momma is at work, I will also be at work. We will be arriving home at the same time at the end of the day. I don't have the desire to go to college, and I think that Momma is disappointed with the decision that I've made not to attend college. The fact of the matter is that deep down inside I am afraid to leave Momma alone for a long period of time. Every now and then, the thought of that awful summer day that I found Momma on the floor in a pool of blood enters my mind. I know she won't ever do anything like that again. However, I'm still afraid to leave her alone for a long period of time. Although momma is a stronger and wiser person now without a doubt, I know that it is my insecurities keeping me at her side.

I have my entire life planned already. I am going to marry Marcus. We are going to have three children, and Momma will live happily ever after with us in our big beautiful mansion.

I have six months left to spend with Marcus before he leaves to go to Georgetown. How will I ever find the strength to live without him? I simply cannot bear the thought. We have become so close.

NO LONGER A VIRGIN

I am no longer a virgin. Marcus and I have already experienced the wonderful joy of sex. When Marcus and I made love for the first time, it was just like in the movies. He took his time and made me feel like I was the most wonderful lady in the world. Our relationship had grown to a higher level. When we make love, we are very careful not to make any mistakes. We use contraceptives. Marcus uses condoms, and I am on the pill.

The only chance we get to make love is when Marcus gets paid every other Tuesday. He and I sneak downtown and check into a motel for about three hours. Marcus is such a gentleman. Although he is the first boy that I have slept with, I am sure at the rate he is going he will truly be my last. I love him so much. I feel bad about sneaking off to the motel to have sex with him. Momma and I share many things. We are also good friends, but this type of information I will kindly keep to myself.

I don't know if Purle is still a virgin or not. We don't have the kind of family that openly discuss sex. What I do know is that lately Purle has been spending an awful lot of time out of the house. I am assuming that she is spending this time out of the house with Tyrone. I like Tyrone. He is very different from the type of guy that I would choose to date. If I were to describe him, I would say he is "Harlemized" as Momma would say. Momma is careful not to emphasize her feelings about Tyrone too much to Purle at this point. I almost get the impression that momma is waiting for Purle to see things for herself regarding Tyrone.

WE DON'T HEAR FROM BOOTSEY

We don't hear from Bootsey too much anymore. Maybe she and momma had a disagreement about daddy. Momma never says anything bad about daddy in our presence, and I know that she would never say anything bad about Bootsey. I miss seeing Bootsey around the apartment. I miss her presence, her voice, and her round cute face. I love when Bootsey is around because momma appears to be happier, it seems. Momma smiles more. There is an abundance of laughter around the house when Bootsey is around. I'm sure that whatever the problem is that's keeping Bootsey away it will resolve itself. I know that she won't go too long without seeing her granddaughters. That's more than I can say for her son.

DIFFERENT PERSONALITIES OF MOMMA'S GIRLS

Out of all of Momma's daughters, Madison is the loner. Madison is always in her bedroom reading books. Her bedroom wall is covered with pictures of black leaders such as members of the "Black Panther Party," Malcolm X, and Martin Luther King Jr. There are many more however. I have no idea of who they are. Madison spends more time in the library than anybody I've ever known.

When I ask Madison how come she is always reading, her response is, "Reading takes me places that I can only dream of going. Reading takes me away from the ghetto for a while." Reading takes me away from this poverty stricken environment that we are all prisoners of at this time. Prisoners because of a lack of education, prisoners because we own nothing."

Madison has such a political way about herself. I know that she will not end up being one of Harlem's statistics, I mean, caught up in the system of welfare. Madison is very bright and continues to do very well in school, and at this point she has not yet found a boyfriend. I do not think that there is a boy in the neighborhood with a strong enough personality to deal with Madison. Madison is physically attractive, about 5ft. 7inches tall, 130 pounds, cocoa colored skin, and big brown eyes. She is just naturally pretty and smart.

Olivia is the baby of the family. All she wants to do is sing. She drives everyone in the house crazy with her singing constantly. Olivia knows the words to every song that comes on the radio. She has a fantastic voice; and I am sure that if she pursued a career in singing when she got a little older, she would probably be an overnight success.

When we get tired of her singing and tell her to be quiet, momma says, "Don't tell her to be quiet. I enjoy listening to her sing." Then she continues to sing for the entire time she's awake until she goes to sleep.

Kim is next to the baby in the family. She is very shy, quiet, and timid. Kim is definitely not a leader but a follower. Kim and Olivia are inseparable. You would very seldom see Kim without Olivia. They are not only sisters, but they are also best friends. Momma likes the closeness of the two. They have separate friends. They always look out for each other. That is one of momma's most important demands, her daughters better not go against each other, wrong or right, for outsiders. Outsiders meaning non-family members. Kim and Olivia would get together and sing for momma, and momma gave them her undivided attention. This was one of momma's favorite past times, she loves music. Momma also loves to sing and has a great voice.

There is a little bit of momma in each and every one of her girls. From looks to personality

GRADUATION DAY

The day finally came for me to walk down the aisle to receive my High School Diploma. Momma was so proud. The first daughter in the family to graduate from High School. Graduating from High School is a big deal in Harlem. A big deal because not too many people graduate. A lot of students drop out of high school and sit for their G.E.D. Momma graduated from High School. She just didn't attend college.

The graduation ceremony so far is beautiful. During the ceremony I had the strong urge, or should I say intuition, to turn my head around. Just as I turned my head around I saw Daddy sitting in the back of the auditorium. As my class marched out of the auditorium after the ceremony was over, I glanced over again to see if Daddy was still sitting in that seat. The seat where he had been sitting was now empty. This made my day for sure. Now, I knew that somewhere deep down inside Daddy must have cared about me.

This was a wonderful day for Momma because as soon as we returned home from the graduation, she took a letter out of the mailbox that had come from Madison's school. The letter was from The Board of Education. Momma opened the letter, ripping the envelope open. The letter read that Madison was recommended by the School Board to be excellerated to the 12th grade instead of the 11th grade where she would normally go. I can honestly say that Madison had it going on academically. The girl was definitely bright. She maintained a G.P.A. score of 4.0 her entire two years in high school. As Momma read the letter her eyes opened wide. Momma began crying and waving the letter in the air while dancing around the room. These were truly happy tears that were way over due and welcomed by us all. This was truly a happy day for Madison and I. This day began as my day, and ended up a special day for Madison and I both.

This letter meant that Purle and Madison would be graduating from high school at the same time. I am not so sure that Purle will like this idea. Speaking of Purle, I haven't seen her all day. She never showed up to my graduation. Purle and I are very close, and this is definitely not like her to not show up to such an important event. I am not going to worry because Purle knows how to take care of herself.

Madison walked through the door as Momma was waving the letter in the air. Momma couldn't wait to tell her the good news from her school. As momma read the letter out loud to Madison, Madison began screaming and jumping up and down with joy also. The two of them together momma and Madison jumping up and down, looked like two jumping jacks. I am so proud of my sister. She is so beautiful, and so smart, what other qualities could anyone ask for. If Momma doesn't hit the number first, I bet that Madison will be the daughter to get us all out of this ghetto.

All of those books that Madison had read, all of the nights she chose to stay at home instead of going out with Purle and I, paid off for Madison. Purle and I could never understand why Madison would rather stay home and read than to go out to the movies or to the Apollo theater with us.

Momma had cooked a good dinner for my graduation, and Marcus was invited over to celebrate the occasion with us. This was also a celebration for Marcus since he graduated from high school just last week. Marcus' graduation ceremony was also very nice. He walked away with about six awards.

Marcus and Tyrone didn't have much parental guidance while growing up. Their mother's name is Miss Lucy, and she is a heroin addict. She has been a heroin addict for a long time. Miss Lucy doesn't care about anyone or anything except for a good high. Momma approached Miss Lucy in the past regarding the possibility of her seeking rehabilitation. Unfortunately, Miss Lucy told Momma to mind her business. Momma never approached Miss Lucy with that concept again. Marcus and Tyrone had the same mother, but their personalities were so different.

Dinner had been served, and the evening was settling in. The day was a nice day, and at this point everyone was tired. Marcus and I had kissed goodnight. He was going home. He only lived in the building right next to ours, so he didn't have far to travel.

Just as I had given up on Purle and had gotten into bed, Purle walked through our bedroom door. Purle had been gone since early this morning. It was now 11:30 at nigh. Where was she all day? I turned the light on that was next to my bed when Purle came into the bedroom. By the look on her face, I could tell that she had something to tell me. Purle and I were just that close. I could feel her emotions, and she could feel mine.

"Purle, where were you?" I asked.

With hesitation she answered, "The police were harassing Tyrone again." I sat up in bed because now Purle had really captured my interest.

I said to Purle, "What do you mean by 'the police was harassing Tyrone.'"

"The police seem to feel that Tyrone has information on who is supplying the drugs in the neighborhood."

I asked Purle, "What would make the police think such a thing about Tyrone?"

Purle shrugged her shoulders and said, "I have no idea sis. All I can say is that Tyrone needed me to hold his gun for him for two days until this mess blows over."

"Purle," I asked, "What is Tyrone doing with a gun?"

"Well," she said, "There are many guys in this neighborhood who are jealous of Tyrone."

"Jealous of what?" I asked.

"Marcey, you know how these people are in this neighborhood. You don't need a reason to be jealous."

"Purle, make sure in two days you give Tyrone back his gun. If momma finds that gun in this house, you will have all hell to pay."

Purle looked at me with those big brown eyes, smiled and said, "I know Marcey."

Purle climbed into bed. I told her all about the graduation and even how I saw Daddy sitting in the back of the auditorium. I don't think that Purle believed that Daddy was at the graduation. The look on her face led me to believe that she might of thought that I had been hallucinating. I told Purle not to mention to Momma that I saw Daddy at the graduation because I didn't know how she would take the news. I knew that Momma didn't invite Daddy, and I didn't want to cause any problems between Momma and Bootsey. If Momma didn't invite Daddy, then Bootsey had to have invited him.

Two weeks had passed, and Purle still had possession of Tyrone's 38-Caliber gun in her duffelbag. I had never mentioned anything else to Purle about the gun. Another four weeks had gone by, and Purle still had the gun in her possession. Afraid of betraying Purles confidence, I never mentioned the gun to Marcus. I didn't want to betray my sister's confidence, neither did I want to burden Marcus with this situation or get him involved. Marcus had only two weeks left before his departure to Georgetown University. I didn't want anything or anyone to interfere with these plans. Marcus was very excited about attending Georgetown. Reverend King from the First Baptist Church had offered to give Marcus a ride down to the University and to help him get situated. This is what Marcus needed; he didn't have a father figure around. The church had taken up a collection for Marcus. The collection was to help with some of his expenses while starting off. The total amount collected by the church was $350.00 from the congregation. I was so proud of Marcus. It is very sad that he has no parents actively involved in his life or the type of parents, I should say, to encourage his goals and accomplishments. Maybe this is the reason why Tyrone is the way that he is, so "Harlemized."

I can tell that Momma is crazy about Marcus. She saved up $50.00 of her hard-earned money to give to Marcus along with the collection. Momma was just that type of person. Whether she had the money to spare or not, she was going to help this boy the best way she knew how.

I cannot believe how fast the time is going by. Before you know it, Marcus will be gone off to college. Madison had received her results from the S.A.T. exam that she had taken last month, and as anticipated her score was well above 1000. The girl is super intelligent with common sense to top it off. Momma is sure that Madison will be able to receive a full scholarship to the college of her choice when the time comes to make those decisions. Madison says that she is not sure if she wants to attend Yale University or Harvard School of Medicine. This was all very exciting. Momma has been on the telephone telling everybody she knew to call about Madison's test scores. Finally Sarah is happy. Momma has a beautiful smile worth more than a billion dollars. Sarah is finally happy.

I love Madison so much for making Momma so happy. Our family is quite different from many families in the neighborhood. We are very close to each other, and we do not have many friends. We have fights and disagreements amongst ourselves, but no outsiders had better get involved. That was the way that Momma had taught us.

CHAPTER FIVE
MARCUS' DEPARTURE TO GEORGE-TOWN

The day has come, August 28, 1978. Marcus is leaving for Georgetown. I have so many mixed feelings about Marcus leaving. He and I spent the entire evening together. The evening was beautiful, except for the fact that it went by too fast.

Reverend King had mentioned in the past that Momma and I could ride with him to take Marcus to school. Georgetown couldn't be that far away. I think we will be traveling south. Momma packed lunch for everybody.

Momma and I awakened early the next morning. The both of us decided to wear comfortable clothes. We wore jeans and a T-shirt. Momma and I arrived at Marcus' door. We knocked on the apartment door. Marcus opened the door. He was looking fine as ever. He also decided to wear blue jeans and a T shirt.

"Are you ready, Marcus?" Momma asked. "Reverend King is waiting downstairs for us in the car."

I asked Momma to take the lightweight bags downstairs to the car. This would allow Marcus and I to have an extra ten minutes alone. We French kissed inside of his apartment at the doorway for about ten minutes. I felt as if a part of me was leaving.

The trip to Georgetown wasn't bad at all. Traffic was light, and Reverend King knew exactly how to get there. The entire ride home I had a knot in my stomach. I was missing Marcus already. Momma sensed that I was feeling the bla blas and tried to strike up conversations the entire ride home.

SIX MONTHS SINCE MARCUS LEFT FOR COLLEGE

Marcus had been gone for six months, and we have been writing each other every week for the entire six months. There are six months remaining before Marcus would be allowed to return home for the summer. I miss him so much. My life isn't the same without Marcus. I work, come home, complete my chores, and begin getting ready for work the next day. Life is completely boring.

Purle and Madison will be graduating from high school this coming June. Momma has already begun making their graduation dresses. Madison had decided that she did not want to attend Yale University or Harvard but decided to stay closer to home. Madison ended up choosing Columbia University as her first choice of schools. Columbia had a wonderful pre-med and medical program. Momma was satisfied with Madison's choice of College.

What Momma really wanted was for Madison to get out of the drug infested neighborhood, A neighborhood that had consumed the lives of so many young people. It was Momma who always said that you can live in an environment, but you didn't have to be a part of it. With this philosophy of hers, there shouldn't be a problem for Madison.

CHAPTER SIX
ROBBERIES IN THE NEIGHBORHOOD

There was a lot of talk in the neighborhood that Mrs. Noobey's son, Jr., had been breaking into apartments in the building and taking neighbors personal possessions while they were asleep at night. Mrs. Noobey's son is a heroin addict and looks like he would take down his mother on a good day. When Momma heard about the robberies and who was suspected of committing them, she just shook her head in disgust.

"You know," she said. "It is bad enough that he is stealing from people, people who live in his neighborhood, people who have watched him grow up, his mothers friends; to cut off the hand that feeds you can be quite dangerous.

The summer had come and gone, and Marcus didn't come home. Unfortunately, he had to work on campus to help pay for some of his books and other expenses. I took a trip down to Georgetown to see him. What a huge campus! It looked as if it stretched for miles. It was great to see Marcus. I was able to purchase my own bus ticket now that I have a job. I am working as a clerk typist in the courthouse downtown Center Street. The job, thus far, has been truly exciting and challenging. Momma got me the job by talking to her director at the rehab center who knew the administrative secretary at the courthouse.

I work Monday through Friday from 9 a.m. to 5 p.m. with weekends off. It's not bad at all. Purle and I both are now able to contribute to the household finances. Momma made me take my first two paychecks and buy some new outfits for work. She said that I couldn't go downtown working with those white folks looking like a rag-a-muffin. What does a rag-a-muffin look like? I have no clue.

Madison and Purle graduated from high school. Their graduation was beautiful. Once again Momma was proud.

Marcus has been at school for three and a half years already. How time flies. I have finally gotten use to the bus ride to Georgetown, and it doesn't seem so long anymore.

Olivia and Kim have started a singing group, and Momma supports their functions whole-heartedly. Between the two of them Olivia is truly the baby at heart. Olivia still gets in the bed with momma at night. Kim and I have become closer lately. I don't know why, but she has been asking for my advice on different subject matters. I guess that's what big sisters are for, advice on subject matters mostly having to deal with clothes, school, and her friends.

Christmas was quickly approaching. Madison is doing well at Columbia University, and Purle is still working at her same job. Financially, the James family is just making ends meet. We're living comfortable, and it is about time.

Momma and I haven't gone Christmas shopping for anyone yet. With three weeks until Christmas I think that we had better start to shop as soon as possible. With Momma's schedule being so busy and my schedule being so busy with me visiting Marcus on weekends, life has been hectic. Momma and I talked about Christmas shopping and set a date to shop for next Tuesday.

Tuesday is here, and Momma and I decided to start the shopping on 34th street. We walked from 8th avenue to 5th avenue. Momma had to stop in every shoe store that we passed by. I hate shopping with Momma. Bootsey is supposed to be here tomorrow. I should have encouraged Momma to shop with Bootsey tomorrow, instead of me shopping with Momma today. Tomorrow I have to meet Bootsey at the Port Authority at 6:00 p.m. I should have really encouraged momma to shop with Bootsey tomorrow. Momma invited Bootsey from New Jersey to spend the holidays with us. Afterall, Bootsey had nothing to do with her son being a deadbeat dad and should not be penalized for his actions. Whatever was keeping Bootsey away had been resolved.

For Christmas momma and I will be making a turkey, some collard greens, macaroni and cheese, and some biscuits. For desert we will make a couple of apple pies and a couple of sweet potato pies. Our family loved to prepare big meals around the holidays. This has been traditional in many African American families.

CHRISTMAS MORNING

It is Christmas morning, and the house is full. Purle is still sleeping. I guess she must have had a late night with Tyrone. Madison is still sleeping; I can hear Olivia and Kim in the living room talking to Bootsey. Momma is in the kitchen putting the finishing touch on the turkey. Everything seems exactly the same as it was before Daddy left.

As I headed back toward the bedroom, I heard a knock at the door, thinking to myself who in the world could be knocking at the door at 10:30 a.m. Momma opened the door. I could hear momma scream, "Marcus!" I ran to the door and sure enough it was my prince charming looking handsome as ever, with the biggest grin on his face. He picked me up with two hands and began spinning me around while kissing me on the lips. My hair was standing on the top of my head. He put me down and gave me another big kiss on the lips in front of Momma. There were so many thoughts going through my head at once. I was truly surprised by his presence. Who cares if I didn't brush my hair or brush my teeth. This is surely the best Christmas that I have ever had.

"Come on in here, and sit down," Momma said after taking her turn giving him a big hug and kiss. "How's school?" Momma asked.

"Fine, Mrs. James," he responded.

Momma said, "Call me Sarah."

"Marcus, have you met my grandmother, Bootsey?"

"Yes, I have." While extending both hands outward to shake Bootseys hands as a friendly gesture.

Bootsey stood smiling from ear to ear and said, "Young man, I don't want to shake your hands. I want a nice kiss like you just gave these two ladies." Marcus smiled. Then he hugged and kissed Bootsey.

"Get dressed, Marcey, I would like to take you out for breakfast at Sylvia's."

I smiled and said, "I'll be right back."

I ran fast to the bathroom to shower and dress. Unaware at the time Marcus had already asked momma for my hand in marriage. It must have taken me, at the most, 45 minutes to shower and get dressed. Marcus must have saved some extra money for the holiday because he was hailing a taxicab to take us only ten city blocks.

Sylvia had the best soulfood restaurant in Harlem. The menu was great. I ordered bacon and eggs with a side order of grits. Marcus ordered the same. We didn't talk much during breakfast. We mostly stared at each other. The atmosphere was just right, and the tunes playing on the jukebox made the atmosphere that much better. Just as I thought that we were ready to leave the restaurant after breakfast, Marcus pulled out of his pocket a small box. Oh my goodness thinking to myself, I know that he doesn't have an engagement ring for me. Sure enough, Marcus removed the ring from the box, reached for my left hand across the table, and put the ring on my ring finger.

"Marcey I would like to spend the rest of my life with you." "Will you marry me?"

I was truly speechless, the tears poured down my face because I knew that this was the man that I truly loved. This was the man that I had wished to spend the rest of my life with.

Without any hesitation I said, "Yes." I said yes so loud that everyone in the restaurant turned around and looked at me. The ring was beautiful, and I couldn't take my eyes off of it. "Marcus, this ring must have cost you a fortune. How did?" I smiled and said, "Oh, never mind. Marcus, as soon as you are finished with school we will get married."

He kissed me on the lips and said, "I can live with that." We held hands and stared across the table at each other for about twenty minutes. Our relationship had been sealed with a commitment.

Marcus and I left the restaurant and went for a long walk after breakfast. We were debating which direction to walk. We were undecided about walking uptown passing off Smalls Paradise or strolling downtown toward Central Park. We decided to walk downtown toward Central Park. Although it was December and cold, we were both dressed for the occasion. We hugged and kissed each other as we slowly walked through the cold empty streets. We had so much to catch up on. Before we knew it, the sky was dark. Where did the time go?

Marcus escorted me back to my apartment, kissed me goodnight and said, "I'll see you tomorrow."

I invited him inside to have dinner with us, but he said that he had to get home to take care of some things.

Marcus was up to something, and I had no idea of what it was. I locked the door behind Marcus after saying goodnight to him. I looked out of my front room window to see if Marcus was truly calling it a night or going back outside as my instincts had led me to believe. I knew that Momma and Bootsey were probably wondering what happened to me.

I was gone all day long. They both sat on the sofa with those wondering looks on their faces. As soon as I got the chance I was going to tell them all about my day with Marcus. First, I had to see what Marcus was up to. When I looked out of the window, I could see Marcus following his brother Tyrone. From my view it seemed as if Tyrone was unaware of Marcus following him. Marcus stayed about fifty feet behind Tyrone while ducking in and out of buildings as he would anticipate Tyrone turning around. Marcus followed Tyrone until I could no longer see either one of them in the distance. It seemed as if Marcus suspected Tyrone of something, and Marcus was the type that would definitely find out what his brother was up to.

The very next day when I saw Marcus I said to him joking around, "I saw you, Marcus, following your brother last night."

Marcus became angry and said, "Marcey please don't ever mention that you saw me following my brother last night to anybody."

Marcus' entire demeanor changed quickly. I had never seen him get so uptight before. It was evident at this point that during Marcus' night out on the town-playing detective he had stumbled upon something very serious. On the other hand it could not have been that serious because Marcus was leaving in the morning to go back to school. Nobody or nothing could stand in the way of Marcus' education. Marcus often said that his education was his ticket to freedom. The same thing that Madison use to say. Those two have a lot in common.

The morning came for Marcus to return to school. These good-byes were becoming very difficult. I finally got the opportunity to tell Momma and Bootsey all about my breakfast at Sylvia's. I didn't leave out any details. I told Momma and Bootsey how the music was playing when Marcus asked for my hand in marriage.

Momma said "Marcey, Marcus is such a fine young man, and he is going to make you very happy in life." I hugged Momma tight.

As the time went on Marcus and I continued to write each other. I continued to work at the courthouse as a clerk typist with having received a promotion to senior clerk typist. I had started saving money towards my wedding. I continued to visit Marcus one weekend a month. Marcus would occasionally ask how his brother was doing, if I ever see him. Now he seldom brings up Tyrone's name. When I mention something about Purle to Marcus, its fine; but the minute I bring Tyrone's name into the conversation Marcus quickly changes the subject. It is almost as if Marcus has conditioned himself to not care about his brother. What did he find out about his brother that had him so emotionally distant with him? I dared not ask. My main concern was Purle, after all she is a strong girl and can take care of herself.

Marcus is doing well in school. He has a part time job working for a law firm. It is part of his internship, and he loves it. The experience he has obtained this far is remarkable. I know that he is going to be a wonderful attorney.

Time is flying by. Marcus has just one-year left of law school. Then he will sit for the Bar exam in the State of New York. He is hoping to land a job working with Lamberg, Stein and Associates downtown on 23rd street. If he does land a job with that firm, he will be financially set for life. He has already sent his resumé with a cover letter to their firm.

WEDDING DATE SET

Marcus and I have set a wedding date for September 5th of next year. I have been diligently saving money to help with the wedding because I know Momma cannot pay for everything especially with her income. I have sent for wedding magazines and all sorts of bridal literature. The thought of being Marcus' wife is so exciting. The wedding is not going to be a big wedding. The only people attending will be family. Marcus' family isn't too big. Neither is mine. I feel very lucky to have the opportunity to marry my first love. It's truly a blessing.

MADISON"S PROGRESSION IN MED SCHOOL

Madison is doing very well at Columbia University. She has been excepted into Harlem Hospital's Residency program after graduation next year. We are all very excited about her accomplishments. It really looks as if we are going to have an attorney and a physician in the family. What more could one ask for.

Momma always said, "All you need is the faith of a mustard seed, and you can move mountains." Momma would also say that "Trust was the maximum measure of success." Although Momma never attended college, she was also a very intelligent woman. Like I said before, Momma held the highest degree one could hold and that was in common sense and wisdom.

Olivia and Kim are singing in the church choir now,

so Momma has been spending a lot of time at the First Baptist Church on Sunday. God has truly blessed Olivia and Kim with beautiful voices. Everytime Momma hears them sing it brings tears to her eyes.

Purle is still in love with Tyrone. Tyrone is still working at Jimmy's grocery store. Purle just landed a new job sewing clothes for some fashion designer down on 37th street. Purle always loved to sew.

Purle and I take turns cooking when we come home from work because Momma is usually beat by the time she gets in from work at 7:15 p.m. After dinner Purle announced that she now had the desire to go to college. We were all shocked. Purle had decided that she loved sewing and designing clothes so much that she wanted to attend The Fashion Institute of Technology. Wow! Were we all surprised. Sewing was truly Purle's calling in life. Actually Purle looked like a runway model herself. Purle stood about 5ft. 9inches tall. She weighs about 127 pounds. She has olive colored skin, with the most beautiful almond shaped brown eyes. If she didn't make it as a designer, she could surely succeed at modeling.

Momma was happy to hear Purle say that she was now ready for college. "Purle, when do you plan on beginning college?" Momma asked.

I knew what Momma was doing. Momma was pinning Purle down for a deadline just in case Purle would attempt to procrastinate or change her mind. Purle said that she had planned on starting school in September. It was too late to begin now. It was already the end of October, and this semester had already begun.

Momma gave Purle a hug and said, "I think that this is wonderful news, and I support your decision 100 percent."

CHAPTER SEVEN
OUR LIVES WILL CHANGE FOREVER

It was just about 11:45 p.m. when everybody decided to turn in for the night. We were all excited about Purle's good news and overall the day had been a good day. As usual Olivia was headed into momma's bedroom for the night where she had often slept. Olivia was such a baby.

Just as I fell into a deep sleep, I felt Olivia shaking me while whispering frantically. Then Olivia ran over to Purle's bed and began to shake Purle and awaken her.

While rubbing my eyes sitting up in bed trying to get my bearings Olivia said, "Marcey, Purle, there is a man in Momma's bedroom with a knife in his hand." Olivia was crying uncontrollably, we could barely understand what she was saying.

Olivia said "Marcey, Purle he is demanding that Momma give him money."

At that point I thought that I was dreaming. Purle quickly jumped out of bed, reached over into the closet, stuck her hand down inside of her duffel bag that she had in the closet. Purle then proceeded to tiptoe into Momma's bedroom. I followed behind Purle.

Everything was happening so fast. I followed Purle not realizing that within a split second Purle had retrieved the 38-caliber pistol that Tyrone had asked her to hold long ago. I thought, OH MY GOD, Purle has the gun. As we approached Momma's bedroom, we could see the man with the knife to momma's throat with one of Momma's arms twisted behind her back while she walked over to the chest drawer in the corner of her bedroom. Purle and I could not see the man's face because he had a ski mask on. I felt like I was going to faint. Just then Purle took a stance and with two hands on the trigger she shot him twice. The man instantly fell to the floor. Purle then fell to her knees with the gun still in her hand. Momma started screaming. I walked over to console Momma, and I could hear the police sirens downstairs. I wondered who had called the police that fast, and I looked over to where Olivia was. By the expression on her face, I knew that it was Olivia who had called 911. Thank God she did.

The police entered into the bedroom where we were. Purle looked terrible. She looked as if she was in shock. Momma was still screaming and crying telling the police that she shot the intruder who was later identified as Mrs. Noobey's son. Momma was trying to protect Purle. The police had no idea of who was telling the truth. How obvious the truth was, a strange man in an apartment at 2:00 a.m. in the morning with a knife in his hand. The police read Purle her rights while at the same time putting handcuffs on her. Purle chose to execute her right to remain silent until we could retain an attorney to represent her. This was all under the advice of Momma. Meanwhile Mrs. Noobey's son was pronounced dead at the scene. Purle must have been taking target lessons because both shots fired hit Jr. directly where she aimed. There were so many questions going through my mind. Why were the police arresting Purle when this man came through my mother's bedroom window demanding money with a knife in his hand? The police wanted to know where Purle had gotten the gun. Of course, Purle refused to say. This was also a concern of Momma's. Momma was so shocked. She had no idea that Purle had a gun in her possession.

When it all simmered down, I'm sure the police didn't care about Jr. being shot dead in our apartment. All the police knew was that Purle had no permit or license to have this gun in her possession. They had a quota of arrests to meet, and they were going to meet their annual quota at any expense. Purle was in big trouble because the gun was not registered.

Momma was broken up emotionally as the police escorted Purle out of the building with handcuffs on into the police car.

Momma, was standing outside of the apartment building with her nightgown on crying her eyes out and yelling, "Please lord, help me. Don't let them take my Purle away."

I put my arms around Momma and held her as tight as I could. I looked into Momma's eyes, and I promised her that I would see to it that Purle was home soon. I was making Momma a promise that I wasn't sure I could keep.

Thinking back in retrospect, this entire scene reminded me of the story that Momma told us about her sister, Purle whom she never met and was taken from my grandmother and put up for adoption. Momma said that grandma never gave consent to the adoption. The baby was taken from grandma after she had given birth and named her Purle. Momma said that her mother did get the opportunity to hold her baby and bond with her for about two hours before having her baby taken away.

Purle was taken down to central booking, and by the time that I had arrived Tyrone was there. I couldn't stand the sight of him. What was he doing here, angrily I asked myself. Then it dawned on me that Purle probably called him. I knew that this gun belonged to Tyrone, and hopefully he would tell the police that the gun belonged to him. Knowing Tyrone the way that I did, if his freedom was in any way jeopardized, he would never tell anyone that the gun was his. I knew that the police really couldn't retain Purle for possession of this gun because there had been laws passed for mandatory jail time for possession of a gun. I really don't know what's going on.

The police ran the gun through ballistics. Now I knew for sure that Purle had a very big chance of being in big trouble. My instincts just told me so. This all seemed like a nightmare, a horrible dream. I needed to wake up.

When it was my turn to see Purle, I reiterated what Momma said to her earlier not to answer any questions until we were able to retain an attorney. Purle had a blank look on her face as if she were still in shock. Purle asked how Momma was holding up? Of course I assured her that momma was fine. I glanced across the room. Thank god I saw a familiar face. A woman who also works at the courthouse was here. I think this woman is an investigator or a detective. She doesn't wear a police uniform; she looks like she is approximately 50 to 55 years old. I looked at this woman again, and we made eye contact. She motioned for me to come over to where she was standing. There was just something about this woman that seemed very familiar to me. It was not the fact that she was the only black face in the precinct, but she just had a very familiar appearance. As I approached her, I could see that her nametag identified her as detective P. Ross.

Detective Ross informed me of all the reasons why Purle was being detained. Everything the detective mentioned to me pointed to Tyrone. It seemed as if the N.Y.P.D. was very familiar with Tyrone and all of his activities in the neighborhood. They were going to build a case against him one way or another.

The detective informed me that until Purle confesses to where she got the gun she will remain in jail or until she could post bail if the judge decides to grant her bail. The detective also said that they had been trying to nail Tyrone for a while now. He knows a lot about the drug activity distribution in the neighborhood. The bottom line is Tyrone must tell the truth or Purle's freedom will be compromised.

This all seemed so unfair to me. If I didn't know any better, I would think that everything that happened tonight was a set up. Growing up in the ghetto just makes you paranoid that way. We have made some progress with receiving respect from community leaders and the police department since the days of Martin Luther King Jr. and Malcolm X. However, we still had more to accomplish. The agenda of equality, civil rights still had some unresolved issues that needed to be addressed. It was clear that Purle's rights were being compromised because of her association with Tyrone.

Momma was home with a neighbor, Miss Delores. Kim, Olivia and myself knew that Momma was fine. The time was passing quickly, and this night will always be remembered as the night that Jr. was murdered in our apartment.

I was worried about Momma. I called home to check

on Momma, Kim answered the phone. Kim said that Momma was getting dressed to come down to the precinct. I asked Kim if someone from the coroner's office had come yet to remove Jr's body from Momma's bedroom. Kim said yes. She also said that the police had drawn an outline of Jr's body on momma's bedroom floor and that Momma was having a hard time looking at it. Momma got on the phone and asked how Purle was doing? I assured momma that Purle was as well as could be expected under the circumstances. I asked Momma not to come down to the precinct. I asked Momma to stay at home until I returned there. I told Momma that there was absolutely nothing that she could do here. She agreed.

Detective Ross allowed me to see Purle again. I advised Purle at this time with a complete change of heart after speaking with the detective that maybe she should tell the police that, indeed, the gun did belong to Tyrone.

Purle looked at me and said, "I can't" in a whispered voice.

I shook my head in disbelief.

Purle said that Tyrone told her that if she told the police that it was his gun that they would both be in jail on conspiracy charges.

I looked at Purle and said, "You have got to be kidding me. Purle, I don't know how we are going to get you out of this mess. Tyrone is lying to you, number one. Number two, he is trying to save his own ass. Purle, I have about seven hundred dollars saved for my wedding. I will use that money to retain a very good attorney for you because you are going to need one."

Purle looked at me and said, "Hold off until we see what Tyrone comes up with, Marcey."

"Where did Tyrone go, Purle?"

"He said that he was going to try and get some money together to post bail for me."

"Post bail? You haven't even gone before the judge

yet to know what your bail is, or if you need to put up bail. Purle, Tyrone is full of it. He is setting you up to take the fall. He is telling you lies."

"No he isn't," Purle said. "Tyrone loves me. He would never do that."

I couldn't believe my ears. Purle and I were raised in the same house by the same mother. How could she have turned out to be so gullible and naive? Is this what love does to a person, blind them from the world of reality?

I won't tell Marcus about this. He has one semester left in school before graduating, and this news will definitely crush him. I won't burden him at this time. Madison doesn't know what has happened as of yet either. I don't know how I will ever keep this from her. Madison is just finishing up her Residency at Harlem Hospital. This type of news is not something that I can keep from everybody.

My God, it suddenly hit me like a ton of bricks. My sister is facing charges of possession of an illegal deadly weapon; and who knows when the ballistics report return, what additional charges will be added. Only if I had done more to encourage Purle to return that gun to Tyrone when I had the chance. I felt as if I let Purle down. On the other hand, perhaps if she had returned the gun to Tyrone maybe Momma wouldn't be alive today. I guess it is true, the saying that everything happens for a reason.

The next morning Momma and I sat at the kitchen table trying to sort things out. We made numerous telephone calls to different attorneys. They were all so very expensive to retain. How would we ever be able to afford one? After trying all day without success, we called it quits. Finally the following day we contacted an attorney who was able to make Momma and I feel comfortable with his skills, and he is affordable. His name was Mr. Fishbein, an older Jewish man with grey hair on the verge of going bald. His experience and tract record was impeccable. Momma and I set up an appointment to meet with him at 11:00 a.m. this morning. That meant that we had to move fast. We didn't have much time to get dressed. Momma and I threw some clothes on and took a cab downtown to his office. This attorney had a great reputation, and we had to keep this appointment. I have personally seen this attorney in action down at the courthouse. Each time I witnessed him defend someone it was very impressive. The grapevine had it that he had never lost a case.

Purle had been transferred to the jail downtown, and an arraignment date was set for tomorrow. Tyrone has not been seen or heard from since Purle's initial arrest two days ago. Momma and I met with the attorney and were able to explain exactly what happened during the night Purle shot and killed Jr. This wasn't premeditated murder. At the time no one knew that the man with the ski mask on in Momma's bedroom was Mrs. Noobey's son.

Poor Mrs. Noobey was taking the death of her son extremely bad. Mrs. Noobey failed to realize that her son Jr. was dead long before Purle pulled the trigger on the gun that awful night. Jr. had become a slave to a new white master by the name of Heroin. Momma made an attempt to give Mrs. Noobey her condolences. Momma's condolences were not excepted. Mrs. Noobey screamed when Momma approached her and called Momma a crazy witch. Mrs. Noobey told Momma that she was going to see to it that Purle would rot in jail. Momma shook her head mumbled under her breath and walked away.

Momma had the weight of the world on her shoulders. Somehow deep down inside I knew that all of this would work itself out. This entire mess will soon be fixed after Purle reveals where she got the gun from. Surely the system cannot detain Purle in custody for defending the safety of our family from an intruder. The intruder had been victimizing everyone in the neighborhood for about three years. What about the victims who had been violated by Jr. in the past. Were they forgotten? The way that I see it, Purle did their job for them. She saved the taxpayers a few dollars; while at the same time she stopped him, Jr., from victimizing anyone else.

Tyrone had been avoiding Purle. The moment he heard that the gun was being put through ballistics he disappeared. I knew by Tyrone's behavior that gun was dirty. Tyrone knew it before he gave it to Purle to hold for him. I'm not sure how dirty, but I knew it would return far from clean. I knew after the ballistics test returned, the D.A. was going to throw the book at Purle. She would be charged with every crime related to the gun.

Momma and I went to visit Purle. It looked as if she had been crying all night. Her eyes were puffy and red, she looked terrible. The sight of Purle broke Momma's heart.

Momma said "Purle what is troubling you besides being here?"

Purle said, "My attorney was here to see me, and he wants me to go before the judge and plead not guilty to all charges."

"Well, isn't that what you want to do honey? Aren't you innocent?"

"Yes Momma I am innocent, but Mr. Fishbein wants me to tell the judge that the gun belongs to Tyrone. I cannot do that. I love Tyrone, Momma. If I confess to that, they will send Tyrone to jail forever, Momma; and you know that. You know how it is for a black man to go through our system. There is black justice, and there is white justice. Momma, you know that he will be considered guilty before he is even tried by a jury NOT of his peers."

Momma looked at me shook her head and looked at Marcey while never verbally responding to what Purle said. Although I knew exactly what Momma was thinking by the expression on her face. The expression revealed pain, the pain of knowing that her daughter, who she taught better, cared for a man more than she cared for herself.

Responding only to what the attorney said, "Yes, Purle, Mr. Fishbein is right. Once you reveal where you got the gun from, honey, you will be free. You will walk."

Purle looked at Momma and said, "I cannot say anything until I speak with Tyrone first."

"Well, where is Tyrone?" Momma asked.

"He is suppose to come here today to visit me."

Momma looked at me and neither one of us said anything.

One month later and Marcus is home. His graduation ceremony from Law school was beautiful. He walked away with honors, and I didn't expect anything less. Now he just had to sit for the N.Y. State Bar Exam. I told Marcus the day after his graduation everything that had happened. It is wonderful to have Marcus home. Maybe he can talk some sense into his brother's head. At least now Tyrone is going up to visit Purle. Marcus and I went to visit Purle today, and finally she is beginning to look like her old self except for the fact that she has to wear that ugly jail outfit. I can tell by the look in Purles eyes she has had enough of this place, and she is ready to talk.

Purle's court date is scheduled for next month. I have a girlfriend who works as a prison guard at Rikers Island where Purle is, and she told me that Tyrone visits Purle frequently. She also said that after he leaves Purle does nothing but cries for hours. Momma is planning on visiting Purle tomorrow, and she is going to attempt one more time to try and talk some sense into Purle.

CHAPTER EIGHT
PURLES PERSONAL ORDEAL WITH JAIL

It has been six months since I have been incarcerated, and no one has been able to help with my release. My attorney says that the maximum amount of time that I could receive was a year and six months. Tyrone still visits on weekends pleading with me not to tell that the gun belongs to him.

The ballistics report came back, and the findings revealed the gun had been used in several other crimes including the murder of a man by the name of Peter Ajuhel. I am not sure exactly of all the details; however, I am sure that I never murdered anyone. And I am sure that this is why I have not been given bail. I believe that the District Attorney is trying to bring different charges against me, the charge of murder in the first degree. I am scared.

Tyrone knows more than he is telling me. I really don't know what to do at this point. I know that Momma, Marcey, and Mr. Fishbein are all right with what they are saying. The fact remains that I love Tyrone so much. I wouldn't be able to live with myself if I were responsible for ratting him out and causing his arrest. I know that I must appear to be crazy with this rationale. It was Tryones fault that I am incarcerated to begin with.

The prison guard came to my cell to tell me that I had a visitor. Finally Momma is here. I hate sitting across the table from her, not being able to hug or kiss her. The prison guards watch you like a hawk. The physical contact allowed is very minimum. Momma is wearing a sharp hat today with a beautiful skirt suit. Momma always made sure that she looked her best when she came to visit me. She says that in our society that a book is definitely judged by its cover. This is totally different than how she use to think. About two years ago Momma didn't give a hoot what anybody thought of her.

Momma looked me in the eyes. I had the feeling that today was D Day the day that she was going to let me have it with both barrels.

"Purle, this situation has gone on long enough, and my intuition tells me that it is not going to get any better, it is only going to get worse. Now is the time to save yourself. You may never get this opportunity to talk on your own behalf to free yourself. Once the verdict comes down, it will be too late, honey. The worst thing in the world is to have to say to yourself - I Wish That I Had Done Things Differently."

Momma looked me in the eyes with a deadlock grip and said, "Baby, life could be hard. This is your life we're talking about not Tyrone's life. If Tyrone loved you half as much as you loved him, you would not be here. You would be free."

I looked at Momma and I could see something different about her. Not the fact that she had looked like she had aged about ten years with gray hair sprouting out at the temples of her head, there was just something very different about Momma. I wasn't sure what it was, but I knew that she wasn't giving up on me now. I think that Momma had finally come to terms with the fact that whatever decision I made that she would have to except that decision and live with it.

I told Momma that I was scared. She said, "You should be. This is your life we're talking about. You only get one go at it. Treat your life like its worth living. I wrote a poem, Purle, about ten years ago when I was going through some tough times; and when I would feel like I was at the lowest point in my life, I would take the poem out and read it. The words that I wrote allowed me to get through many sleepless nights and many difficult times and not having the answers to many questions that I needed the answers to to carry on my life."

Momma showed me the faded scars on her wrist. Purle, she said, "Anybody can promise you the world, but it is the promise that is kept that is most important. My advice to you is to never love any man more then yourself. That is the number one rule in life. Always remember that no one owes you a thing in life except for your self."

Deep down inside I knew everything Momma was saying was true. I opened up the folded paper that Momma had given to me and began to read the poem out loud while she sat there looking at me.

TRUE SURVIVAL

For every man a story could be told
For every mother a baby she will hold
A river sways and with wind and sometimes deep
For every broken promise that just won't keep
My life's plans unraveled twine
A foundation of history that is only mine
Who will peep the perfect way, or stand without fear
    if you may
My superior man wear your armor of steel and sword
    of gold
Courage, dignity, power to uphold
Will the powers that be ever decide
Winners of success, losers striped of pride
The Epitaph written, silence with his voice he shouts
    and at rest
Step up, time stops, smile sigh and say I've done my
    best

I started crying. Momma said "Purle, can you live with yourself knowing what you are doing? I didn't raise you to fall down and play dead when the going got rough. I sacrificed my entire life for my daughters. Don't go out like this, Purle. Purle honey, it is almost like you are punishing yourself for shooting Jr. Purle, you didn't kill that young man. He killed himself. Honey, our days are numbered, and it is the mark in life that we make that is important to our real judge and jury. I'll probably never know how you feel, Purle, deep down inside, but I will tell you this I am thankful and grateful that you saved my life that dreadful night. I have already asked for forgiveness for Jr's soul. Purle it is time to stop punishing yourself and to take back control of your life."

"Thank you, Momma, for that wake up call. Thank

you for saving my life. Please have my attorney come to see me right away."

Momma looked at me and winked her eye and said, "Now the ball is in your court, and its up to you now."

The night came; I tossed and turned all night. I hated the night. It brought a feeling of loneliness and despair to me. All I could think about was Tyrone, the good times along with the bad. Everything was just so painfully right now. The way that I am feeling right now is that I have to tell my attorney everything. When I say everything, I mean everything. I cannot tell that I intend on telling the entire truth about the gun being his. Tyrone has a way about him that makes me weak regardless of what I know is wrong or right.

Morning was here. The night had passed by fast. During the night I thought about my entire future over and over. I thought about the fact that one day I would like to get married and have children. I thought about one day I would like to also graduate from college with a degree in fashion design. I cannot allow anyone or anybody deprive me of the right to freedom. Oh how I long to be able to smell the fresh air again. I dream of being free. Without a wink of sleep all night, I knew that this was the day that I had to do what I had to do to get my life back.

Momma must have contacted Mr. Fishbein yesterday as she said she would. It is 9:00 a.m., and the prison guards are here to escort me to the waiting area. There sat Mr. Fishbein and that lady detective from the precinct Miss. P. Ross.

"Are you ready, Purle, for me to represent you?"

I looked at Mr. Fishbein and said, "Yes."

He looked at me smiled and said, "Alright. Purle, this is Detective Ross. She insisted on coming along to visit. Purle, she is here because she believes in your innocence. Is that O.K. with you?"

Detective Ross looked on with a warm smile. I smiled at the detective and said that I don't mind her being here.

There was something about this lady that made me feel very comfortable and at ease.

Mr. Fishbein said, "Purle, tell me how you gained access of the 38 caliber gun that was fired by you on the night in question."

I began to tell Mr. Fishbein the entire story as detective Ross looked on.

CHAPTER NINE
PURLE'S CONFESSION

"Tyrone and I had gone to the movies; and after we had returned from the theater, he said that he needed a small favor from me."

"Purle," Mr. Fishbein asked as he interrupted my conversation, "Would you mind if I recorded this conversation?" I shook my head no.

"Continue," he said after pulling out his tape recorder. "Pick up from where you said that you and Tyrone exited the movie theater."

"Well Tyrone said to me that he needed a big favor. As we proceeded to walk to the bus stop, Tyrone handed me a bag to hold for him. I asked Tyrone what was in the bag and he said a piece. At first I didn't understand what he meant by a piece, and then it dawned on me that he was referring to a gun. My response to Tyrone at that time was that I could not hold this gun for him because my mother would kill me if she had found it in her house. Tyrone then began to beg me to hold the gun and his reason for wanting me to hold the gun was that the police were hassling him about some things going on in the neighborhood that he knew nothing about."

"Purle, why did you decide to hold the gun after all?"

"Well, I decided to hold the gun after all because Tyrone said that he just needed me to hold it for two days and at the most a week. And thinking back in retrospect, a week is seven days, and what difference I thought would seven days make?"

"After a week I confronted Tyrone about taking the gun back, and he said that he needed one more week. Each time I approached him he would say that he just needed one more week. The gun was still in the duffel bag in my bedroom closet, and I had completely forgotten about it until the night JR. came into our apartment."

Mr. Fishbein asked, "Purle, would you be willing to appear before the judge if I can arrange a special hearing to allow you to give your statement."

I said, "Yes," without any hesitation.

"I'll tell you right now, Purle, this just might ball down to your word against Tyrone's word."

"No, it won't," I said. "Tyrone will admit that it was his pistol that I used to defend my mother against Jr."

"I want you to know, Purle, that this is not a cut and dry case. A lot of time has passed. Ballistics have shown the gun to have been involved in another murder besides Jr's. We are going to need a witness that could substantiate your story, a witness that could place Tyrone at the scene of the crime that was previously committed. The judge is going to want to know why it took you so long, Purle, to tell your side of the story." Mr. Fishbein stood up shook my hand and said, "I'll see you on Friday, Purle. We have a lot of work ahead of us."

Detective P. Ross winked at me and said, "I'll be in touch."

It really felt good to have detective Ross on my side. It seemed as if she carried a lot of weight at the jail and precinct. Everyone seemed to know her. She may have some influence as to whether or not I can get a special hearing.

Hopefully Mr. Fishbein will be able to convince the judge to allow a special hearing. While walking back to the cell I heard a voice call out, "Miss James," a correction officer said, "you have another visitor." I turned around; it was Marcey and Marcus.

"Marcey and Marcus, what a pleasant surprise." I had no idea that you two would be visiting me today."

Marcus said, "Purle, I just wanted you to know that

if there is something that I could do to help with your release, I will do. I do not condone what my brother has put you through. I am morally against what he is doing. Of course, our levels of integrity are totally incomparable."

I smiled and gave Marcus a thumbs up and told him it was good to see him. I really didn't feel up to discussing my feelings about Tyrone with anyone at this point.

"Purle," Marcus said. "I haven't sat for the Bar exam yet, but that won't stop me from doing everything in my power to get you out of here.

"Thank you, Marcus. I spoke with my attorney today, Marcus, and he said that what we have to do was to prove that the gun belonged to Tyrone." This is not going to be easy. For some reason deep down inside, I thought how in the heck would we be able to prove that? Why was I telling this to Marcus, especially after my attorney asked me not to discuss the case with anyone?

"I am so sorry, Purle, that my brother is putting you through this horrible ordeal."

"I know, Marcus, you have nothing to do with this. I am just sorry that I didn't speak up sooner. Now it may be too late. I might have ruined all of my chances to be released by remaining silent for so long."

Marcey said, "Purle, we are not going to stay long. We promised Madison that we would take her out to dinner for her birthday. That's right today is Madison's birthday. Has she been here to visit you yet, Purle?"

"No she has not been here to visit, but I understand why she hasn't visited. When Madison has a hard time dealing with something, she pretends that it doesn't exist by ignoring the situation. Where are you guys going for dinner?"

"Probably to Lorraines uptown."

"I smiled and said, "Well have a spare rib dinner for me."

Marcey said, "You'll be out soon enough to have your own spare rib dinner."

I smiled and said that I could not wait for that day. We looked at each other for about two minutes, and they left. As I was escorted back to my cell-block I felt so lonely. I think the loneliest that I have felt since I've been incarcerated.

I really don't know if I am strong enough emotionally to get through this. Do I really have a choice, I thought to myself?

MADISON'S BIRTHDAY

Just as Marcus and I approached Lorraine's restaurant, my God, I couldn't believe my eyes. We saw Tyrone walking arm and arm with another woman. I could tell that Marcus was embarrassed and ashamed. He walked over to Tyrone, and they exchanged words.

All I could hear was Tyrone saying, "Mind your damn business, Marcus."

Marcus said to Tyrone, "You're a bum."

Throughout the dinner no one said a word. We all felt so bad for Purle. Here she put her life on hold for someone who didn't care half as much about her as she did for him. I think if Tyrone wasn't Marcus's brother, Madison and I would have probably beaten the crap of him with our bare hands. That's how upset we were. I knew that I wasn't going to tell Purle that Tyrone was cheating on her, and I knew that Madison wasn't going to mention it either. We both agreed while on the way home not to mention it to Momma. She has also been through enough. Why burden her with more problems especially one of this nature.

PURLE SPEAKS OUT

I am so happy that Purle finally decided to tell the judge and the District Attorney where she got the gun. Hopefully this nightmare will be resolved soon. We have all had enough and long for our lives to return to normal.

Mrs. Noobey finally had enough of seeing Momma and all of us coming and going in and out of the building. She decided to move. It was best for everybody. Momma often said that her heart went out to Mrs. Noobey because nobody deserved to loose a child to death. One thing Mrs. Noobey didn't realize was that when her son Junior became a heroin addict that's when he died, not when Purle pulled the trigger of the gun on the night in question.

KIM CONFIDES IN MARCEY

Kim walked into the living room and said, "Can I talk to you Marcey?"

"Sure," I said and got up off the couch to go into her bedroom to give us more privacy.

We sat on her bed and Kim said, "Marcey, my friend, Ashley asked me if Momma was crazy? Marcey how could she ask me something like that? She is supposed to be my best friend."

"Well, what did you say to Ashley?"

"I said no, my mother is not crazy. She is just a little different from everybody else. I told Ashley that Momma was a very kind, gentle woman who loved just about everybody. Sure I said her taste in music is different and her style in clothes and hats are different, but not by any means is my mother crazy.

Just at that point Momma came into the room and said, "Is everything all right?"

I looked up and smiled at her and said, "Yes, Momma, everything is all right."

As Momma left the room Marcey said, "Kim, as long as you know that Momma is not crazy that's all that matters. But Marcey, I don't want anybody to think that Momma is crazy. I love her."

"Kim, people are going to think what they want to think. People are going to say what they want to say."

You cannot go through life worrying about what people say or think. You cannot change the world. I put my arms around Kim and said, "Be strong girl. You are Sarah James' daughter,and that accounts for a lot."

With everything going on with Purle, all I could think about was Purle's freedom. In the process I was neglecting Kim and Olivia. Not intentionally but I just felt as if I had no energy for anything except getting Purle out of jail.

Friday will be the day that will determine the future for all of us. This family should be able to get through the next two days without falling apart.

Friday came and Mr. Fishbein was in early to see Purle.

MR. FISHBEIN VISITS WITH PURLE

Lying on the bed in my cell with one blanket, cold, nervous, unable to sleep, the correction officer opened my cell lock while pulling the steel door back at the same time and said "Miss James, you have a visitor." Thinking to myself who would be visiting me at 8:30 a.m. it came to me. That's right, Mr. Fishbein was due to come back today.

Brushing my hair back and washing my face slowly blotting my face dry with a towel thinking to myself, why is he here so early? Yes, he did say that he would be here on Friday. However, today is Wednesday. I could feel my heart beating through my skin and uniform.

The prison guard escorted me to the visiting area. I could see from a short distance by the look on Mr. Fishbeins face that he had some good news. My heart continued to beat very fast and hard. Sitting down slowly in the chair not taking my eyes off of this guy for one second, I asked, "What's up?"

"Well, he said. You are not going to believe this, Purle." I received a call yesterday from a potential witness who could place Tyrone at the scene of the crime of the murder of our Arab victim, Peter Ajuhel."

Needless to say I was in total shock. I knew that Tyrone had betrayed me as far as leaving me holding the bag with the gun, but I never thought or believed for one moment that he was capable of shooting someone in the head. When did Tyrone turn into this monster?

I put my hand over my mouth to keep from screaming. I closed my eyes for a second. I surely knew that I was going to puke. Would you believe that somewhere deep down inside that I still loved Tyrone? As a matter of fact, I am sure that I will always love him.

As my mind drifted, Mr. Fishbein said, "Purle, are you all right?"

"Yes," I whispered. "Who is this witness?" I asked. "Is this person credible?"

Mr. Fishbein responded, "Yes, the witness is credible, and for now his identity will be and must be withheld for safety purposes.

This was surely the worst news that I had received in my entire life. This confirmed the fact that I had no clue to who Tyrone really was. My mind was racing at this point. "My god I slept with a murderer."

Mr. Fishbein said that he had to meet with the prosecutor to present the new evidence that had come forth and to make a motion to drop all charges. I was so curious to find out who this secret witness was. I wanted to decide for myself if this person was credible or not. Maybe I had just better sit back and allow everybody to do their jobs so that I can be released. Like Momma said, never look a gift horse in the mouth. Sure I felt relieved to a certain degree, but I also felt a deep sense of betrayal by Tyrone.

How could Tyrone allow me to serve all of this time knowing what he knew all for the purpose of saving his own tail. We grew up together. Not only was he my boyfriend, but he was my best friend. How could I be so wrong in judging his character? At least now I know that there will be brighter days ahead.

"There is just one thing, Mr. Fishbein said.

"What is it?" I asked.

"Purle, you cannot tell anybody about what we just discussed."

"I won't tell anybody, not even Momma." I stood to my feet while my knees were shaking, gave Mr. Fishbein two thumbs up and said thank you for everything. While walking back to the cell, I kept thinking over and over in my mind who could this witness be? Do I know him? Finally I gave up on trying to figure out who this witness could possibly be. At this point it is irrelevant to me.

As time passed I got to know the prison guards better. There was a certain amount of trust that I had established; I stayed out of trouble and didn't bother with anyone. They allowed me to have a little more physical contact with Momma. My court date was quickly approaching. Momma came to see me, and it was very difficult not to share the information with her that my attorney had given me a couple of days ago. Somehow I knew this information had to stay with me.

Momma hugged and kissed me. The prison guards didn't say anything. Momma said that Bootsey sends her love.

"Oh Momma, I wish that she didn't have to know that I was here."

Momma said. "I know, but how long could we keep something like this a secret from her? She is bound to find out."

"Purle," Momma said. "Your attorney telephoned me, and he is trying to get your court date moved up to an earlier date."

It took everything that I had inside to try to contain myself to keep from sharing what Mr. Fishbein said. She had suffered so much already during this tragedy. Just listening to Momma not saying anything, "What else did he say Momma?"

"Nothing else. Marcey and I went out and bought you a beautiful suit for you to wear when you go to court. That's if they'll let you wear it."

I smiled, looked at Momma and said, "What kind of a suit."

"Purle, it is a fine suit."

Momma's taste was different from mine, but I knew that Marcey would know what I liked. Our taste was similar. I love clothes, and hopefully one day I'll be able to fulfill my dreams of becoming a fashion designer. All I had was my hopes and dreams to hang on to at this point. This is what was keeping me alive in this place, alive emotionally and physically.

CHAPTER TEN
DETECTIVE P. ROSS

Detective Ross had come up to talk to me about the case to give me an update on what she had uncovered in the investigation. She said that she always believed in my innocence and that I was doing the right thing by saving my self. Saving myself from what I thought? Seven years in prison or saving myself from the man that I thought I would be spending the rest of my life with? She also said that life was full of unfair situations and that a lot of the unfair situations are out of our control. But what we can control, we should control. Her concept of survival was reasonable but to me was not acceptable.

She began to tell me a little bit about herself. She said that she had no children and that she didn't want any because she had no real clue to who she was. I thought to my self how sad. Detective Ross also said that all of her life growing up in the Bronx, she wished for a large family. She said that she had no brothers or sisters, and she never got married because of her line of work as a law enforcement agent, a cop. I couldn't believe when she said that she used to be a cop. She didn't fit the rough tough looking profile of a cop, (How stereotypical of me). The bottom line was, this woman was a lonely woman and probably regrets the choices she made in life. The choice of not to have gotten married and have a family was obviously a bad choice for her. It was obvious that I probably fit her profile of what her daughter would have looked like and behaved like. Why else would she have taken such an interest in my case? Why would she be so eager to share with me, someone she recently met, her most intimate feelings about her life in general? Truly I felt sorry for her.

I began telling the detective about Momma growing up as an only child also. The difference between her and Momma was that Momma always wanted a lot of children because she was also an only child and expressed how lonely she was as the only child. I mentioned to Ms. Ross that Momma's mother died when she was a little girl. I also told Ms. Ross that Momma was adopted after her mother died by a nice couple who were killed in a car accident.

Ms. Ross said, "Gee, Ms. James, your Momma and I have a lot in common."

I smiled and said, "You can call me Purle."

"The detective smiled at me and said, "You can also call me Purle." I thought to myself what a sense of humor this detective has.

"Purle, another reason I am here is because I am concerned for your safety. The word on the street is that Jr's brother Lucas, another slime ball of the earth, has mentioned to people in the neighborhood that you had better stay in jail forever because when you come out he is going to kill you."

"I doubt that. He doesn't know me from Adam. He has no idea of what I even look like, Miss Ross. The entire time that his mom, Mrs. Noobey, lived in the building I have never seen him, not once laid eyes on him."

"Well, Purle, the detective said we have to take what he is saying serious for now. During my career I have seen many threats carried out. Do you have someplace else to stay other then your mother's apartment when you are released?"

I laughed and said, "No." I told the detective that she was behaving worse then my mother with her over protective behavior. She smiled and said that you could never be too careful while reaching down into her pocket taking out a weird looking necklace.

She said to me, "Believe it or not, this is my protection."

She showed me an old beaded necklace and asked me, "What do you have?"

I answered while pointing upward, "The man upstairs."

Once again she smiled and said, "I have him too."

MARCUS AND MARCEY

Marcus and I are supposed to meet later for dinner at approximately 6:30 p.m. Originally we had set the time to meet for 5:30 p.m. Marcus said that he had a very important meeting at the same time, so we made the dinner date for one hour later.

I decided to wait in the area for Marcus just a little earlier than we had agreed upon. I was early and had some time to kill. As I walked down 57th street and 6th avenue I could see Marcus from a distance. Marcus was with the District Attorney who was prosecuting Purle. I rubbed my eyes to make sure that I wasn't seeing things. After all, it was raining outside. Sure enough as I got a little closer it was Marcus with the D.A. who was prosecuting Purle. I thought to myself that Marcus must have had a job interview with this man. How unethical the situation had seemed. My husband to be working for the same side that is responsible for incarcerating my sister.

I will not, absolutely won't question him about what I just saw when I see him. If he brings up the topic or initiates the conversation of his meeting with the D.A., then and only then will I ask him questions of my concern. I watched in the distance as Marcus held his umbrella in one hand and shook the D.A.'s hand with his free hand. The D.A. proceeded to walk away while hailing a taxicab. I hid inside a storefront until Marcus was out of sight. I am sure that he is now on his way to meet me for dinner. I wanted to arrive at the restaurant before he did. I began to walk fast. I did arrive at the restaurant before he did and sat in the waiting area waiting for him to walk up any minute, and he did.

We sat in the restaurant, ordered a carafe of Chardonnay and two spaghetti dinners. Marcus mentioned nothing about his meeting with the D.A., and neither did I. I felt like I was going to bust wide open. I was so anxiety ridden. I knew that I had to contain myself. The only way to manage that was to not allow my curiosity to get the best of me. I managed to get through the dinner without allowing my curiosity to over ride my judgement.

CHAPTER ELEVEN
PURLES DAY IN COURT

The day finally came for the courts to hear the case, "The State Verses Purle James." We all sat together in the courtroom, and on the other side of the room sat Mrs. Noobey. I felt so bad for Mrs. Noobey sitting in the courtroom alone with no one sitting next to her to comfort her. Momma, myself, Olivia, Kim, Madison, and Marcus were all there to support Purle and to be her pillar of strength.

Tyrone was there; he sat in the back of the courtroom. He thought that we didn't notice him, but we did. He was not there on behalf of Purle but on behalf of himself. I'm sure that he needed to know where he stood with this case. He needed to know if the prosecutor was going to come after him. Purle was escorted into the courtroom by a security guard. She was allowed to wear that beautiful suit that Momma and I bought for her. She looked sharp. How did she ever get the court to allow her to wear civilian clothes? I thought to myself, after Purle gets out of here she had better not look Tyrone's way.

I knew even after all of this that she was still in love with Tyrone. After all, he was her first and only love. I think that it hurt Purle most of all to know that he literally left her holding the bag and kept going.

As the judge entered the courtroom, everybody had to stand. He said with a deep voice, just like on television, you all may be seated. Thank god, it was a black judge. For some reason I felt because the judge was black he would be more likely to understand the entire situation at hand. The situation that dealt with "poverty, the rights and justice for all not for some." I felt such a surge of relief because my intuition told me that this judge would be fair. The entire time the case was being heard, Mrs. Noobey was looking over at us with the meanest look on her face.

The prosecutor stood up and said, "Your Honor, the state has decided to drop all charges against the defendant due to new evidence that was presented to the courts."

The judge summoned Mr. Fishbein and the prosecutor to the bench. They whispered for about two minutes. We could not hear what they were saying. They returned to their original places.

The judge banged his gavel and said, "This case is dismissed."

Momma put her hands over her face and sobbed uncontrollably. Purle looked back at us and gave us the two thumbs up. I put my arms around Momma and hugged her. We were all hugging each other. When we looked back to see if Tyrone was there sitting in the back of the courtroom, his seat was empty. He must have smelled a rat. I'm sure that Tyrone knew at this point that he was in deep trouble way above his knees.

Mrs. Noobey screamed out loud, "NO!" Her voice seemed as if it echoed. "This murdering tramp is going to walk? NO!"

The judge said to Mrs. Noobey after banging his gavel again, "I would suggest that you try to contain yourself before I hold you in contempt. Mam, you should try to find out why and accept why your son was in someone else's apartment at 2:00 a.m. demanding money that didn't belong to him with a ski mask on flailing a knife."

I looked at Marcus, and he didn't appear to be surprised by any of this. Something just didn't jive to me. Could Marcus have known something that nobody else knew? Was it Marcus who had given the prosecutor the evidence that they needed to lock up his brother and to set Purle free? NA, thinking to myself. I know Marcus. I know that he doesn't condone what his brother has done, but he would never turn him in.

We were all in shock. This was truly a great surprise to all of us. We all hugged each other. Momma was crying. Mr. Fishbein shook Marcus's hand. They didn't say much to each other, but the look they exchanged said it all. Mr.

Fishbein told Marcus and I that he would take care of all of the paper work that was related to Purles discharge. I felt so bad for Mrs. Noobey. As we left the courtroom, she sat alone sobbing her eyes out. Her head buried in her lap this was truly a pathetic sight. Marcus hailed a taxi for us, and the ride home was short. Purle began sharing her jail stories with us immediately; she was glowing with happiness. The day finally came when justice prevailed.

Purle was home, and everyone was happy. Now we had to try and resume life where we left off. Purle had no problems adjusting to her original routine. The real challenge would be for her to reject Tyrone if he makes an attempt to resume their relationship. I trust that she is smart enough to decide what is good and what is not good for her in life. She has had enough policing in her life for now.

MADISON'S JOB OFFER

Almost finished with my residency at Harlem Hospital I was already offered a job as a medical emergency physician on an emergency medical van. It all sounds exciting except I will be working the streets in which I grew up. Harlem is definitely familiar territory to me. Every side street every hidden alley, it's all very familiar. At this point I am almost sure that I will accept the offer. I look at the offer as a challenge, and I love a good challenge.

Purle is home, Momma is happy and the family is back to its old routine. Purle has even gotten her old job back. Tyrone was picked up and arrested two days after Purle's release. I'm not sure of the exact charges. Purle is aware of Tyrones arrest by the police yesterday; however, she hasn't mentioned it to anyone. Purle is a little less talkative with a little more subdued demeanor. I guess she has made the right choice of what is good for her. We all know it, but the important thing is that Purle has to know it.

TWO WEEKS BEFORE MARRIAGE

Marcus and Marcey had just two weeks left before their wedding day. The dress Marcey has picked out to wear is beautiful. It isn't the traditional white wedding dress.

Purle had sent for some African raw silk from Zimbabwe and designed the dress for Marcey. It was beautiful, breathtaking.

Marcus was getting his suit tailor made also. This was going to be the day that everyone had been waiting for. Therefore, it had to be perfect. Marcey wanted all of her bride's maids who happen to be all of her sisters to wear something similar to what she was wearing.

Purle designed and made everybody's dresses. Purle did a fantastic job, and Marcey must have saved thousands of dollars by having Purle make the dresses. After each dress Purle completed, the excitement of trying it on was awesome.

Momma designed her own dress. It was nice, but you know Momma. With her taste being quite different everyone held their breath until the dress was complete. Marcey suggested a couple of changes to Momma's dress, and Momma was o.k. with the minor changes. Marcey approved of Momma's three zippers on the dress. Actually, Marcey really wouldn't care what Momma wore to her wedding just as long as she was there.

Marcus chose a buddy of his from college named Cliff to be his best man. Marcus had three cousins from Georgia that he also asked to be in the wedding. All three cousins were brothers, with very strong southern accents. I believe they were Miss Lucy's sister's boys. They were very polite young men and expressed that they were honored to be a part of such a joyous occasion.

They wore a smile the entire time I saw them. It was as if the smiles were pasted on their faces. They had the whitest teeth that I'd ever seen in my life.

Marcus managed to finally talk his mother, Miss Lucy, into seeking professional help for her drug addiction. Marcus thought that it would be best for her to complete her rehab Up State New York. It is a shame that Miss Lucy would miss her own son's wedding. Marcus was the type of man who always set his priorities according to logic. This quality was what was going to determine his professional outcome as an attorney.

CHAPTER TWELVE
MORNING OF THE WEDDING

Momma and Bootsey were up early making breakfast for everyone. Momma is so happy. She truly loves Marcus. The wedding is scheduled to start at 1:00 p.m. at the First Baptist Church. Reverend King is going to marry Marcey and Marcus. Jimmy from the grocery store requested to give Marcey away. Afterall, he has watched Marcey grow up from a shy quiet young girl to an out going smart young lady. Momma was grateful to Jimmy for offering such a wonderful gesture of love. She didn't know how to contact daddy. It was best that she didn't contact him. It would just make everyone feel uncomfortable anyway.

Olivia and Kim prepared two songs to sing at the wedding and at the reception which was to follow in the basement of the church. Marcey and Marcus had spent most of their savings to help with the expenses of Purle's defense. Financially, things were tight.

Purle and Madison were helping Momma and Marcey put the finishing touches on everyone's make-up. Purle and Marcey looked as if they had just stepped out of a wedding magazine from Africa. Bootsey looked beautiful also with her gold tea length dress. Marcey looks like an Ebony Princess. She is the most beautiful bride that I have ever seen in my life. When Marcus sets eyes on her he is going to be filled with everlasting joy. Momma was beautiful. If only daddy could see her now.

The limousine was waiting downstairs to drive us around the block to the church. Marcus's cousins had already informed us that Marcus was at the church. It was believed by our family that if the groom saw the bride before the ceremony, the marriage wouldn't last. I guess Daddy must have seen Momma before their ceremony I thought to myself.

As we approached the church, Bootsey began to cry. I cannot believe my son is missing all of this. Was she crying because her son was missing the wedding or was she crying because she was embarrassed that he was not here?

Momma looked at Bootsey and said, "Don't do this to yourself Bootsey, not today."

"Besides," Madison said. "You'll mess up your make-up."

Momma reached in her purse and pulled out a tissue and gave it to Bootsey to wipe her eyes with.

The ceremony began after everybody was seated. Olivia and Kim began to sing. Everyone in the church began to clap and say amen after they were finished singing. They were truly blessed with voices. Marcus was standing at the front of the church with his three cousins and his best man, my was he handsome. Marcey entered the church through the back entrance.

Marcey marched in with Jimmy escorting her down the isle. Myself, Madison, Olivia and Kim followed in step. Marcey and Marcus didn't want the traditional wedding. They agreed upon a ceremony to represent the history of their African American Culture. As Kim began to sing The National Negro Anthem, "Lift Every Voice and Sing," everyone in the church stood to their feet once again. I am happy Olivia and Kim decided to sing three songs instead of two. With their voices two songs simply would not be enough.

The entire ceremony was beautiful. Momma got up to read a poem to Marcey and Marcus. Momma loved to write poetry. " I have chosen you to spend the rest of my life with. Why, because I love you with every breath. Every waking moment I treasure your being." Momma took a deep breath between each line and looked out at the crowd, and continued. "With much respect, I will forever trust and honor you as my equal partner in life and in death. Giving you an abundance of love, along with my heart for you to keep for eternity."

Everyone clapped after Momma read her poem. It was beautiful. Reverend King began to preach about commitment.

Then he went on "Marcus, do you take Marcey to be your lawful wedded wife?"

After Reverend King pronounced Marcus and Marcey husband and wife, at that point they kissed each other for about one minute straight. The entire ceremony was beautiful. It was hard to believe that my big sister was now somebody's wife. I didn't mind sharing her with Marcus. He was deserving of her love.

All of the invited guests followed downstairs into the church basement for the reception. The food was fantastic. Everyone danced and ate until about 1:00 a.m. If I didn't know any better I would have bet that Reverend King was sipping on more then just punch. Olivia and Kim sang their last song, it was beautiful.

Marcus and Marcey received two thousand dollars in gifts and lots of dishes, glasses, pots and pans. They received more money then anyone had anticipated. Now they had enough money to buy their first living room set. They hadn't planned a honeymoon. Marcus's idea of a honeymoon was having Marcey alone all to himself. They had been looking at houses for the past year; and after looking at about ten houses in New Jersey, they didn't like any of them. They finally started looking in Pennsylvania.

They finally found the house of their dreams in Marshalls Creek, Pennsylvania, a beautiful four bedroom Colonial house. They tried to convince Momma to move out of the tenement apartment and in with them, but she refused. Momma said that the apartment held too many memories that she wasn't ready to part with just yet. In other words, she became a part of the structure. I think the memories that she wanted to hold on to were memories of her and Daddy.

Marcus had been studying for about two months for the bar exam. He would stay awake for hours and hours at night, and sometimes he never got to bed. When he set his mind to do something, there was no detouring for Marcus.

He would say that our lives together depended on whether or not he passed the boards. He felt that if he didn't pass the boards, financially we would go under. The mortgage had to be paid, simple as that; and there was no way we could make the payments on an average income. The day finally came for Marcus to take the State Board Exam.

He was extremely calm before he left the house. I made sure that he had a good night sleep the night before and had eaten a healthy breakfast before leaving the house. Momma called to say goodluck and so did Purle and Madison. I had no doubt in my mind that Marcus would pass. It took forever for us to find out the results of his test. Finally the day came that we received the news. The letter was great! This was the happiest day of our life. We telephoned everyone with the results. Momma cried with joy. If we had a penny for everytime Momma cried, we would be rich.

MARCUS PASSES THE BAR EXAM

Marcus passed the Bar exam and landed that job with Landberg, Stein and Associates. They were pretty much set financially to begin their life together.

MARCEY MOVES AWAY

Momma was so sad the day that Marcey moved out of the apartment. Purle was looking for an apartment. She said that the apartment held too many bad memories for her. Madison found a beautiful studio apartment on 72nd street and Central Park West. Olivia and Kim were not looking to move anywhere anytime soon. The both of them graduated from high school and wanted no parts of college at this time.

The both of them, Kim and Olivia, managed to land jobs working at a recording studio on 61st Street not far from Lincoln Center. Determined to become successful female vocalist they proceeded to make demos at the studio. Momma continued to work at the rehab center on 123rd street but only part-time. She had a little more free time on her hands with everyone going about with their lives.

CHAPTER THIRTEEN
PURLE HOME WITH MOMMA

We were all so very happy that Purle was still at home with Momma. Purle was very content with her living arrangements at this point in her life and decided not to move away afterall. This was great because she could look out for Momma.

Although Olivia and Madison were also living with Momma, their schedules were too busy at this time. Purle spent much of her time after work in her bedroom reading. I asked Purle how Tyrone was doing, but she quickly changed the subject. Purle was on a new mission. For some reason she began asking Momma many questions about her past questions about her mother.

PURLE REMEMBERING CONVERSATIONS
WHILE IN JAIL

For some reason I just could not get Detective Ross out of my mind. There were certain things that she said during her visit with me at Rikers Island that lit a spark. Her and Momma had so much in common. As a matter of fact they had similar mannerisms their facial expressions, the way they smiled. I need to find out a little more about Det. Ross' past.

"Hello, may I speak with Detective Ross?"

Some guy with a deep voice answered, "She just left to go home for the day. Can I take a message?"

"When will she be back?"

"She will be in tomorrow morning at 9:00 a.m."

"Thank you."

My mind began to wonder again. Could her name also be Purle? She said for me to call her Purle, and her nametag read Detective P. Ross. Momma said that she named me after her sister, Purle, who was put up for adoption as a baby. Also, what about this necklace that she carries around for protection? Where did she get it? Momma said that her mother gave her sister Purle rosary beads before she was taken away from her. Oh my God, thinking to myself, what a coincidence. I have to ask Detective Ross some questions as soon as possible. The first question being how does she spell her name. Does she spell it Pearl or Purle?

I asked Momma if she had any pictures of her mother hanging around, and she said yes. I told her that I needed to see them as soon as possible. Momma reached under her bed, pulled out a shoe box, and opened it. The both of us sat on the bed looking through the pictures. Of course, Momma wanted to know what I was up to; but there was no way that I was going to get her hopes up without some real proof of their relationship as sisters. Besides I needed to know where Detective Ross stood about wanting to know who her family was.

Momma pulled out a picture of her mother, and I thought that I would faint. Her mother and Detective Ross looked like the same person. My grandmother had the same weird looking beaded necklace around her neck that Det. P.Ross showed me.

Momma looked at me and said, "Child, what's wrong with you? You look like you just saw a ghost."

"Nothing, Momma, I said. There is nothing wrong with me."

I asked Momma if I could hold on to the picture of my grandmother. Momma smiled and said yes. Momma had been through too much in life, and I didn't want her to get hurt again. I had to be sure of what I was thinking, and I had to be sure if Det. Ross wanted a sister in her life at this time. I knew Momma would be thrilled.

The next morning I called the precinct again. "Hello,

may I speak with Det. Ross?"

"She is working in the field today," the man answered.

"Well, do you know what time she should be stopping in the office?"

"No I don't. Can I take a message?"

"Yes, can you have her call Purle James when she gets in?"

"Sure, what's your phone number?"

"555-1212, please tell her that it is urgent."

"Will do."

"Thank you, sir."

DETECTIVE P.ROSS

"Detective Ross you had a phone call from a Purle James this morning."

"Did she say what she wanted?"

"No, she just left a message for you to call her back when you got in."

"I needed to speak with her anyway. I'll just pay her a visit. I've been doing some investigating, and it seems as if this Lucas guy, Mrs. Noobey's other son, is planning on seeking revenge against Purle James for his brother's murder. If Miss James calls back, tell her that I went to grab a sandwich, and then I'll be stopping over to see her."

"O.K. will do."

PURLE ATTEMPTING TO CONTACT DETECTIVE ROSS

"Hello, this is Purle James again. Did Detective Ross return yet?"

"Yes, Miss James, she left a message for you that she was stopping off to get a sandwich, and then she was going over to your house to discuss some unfinished business."

"Do you know, sir, what the unfinished business is about?"

"She mentioned something about a man named Lucas and revenge."

"Oh, that again. How long ago did she leave?"

"Just about 45 minutes ago"

"Thank you, sir. I'll be looking out for her."

I'll look out of the window for her, meet her in the hallway and take her down the street to have another sandwich because Momma is home, and we really need to talk in private. While looking out of the front room window I could finally see her pull up in her old Navy Blue Buick. Waving to her out of the window I caught her eye, and she waved and smiled at me. I ran out of the house to meet her in the hallway. While standing at the ledge of the 3rd floor I could hear her panting while walking up the steps. I couldn't wait to tell her what I knew.

I yelled out to her, "Purle." After all, while I was in jail she told me to call her Purle.

"I yelled out again, Purle, I'm up here."

She looked up while continuing to walk up the stairs, and all of a sudden I heard a loud bang and then another loud bang. Thinking to myself what in the heck was that, I could see Purle fall back while holding her chest. It all seemed as if it were happening in slow motion.

I began screaming and calling for someone to help me. I could see a man running past her down the stairs.

"Help me, my god, somebody call an ambulance." Help me," I yelled.

I held Detective Ross' head in my hands.

She looked at me and said in a whisper, "I came over to warn you that Lucas was going to try and hurt you."

I managed to ask Detective Ross if she spelled her name Purle. She nodded her head yes before passing out. I don't know why I decided to ask her something like that at a time like this. This was the last question, I guess, to validate if she was truly Momma's sister.

I said, "God, don't you die on me. You are my Auntie Purle. You are Momma's Purle." I took her Rosary beads out of her pocket held them tight and began to pray out loud while crying. "God Please, Please God let her live." By this time Momma was looking on. "She is my Momma's Purle, God. They need each other. Please God don't let it end like this. I'll do anything God anything you ask me to do. Let her live." Deep down inside I had truly grown to care about Detective P. Ross, not because she was my mother's sister but because she truly cared about me.

I looked up and could barely see through my tears. Madison and her emergency crew had arrived. It felt as if time was moving slow. I began to scream and cry while on my knees banging my hand into the concrete floor.

I could hear Madison say in an echoed voice, "I have a pulse. It's weak, but it's there."

Madison went into motion along with her medical crew. I could hear walkie talkies. I could see Madison working fiercely and screaming, "I need a line. I need an airway. She is going into Ventricular Tachycardia now."

"Probably because of the blood loss," a voice said.

I could hear Madison say, "Give me 200 Joules all clear. I heard a thumping sound. Give me 300 Joules all clear. I heard another thump. O.K. 360 Joules and some epi stat. Let's get her going. Let's move it. Alright, normal sinus rhythm," Madison said. "Let's move it."

I could hear a police officer say, "Yes they caught Lucas two blocks away with the gun in his hand."

I felt no relief of pain or disappear. I wanted to die. I

knew that Lucas' bullets were meant for me. Momma held me tight. I just wanted to die.

As The Medical team proceeded to the emergency vehicle with Purle on the stretcher, I kissed her on the cheek and whispered in her ear that I needed her to live as they carried her away. I whispered in her ear that she had a big family waiting for her to recuperate and that I had a lot of stories to tell her about her real mother and her real sister and all of her nieces.

As they took her away, Momma looked at me and said, "Purle, I am not going to ask you right now what happened and what's going on." Momma squeezed me tight and said, "Purle, I love you. Let's go inside so you can lie down."

I said, "Momma that lady that just got shot in our hallway is your sister, Purle." Momma looked at me and said, "I believe that Purle. She looks exactly like my mother, your grandmother. When I saw the rosary beads you took out of her pocket, I nearly fainted. Those beads are one of a kind. Purle, how did you find out?"

"Well Momma, it's a long story. When I was in jail, she came to visit me and we began talking. I began to put two and two together. Momma, you two were destined to meet. Your paths were bound to cross; and for some reason, God used me as the bridge of contact."

"Well, Purle, I am going to go over to the hospital to see how Purle is doing. You stay here and get some rest."

"No Momma, I'm going with you. I need to know how she is doing."

When we arrived at the hospital, the Doctor's wouldn't give us any information. About an hour later we saw Doctor Madison James. Madison looked up at Momma and I and said, "Well, since you are the next of kin I guess I can tell you what her present condition is.

Madison said, "Right now she is in the O.R. with the best two surgeons that I know. She sustained two gunshot wounds, one to her right shoulder and one to her abdomen. The wound to her abdomen is the one that is of concern. The surgeon has been able to stop the bleeding. However, she is not out of danger.

I hugged Madison and said, "You are the best."

Madison looked at me and said, "No" while pointing up in the air God is the best.

I began to cry again. Momma held me tight. Madison looked at us and said "You had better be right, Purle, that this is Momma's sister because I signed consent for surgery as next of kin." And she walked off wearing her Green Doctors' Scrubs and clogs.

Momma and I continued to wait at the hospital. Six hours passed. Eight hours passed and after the ninth hour, Madison returned.

"The surgery went well. Purle was transferred to the Intensive Care Unit. She is intubated and on a ventilator to help with oxygen exchange. She has a lot of I.V. fluids going, and her face is a little puffy from the trauma of falling."

Madison told us that we could only visit for 15 minutes. That was fine with us. We would have been happy with just one minute.

Momma went in first; I could see Momma holding her hand. I could hear Momma saying, "Thank you, God, for giving me back my sister after all of these years. Please keep her safe. I need her to know that I welcome her into my family as my sister with open arms. Purle, you look just like Momma. I know that you cannot hear me, but when you wake up I'm going to tell you all about our mother. Purle, you gotta know that she didn't want to give you away. She had no choice at that time. If you can hear me, Purle, squeeze my hand." Purle squeezed my hand. I began to cry. This was confirmation that she knew that I was with her and that she had heard everything that I said.

To think that I went all of these years not knowing whether or not my sister was dead or alive not being emotionally strong enough to try to attempt to find out. I guess it was the fear of not knowing whether or not she would accept me as her sister.

Purle went in next. Threw her hands in the air and said, "Thank you, Lord. Please continue to answer my prayers by keeping her safe through the night. I meant everything I said lord in that hallway back there. Continue to watch over her and keep her guardian angel with her throughout the night." As Momma and I left the hospital, there were police officers everywhere. Afterall, this was one of their fellow officers who went down. The news was all over the radio and television stations.

Lucas was going away for a long time. Sure, he shot Purle but the wrong Purle. Poor Mrs. Noobey, I cannot imagine the state of mind she is in right now. Momma called Reverend King and asked him to have a special prayer meeting for Mrs. Noobey. Momma was special that way.

When Momma and I returned home, Marcey and Marcus were there waiting. They had heard about what happened and came over right away to make sure that we were all right. I began to tell Marcey and Marcus the entire story and how I found out that Detective P.Ross was Momma's long lost sister Purle. Marcus and Marcey were shocked.

CHAPTER FOURTEEN
MARCEY'S PREGNANCY

Marcus told Momma that she was going to be a grandmother. Momma hugged Marcus and Marcey and said thank you. Momma was elated. She threw both hands up in the air and yelled "alright" WHILE DANCING TO ONLY THE SOUND OF HER MUSIC while singing. Momma has a great voice.

This day had been a very emotional day for us all. Marcey confided in Momma that she had a dream that she was going to have twins.

Momma looked at Marcey and said with a big grin on her face, "One for me, and one for you." Momma hugged Marcey and said, "I wish you and Marcus the best."

Marcey looked at Momma and said, "I know, Momma. I love you."

It seemed as if Momma's life was now on a positive roll. These last couple weeks that we have had had been happy times. This was unusual for our family.

Bootsey had given Momma a phone call at last. She wanted to visit with Purle whom she hadn't seen in over a year due to Purle's incarceration. Momma agreed to meet Bootsey at the 42nd Street bus terminal next Tuesday. Momma had every Tuesday off from work.

Bootsey came and left, and her visit was wonderful. It looked as if she might have lost a couple of pounds, and her upper body appears to be a little bent forward. Hopefully, she does not have something that Madison calls "Osteoporosis". Madison went out and picked up some calcium vitamins for Bootsey and made a big deal about her taking them everyday. Bootsey agreed to take a vitamin every day. Momma escorted Bootsey back to the bus terminal when leaving.

TWO WEEKS LATER

Detective Purle is out of the hospital doing quite well. She and Momma are getting to know each other. They have about fifty years to catch up on. Momma has decided to move to a different location finally agreeing that this neighborhood has given this family more than its share of grief. Momma and Purle began looking in the newspaper for an apartment in a better neighborhood. Deep down inside I could sense that Momma didn't really want to move. Momma was just trying to keep her family from worrying anymore. Afterall, it was always Momma who wanted and expressed her desire to get out of the ghetto. Could it be that perhaps this was no longer her main objective because we are all grown.

We are at the point in our lives where we are no longer impressionable. The foundation of our personalities are firm and strong; and truthfully, we are who we are going to be. I am the oldest. I am now 30 years old. Purle is 29, Madison is 28, Kim is 24, and Olivia is 22. There are no babies left for Momma to take care of. Although she never did get us physically out of Harlem, she got us out of Harlem emotionally and spiritually, meaning we were never a part of the lifestyle or thinking of the environment in which we lived.

We have all grown up and with our very different personalities have gone separate ways as far as careers are concerned. Olivia and Kim are pursuing a singing career, Madison is a physician, Purle is a seamstress down in the garment district, and I am a wife and a mother soon to be. With Purle still not seeing Tyrone, she has a lot more time on her hands to spend with Momma and to do the things that she want to do. Purle has been spending a lot of time with Detective Ross. Detective Ross has done a great job with helping Purle overcome a lot of her emotional turmoil regarding Tyrone. I know that Purle has grown to love Detective Ross who I must get use to calling "Auntie Purle". They are good for each other. Purle also helps to fill the void in Auntie Purle's life. Truthfully she is the daughter to Auntie Purle that she never had.

Momma's two Purles have become very close. They spend a lot of time together just like with Momma. It is so nice having an auntie in the family. Momma and her sister go shopping together. They go to the movie theater every Saturday night and out for dinner every other Tuesday. It is wonderful. Momma seems so happy. What an improvement in Momma's quality of life. She had struggled so long trying to raise us alone without any real financial stability. The most important thing was that she was and still is the best mother to us.

CHAPTER FIFTEEN
MOMMA'S ENCOUNTER WITH DADDY

Just getting off of work, tired, feet hurting, I approached my apartment building. I could see a man sitting on the stoop with a bag beside him. Thinking to myself, oh God, what now? As I got closer I could see that it was Bootsey's son.

My goodness, it has been years since I had seen him. Although by law we never got divorced, it was hard for me to refer to him as my husband. Thinking to myself, how convenient, he shows up after all of the hard work is done. The girls are all grown, and here he sits. Saying to myself, "Sarah, don't be mean. Don't be nasty. He is also human and subject to make mistakes."

"Lee James, you still look the same with the exception of some gray hair at the temples."

Looking up at me smirking with that same old slick grin, "It's been a long time, Sarah," he said, "and you're still looking fine as ever." I didn't respond to his compliment. "Sarah," he said, "I've been doing a lot of thinking, and I know in the past that I haven't been the best husband in the world." He looked up at me and said, "If you give me another chance, I'll make up all of the years that I deserted you and the girls."

I said, "Lee that time is lost forever. I looked him straight in the eyes and said, "Lee that time is lost forever, and we will never see it again. When you decided that night to pack your clothes and leave, I got through it. It nearly killed me, but I got through it. The girls and I had each other, and we got along just fine. There were some rough times, but we made it through. The sad part, Lee, is that you

missed the best years of your daughters lives - the gradua-
tions, Madison's graduation from med school, Marcey's wedding, Purle's arrest (we cannot forget about that), and now
I'm going to be a grandmother."

Lee looked up at me with that old sorry expression
and said, "Sarah I'm sorry. I'm sorry that I wasn't here for
you when you and the girls needed me."

I looked at Lee and said, "Lee your apology is accepted. I hold no malice or contempt for you, but what I do hold
is sympathy. All that time that you have missed with your
daughters, those special moments of hearing Olivia and
Kim sing, that time is gone forever. Lee they don't know you.
They only know you by name. Your daughters have grown
up to be fine young women. They are all different in their
own ways, but what they all have in common is their self
respect and level of integrity. I am grateful for that Lee."

I knew what Lee was working up to asking me; he
still has the same nerve that he had before he left fifteen
years ago. I couldn't believe what this man was about to ask
me. "Sarah can I come back home?"

I shook my head thinking to myself, this man is
pathetic. "Lee, home is where your heart is. Your heart has
never been with me. This is not your home, Lee, not anymore; and I cannot direct you to where your home is because
even I don't know that." I shook my head, in disgust,
reached down into my purse took out a fifty dollar bill and
gave it to him. It was my last $50.00 bill, but I know that
when you give from your heart you receive. I had experienced this idea of giving in the past. He took the money
without hesitation. It was apparent that he had no place
else to go.

Lee handed me his phone number on a piece of torn
paper and said, "If you decide, Sarah, to change your mind
about taking me back, give me a call." I winked at him, nodded my head O.K., smiled, and walked inside my apartment
building.

Olivia and Kim were looking out of the window the
entire time I was having this discussion with their father.

They said, "Could you believe, Momma, after all these years Daddy decides to show up?

I looked at Olivia and Kim and said, "It's a crazy world out there," while handing them Lee's phone number that he had given to me. I said to Olivia and Kim, "If you ever want to get to know him better, give him a call; but if you ever expect something from him, my advice to the both of you is, 'Don't expect and you won't be let down.'"

They looked at each other and said at the same time, "WE KNOW." The three of us began to laugh.

Momma never had a bad thing to say about Daddy, and I could appreciate that quality in her. She was truly a positive person, word, thought, and deed. If there was truly a place in heaven, I knew Momma would be there. Never had any bad gossip about anybody and never came home drunk. How did she maintain her composure in this crazy neighborhood?

Bootsey would still come to visit Momma from time to time. However, she was getting older and was having more trouble ambulating with those bad knees. Momma would call her at least once a week to check up on her and to make sure that she was doing fine. I knew also that Momma was sending her money from time to time. Momma truly loved Bootsey, and Bootsey adored Momma. Momma was the daughter that Bootsey never had. Bootsey's birthday was coming up and Momma planned a surprise birthday party for her. Momma told Bootsey that she was taking her out to dinner and for her to come into the city from New Jersey already dressed up.

By the time Momma picked Bootsey up from the Port Authority it was already 6:00 p.m. This was close to Bootsey's bedtime and made us a little nervous. We decorated the house, laid out the snacks, and turned the music down low when Olivia warned us that they had just gotten off of the bus and were on their way upstairs. We turned the lights out and hid behind the drapes. Momma walked into the apartment turned the lights on, and we yelled "Surprise!" Bootsey almost had a heart attack, but she was tickled pink. She laughed and laughed.

We hugged and kissed her and gave her gifts. She loved the new dress Purle made for her, the perfume and blouse that Marcus and I bought for her, and the four new night gowns Olivia and Kim bought for her. Madison brought her the best gift of all a gift certificate to the furniture store to buy a new posturepedic bed. Bootsey had been complaining to Madison about her back hurting.

Momma gave Bootsey a big hug. We turned the music up, ate all night, and danced. We had a great party. The birthday cake was beautiful that Kim baked with two candles. There was no way that we were going to fit 78 candles on that cake. Bootsey kept saying that she was 75 years old, but we knew her true age. Actually she didn't have one wrinkle in her face; and she could have truly passed for 55 years old. That's how well she looked.

SEVEN MONTHS LATER

Marcey finally gave birth to two healthy baby boys. Momma was ecstatic. Twins in the family We couldn't believe that Marcey's dream was accurate. Did Marcey have psychic abilities or what? Marcus was so proud. They named the boys Michael and Matthew. They were the cutest little bundles of joy. Marcey's labor was terrible. She suffered for seven hours before the doctors decided to perform a cesarean section.

Michael weighed four lbs. and three ounces and Matthew weighed five lbs. even. Momma and Aunt Purle went out shopping for the boys and returned with the entire infant section from the department store. The twins were identical and nobody could tell them apart except for Marcey. Marcus couldn't even tell them apart, and he is the daddy.

Marcey had to keep the babies with different color outfits on for knowing who was who. Momma and Auntie Purle also bought Marcey and Marcus a beautiful twin baby carriage. Knowing Momma, she must have been saving her money from the first day Marcey told her that she was pregnant.

Marcus' mother Lucy was home from rehab and also

brought the baby a few things. Lucy was doing fine. Marcey and Marcus often had her over to visit with them. Miss Lucy has been drug free now for almost two years. She still looks awful, but I guess it will take more years to come before she looks normal. Marcus is very proud of her accomplishments, and often reminds her of how proud of her he is.

It seems as if Marcus and Marcey spend more time visiting Momma these days then ever. Madison is dating a nice young doctor who is a surgeon. She met him at the hospital. His name is Dr. Frances Obilae. He is African and very handsome. Of course Momma likes him. Madison loves him. Ever since she has been dating this guy she has had such a magical glow to her eyes and skin. I think the relationship is serious at this point. They spend working hours together and off duty time together. Madison has been shopping for perfume, negligees, and fancy underwear. This is very different for Madison. These days her nails are done, and her hair is fine. She has done a 360° as far as her outer appearance is concerned. She is simply beautiful.

Olivia and Kim are dating two rappers from the Bronx with whom they have a lot in common with. The two fellas just came out with their first single, and Olivia and Kim have been touring with them hoping to also get some recognition.

It's just Purle left at home with Momma most of the time, and she hasn't found anybody to date since Tyrone. She enjoys spending her time with Momma and Aunt Purle. The talk of finding a new apartment has dissolved. Momma and Purle I guess are truly happy with where they are living, and that is o.k. if that's what they want.

Everybody's life seems like it is on the right track, Olivia, Kim, Madison, Purle, Momma, Aunt Purle, and myself. Marcus and I spend a lot of quality time together with our boys when he is not at work. We often visit the Central Park Zoo. The twins adore the monkey's.

Marcus loves his job at the firm, and I loved staying home taking care of the twins. Marcus is a terrific husband and a wonderful father. Marcus informed me that Tyrone was due to come home in eight months on parole. We didn't tell Purle. We felt that she was just better off not knowing.

Olivia and Kim moved out and found a place of their own. They both decided to share an apartment not far from Madison. Momma was O.K. with the idea as long as they were not going to, as Momma called it, shack up with their boyfriends. Purle was the only one left at home with Momma. I felt bad for Purle because I knew that she would be living with Momma probably forever.

TYRONE OUT OF JAIL

Tyrone had been out of jail a year now and had made no attempts to contact Purle which was great as far as we were concerned. Marcus would hear from him occasionally when he needed a loan from time to time. Tyrone had that kind of personality. He only wanted to be bothered when he needed something.

It was Friday evening the weather was beautiful and Marcus and I decided to pay Momma a visit with the children. They adored Momma. She had those boys spoiled rotten. They called Momma, "MeMa", and she loved it. We didn't call Momma before coming over because we wanted to surprise her as we often did. When we entered into the apartment, the radio was on as usual.

"Momma," I yelled out. She didn't answer. "Momma are you in the back?" Still no answer. Michael broke away from me and ran into Momma's bedroom while I continued to inspect the refrigerator. Marcus had already gotten comfortable at the kitchen table waiting for Momma to come out of the room to offer him a warm plate of something delicious as she always did in the past.

Michael ran from Momma's room saying, "MeMa is on the floor and her won't answer me when I talking to her, Mommy."

I ran into Momma's room and screamed for Marcus who was right behind me. Momma looked terrible. She wasn't breathing. Marcus called 911. I yelled out for Marcus to keep the twins out of the bedroom. I begged for Momma to answer me, but she didn't. Her body was cold. I grabbed a blanket off of her bed and wrapped it around her. Her eyes were closed. My knees began to buckle. I tried frantically to breath into Momma's mouth. She wasn't breathing. I began to cry out loud unable at this point to contain my emotions. I was totally aware of what was going on, the boys in the next room. However, I let out a scream that if Momma wasn't dead she would have surely awakened at this point. I cried for Marcus to help me bring Momma back. Marcus knelt down beside Momma's lifeless body on the floor and began to pray. "Our father, which art in heaven." All I could do was cry. I never felt so helpless in my entire life. The twins watched on quietly.

CHAPTER SIXTEEN
MADISON'S TURMOIL

I had just gotten to work ready to round up my emergency medical crew when Dr. Frances Obilae who is also my fiancé said to me, "Matti you just got a page over the system to call the office."

I said I didn't hear it. "I'll respond after I get my team together Frances."

At the same time my personal pager went off to respond to a code blue at 220 west 114th street apartment 5B. A women approximately in her fifty's early sixty's found not breathing no heart beat lying on the floor of her bedroom.

"No this can't be. This is Momma's apartment. No, No, No!" I threw the pager against the wall.

Frances pulled me close to him and said, "Matti get a grip."

"Frances, I cannot go on this call. It's my mother. Oh my God, it's my mother."

Frances looked at a member of my team and said, "Stay with her while I get the team ready to move out. LET'S GO NOW."

I ran into the bathroom and began to puke. I broke out in a sweat and felt as if I were going to pass out. Frances had left with the emergency team to the address called in. I felt as if someone had put their hand over my mouth and was interfering with the process of my breathing. I felt a ringing sensation in both ears, and the room I was in began spinning fast. When I woke up, Marcey and Frances and Purle were standing around my bed. I had passed out, I guess, and was taken to a room and put into bed.

Marcey said, "Madison, I'm so sorry."

Purle said "Momma went fast."

Frances held me and said, "Matti, my love, I am so sorry. We did everything, but she was already gone when we got there, massive heart attack." I cried so bad.

This was the woman who nurtured me, the woman who made me the physician that I am today. This was the woman who stayed up more then 24 hours sewing Easter outfits for five daughters when she didn't have a dime in her pocket to buy us new outfits so that we would feel all dressed up like the other kids in the neighborhood. This was truly the woman that built the walls of Jericho. I was consumed with grief.

I could not stop crying.

Olivia and Kim are at the house with Aunt Purle. They are devastated.

Frances looked at me and asked "Do you feel well enough, my love, to leave with your sisters?"

"Yes," I said. "Frances come home with me." This was truly the saddest day of my life. I felt like my heart was ripped out of my chest. The pit that I had in my stomach was wrenching. With each breath that I took was a struggle.

I thought if only I had stopped by to see Momma earlier today, I might have been able to assess that something was wrong.

Frances said, "Matti don't torture yourself like this. We can all ride through life on a big IF. If we knew the future, Matti, we would not be able to get through today."

"Yeah, I guess your right, Frances."

The very next morning Purle, Marcey, Kim, Olivia, Aunt Purle and myself went to the funeral parlor to make the arrangements. Momma had a small insurance policy that we were unaware of until searching through her belongings.

Marcus sent a limo out to N.J. to pick up Bootsey. She was devastated. Olivia and Kim were also devastated. Our family was not prepared for this tragedy. We were all consumed with grief.

The funeral was set for three days from the day she died. Reverend King was going to do the eulogy. I knew for sure that Momma was in heaven. The only way that I can accept her death is by believing that God needed her to take care of somethings for Him. She did everything that she could do while she was here. I guess there was nothing else left for her to do here.

Momma had a heart of gold and was going to be missed terribly by her family. We had to figure out how in the heck we were going to live without Momma. We always relied on Momma's advice. Now we had to rely on our own common sense and intuition to survive life's unpredictable encounters. We have to coast through life on what Momma had given us as life's guide to succeed, all of the little do's and don'ts she had told us about.

The day of the funeral we all stayed together at Momma's apartment like old times. We talked about old times good and bad, happy and sad. Bootsey cried so bad.

Bootsey kept crying and saying, "I wanted to go first."

She truly loved Momma. Aunt Purle had come into our lives just in time.

We truly learned to love her, and I know that Momma loved aunt Purle. The twins kept asking when God was going to send Momma back for a visit. I was mentally drained and didn't have any more answers for anybody. Purle decided that she no longer wanted to move out of the apartment. We all knew she had no real intentions of going anywhere.

As we proceeded to get into the limousine to take us to the funeral home, we could almost hear each others heart beating. Momma had more friends then we ever knew.

There were many ex-addicts waiting to go inside the funeral home. As I looked at the big black hearse carrying Momma's body, I broke down and sobbed. My entire four years as a medical physician, I had never felt such despair and helplessness.

The service began and Reverend King began to preach. His sermon was fantastic. He spoke on life after death. This was truly refreshing for all of us. After he was done preaching, Olivia and Kim got up to sing. I knew surely now that I would have to be carried out. They sang "I'll Trade A Lifetime." After they were done there wasn't a dry eye in the building.

Purle stood up to read the poem that Momma had given her while she was in jail titled, "TRUE SURVIVAL"

"For every man a story could be told.
For every mother a baby she will hold
A river sways and with wind, and sometimes deep
For every broken promise that just won't keep
My life's plans unraveled twine
A foundation of history that is only mine
Who will peep the perfect way
Or stand without fear if you may
My superior man wear your armor of steel and sword
    of gold
Courage, dignity, power to uphold."

Purle looked up at everyone crying took a deep breath with a straight face and continued to read.

"Will the powers that be ever decide
Winners of success, losers stripped of pride
The epitaph written, silence with his voice he shouts
    and at rest
Step up, time stops, smile sigh and say I've done my
    best."

Purles voice didn't crack once.

After Purle read the poem everyone began to sob very loudly. Marcus stood up and talked about how Momma was a mother to him and how Momma showed him how to

love unconditionally and how to be a man. The entire service was beautiful. Bootsey had to be carried out. I got really
nervous when I saw the three ushers carrying her out. I
thought perhaps she had died. They were taking her into
Reverend King's office to lie down.

At the burial site Kim and Olivia sang "I'm going Up
Yonder." After they were finished singing, I looked over to
see Daddy standing in the midst of things with a beautiful
bouquet of red roses. He looked terrible. He had on an old
blue suit that was much too small for him. I motioned him
to come closer, and he walked slowly closer toward us and
blended into the crowd. I guess his guilt kept him from getting any closer to his girls at this time.

As we laid the flowers on Momma's grave and Pastor
King was closing the ceremony Daddy yelled out, "Sarah,
Sarah, I'm so sorry, Sarah. I love you, Sarah." He walked up
to the coffin and placed his roses gently down on top of the
coffin while crying uncontrollably. Bootsey put her arms
around him and whispered something into his ear. Daddy
nodded his head yes to Bootsey and kissed her on the cheek.
This was the first time that we had ever seen Bootsey com-
municate positively with her son.

Purle was visibly upset that Daddy showed up. The
look on Purle's face was one of total disgust. I was hoping
that Purle kept her cool out of respect for Momma and
Bootsey. If looks could kill, Daddy would be dead.

Everybody followed us back to the church basement,
and food was served. Friends and family prepared all of the
food. I didn't have an appetite and neither did Marcus. The
twins hadn't eaten all day. Marcus fed Matthew, and I fed
Michael. They shoved the food into their little mouths as if
they hadn't eaten in months. I felt terrible.

Purle still had that look of disgust on her face. I did-
n't have the opportunity to talk with her as of yet, and I
don't know if I will. She is surrounded constantly by friends
and family. Daddy didn't come to the church, thank God or
else Purle would have probably ripped his heart out of his
chest.

Bootsey went to the house to lie down. The day has been too much for her. She looked as if she had aged ten years. Marcus and I tried to convince Bootsey to come back home with us, but she declined. Auntie Purle has been so very busy serving food that she hasn't sat down all day. I also thank God for her. She is a pillar of strength for us all. Momma looked just like her.

I finally got the chance to speak to Purle alone. I asked her if she was holding up O.K., and she said yes. Purle assured me that she was just very tired. Olivia and Kim are dressed exactly alike. Momma would be so proud of the way that they sang for her today. Madison and Frances are busy talking with their doctor friends. Madison looks beautiful with her form fitting black velvet dress on.

After everyone left the church, we all packed up the food that was left over and put it into the refrigerator for the congregation to eat for lunch tomorrow; and the flowers were also left for their enjoyment. We all stayed at Momma's house with Purle so that she and Bootsey wouldn't be alone. Even Madison and Frances found a spot on the floor with a blanket. We talked all night. Auntie Purle got the chance to hear some of the family stories, and she seemed to truly enjoy them all. Her sadness was abundantly visible. She would break down and cry every so often between stories.

TWO WEEKS LATER

Everybody was doing fine adjusting to their new lives without Momma, everybody except for Purle. Purle looked drawn, tired, and frankly peculiar. Her attention span was extremely short, and she truly appeared to be preoccupied with thoughts at all times.

Auntie Purle telephoned Madison and I because she was worried about Purle. Madison and I quickly responded to Auntie Purles' concerns. Purle said that she had no appetite and said that she was having trouble sleeping at night. Madison offered to move back in with Purle for a while to help her get herself together. We suggested to Purle that she consider moving out of the apartment and start fresh somewhere else. We encouraged her to find a new apartment, but she totally refused. Madison examined Purle and diagnosed her with a bad case of depression. Madison wouldn't write a prescription for an antidepressant. Madison referred Purle to one of her friends who specialized in psychiatry. Madison felt that because she had such an emotional bond to Purle that perhaps she couldn't be objective enough to diagnosis her problem accurately.

Madison explained to Purle that it was very important for her to contact her friend who is a psychiatrist. If she were depressed, medicine would make her feel much better. Purle acknowledged Madison's advice and said that she would telephone tomorrow morning for an appointment. This made us all feel a lot better. Purle verbalized that she did not want Madison moving in with her. She said that she did not need anybody babysitting her. She stressed the point that she needed her privacy. Purle managed to get Bootsey to leave to go back to New Jersey a week earlier than she had planned. Bootsey didn't like the idea at all and was upset with Purle. Purle's personality had become mean. This was so unlike Purle. The Purle we knew was loving, caring, and patient.

THREE WEEKS LATER

Madison telephoned me to inform me that Purle hadn't contacted her friend who is a psychiatrist. When I tried to contact Purle by phone, a recording came on saying that the number had been temporarily disconnected. When Marcus came home, I asked him to drive me over to check on Purle. I really didn't want to ask Marcus to drive me. It was after 9:00 p.m., and I knew that Marcus had a very busy day in court. As usual, Marcus was more than willing. He said give me 15 minutes, honey, to change my clothes.

Lucy was over visiting for the week, and this meant that I didn't have to awaken the twins and carry them out of the house so late at night. Lucy loved those little boys. I guess this allowed her to give the love to her grandsons that she was not able to give to her sons. Marcus is really good to Lucy considering her poor tract record as a mom.

I yelled into the study downstairs where Lucy was

reading, "Lucy, the boys are sleeping in their room upstairs. Marcus and I will be back late. Don't wait up for us."

Lucy yelled back, "O.k. take your time."

The ride to the city seemed so long. There has been so many tragedies in our family.

"I don't think that my heart can take anymore," I said to Marcus.

He looked at me and said, "Honey, don't worry. Purle is fine. She just needs a little more time to adjust to not seeing your mom."

"Maybe I should have insisted that she come to spend time with us, Marcus. I should have told her that the twins wanted her to spend some time with them. You know how she feels about those boys."

When we got to the apartment, it took Purle forever to come to the door. Her hair was standing on top of her head. The house was a total mess, and she smelled like she hadn't taken a bath in weeks.

"Marcus can you give me a few minutes with my sister alone?" He nodded his head yes and went into the kitchen.

"Purle," I said. "This has got to end now," slamming my fist down on Momma's dresser.

Purle I said, "I'm so tired. Do you understand me girl?"

"I miss Momma too, but I know that Momma would not want me to curl up in her bed and die because she is gone. Besides! Momma moved on, Purle. Her spirit is as alive as you and I are right now. I feel her presence every day. Purle, I cannot worry about you. I cannot have my husband work all day and come home to have to drive all night. Purle, can you hear what I'm saying to you?" I screamed, "Listen to me" as I pulled the blanket off of her. "Get up and get in the shower now! Enough is enough," I screamed. "When is the last time that you have been to work?"

Purle sat up in bed and looked at me as if she were possessed by the devil. Her eyes were blood shot and bulging out of her head. This didn't look like my sister, Purle.

"Marcey, when is the last time you have been to work?"

"Purle, I don't have a job outside the house, but I WORK EVERYDAY. I take care of my children which is an on going job -nonstop."

Purle looked at me and said, "Yeah! What a job!"

I looked at Purle and said, "How dare you? How dare you belittle my role as a mother? Purle, if you want to wattle in self-pity and lie down in bed to die, that is your choice. I am not going to waste my time and energy worrying about you if you don't have sense enough to take care of yourself."

Purle looked at me and said, "Get out of here little Miss Fucking rich girl!"

I looked at Purle and said, "I love you" and left without looking back.

I cried all the way home for two hours straight. My sister Purle had never used bad language and for her to use the F word was totally out of character for her. Marcus heard the entire conversation between Purle and I. He never gets involved. He knew there was a serious problem with Purle.

"Gee Marcey, that didn't sound like Purle."

"I know."

The following day I telephoned Madison and told her what had happened. Madison said that she would make an attempt to try and get through to Purle. Auntie Purle had already tried over and over again without success. Purle had gone stole cold crazy if you ask me.

The thought came through my mind to perhaps contact Tyrone. It may seem like a crazy thought. However, Marcus says that his brother has joined some church in the Bronx and has gotten his life together. Marcus says that his brother has had a steady job working for a brokerage firm for the past year and now. If Tyrone has gotten himself together, maybe just maybe, Purle will see a gleam of hope for her future. I'm not really sure if Tyrone is seeing someone now or not. Well anyway, it's an option to consider if Purle does not pull herself together.

I discussed the idea with Marcus, and he seemed to think that whatever will save her life would be a good option whether it is to contact Tyrone or any other way of getting through to her. It may seem bizarre at the moment, but I'm going to give it a try. Marcus was the only one that I discussed this with. Hopefully, Tyrone could talk some sense into Purles head. It could make matters worse, or it could turn the situation around for the better. This is a tough call. Then I asked myself what would Momma say about all of this? Knowing Momma she would do whatever it took to save any of her children.

The following day I discussed the situation of Purle's depression over again with Marcus. Her condition had not improved at this point. Purle was still deeply depressed and growing deeper and deeper into depression as the days went on without seeking help. Purle was beginning to look like a bum. I asked Marcus to invite Tyrone over for dinner so that I could plead my case to him. This of course would be a very awkward situation for me considering I haven't spoken with Tyrone since the days of the court ordeal. I didn't care. Whatever it took to save my sister, I would do it. I was desperate at this point and knew that I had to work fast at whatever I was going to do.

Marcus said that he would telephone Tyrone from work and invite him over to dinner as soon as possible. I was relieved. I just had to wait to see if Tyrone would accept Marcus' invitation. Lucy was still visiting, and I knew that she would be thrilled to see her son. After all, the past was the past and whatever happened back then should be left there. It's time for this family to move on. We have all grown up emotionally and have gained more of life's experience and knowledge. With this we must pull together to make the best out of a bad situation. Momma always said, "Out of every bad situation comes something good."

Meanwhile, I had received a phone call from Madison. She informed me that she went over to check up on Purle, and Purle yelled to her through the door that she was not up to seeing any visitors.

Madison cried on the telephone, "Marcey, I never considered myself a visitor. I'm her sister."

"I know this, Madison, and you know this, Purle is not rationale right now. You are a physician. You should know this behavior is expected of someone who is not mentally stable.

Madison was devastated over the phone. We were quickly running out of options. Purle was definitely in a situation that warranted drastic measures. At this point I decided to share my idea with Madison of having Tyrone try and talk some sense into Purle. Madison didn't agree with the idea because she said that Purle had lost trust in Tyrone a long time ago. I mentioned to Madison that Tyrone has changed his life around. He has given his life to God. He is saved and has been holding down a good job for the past year. I also explained to Madison that Purle may have lost some trust in Tyrone; however there definitely has been no love lost. Madison pondered over the idea; and after about 30 minutes, going back and forth with the pros and cons, she finally agreed the idea was worth a try.

I told Madison that I would keep her informed from this point on of all the details concerning this particular plan.

When Marcus returned home from work, he kissed me as he walked through the door hugging me tight and picked me up and spun me around. The twins were still awake, and they were screaming daddy, daddy. They could even sense the rejuvenated demeanor he had developed.

Marcus said, "Sweetheart, I had lunch with Tyrone today. Marcey, he looks fantastic."

As I sat with an overflow of anticipation not able to contain myself, I felt a rush of adrenaline go through my body and began jumping up and down with joy. The twins followed my behavior by also jumping up and down and clapping their little hands.

"Marcus, did Tyrone agree to talk to Purle?"

"Honey, I didn't get that far with asking him that much. He did agree to come over for dinner tomorrow. He did ask about Purle."

"Well, what did he ask?"

"He asked how she was doing, and what she was doing with her life."

"Marcus, what did you say?"

"I didn't say anything. I just looked at him and smiled."

What should I make for dinner tomorrow?"

"Marcey, Tyrone was never choosy with what he ate. He always had an appetite like a bull."

"I'll make some fried chicken, collard greens and macaroni and cheese."

"Marcey, just looking into my brother's eyes I could see that he has grown up. Marcey, I can see his humbleness and his spiritual growth."

"Marcus, that is wonderful!" I am truly excited about all of this. I pray this will all work out for the best."

I woke up very early the next morning to begin preparing supper. I wanted everything to be perfect. I wanted Tyrone to know that I had truly forgiven him for all of the turmoil he has put my family through. I wanted him to know that if he chose not to speak with Purle to help us to help her come around that I would understand.

Marcus said that he would be getting off of work early tonight so that he could pick his brother up to bring him over for dinner. Marcus also said that all of the arrangements were made yesterday when they had lunch together. They discussed a pick up time and transportation to and from work.

I finally finished cooking. Lucy had offered to help with the cooking but I needed her to keep an eye on the twins instead. Everything smelled so good. Lucy was very excited that Tyrone was coming for dinner. She put on her favorite suit that Marcus and I bought her last month for her birthday. Lucy looked great! Tyrone is going to be surprised when he sees his mom. It has been years since he has seen Lucy. Lucy finally looked like she belonged to the human race. She must have gained about 30 pounds since she has been visiting with Marcus and I. She is very happy in this environment. As a matter of fact, Marcus and I had discussed the possibility of Lucy coming to live with us for good. The twins adore her and so do we. There is nothing left for Lucy back where she lives except the possibility of her meeting up with her old druggy friends and taking a fall into the past life she has fought so hard to relinquish.

The doorbell rang. I knew it was Marcus although Marcus always uses his house key. This was his way of warning me that Tyrone was with him. I looked in the mirror one last time before opening up the door. I looked great! Tyrone looked great, extremely handsome with a special glow that radiated! I motioned him to step inside the house, gave him a hug, and told him that it was a great pleasure to see him again.

"Likewise, Marcey."

"Come on in Tyrone and sit down. Say hello to your nephews. This is Michael, and this is Matthew.

Tyrone picked up both of the boys at the same time and said, "My name is Uncle Tye."

The boys looked at him and smiled. At that point Lucy came out extended her two arms, and they embraced for about five minutes. It was beautiful.

Everything was going perfect so far. We all sat down to talk. I offered Tyrone a drink. He declined and said, "Thanks, sis, but I don't drink alcohol."

This was definitely not the same Tyrone that I knew

a few years ago. That Tyrone would throw down anything that had alcohol in it including the rubbing alcohol that I kept in my cabinet. I noticed that after a conversation or the completion of a topic Tyrone would say, "Praise the Lord." I could see that this man had drastically changed.

The time came for dinner to be served and Tyrone said, "Marcey, if it is o.k. with you before we began eating, I would like to bless the table." We all looked at each other in disbelief, including Lucy.

Tyrone began to pray. "Lord I would like to first and foremost ask for your forgiveness for all of our sins. Lord, I thank you for allowing me to have the opportunity to sit with my family for this fine meal that has been served on this fine evening. Thank you Lord for my mother, my brother, and his wife, and my two nephews. Lord, thank you for waking us up this morning so that we would have the opportunity to dine together this evening. Thank you God for the forgiveness that has been shown to me by my family because I am truly undeserving of it. Thank you God for answering my prayers of being able to see my family in an atmosphere of peace and harmony. Thank you for this food that we are about to receive from thy bounty through Christ thy Lord. Amen." I couldn't believe my ears. Thinking to myself again, Tyrone has definitely changed.

After dinner was served we returned to the study to catch up on things in our lives that were missed. We experienced a lot of problems the past couple of years. Lucy was never happier in her entire life. Tyrone extended an invitation to us to visit his church next Sunday and stressed to Lucy how important it was to him if she was his special guest next Sunday. Lucy didn't answer him. I think that she was in shock. Finally the big question, Tyrone asked me how Purle was doing.

"Tyrone," I answered, "Not so well," I just belted right out.

"What do you mean not so good?"

I began to explain that Purle was extremely depressed. And how none of her sisters, not even Madison could help her out of this one.

Tyrone said "You know, Marcey, no matter how crazy that situation was between your sister and I, I never stopped loving her. No matter how crazy it looked at that time, I loved your sister more than anyone would ever know. I was a very weak person back then, Marcey. I was without guidance. I was just wild and crazy and didn't know how to relate to new situations. Running was the only thing I knew how to do. I regret every day of my life not treating Purle the way I should have. Marcey, I really didn't know how to show Purle the love that I felt or the love that she deserved. The peer pressure from the 'home-boys'. Being in love just wasn't cool back then for a young man."

I wish that I had the opportunity to change things. I am in love with Purle still after all these years, and I miss her. I have to live with myself every day knowing that I have lost the only woman in the world that I would ever consider marrying."

At that point I stopped Tyrone. "Tyrone you have made this favor that I am going to ask of you very easy for me to ask. I am going to cut through the chase."

Tyrone looked at me with a perplexed look on his face. "I need you to go over to see Purle. I need you to talk some sense into her head."

Tyrone looked at me as if I was crazy. "Marcey, I would love to talk to Purle, but she doesn't trust me. Marcey, Purle doesn't know that I am saved. She has no idea that I am not the same person she knew back then."

"Tyrone, all you have to do is be yourself, and she will see exactly what we have seen in you this evening. Tyrone you are our last hope of saving Purle. Her life is at stake."

Tyrone looked at Marcus and myself and said, "I'll do my best. When should I go to see Purle," Tyrone asked.

"As soon as possible," I said.

Tyrone nodded his head O.K. What a feeling of relief that came over me. Somehow I knew now that this would all work out for the best.

Tyrone hugged me and said, "Marcey, I am so sorry to hear about your mom."

I know, Tyrone."

Tyrone said, "I had better get going, you guys. I have to work in the morning."

Marcus said, "Why don't you stay the night, and I'll give you a ride to work in the morning with me."

"I don't think so, Marcus. I don't have a change of clothes."

"I'm sure that you could fit one of my suits."

Tyrone smiled and said, "Oh yeah, I can fit one of your expensive suits. I guess if you guys have a room for me, I can stand to stay over; and he smiled. I began to clear the dinning room table. Marcus showed Tyrone around the house and to the bedroom where he was to sleep. Lucy followed. The night had gone well. We were all tired. It had been a long day. We all said goodnight and turned in for the evening.

Madison telephoned the following morning to see how the evening had gone with Tyrone's visit. I told her all about last evening not leaving out any details. Madison had a hard time believing how much Tyrone has changed. I guess if I were her I would have a hard time believing also without actually seeing for myself.

After all was said and done, Madison agreed that this attempt to have Tyrone talk to Purle was the only option left. All we could do now was to sit, wait, and be patient. Purle had gotten so crazy that she was at the point where she wouldn't open the door for anybody. Her perception of reality must have been severely distorted. For her to even think for a moment that we meant her any harm was inconceivable if that was truly her rationale for not opening the door for us. Tyrone is going to have to call upon every angel from the heavens to help him get through to Purle. I know Momma will be right at his side helping him.

Olivia and Kim have no idea of what's going on with Purle. All they know is that Purle is suffering from what they have named the Bla Blas. It was the Bla Blas after Momma died; however, it has exacerbated to the deepest state of depression larger than the state of Texas. They have not seen Purle since a week after Momma died. They are due home from tour next week. Hopefully, by then Madison and I will have everything under control with Purle. Auntie Purle has been calling me every day from work. She is so upset that Purle will not open the door for her.

The phone is still disconnected even though Madison paid the phone bill yesterday. Purle's phone should be reconnected at some point today. I telephoned Purle's job to try and find out if she has been calling in sick. The receptionist answered the phone and said that Purle James was no longer employed at the Fashion Industry. Now I knew that Purle was not paying the phone bill or her rent.

CHAPTER SEVENTEEN
TYRONE'S ORDEAL WITH PURLE

Thinking to myself, this was a heavy burden bestowed upon me to have to try to talk to Purle after all of this time. Her present state of mind is not going to help at all. I fast and prayed for three days because I knew that I needed the power of the almighty to help rebuke those demons that invaded Purle's temple, temple meaning the body and soul that God had given her to use while here on earth. I had so many mixed feelings about this entire ordeal. The strongest feeling of all was the feeling of love, love not lust, that I still carried for this lady. I knew this would make my job of allowing God to use me to deliver Purle from her demons much more difficult.

I hadn't seen Purle in so long; I had no idea of what to expect. One thing I knew for sure was that I was going to be right there with Purle until I was sure she was out of the danger zone. I couldn't sleep. I tossed and turned all night. After praying, I knew that tomorrow was the day of approach the day that I would lay eyes on Purle for the first time since her release from prison.

I must have fallen asleep at some point; I awakened to the alarm of my bedside clock. At 7:30 a.m. I jumped out of bed, took a fast shower, and shaved. I allowed myself 45 minutes for prayer. I had decided to wear something comfortable and casual. From this point on God was going to make all of the decisions for me. I was going to rely on him to guide me in the right direction. I started to put different items into my shoulder bag. Items that I had no idea of why I was taking. I was very nervous, anxious, and filled with anticipation.

I decided not to eat breakfast. After fasting for three days, I needed to remain spiritually elevated. The last item to go inside my bag was my Bible.

As I proceeded down the stairs of my apartment building, I hailed a taxicab and approached Purle's apartment building. I could see the alleyway where I use to play stickball as a child. As I got closer to the building, I could see the small entrance to her basement where I made many drug sales. The same fellas were on the same corner, just a little bit older now.

I looked up at the sky, and I thanked God for rescuing me from this terrible life of bondage. I quickly paid the cab driver and got out of the taxi cab holding on to my bag tight. I could feel a hand on my shoulder. It startled me. I turned around. It was Jimmy from the grocery store down the street. I gave Jimmy a big bear hug.

"Kid, its good to see you," he said. "You look Great."

"Jimmy, you look great also, look like you haven't aged a day from the last time I saw you."

Jimmy smiled. Jimmy asked, "What brings you back to our neck of the woods?"

I smiled looked at Jimmy and said some unfinished business. Jimmy slapped me five, said for me to tell everybody hello, and walked off. Never once asking me about the unfinished business or did he already know that the unfinished business was related to Purle.

The neighborhood seemed a little different; it didn't seem as loud or crowded. I guess all of the hoodlums were in jail or either dead. I proceeded to walk up the steps inside of the building where Purle lived. I passed some Jehovah's Witnesses on the way; I wanted to get to Purles apartment before they did. As I got to the door, I listened first. I put my ear to the door to see if I could hear any movement inside. I couldn't hear anything. I knocked three times, paused waited for her to ask "who is it". No one answered. I knocked on the door three more times and waited another five minutes.

Purle didn't answer.

I put my ear to the door again to try and hear some type of movement on the inside. While my ear was to the door, the two Jehovah's witnesses looked at me. The look they gave me was one that I was familiar with, "move out of the way it is our turn to knock", while rolling their eyes.

I took a seat on the floor outside the door as the two sisters proceeded to knock on the door for about ten minutes and then came to the conclusion that maybe no one was home. They looked at me. I looked at them, and they continued up the next flight of stairs.

At this point I had a very bad feeling inside. I put my head into my hands and began to pray silently. I asked God to tell me what I needed to do next because at this point I had no clue. The thought came into my mind, Well Tyrone, you were the one who said that you were going to stay as long as you needed to. Thinking to myself after an hour had passed by, why am I here? I don't know what to do next. Just at that point I heard some movement inside the apartment. I knocked on the door again. Three more knocks this time and I said, "Purle, Purle are you in there?" I could hear some fast shuffling on the other side of the door. Thinking to myself what is going on in there? I could hear Purle saying something, but I could not make out what she was saying. I began to bang on the door harder and louder especially now knowing that she was inside. "Purle, open the door. It's Tyrone. I need to talk to you. Its urgent." I could feel inside my soul that something was definitely wrong. I could faintly hear Purle calling my name.

I definitely knew that I had to remove this front door to allow me access inside the apartment. I dumped everything out of my bag onto the floor in the hallway to see exactly what I had to work with. I had an electric razor, a bible, a blanket and some snapshot pictures of my twin nephews and a screwdriver. I grabbed the screwdriver and began to pry the lock off of the door. Pushing my body against the door as hard as I could to try and loosen up the lock, I was able to fit my hand on the inside of the door to remove the bar that would not allow the door to budge any further. I stood back and gave the door a big kick with my foot.

The door flew opened. I ran inside and there was Purle on the bathroom floor. Blood was everywhere. My God, she slit her wrist. I grabbed a towel off of the shower line and wrapped it around her wrist as tight as I could. I picked her up and ran with her down four flights of stairs. I cried, "Don't you die on me, no. Don't you die on me, no." I picked her up in my arms and ran as fast as possible. As I got outside the building, there was a taxi-cab waiting for the light to change. I jumped inside, "Take me to Harlem Hospital. Move it." The cab driver was frightened. I could see the fear in his eyes. He had no idea of what was going on. I held the towel tightly around Purle's wrist. Her eyes were closed, but I could see her stomach moving up and down. That's how I knew that she was breathing. I yelled to the cab driver, "Drive faster." I could see that Purle was loosing a lot of blood. Blood was all over me.

"Purle, I do love you. I am so sorry for all of the pain that I have caused you. I have never stopped loving you. Please forgive me, Purle, for not knowing back then how to love you." I kissed Purle while crying for the first time in my life. I moved her hair back out of her face and whispered into her ear, "Hang in there. I love you." The taxi stopped on 135th street and Lenox Avenue in front of Harlem Hospital. I saw two doctors standing in front of the Hospital. I yelled out to them that I needed help. One of the doctors ran inside and came out with a stretcher.

I reached in my back pocket to get my wallet to pay the cab driver and realized that my wallet was in the duffel bag left at Purle's apartment. The cab driver was nice; he motioned me inside the hospital with his hand and said next time. As we proceeded to put Purle on the stretcher, one of the doctors asked me what had happened. I told him that I found Purle on the bathroom floor with her wrist slit and that her family said that she was suffering from depression.

Purle was unconscious. As the doctors rolled her inside of the hospital they confirmed a pulse and confirmed that she was breathing. I knew that God wouldn't bring me this far to let me down now. I knew that he would keep Purle safe. I ran behind the stretcher that was carrying Purle.

Another doctor approached us as they rolled the stretcher into a small room in the ER; he was the doctor who was going to repair the wound that Purle inflicted upon herself.

I could hear this doctor say "My Goodness this is Matti's sister. Thank goodness, Matti just left for the day." This doctor had a very strong African accent.

"What happened?" the doctor asked. I began to tell the doctor how I went to Purle's apartment to talk to her as her family asked me to do. When I got there, she wouldn't open the door. I pushed the door in after approximately an hour and a half and found her on the bathroom floor with her wrist slit.

The doctor said that she is lucky that you found her when you did. "She lost a lot of blood." The doctor asked me if I had contacted any family members?

"No," I said. All I could think about was getting her here to the hospital as soon as possible."

This doctor who was asking all of the questions began to stitch Purle's wrist. Within a couple of minutes they had a blood transfusion in progress. She had lost a lot of blood. Her wrist was stitched up, and she was being taken to another room on the second floor. I asked the doctor if Purle was going to be all right?

He looked at me and said, "Call me Frances," as he removed the bloody rubber gloves and extended his hand for me to shake.

I shook his hand and he said, "Physically, she will be fine. Mentally and emotionally she's going to need a lot of help. Who are you?" Dr. Frances asked me.

I looked at him hesitant to answer. I answered, "I am a person from her past who loves her dearly, and at this point she has no idea of how I feel about her." I knew that I wasn't making any sense to this man.

I looked at the doctor and said "I use to be a different person, never mind."

The doctor looked at me and said while nodding his head with a half grin on his face, "I know who you are." How could this doctor know me, and I know for a fact that I have never seen him in my entire life.

"Madison James is my fiancée."

OH! Now I really felt awkward. I knew how much Madison didn't like me for the way that I treated her sister. I could imagine what this doctor must be thinking.

"I could see in your eyes that you are a changed person, Tyrone. I don't think you are anything like the stories that I have heard about you. Sometimes it takes some people a little longer than others to mature." I nodded my head in agreement with the doctor.

"Well!" I said. "Somebody had better call the family to let them know that Purle has been admitted into the hospital."

The doctor said, "I agree."

I used the pay phone down the hall from the emergency room to call Marcey. I forgot that it was Saturday and that Marcus was home. Marcus answered the phone, and I told him what had happened. While I was talking to Marcus over the phone, he was telling Marcey at the same time what had happened as I was telling him. Marcus said that they were going to have Momma Lucy watch the kids and that they were on their way to the hospital. I didn't feel right calling Madison, so I left it up to Marcey or Dr. Frances to make that call.

While the family was visiting Purle, I waited outside of her room. Madison was cordial to me when she arrived. Olivia and Kim were still on tour and due home in a week. They had no idea of what had happened, and Marcey didn't want to call them with this news especially since Purle was going to live. Auntie Purle visited and cried her eyes out. She had become very fond of her niece Purle.

The doctors had Purle heavily sedated. They wanted to make sure that physically she would be O.K. They were infusing electrolytes intravenously due to Purle's severe dehydration. Doctor Frances had written a consult for Purle to see a Dr. Crane. He is an old psychiatrist who has been working at Harlem Hospital for many years.

Purle had been in the hospital for almost a week. I thought to myself, its time that I faced the music. I'm sure that her sisters told her how she had gotten to the hospital. I was hoping that when I got to the hospital that nobody would be there. I needed to see Purle alone.

Purle was still on the second floor in the same room. I got there to visit during the first set of visiting hours. I made up my mind that if someone was there visiting her, that I would come back later. Lucky me, no one was in her room. She was sitting up watching television with her hair pulled back. She was still beautiful. I stood outside of her room peeking in for about three minutes before I conjured up the courage to walk inside of the room.

I walked inside the room. She looked up at me. I thought that my heart would stop. Those big beautiful brown eyes looking at me, It was almost like she had been expecting me today. "Hello Purle," I said.

She gave me the biggest smile and said, "Hi, Tyrone." The sound of her soft voice saying my name again made me feel great. "Sit down," she said.

I sat next to her on the edge of her bed. I began to speak. "There are so many things that I want to say to you."

She put her finger to her lips and said, "SHH. I heard you already in the taxicab." I couldn't believe that she heard everything that I said in the taxicab. "Thank you for saving my life, Tyrone." I looked into those big brown eyes. She still had that same innocence about her as she did a few years ago. My heart began to beat fast. I knew that I loved this girl more than anybody I had ever loved in my entire life. She looked at me and said, "I have had a change of heart also, and I do forgive you. I never stopped loving you either, Tyrone. We were both so young and immature and didn't know the first thing about maintaining a relationship."

Tears began to roll down my face because truly I

have prayed many nights for this moment. I thought to myself, am I dreaming or is this for real?

"Purle, I don't want to sit here and tell you that I have changed. I want to show you that I have changed if you will afford me the opportunity to."

Purle looked into my eyes and said, "Give me one reason why."

I looked back into her eyes and said, "because I still love you."

She smiled and gave me the two thumbs up as she had done many times in the past when things were O.K. "Before I am able to get out of here, Tyrone, I have to meet with a psychiatrist named Dr. Crane first. He has to determine whether or not I am a hazard to myself or not."

"Well, when do you have to meet with him?"

"Monday morning is my first session with him."

"When you are discharged from this hospital, I want to take you to my church to meet my pastor."

"I would love to meet the pastor of your church, Tyrone."

I picked up Purle's hand, and kissed it.

She smiled and winked at me and said, "I am going to be fine."

I never told Purle that I was sorry to hear about the death of her mother. I felt that the time wasn't right to say that. I didn't know how strong Purle was mentally at this time to hear those words, but I wasn't taking any chances.

Marcey and Marcus walked in the room. If they hadn't, I might have kissed Purle on the lips. I could tell that Marcey and Marcus were happy to see me here visiting Purle. I hugged Purle and told her that I would be back to visit her tomorrow. She smiled and gave me two thumbs up. I hugged Marcus and Marcey and said goodbye. I felt totally rejuvenated. I thanked God for this day all the way home.

CHAPTER EIGHTEEN
PURLE'S MEETING WITH DOCTOR CRANE

"Dr. Crane, how long do you think that it will be before I am able to go home?" Without answering my question, Dr. Crane starred at me for about five minutes without saying a word. Thinking to myself is this man crazy or what?

Dr. Crane sat in his straight chair with his straight face expressionless. He had the scariest black piercing eyes. Looking over his eye glasses he said, "Purle, I will not be able to discharge you unless you can tell me why you felt the need to try to commit suicide last Thursday."

What in the heck is this Dr. talking about? Thinking to myself, it wasn't last Thursday; it was last Saturday.

"Dr. Crane I felt the need to attempt suicide last Saturday because I was feeling desperate. Have you ever gotten to a point in your life where you felt you didn't have the answers anymore?"

"The answers to what Sarah?"

This Dr. was definitely a quack. "My name is not Sarah, Dr. Crane. My name is Purle."

"I'm sorry. You have a striking resemblance to a patient that I treated many years ago."

"To finish answering your question, Dr. Crane, I wasn't thinking clearly at the time I tried to kill myself. I hadn't eaten or slept for days. I was depressed. I had just lost my mother and was feeling very lonely. You see, my mother and I were very close. We did everything together, and her death was very sudden."

The Dr. was writing in his pad the entire time I was talking. Never once looking up, "O.K. Sarah, I will fill out the discharge forms for your release. You seem well enough to go home.

I will have you come back once a week to our out patient follow up clinic for evaluation."

"My name isn't Sarah. I told you, its Purle."

"I'm sorry Purle. Like I said, you bear a remarkable resemblance to a patient I had many years ago named Sarah."

I extended my arm out to shake Dr. Crane's hand forgetting about the bandage around my wrist. Embarrassment had completely taken over me at this point, and I dropped my head.

The doctor looked at me with a peculiar look, shook his head almost in disbelief, and said, "Purle, take care of yourself."

I was so happy. It felt as if I was in this hospital for weeks. I ran to my room to get my belongings, and Tyrone was sitting on the chair in my room with a dozen of long stem roses. I was so happy to see him. I told him about my consultation with the psychiatrist and how the psychiatrist kept referring to me as Sarah. We joked and laughed about it.

"Purle, I don't want you to go back to that apartment. I had the door fixed for you. However, I think that apartment holds too many bad memories for you."

"Tyrone where do you suppose that I go?"

"I rented a different apartment for you not far from where your sister Madison lives. You don't have to stay there if you don't like it; but please, Purle, first see it."

"O.K., lets go." The outside of the building was beautiful. How in the world could Tyrone have afforded something like this? The doorman opened the door for us. We stepped inside of the elevator, and it stopped at the second floor. Tyrone put the key in the door, and the place was beautiful. "I'm never leaving here Tyrone. I love it."

"Good, I'll arrange to have your belongings brought over. Purle, I cannot imagine spending one more day without you. Purle, will you marry me."

I looked at Tyrone in disbelief. He was never the marrying type. "We don't have any money saved for a wedding," I said.

"Purle, I don't want a wedding. My pastor said that he would marry us tonight if we wanted."

"Tyrone, the only way that I would marry you tonight was if my sisters could be there."

Olivia and Kim will be back tomorrow. Surely we can wait one more night."

"Well, I will sleep over here on this chair because I am not leaving you for one second."

"I need to telephone Marcey and Madison to let them know that I am fine and to give them the phone number here."

"Hi Marcey, how are you?"

"Fine, Purle?"

"Yeah, its me."

"Where are you?"

"Well, I'm in my new apartment that Tyrone rented for me."

"Are you serious?"

"Yes."

"How are you feeling honey?"

"Never better. Marcey, take down my new telephone number, 555-6848. Marcey, do me a favor and call Madison and Auntie Purle and tell them not to make any plans for tomorrow night."

"Why?"

"Well, because Tyrone and I are getting married."

Marcey threw the phone down and started screaming, "Marcus, Marcus, they're getting married tomorrow."

Marcus picked up the phone and said congratulations. "You two have come a long way from almost nowhere."

"I laughed and said to Marcus, "It's the power of love."

"I can attest to that," Marcus said. "I am very happy for the both of you."

I was exhausted from the busy day that I encountered, and it was definitely time for me to get some shuteye. I took off my shoes; ah, did my feet feel a thousand times better. Tyrone massaged my feet one at a time taking his time and I was in ecstasy. After he was done massaging my feet, I decided to take a nice hot shower to relax my muscles that were extremely tensed. The bathroom was huge. It was beautiful. Everything was light peach and green. The shower had two showerheads; I had never seen anything like this before. As I stepped into the shower turned the water on and let the water beat down on my head and back, it felt wonderful. I could hear Tyrone on the phone.

A part of me wanted him to join me in the shower. That would have made the entire day perfect, but I knew that he wouldn't. He was determined to wait until we were married to make love. In the past we have made love, but that was before his rebirth. I was exhausted for sure now after that relaxing shower. I lied across the bed with my nightgown on to rest my eyes for a few minutes. I could feel Tyrone's eyes on me as he sat in the chair all night watching me sleep. I never felt more safe in my entire life.

The next day Marcey informed Olivia and Kim when

she picked them up from the airport that Tyrone and I were getting married. They trusted Marcey's judgement so much that they never questioned Tyrone's authenticity of his sudden change of character. Marcey was happy for me; and therefore, they, too, showed their appreciation for the good news.

Auntie Purle was happy after she had the opportunity to speak with Tyrone directly for about 45 minutes. Madison was also in the spirit of forgiving after verbally slapping Tyrone around for a bit. Tyrone and I went down to City Hall and applied for a marriage license. The clerk informed us that it would take two days. I guess we could wait two days. After all, we had waited about five years or more.

Dr. Frances Obilae was so intrigued by Tyrone's genuine love for Purle that he was touched to ask for Madison's hand in marriage also. Unfortunately, Madison declined his offer. She told Frances that she wasn't ready at this point in her life for marriage. She assured Dr. Obilae that it had absolutely nothing to do with her love for him. Her rationale for declining his marriage proposal was that she had to come to terms with sharing herself. Madison said that she wasn't ready to give up her name. There were so many reasons, excuses she gave for not being ready for marriage at this time. Madison was so unbelievably political it was ridiculous. Dr. Obilae accepted Matti's decline graciously and mentioned that he would not give up on his request to have Matti's hand in marriage. Truthfully, I don't think that Madison will ever be ready for marriage.

Tyrone and Purle were married two days later, and the ceremony was private and sacred. Truly Tyrone had become a changed man; his behavior validated what he verbally professed. That was that God had saved his spirit by delivering him from his past and forgiving him and allowing him to live a better future, a future with love and respect not only for himself, but for everyone around him.

Purle eventually became saved along with Tyrone. When I say saved, I mean saved from the concept of eternal hell as we know it from the book of revelations; and she was convinced that God had it all planned from the very start of her long journey to freedom, freedom from the turmoil that lived within her spirit making life impossible for her to cope with on a daily basis.

Madison never did marry Dr. Frances Obilae, although they remained inseparable throughout the years. Madison left her position working the emergency medical van in Harlem, and went on to teach pre-med at Columbia University down the street from where she grew up.

Kim and Olivia continued to sing. They reached stardom, came out with two songs that hit the charts number one list. They, too, joined the church and eventually married and had children.

Auntie Purle never married. She died at the age of 75 and never went a day without calling her niece Purle on the telephone. We buried Auntie Purle next to Momma.

Bootsey lived to a ripe old age of 92 and died with all of her granddaughter's at her side at Metropolitan Hospital here in New York. This was exactly how Bootsey mentioned many times she wanted to make her exit and enter into the Pearly Gates.

We never did hear from Daddy again, never knew what happened or became of him. But we all have forgiven him within our hearts. Like the words from Momma's mouth "what is life without forgiveness, and what is love without a free spirit".

Sarah James' Family

About the Author

Bridget Davis grew up in Harlem in the early 70's and 80's. She began writing short stories and poetry as a young girl for enjoyment and a means of escape.

Momma's Purle is her first published novel.

Bridget Davis is also a Registered Nurse who works in an Intensive Care Unit at a local New Jersey hospital.

She lives in the Pocono Mountains of Pennsylvania with her husband and two children.

CLASSIC HOME PLANS

230 New Designs in Traditional Styles

HOME PLANNERS
TUCSON, ARIZONA

Published by Home Planners
A Division of Hanley-Wood, Inc.
Editorial and Corporate Offices:
3275 West Ina Road, Suite 110
Tucson, Arizona 85741

Distribution Center:
29333 Lorie Lane
Wixom, Michigan 48393

Rickard D. Bailey, CEO and Publisher
Cindy Coatsworth Lewis, Publications Manager
Jan Prideaux, Senior Editor
Laura Hurst Brown, Editor
Jay C. Walsh, Graphic Designer

Design/Photography Credits

Front Cover: Plan 8186 by Larry E. Belk Designs
                 Photo by Scott Ramsey

Pages 4-5:   Plan 8186 by Larry E. Belk Designs
                 Photos by Scott Ramsey

Back Cover: Plan 9565 by Alan Mascord Design Associates, Inc.
                 Photos by Bob Greenspan

First Printing, February 1998

10 9 8 7 6 5 4 3 2 1

Printed in the United States of America

Library of Congress Catalog Card Number: 97-077085

ISBN softcover: 1-881955-43-5

C·O·N·T·E·N·T·S

Photos by Scott Ramsey
Courtesy of Larry E. Belk Designs
Plan 8186, page 165

F·U·N·D·A·M·E·N·T·A·L·S

*C*lassic is a word that's been tossed around a lot, used to mean nearly anything—from Greek and Roman classicism to simple, lasting elegance. The term implies a standard of excellence and calls to the senses a balanced formality, tempered with both restraint and imagination. And, while the architectural styles we've conceived to be classic speak softly of our heritage, they also point honestly to what we hold priceless in this moment.

Simple ingredients outlast the past. Monticello's Doric columns, pedimented portico and spare lines have no real sense of time in today's traditionals. A uniquely American vernacular has set its own plural definition of classic style, with an untamed bevy of elements drawn from our already-rich history. We've lovingly revived the refined detail of Queen Anne style and, at the same time, regarded Frank Lloyd Wright's pure, organic architecture with undiminished pleasure.

This portfolio of house plans weds vintage styles with visional ideas, and holds that the meaning of classic is intrinsically woven into the notion of home. We've placed the cream of the crop in the front of the book, in full color; the Masterworks Collection begins on page six. Charm and comfort work together in "A Turn in Tradition," a look at the new Americana in a wide range of square footages.

Our "American Heritage" homes reinterpret the architectural past to create a new breed of authentic designs that are formal and sophisticated but also friendly and livable. Rustic country kitchens live side-by-side with finished formal rooms in our "Harvest Gold" section. Keystone arches and corner quoins introduce

Photos by Scott Ramsey Courtesy of Larry E. Belk Designs
Plan 8186, see page 165

tiled foyers and transatlantic styles that go straight to the heart; see "Cultural Influences," page 153. Ready for really new digs? "Novel Concepts" shows off the latest in Contemporary and Coastal designs, well-planned for the unpredictable future.

A true classic preserves the best of what's gone before and boldly adds vibrant thought, to create a compelling whole that won't fade with fashion. The home designs featured here are both regional and universal, eclectic yet intimate, stylish but elemental. They're better by design not only because of the way they look, but because of the way they make you feel—like you have a style of your own and a place to forever call home.

This home, as shown in the photograph, may differ from the actual blueprints.
For more detailed information, please check the floor plans carefully.

Photo by Andrew D. Lautman

Width 60'
Depth 32'

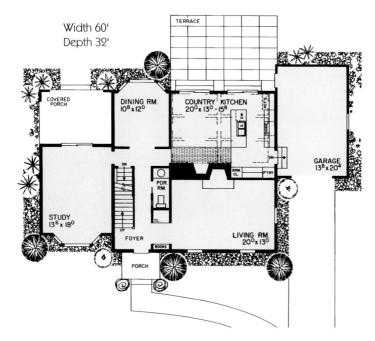

TERRACE

COVERED PORCH

DINING RM.
10⁸ x 12⁰

COUNTRY KITCHEN
20⁰ x 13⁰ - 15⁸

GARAGE
13⁸ x 20⁴

STUDY
13⁶ x 18⁰

PDR. RM.

DN

UP

FOYER

CL.

BOOKS

PORCH

LIVING RM.
20⁰ x 13⁰

BRM CL.

P'TRY

DESIGN 2682

First Floor (Expanded Plan):
1,230 square feet
Second Floor:
744 square feet
Total (Expanded Plan):
1,974 square feet

L D

QUOTE ONE®

Cost to build? See page 230
to order complete cost estimate
to build this house in your area!

Design by
Home Planners

Here's an expandable Colonial with a full measure of Cape Cod charm. A spider beam ceiling dresses up the country kitchen, which offers a gourmet island counter and a sitting area with a hearth. Upstairs, a spacious master suite shares a gallery hall which leads to two family bedrooms and sizable storage space. The expanded version (shown here) of the basic plan adds a study wing as well as an attached garage with a service entrance to the kitchen.

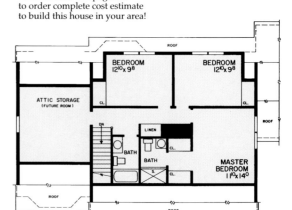

ROOF

BEDROOM
12¹⁰ x 9⁸

BEDROOM
12¹⁰ x 9⁸

ATTIC STORAGE
(FUTURE ROOM)

DN

LINEN

CL.

BATH

BATH

MASTER BEDROOM
11⁰ x 14⁰

ROOF

ROOF

ROOF

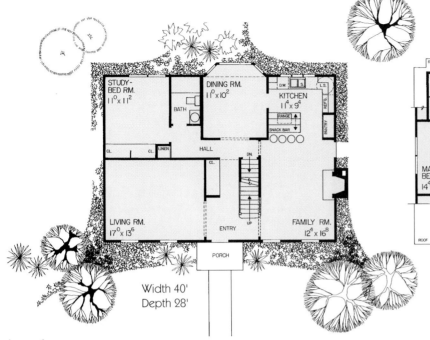

Width 40'
Depth 28'

Design by
Home Planners

T his cozy Cape has an efficient plan that's long on style and comfort. Multipane windows and mock shutters lend a welcoming appeal to the charming exterior. Inside, to the right of the foyer, the comfortable family room features a fireplace and snack bar. The separate dining room has a gorgeous bay window and is just steps from the efficient kitchen. The formal living room and study-bedroom, with nearby full bath, round out the first floor. Upstairs, the master suite has a walk-in closet and large bath. Two spacious family bedrooms share a full bath.

DESIGN 2571
First Floor:
1,137 square feet
Second Floor:
795 square feet
Total:
1,932 square feet
L D

This home, as shown in the photograph, may differ from the actual blueprints. For more detailed information, please check the floor plans carefully.

Photo by Andrew D. Lautman

This home, as shown in the photograph, may differ from the actual blueprints. For more detailed information, please check the floor plans carefully.

Photo by Andrew D. Lautman

Width 74'
Depth 46'

Design by
Home Planners

Here's a traditional farmhouse design that's made for down-home hospitality and the good grace of pleasant company. Star attractions are the large covered porch and the entertainment terrace. The hardworking interior offers separate living and family rooms, each with their own fireplace, and a formal dining room with separate access to the terrace. The U-shaped kitchen shares natural light from a bayed breakfast nook and offers a sizable pantry and lots of counter space. The mud room and laundry offer access from the garage and from the rear terrace, while the adjoining workshop enjoys its own entries.

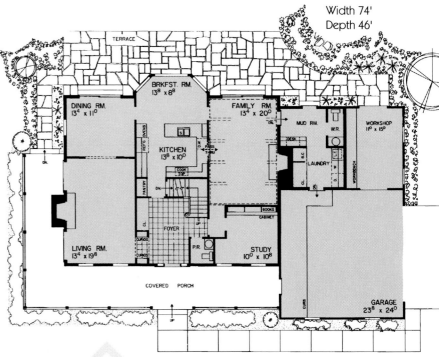

DESIGN 2946

First Floor:
1,581 square feet
Second Floor:
1,344 square feet
Total:
2,925 square feet

L **D**

QUOTE ONE®

Cost to build? See page 230 to order complete cost estimate to build this house in your area!

*This home, as shown in the photograph, may differ from the actual blueprints.
For more detailed information, please check the floor plans carefully.*

Photo by Carl Socolow

Design by
Home Planners

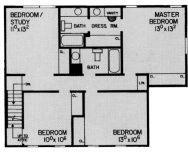

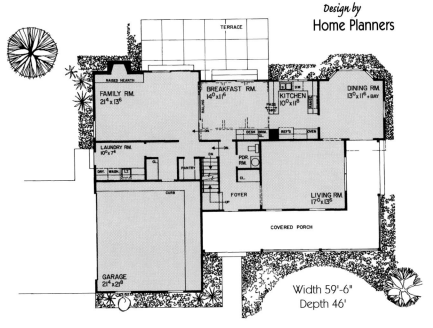

Width 59'-6"
Depth 46'

D E S I G N 2 7 7 4

First Floor:
1,366 square feet
Second Floor:
969 square feet
Total:
2,335 square feet

L **D**

Cost to build? See page 230
to order complete cost estimate
to build this house in your area!

Here's a best-selling farmhouse adaptation with deluxe amenities. The quiet corner living room opens to a sizable dining room with bumped-out bay, while the U-shaped kitchen offers built-ins and a pass-through to the breakfast room, which features a rustic beam ceiling. Sliding glass doors open to outdoor areas from the family room and breakfast area, and let in natural light. The service entrance to the garage offers a coat closet and a walk-in pantry. Second-floor sleeping quarters include a master suite with a private dressing room and bath, and three family bedrooms—or make one a study—and a hall bath.

This home, as shown in the photograph, may differ from the actual blueprints. For more detailed information, please check the floor plans carefully.

Photo by Jon Riley, Riley & Riley Photography

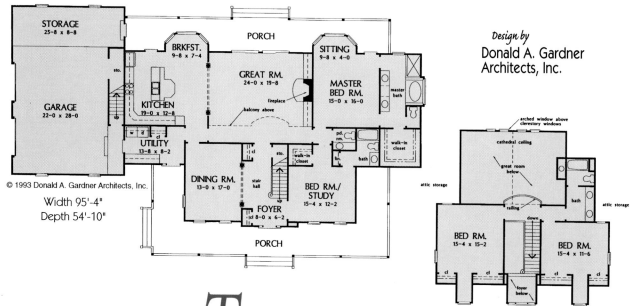

STORAGE
25-8 x 8-8

GARAGE
22-0 x 28-0

BRKFST.
9-8 x 7-4

PORCH

GREAT RM.
24-0 x 19-8

fireplace

balcony above

SITTING
9-8 x 4-0

MASTER
BED RM.
15-0 x 16-0

master bath

walk-in closet

KITCHEN
19-0 x 12-8

UTILITY
13-8 x 8-2

walk-in closet

pd. rm.

lin.

bath

© 1993 Donald A. Gardner Architects, Inc.

Width 95'-4"
Depth 54'-10"

DINING RM.
13-0 x 17-0

stair hall

sto.

up

BED RM./
STUDY
15-4 x 12-2

FOYER
cl 8-0 x 6-2

PORCH

Design by
**Donald A. Gardner
Architects, Inc.**

arched window above clerestory windows

cathedral ceiling

great room below

attic storage

railing

bath

attic storage

BED RM.
15-4 x 15-2

down

BED RM.
15-4 x 11-6

foyer below

DESIGN 9721

First Floor:
2,316 square feet
Second Floor:
721 square feet
Total:
3,037 square feet

The elegant foyer to this new country home enjoys a Palladian clerestory window that fills the entrance with natural light. A balcony overlooks the great room, which provides access to the rear covered porch. To the right of the first-floor plan, a spacious master suite offers a sitting bay and a sumptuous bath with a dressing area and U-shaped walk-in closet. A private hall leads to a study or guest suite with a private bath. Upstairs, two additional bedrooms share a full bath and a balcony hall.

QUOTE ONE®
Cost to build? See page 230 to order complete cost estimate to build this house in your area!

Casual areas are free-flowing while formal, more traditional rooms are secluded and well-defined in this new country home. A two-story foyer with a clerestory window leads to a quiet parlor with a vaulted ceiling and a Palladian window. The formal dining room opens from the foyer and enjoys service from a spacious gourmet kitchen through a butler's pantry. Casual living space, defined by columns, has an angled corner hearth and is open to the kitchen. The first-floor master suite boasts a sumptuous bath with a corner whirlpool tub and a twin vanity. The second floor includes two family bedrooms which share a full bath.

Design by
Alan Mascord
Design Associates, Inc.

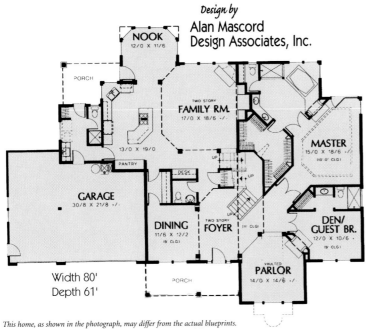

Width 80'
Depth 61'

DESIGN 7403

First Floor:
2,642 square feet
Second Floor:
603 square feet
Total:
3,245 square feet

This home, as shown in the photograph, may differ from the actual blueprints. For more detailed information, please check the floor plans carefully.

Photo by Bob Greenspan

Meadow Lark

An arched, columned entry provides a touch of class to this contemporary home, while shingles and siding add a country flavor. Inside, the foyer opens to a formal dining room, set off by decorative columns and a triple transom window. An expansive great room opens to the rear deck with spa. The well-organized gourmet kitchen serves both the dining room and a breakfast area with its own doors to the outside. The private master suite enjoys two walk-in closets and a windowed whirlpool tub. Upstairs, two family bedrooms share a full bath with two vanities. Please specify basement or crawlspace foundation when ordering.

Design by
Donald A. Gardner
Architects, Inc.

DESIGN 9661

First Floor:
1,416 square feet
Second Floor:
445 square feet
Total:
1,861 square feet

DECK

seat

spa

GREAT RM.
15-4 × 18-0
(cathedral ceiling)

arched window above door

KIT./BRKFST.
16-8 × 16-0

fireplace

master bath

walk-in closet

walk-in closet

MASTER BED RM.
13-0 × 13-6

pd. rm.

up

sto.

FOYER
7-8 × 9-0

DINING
12-4 × 12-4

UTILITY
10-0 × 6-4

w
d

up

storage

PORCH

© 1991 Donald A. Gardner Architects, Inc.

GARAGE
20-0 × 20-0

Width 58'-3"
Depth 68'-9"

BED RM.
10-4 × 11-9

walk-in closet

down

bath

cl

BED RM.
12-4 × 13-6

down

BONUS RM.
11-0 × 20-0

QUOTE ONE®

Cost to build? See page 230 to order complete cost estimate to build this house in your area!

This home, as shown in the photograph, may differ from the actual blueprints. For more detailed information, please check the floor plans carefully.

Photo by Jon Riley, Riley & Riley Photography

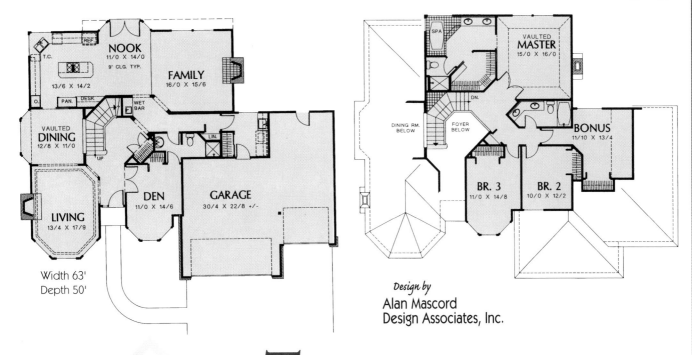

Width 63'
Depth 50'

Design by
Alan Mascord
Design Associates, Inc.

DESIGN 9478

First Floor:
1,586 square feet
Second Floor:
960 square feet
Total:
2,546 square feet

This country home offers a fresh face and plenty of personality, starting with its sunny bay with transom windows and a two-story turret. Inside, the foyer opens to a quiet den—the lower bay of the turret— through French doors. A formal living room with a tray ceiling leads to the vaulted dining room, which is served by a gourmet kitchen. To the rear of the plan, a spacious family area offers its own fireplace with a tiled hearth. Upstairs, a secluded master suite boasts a corner tiled-rim spa tub and an angled walk-in closet. Two family bedrooms share a full bath and a hall that leads to a sizable bonus room.

This home, as shown in the photograph, may differ from the actual blueprints.
For more detailed information, please check the floor plans carefully.

Photo by Bob Greenspan

This home, as shown in the photograph, may differ from the actual blueprints.
For more detailed information, please check the floor plans carefully.

Photo by Andrew D. Lautman

T he classic American homestead is all dressed up with contemporary character and country spirit. Well-defined rooms, flowing spaces and the latest amenities blend the best of traditional and modern elements. The spacious gathering room offers terrace access and shares a through-fireplace with a secluded study. The second-floor master suite shares a balcony hallway, which overlooks the gathering room, with two family bedrooms. Dual vanities, built-in cabinets and shelves, and triple-window views highlight the master bedroom. In an alternate plan, the formal dining room and the breakfast room are switched, placing the dining room to the front of the plan.

DESIGN 2826

First Floor:
1,112 square feet
Second Floor:
881 square feet
Total:
1,993 square feet

D

QUOTE ONE®

Cost to build? See page 230
to order complete cost estimate
to build this house in your area!

Design by
Home Planners

Width 49'
Depth 54'-4"

Alternate Kitchen / Dining Rm /
Breakfast Rm Floor Plan

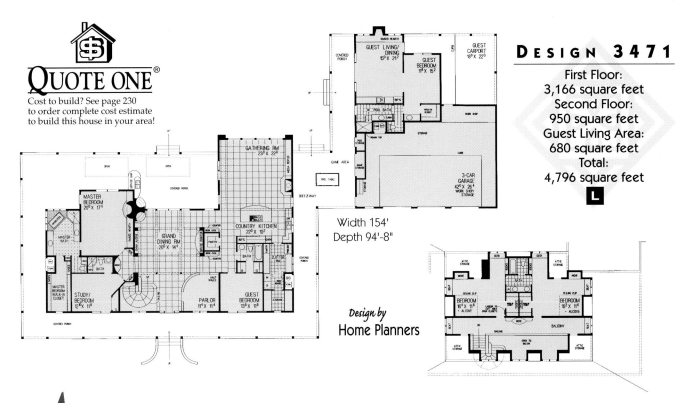

QUOTE ONE®

Cost to build? See page 230
to order complete cost estimate
to build this house in your area!

DESIGN 3471

First Floor:
3,166 square feet
Second Floor:
950 square feet
Guest Living Area:
680 square feet
Total:
4,796 square feet

L

Width 154'
Depth 94'-8"

Design by
Home Planners

A long, low-pitched roof distinguishes this Southwestern-style farmhouse design. The tiled entrance leads to a grand dining room and opens to a formal parlor secluded by half-walls. A country kitchen with cooktop island overlooks the two-story gathering room with its full wall of glass, fireplace and built-in media shelves.

The master suite satisfies the most discerning tastes with a raised hearth, an adjoining study or exercise room, access to the wraparound porch, and a bath with corner whirlpool tub. Rooms upstairs can serve as secondary bedrooms for family members, or can be converted to home office space.

This home, as shown in the photograph, may differ from the actual blueprints. For more detailed information, please check the floor plans carefully.

Photo by Allen Maertz

This home, as shown in the photograph, may differ from the actual blueprints.
For more detailed information, please check the floor plans carefully.

Photo by Andrew D. Lautman

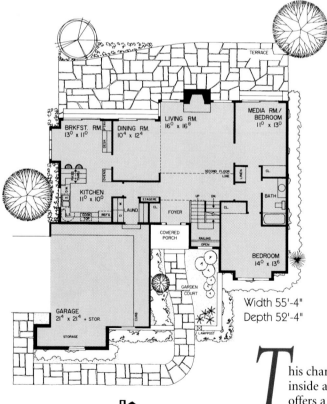

Width 55'-4"
Depth 52'-4"

DESIGN 2927

First Floor:
1,425 square feet
Second Floor:
704 square feet
Total:
2,129 square feet

D

Design by
Home Planners

QUOTE ONE®

Cost to build? See page 230
to order complete cost estimate
to build this house in your area!

This charming Early American adaptation offers a warm welcome—inside and out. The first floor features a convenient kitchen which offers a pass-through to the breakfast room, and easily serves the formal dining room. A spacious living room in the heart of the home enjoys a centered fireplace with flanking windows and leads to a media room, which could also be used as a guest bedroom. The second floor includes a spacious master suite with two walk-in closets and a luxurious bath with a tiled-rim, windowed tub. A balcony hall leads to a sizable studio with closet space.

DESIGN 2947

Square Footage: 1,830

L D

Design by
Home Planners

Rear Elevation

This charming, one-story traditional home greets visitors with a covered porch, decked out with columns and balusters. Inside, a galley-style kitchen shares a snack counter with the gathering room, which offers a fireplace and opens to the formal dining room. The lavish master suite nestles to the rear of the plan and boasts a sloped ceiling, a dressing room and a relaxing bath with a whirlpool tub and a separate shower. Two additional bedrooms—one could double as a study—enjoy views of the front property.

QUOTE ONE®

Cost to build? See page 230
to order complete cost estimate
to build this house in your area!

Width 75'
Depth 43'-5"

This home, as shown in the photograph, may differ from the actual blueprints.
For more detailed information, please check the floor plans carefully.

Photos by Andrew D. Lautman

Design by
Home Planners

Width 44'-8"
Depth 52'-4"/54'-4"

Design 3655

Design 3656

QUOTE ONE®
Cost to build? See page 230
to order complete cost estimate
to build this house in your area!

DESIGN
3655/3656

Square Footage:

1,418/1,414

L

This cozy cottage offers the choice of a three- (Design 3656) or four-bedroom (Design 3655) plan. Both designs feature a front-facing office/guest suite which provides privacy for the entry courtyard. With its separate entrance it offers the perfect haven for an in-home office or for those with live-in parents. The remainder of the house is designed with the same level of efficiency. It contains a large living area with access to a covered patio and a three-sided fireplace that shares its warmth with a dining room featuring built-ins. A unique kitchen provides garage access. The bedrooms include a comfortable master suite with a whirlpool tub, a double-bowl vanity and twin closets.

This home, as shown in the photograph, may differ from the actual blueprints.
For more detailed information, please check the floor plans carefully.

Photo by Andrew D. Lautman

DESIGN 2878
Square Footage: 1,521
L D

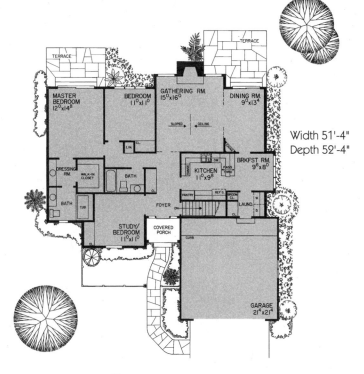

Width 51'-4"
Depth 52'-4"

T his charming, compact design combines traditional styling with sensational commodities and modern livability. Thoughtful zoning places sleeping areas to one side, apart from household activity. The plan includes a spacious gathering room with sloped ceiling and centered fireplace, and a formal dining room overlooking a rear terrace. A handy pass-through connects the breakfast room and an efficient kitchen. The laundry is strategically positioned nearby for handy access. An impressive master suite enjoys access to a private rear terrace and offers a separate dressing area with walk-in closet. Two family bedrooms, or one and a study, are nearby and share a full bath.

QUOTE ONE®

Cost to build? See page 230
to order complete cost estimate
to build this house in your area!

Design by
Home Planners

DESIGN 3651

Square Footage: 2,213

L D

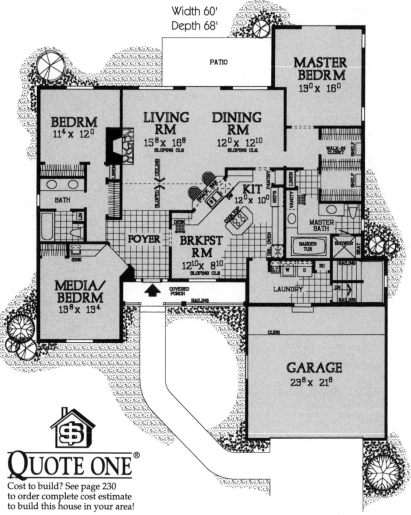

Width 60'
Depth 68'

PATIO

MASTER BEDRM
13⁰ x 16⁰

BEDRM
11⁴ x 12⁰

LIVING RM
15⁸ x 16⁸
SLOPING CLG.

DINING RM
12⁰ x 12¹⁰
SLOPING CLG.

WALK-IN CLOSET

KIT
12⁰ x 10⁰

PANTRY

BATH

MASTER BATH

FOYER

BRKFST RM
12¹⁰ x 8¹⁰
SLOPING CLG.

GARDEN TUB

SHOWER

MEDIA/BEDRM
13⁸ x 19⁴

DESK

DBL. OVEN

LAUNDRY

COVERED PORCH

RAILING

RAILING

CURB

GARAGE
23⁸ x 21⁸

*T*his home's two projecting wings with low-pitched, wide, overhanging roofs provide a distinctive note. The compact, efficient floor plan assures convenient living patterns. In the kitchen, a planning desk, an island cooking counter with storage below, double ovens, a pantry, fine counter space and an opening to a handy snack bar capture attention. The open planning of the living and dining rooms provides one big, spacious area for functional family living. The master bedroom has French doors to provide outdoor living potential.

Design by
Home Planners

QUOTE ONE®

Cost to build? See page 230
to order complete cost estimate
to build this house in your area!

Width 71'
Depth 43'-5"

QUOTE ONE®

Cost to build? See page 230
to order complete cost estimate
to build this house in your area!

Design by
Home Planners

DESIGN 3487
Square Footage: 1,835

L

*C*ountry comfort is the focus of this charming plan, ready for any region. A cozy covered porch offers a warm introduction to the tiled foyer, which leads to the living areas and opens to the breakfast room and kitchen. The expansive gathering room features an extended-hearth fireplace and adjoins the formal dining room, served by the kitchen. The entertainment terrace enjoys access from the dining room as well as the master suite. A sumptuous master bath provides a relaxing retreat for the homeowner, with a windowed whirlpool tub, a separate shower, two vanities and a sloped ceiling. A study at the front of the plan could be used as a bedroom.

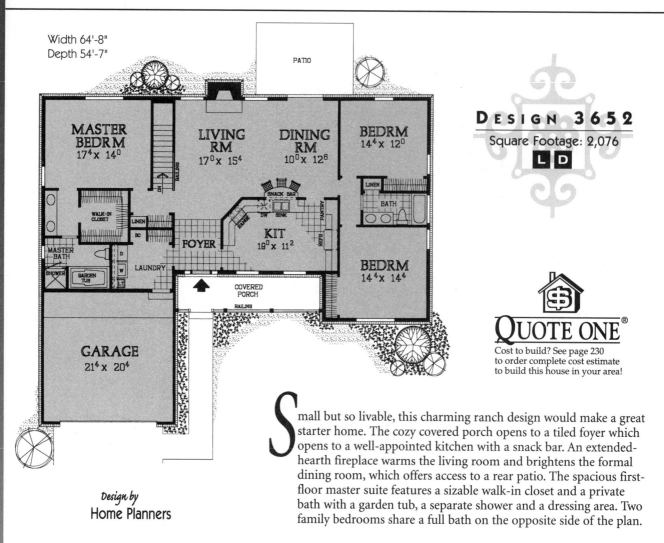

Width 64'-8"
Depth 54'-7"

MASTER BEDRM 17⁴ x 14⁰

LIVING RM 17⁰ x 15⁴

DINING RM 10⁰ x 12⁸

BEDRM 14⁴ x 12⁰

WALK-IN CLOSET

LINEN

BC

MASTER BATH

SHOWER

GARDEN TUB

D

W

LT

LAUNDRY

FOYER

SNACK BAR

DW SINK

RANGE

KIT 19⁰ x 11²

PANTRY

REFG

LINEN

BATH

BEDRM 14⁴ x 14⁴

COVERED PORCH

RAILING

RAILING

DN

PATIO

GARAGE 21⁴ x 20⁴

Design by
Home Planners

DESIGN 3652

Square Footage: 2,076

L D

QUOTE ONE®

Cost to build? See page 230
to order complete cost estimate
to build this house in your area!

Small but so livable, this charming ranch design would make a great starter home. The cozy covered porch opens to a tiled foyer which opens to a well-appointed kitchen with a snack bar. An extended-hearth fireplace warms the living room and brightens the formal dining room, which offers access to a rear patio. The spacious first-floor master suite features a sizable walk-in closet and a private bath with a garden tub, a separate shower and a dressing area. Two family bedrooms share a full bath on the opposite side of the plan.

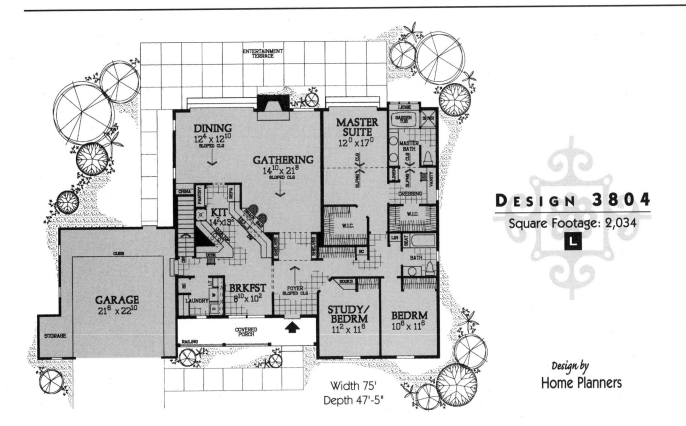

DINING
12⁴ x 12¹⁰
SLOPED CLG

GATHERING
14¹⁰ x 21⁸
SLOPED CLG

MASTER SUITE
12⁰ x 17⁰

GARDEN TUB

SHWR

MASTER BATH

DRESSING

VANITY

W.I.C.

LIN

SEAT

BATH

CHINA

PANTRY

KIT
14¹⁰ x 19³

SNACK BAR

W.I.C.

SHELVES

SHELVES

DESK

GARAGE
21⁶ x 22¹⁰

CURB

LAUNDRY

BRKFST
8¹⁰ x 10²

FOYER
SLOPED CLG

BOOKS

STUDY/ BEDRM
11² x 11⁸

BEDRM
10⁶ x 11⁸

STORAGE

RAILING

COVERED PORCH

ENTERTAINMENT TERRACE

LEDGE

Width 75'
Depth 47'-5"

DESIGN 3804
Square Footage: 2,034

L

Design by
Home Planners

H orizontal siding, multi-pane windows and a simple balustrade lend a Prairies 'N' Plains flavor to this traditional home. A roomy foyer with a sloped ceiling leads through a tiled vestibule with built-in shelves to the spacious gathering room, complete with a warming fireplace. An angled kitchen with a snack bar easily serves the formal dining room, which leads outdoors to the rear entertainment terrace. The luxurious master suite has its own door to the terrace as well as a fabulous private bath with a windowed whirlpool tub. Two additional bedrooms share a full bath and a hall that offers more wardrobe space.

Width 76'-4"
Depth 46'

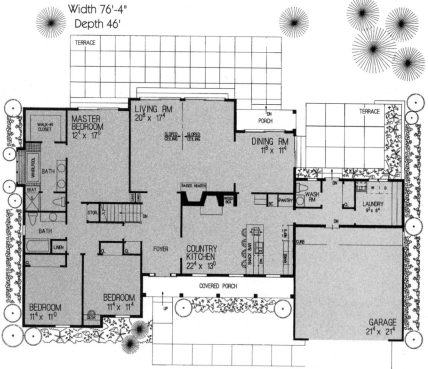

TERRACE

MASTER BEDROOM
12⁴ x 17⁵

WALK-IN CLOSET

LIVING RM
20⁸ x 17⁴

SLOPED CEILING   SLOPED CEILING

WHIRLPOOL

BATH

SEAT

STOR.

DN

BATH

LINEN

RAISED HEARTH

WOOD BOX

DINING RM
11⁸ x 11⁴

PORCH

DN

TERRACE

WASH RM

PANTRY

BC

CL

LAUNDRY
9² x 8⁴

W   D

DN

FOYER

COUNTRY KITCHEN
22⁴ x 13⁰

SNACK BAR

DW

REF

RANGE

CURB

BEDROOM
11⁴ x 11⁰

BEDROOM
11⁴ x 11⁴

DESK

COVERED PORCH

UP

GARAGE
21⁴ x 21⁴

DESIGN 3332

Square Footage: 2,168

L

Design by
Home Planners

othing completes a traditional-style home quite as well as a country kitchen with a fireplace and built-in wood box. Notice also the second fireplace (with raised hearth) and the sloped ceiling in the living room. The nearby dining room has an attached porch and separate dining terrace. Besides two family bedrooms with a shared full bath, there is also a marvelous master suite with rear terrace access, walk-in closet, whirlpool tub and double vanities. A handy washroom is near the laundry, just off the two-car garage.

QUOTE ONE®
Cost to build? See page 230
to order complete cost estimate
to build this house in your area!

QUOTE ONE®

Cost to build? See page 230 to order complete cost estimate to build this house in your area!

Design by
Home Planners

Width 88'-8"
Depth 53'-6"

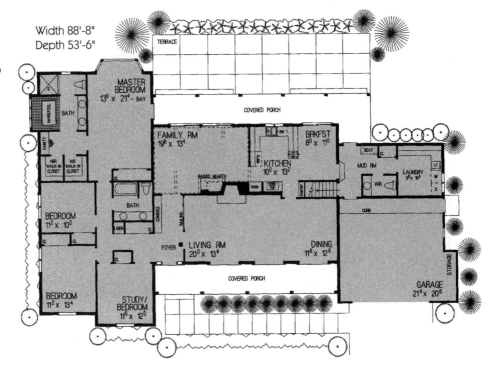

DESIGN 3348
Square Footage: 2,549

L

Covered porches front and rear will be the envy of the neighborhood when this house is built. The interior plan meets family needs perfectly in well-zoned areas: a sleeping wing with four bedrooms and two baths, a living zone with formal and informal gathering space and a work zone with U-shaped kitchen and laundry with washroom. The two-car garage has a huge storage area.

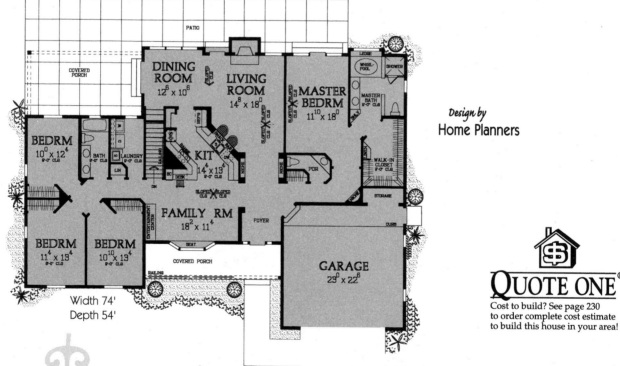

DINING
ROOM
12⁸ x 10⁶

LIVING
ROOM
14⁸ x 18⁰

MASTER
BEDRM
11¹⁰ x 18⁰

MASTER
BATH

WHIRL-
POOL

SHOWER

LEDGE

COVERED
PORCH

BEDRM
10⁰ x 12⁴

BATH

LAUNDRY

KIT
14⁴ x 13⁰

WALK-IN
CLOSET

PDR.

STORAGE

BEDRM
11⁴ x 13⁴

BEDRM
10¹⁰ x 13⁴

FAMILY RM
18² x 11⁴

FOYER

SEAT

COVERED PORCH

RAILING

GARAGE
23⁰ x 22⁶

PATIO

Width 74'
Depth 54'

Design by
Home Planners

DESIGN 3685
Square Footage: 2,415

A quaint covered porch, country shutters and a clerestory dormer window decorate this traditional design with blue-ribbon style. The family room boasts a bay window with a seat, and a built-in entertainment center. An angled kitchen offers a snack bar which overlooks the living room and enjoys the glow of its hearth. The living area has a sloped ceiling and leads outdoors to a rear patio and, through the dining room, to a covered porch. Three sizable family bedrooms complement a sensational master suite, which features a whirlpool bath and an oversized walk-in closet.

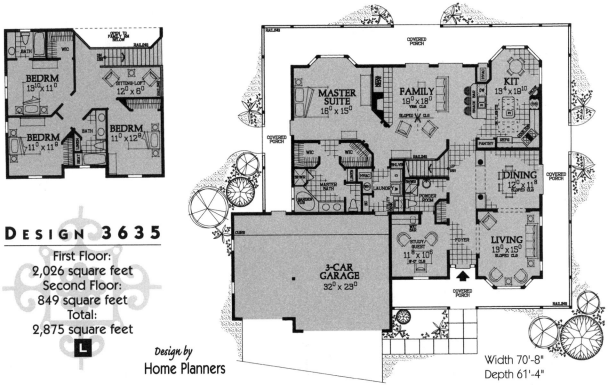

DESIGN 3635

First Floor:
2,026 square feet
Second Floor:
849 square feet
Total:
2,875 square feet

L

Design by
Home Planners

Width 70'-8"
Depth 61'-4"

Sunny bay windows create a charming facade that's set off by an old-fashioned country porch on this farmhouse design. Inside, the ceramic-tiled foyer opens to a formal living room and to a study, or guest suite, with a powder room. The casual living area, set off by a sloped ceiling, enjoys a raised-hearth fireplace and a media niche. The nearby gourmet kitchen enjoys natural light from a sunny breakfast bay and from a skylight. The sensational master suite offers private access to the covered porch, and a lavish tiled bath. Two family bedrooms share a full bath on the second floor, while a fourth bedroom, or guest suite, enjoys a private bath.

RAILING
COVERED PORCH RETREAT

MASTER SUITE
15⁸ x 13⁴
SLOPED CEILING

MASTER BATH
GARDEN TUB
LINEN
SHWR
PLANT SHELF ABOVE

FAMILY RM
12⁸ x 13⁰
VAULTED CLG

BAY WINDOW

LAUNDRY
W
D

WALK-IN CLOSET

COVERED PORCH

PANTRY
BC

DW
KIT
12⁹ x 10⁰
RANGE
REFG

BEDRM
10⁰ x 12⁰
VAULTED CLG

RAILING

LINEN

BATH

BEDRM
10⁰ x 10⁸
VAULTED CLG

BAY WINDOW

DINING

LIVING RM
15¹⁰ x 19⁰
VAULTED CLG

PLANT SHELF ABOVE

HVAC
WH

LOW WALL
ENTRY

CURB

COVERED PORCH

2-CAR GARAGE
21⁴ x 23⁸

RAILING

Width 64'
Depth 44'-8"

Design by
Home Planners

*F*rom its wraparound covered porch to its two bay windows, this design offers plenty of amenities. The foyer opens directly into the attractive living room, which is enhanced by a warming fireplace, a vaulted ceiling and a bay window. A U-shaped kitchen with a snack bar works well with both the dining area and the family room. Two secondary bedrooms share a full bath and easily accommodate family or friends. At the back of the plan, a master suite with a sloped ceiling waits to pamper the lucky homeowner with a lavish bath plus private access to the porch.

DESIGN 3688
Square Footage: 1,646
L

DESIGN 3609

First Floor:
1,624 square feet
Second Floor:
596 square feet
Total:
2,220 square feet

L D

Design by
Home Planners

A front-projecting garage dressed up with siding, fishscale shingles and a sunburst adds charm and allows building on a narrow-lot. Open planning, sloped ceilings and an abundance of windows highlight the dining room, while the great room features a focal-point fireplace and twin picture windows. The family kitchen steps out in style with angled counters, a sloped ceiling, a bay window and a ceramic tile floor. Upstairs, two additional bedrooms share a full bath and a gallery hall that leads to a study area with space for computers.

Width 54'-4"
Depth 56'-4"

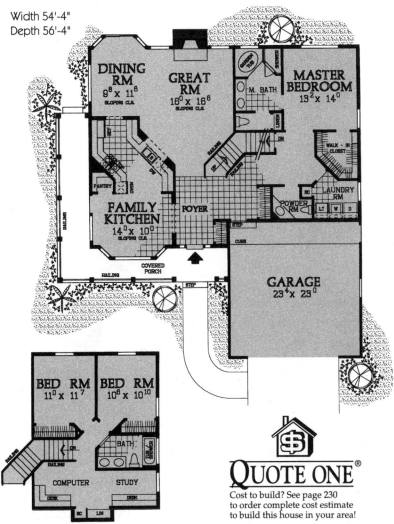

Quote One®

Cost to build? See page 230 to order complete cost estimate to build this house in your area!

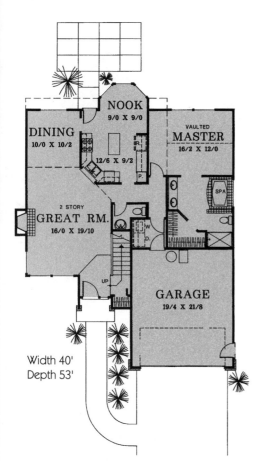

NOOK
9/0 X 9/0

DINING
10/0 X 10/2

VAULTED
MASTER
16/2 X 12/0

12/6 X 9/2

2 STORY
GREAT RM.
16/0 X 19/10

SPA

UP

GARAGE
19/4 X 21/8

Width 40'
Depth 53'

A perfect blend of siding and brick on this traditional exterior introduces a floor plan with great living spaces within the home. The highlight of the interior is the two-story great room, complete with a tiled-hearth fireplace. The gourmet kitchen and the bay-windowed breakfast nook open to the formal dining room. The first-floor master suite boasts a vaulted ceiling, whirlpool spa, two vanities and a corner walk-in closet. Upstairs, two family bedrooms share a full bath.

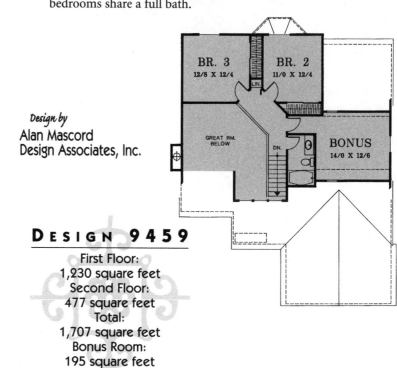

BR. 3
12/8 X 12/4

BR. 2
11/0 X 12/4

LIN.

GREAT RM.
BELOW

DN.

BONUS
14/0 X 12/6

Design by
**Alan Mascord
Design Associates, Inc.**

DESIGN 9459

First Floor:
1,230 square feet
Second Floor:
477 square feet
Total:
1,707 square feet
Bonus Room:
195 square feet

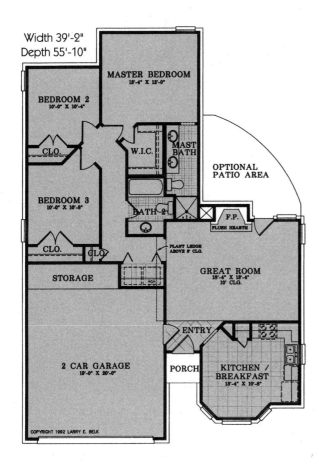

Width 39'-2"
Depth 55'-10"

BEDROOM 2
10'-0" X 10'-4"

MASTER BEDROOM
18'-4" X 12'-0"

CLO.

W.I.C.

MAST
BATH

OPTIONAL
PATIO AREA

BEDROOM 3
10'-0" X 10'-8"

BATH 2

CLO.

CLO.

F.P.
FLUSH HEARTH

STORAGE

PLANT LEDGE
ABOVE 8' CLG.

GREAT ROOM
18'-4" X 18'-4"
10' CLG.

2 CAR GARAGE
19'-0" X 20'-0"

ENTRY

PORCH

KITCHEN /
BREAKFAST
13'-4" X 10'-8"

COPYRIGHT 1992 LARRY E. BELK

Design by
Larry E. Belk Designs

DESIGN 8197
Square Footage: 1,178

*T*his cozy traditional charmer is set off by a bay window and asymmetrical gables. The inviting entry leads to a spacious great room, complete with a fireplace as well as access to an optional patio area. The front bay window brings in natural light to the kitchen/breakfast room with an ample pantry and wrapping counters. A gallery hall connects the sleeping quarters, which include two family bedrooms, which share a full bath, and a generous master suite with a private bath. Please specify crawl-space or slab foundation when ordering.

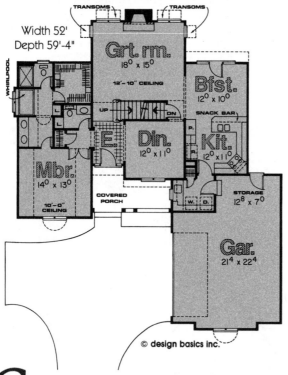

Width 52'
Depth 59'-4"

TRANSOMS   TRANSOMS

Grt. rm.
18⁰ x 15⁰

12'-10" CEILING

Bfst.
12⁰ x 10⁰

WHIRLPOOL

UP   DN   SNACK BAR

P.

Din.
12⁰ x 11⁰

Kit.
12⁰ x 11⁰

Mbr.
14⁰ x 13⁰

10'-0"
CEILING

COVERED
PORCH

STORAGE
12⁸ x 7⁰

W.   D.

Gar.
21⁴ x 22⁴

© design basics inc.

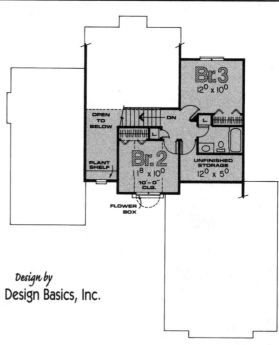

Br. 3
12⁰ x 10⁰

OPEN
TO
BELOW

DN

PLANT
SHELF

Br. 2
11⁸ x 10⁰

UNFINISHED
STORAGE
12⁰ x 5⁰

10'-0"
CLG.

FLOWER
BOX

Design by
Design Basics, Inc.

Circle-top windows deliver an extra measure of natural light into this 1½-story home. Inside, a two-story entry provides a fine introduction to the formal dining room and the sun-filled great room. A warming fireplace bordered by transom windows extends a gracious welcome. Adjoining the kitchen and snack bar, the breakfast room completes the casual living space. French doors open onto the first-floor master suite with its grand bath. The second floor contains two family bedrooms, a full bath and storage space.

DESIGN 7309

First Floor:
1,316 square feet
Second Floor:
396 square feet
Total:
1,712 square feet

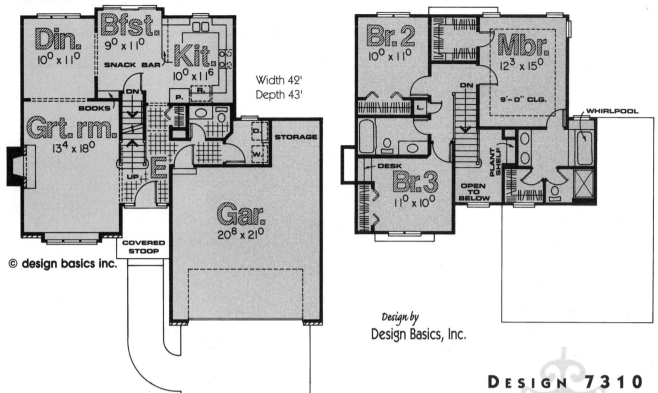

Din.
10⁰ x 11⁰

Bfst.
9⁰ x 11⁰

Kit.
10⁰ x 11⁶

SNACK BAR

DN

P.

R.

BOOKS

Grt. rm.
13⁴ x 18⁰

UP

D.

W.

STORAGE

Gar.
20⁸ x 21⁰

COVERED STOOP

© design basics inc.

Width 42'
Depth 43'

Br. 2
10⁰ x 11⁰

Mbr.
12³ x 15⁰

9'-0" CLG.

DN

L.

WHIRLPOOL

DESK

Br. 3
11⁰ x 10⁰

PLANT SHELF

OPEN TO BELOW

Design by
Design Basics, Inc.

U nique window treatments, brick accents and classic siding dress up this impressive two-story home. The entry, topped by a plant shelf, opens on the left to a cozy great room with a warming fireplace. A sun-filled breakfast room with a built-in bookcase provides a place for casual meals and conversations with the resident gourmet. Upstairs, two family bedrooms share a full bath. A terrific master suite offers a compartmented whirlpool bath.

D E S I G N   7 3 1 0

First Floor:
831 square feet
Second Floor:
790 square feet
Total:
1,621 square feet

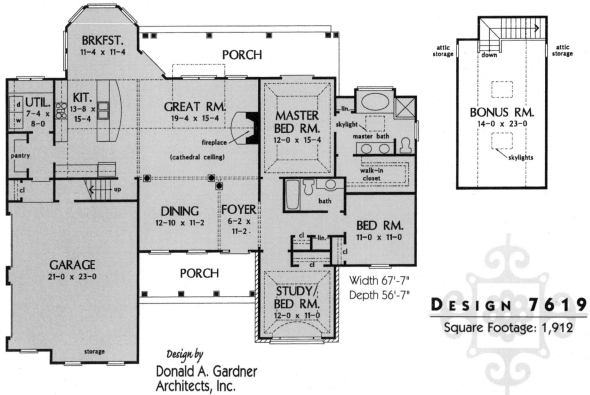

BRKFST.
11-4 x 11-4

PORCH

UTIL.
7-4 x
8-0

KIT.
13-8 x
15-4

GREAT RM.
19-4 x 15-4

MASTER
BED RM.
12-0 x 15-4

pantry

fireplace

(cathedral ceiling)

skylight

master bath

lin.

cl

up

DINING
12-10 x 11-2

FOYER
6-2 x
11-2

walk-in
closet

bath

GARAGE
21-0 x 23-0

PORCH

cl lin.

cl

cl

BED RM.
11-0 x 11-0

storage

STUDY/
BED RM.
12-0 x 11-0

Width 67'-7"
Depth 56'-7"

attic
storage

down

attic
storage

BONUS RM.
14-0 x 23-0

skylights

DESIGN 7619
Square Footage: 1,912

Design by
Donald A. Gardner
Architects, Inc.

An appealing blend of stone, siding and stucco announces a 21st-Century floor plan. A formal dining area defined by decorative columns opens to a grand great room with a centered hearth. The gourmet kitchen overlooks the great room, and enjoys natural light brought in by the bayed breakfast nook. The sleeping wing, to the right of the plan, includes a sumptuous master suite with a tray ceiling and a skylit bath with twin vanities. A secluded study is near a family bedroom and shares its bath.

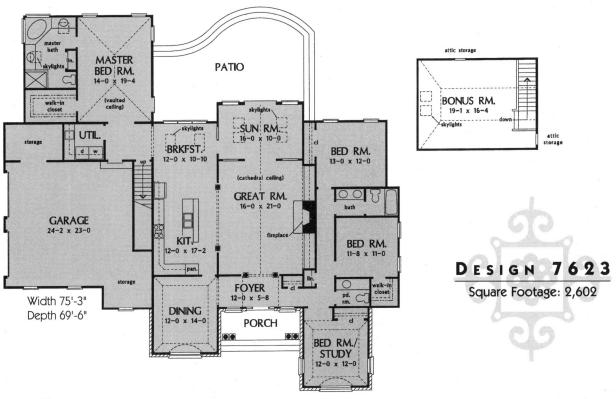

MASTER BED RM. 14-0 x 19-4 (vaulted ceiling)

master bath

skylights

lin.

walk-in closet

storage

UTIL.

d w

up

PATIO

skylights

SUN RM. 16-0 x 10-0

skylights

BRKFST. 12-0 x 10-10

(cathedral ceiling)

GREAT RM. 16-0 x 21-0

fireplace

KIT. 12-0 x 17-2

pan.

BED RM. 13-0 x 12-0

cl

bath

BED RM. 11-8 x 11-0

GARAGE 24-2 x 23-0

storage

FOYER 12-0 x 5-8

lin.

cl

pd. rm.

walk-in closet

cl

Width 75'-3"
Depth 69'-6"

DINING 12-0 x 14-0

PORCH

BED RM./ STUDY 12-0 x 12-0

attic storage

BONUS RM. 19-1 x 16-4

skylights

down

attic storage

D ESIGN 7623
Square Footage: 2,602

Classic brick and siding dress up this traditional home and introduce a well-cultivated interior. The foyer opens to an expansive great room with a centered fireplace flanked by built-in cabinets. The secluded master suite nestles to the rear of the plan and boasts a vaulted ceiling and a skylit master bath. Three additional bedrooms—or make one a study—share a full bath and a convenient powder room.

Design by
Donald A. Gardner
Architects, Inc.

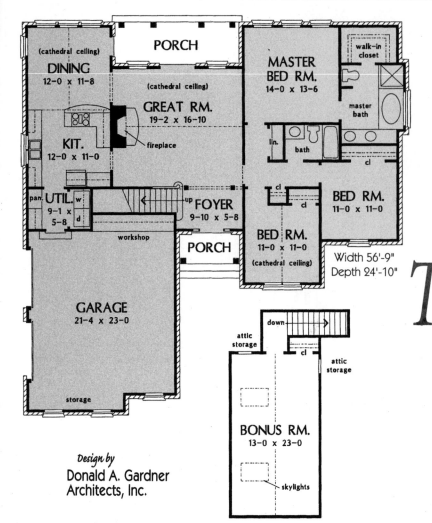

DINING
12-0 x 11-8
(cathedral ceiling)

PORCH

MASTER
BED RM.
14-0 x 13-6

walk-in
closet

master
bath

GREAT RM.
19-2 x 16-10
(cathedral ceiling)

KIT.
12-0 x 11-0

fireplace

lin.

bath

cl

UTIL.
9-1 x
5-8

pan.

w
d

up FOYER
9-10 x 5-8

cl

cl

BED RM.
11-0 x 11-0

workshop

PORCH

BED RM.
11-0 x 11-0
(cathedral ceiling)

Width 56'-9"
Depth 24'-10"

GARAGE
21-4 x 23-0

storage

down

attic
storage

cl

attic
storage

BONUS RM.
13-0 x 23-0

skylights

DESIGN 7639

Square Footage: 1,666
Bonus Room:
335 square feet

Design by
**Donald A. Gardner
Architects, Inc.**

This lovely traditional plan says "welcome home" to modern homeowners. Inside, cathedral ceilings add an aura of hospitality, while flexible bonus space over the garage invites future development. A luxurious master suite boasts a windowed whirlpool tub, a sizable walk-in closet and twin vanities. The spacious dining room works well for both casual family meals and formal events, with elegant touches such as a cathedral ceiling and a wall of windows. The kitchen is designed for easy meal preparation and service. A two-car garage has a designated workshop area plus separate space for storage.

© 1996 Donald A. Gardner Architects, Inc.

B. NATHAN

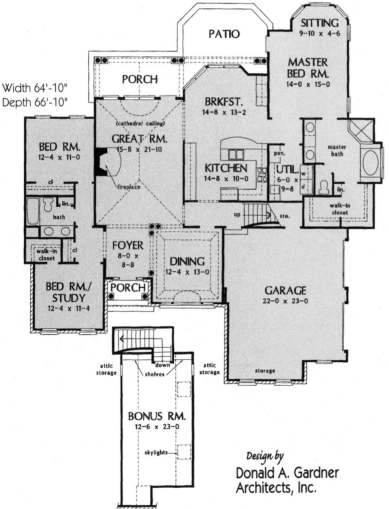

Width 64'-10"
Depth 66'-10"

BED RM.
12-4 x 11-0

cl · lin.

bath

walk-in closet · cl

BED RM./ STUDY
12-4 x 11-4

PORCH

FOYER
8-0 x 8-8

DINING
12-4 x 13-0

GREAT RM.
15-8 x 21-10
(cathedral ceiling)

fireplace

up

KITCHEN
14-8 x 10-0

BRKFST.
14-8 x 13-2

PORCH

PATIO

SITTING
9-10 x 4-6

MASTER BED RM.
14-0 x 15-0

pan.

UTIL.
6-0 x 9-8

w d

sto.

master bath

lin.

walk-in closet

GARAGE
22-0 x 23-0

storage

attic storage

down shelves

attic storage

BONUS RM.
12-6 x 23-0

skylights

Design by
Donald A. Gardner
Architects, Inc.

DESIGN 7636

Square Footage: 2,196
Bonus Room:
326 square feet

This plan's stunning brick-and-siding exterior surrounds well-planned living spaces to create a home where formal gatherings or casual family moments are equal pleasures. The heart of this comfortably elegant home is the great room, which opens to the breakfast area, the formal dining room and the foyer. Bay windows in the breakfast area and the master bedroom echo one another to provide a great master sitting area and a dramatic rear elevation. The master suite is also equipped with a spacious, pampering bath with a corner shower, a garden tub, an enclosed toilet and a sizable walk-in closet.

BATH

BEDROOM NO. 3
11'-6" X 11'-0"

BEDROOM NO. 2
11'-4" X 11'-0"

SUN ROOM
12'-0" X 13'-8"

PORCH

MASTER
BATH

W.I.C.

PORCH

BREAKFAST
10'-0" X 9'-0"

FAMILY ROOM
18'-0" X 14'-0"

MASTER BEDROOM
13'-4" X 15'-6"

LAUNDRY

KITCHEN
12'-0" X 13'-2"

BATH

STORAGE

DN

DINING ROOM
11'-4" X 11'-4"

FOYER
6'-8" X 11'-10"

DEN/GUEST
BEDROOM
11'-4" X 14'-0"

TWO CAR GARAGE
20'-4" X 19'-8"

PORCH

Width 62'-4"
Depth 62'-2"

DESIGN 9862
Square Footage: 2,170

Design by
Design Traditions

QUOTE ONE®
Cost to build? See page 230
to order complete cost estimate
to build this house in your area!

*T*his classic cottage boasts a stone and wood exterior with a welcoming arch-top entry that leads to a columned foyer. An extended-hearth fireplace is the focal point for the family room, while a nearby sun room with covered porch access opens up the living area to the outdoors. The gourmet island kitchen opens through double doors from the living area, and the breakfast area hugs a private porch. Sleeping quarters include a master wing with a spacious, angled bath and a sitting room or den which has its own full bath—perfect for a guest suite. On the opposite side of the plan, two family bedrooms share a full bath. This home is designed with a basement foundation.

© Design Traditions

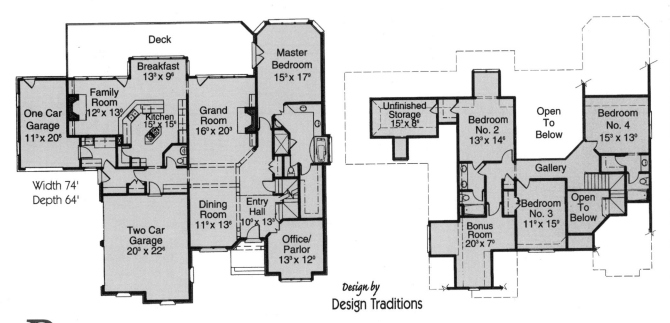

First Floor labels:

Deck

Breakfast
13³ x 9⁶

Family Room
12⁰ x 13⁰

One Car Garage
11³ x 20⁶

Kitchen
15³ x 15⁶

Grand Room
16⁰ x 20³

Master Bedroom
15³ x 17⁹

Width 74'
Depth 64'

Two Car Garage
20³ x 22⁶

Dining Room
11⁹ x 13⁶

Entry Hall
10⁰ x 13³

Office/Parlor
13³ x 12⁰

Second Floor labels:

Unfinished Storage
15³ x 8⁶

Bedroom No. 2
13³ x 14⁶

Open To Below

Bedroom No. 4
15³ x 13⁰

Gallery

Bonus Room
20³ x 7⁰

Bedroom No. 3
11⁹ x 15⁹

Open To Below

Design by
Design Traditions

R ustic brick, vertical siding and a distinctive center gable add up to world-class style with this traditional plan. Gently flavored with both European and country accents, the exterior architecture introduces a modern floor plan. The entry hall opens to an elegant formal dining room and to the vaulted grand room, complete with a fireplace and views to the outdoors. A gourmet kitchen boasts a center cooking island and an adjoining breakfast room with a box-bay window. The master bedroom and bath provide a rambling retreat to the right of the plan, with an L-shaped double vanity, an extended walk-in closet and a step-up whirlpool tub. Upstairs, the family sleeping quarters are connected by a gallery hall with interior vistas to the grand room. This home is designed with a basement foundation.

DESIGN 7822

First Floor:
2,323 square feet
Second Floor:
1,060 square feet
Total:
3,383 square feet
Bonus Room:
234 square feet

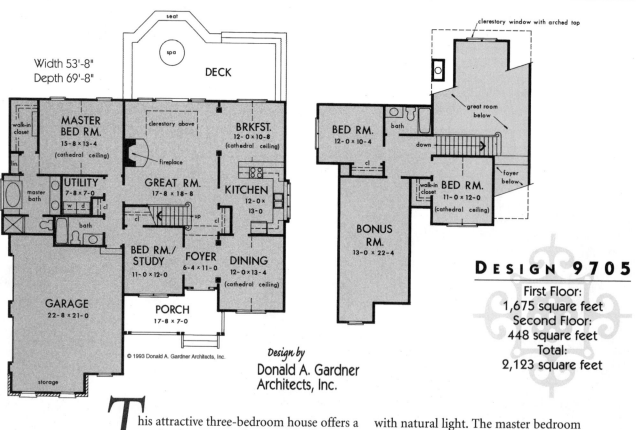

Width 53'-8"
Depth 69'-8"

DECK

seat

spa

MASTER BED RM.
15-8 x 13-4
(cathedral ceiling)

walk-in closet

clerestory above

fireplace

BRKFST.
12-0 x 10-8
(cathedral ceiling)

UTILITY
7-8 x 7-0

master bath

bath

w d

cl

GREAT RM.
17-8 x 18-8

KITCHEN
12-0 x 13-0

up

cl

BED RM./ STUDY
11-0 x 12-0

FOYER
6-4 x 11-0

DINING
12-0 x 13-4
(cathedral ceiling)

GARAGE
22-8 x 21-0

storage

PORCH
17-8 x 7-0

© 1993 Donald A. Gardner Architects, Inc.

clerestory window with arched top

BED RM.
12-0 x 10-4

bath

great room below

down

foyer below

walk-in closet

BED RM.
11-0 x 12-0
(cathedral ceiling)

BONUS RM.
13-0 x 22-4

Design by
Donald A. Gardner Architects, Inc.

DESIGN 9705

First Floor:
1,675 square feet
Second Floor:
448 square feet
Total:
2,123 square feet

his attractive three-bedroom house offers a touch of country with its covered front porch. The foyer, flanked by the dining room and the bedroom/study, leads to the spacious great room. The dining room and breakfast room have cathedral ceilings with arched windows filling the house

with natural light. The master bedroom boasts a cathedral ceiling and bath with whirlpool, shower and double-bowl vanity. Two family bedrooms reside upstairs. Please specify basement or crawlspace foundation when ordering.

DESIGN 7641

Square Footage: 2,027
Bonus Room:
340 square feet

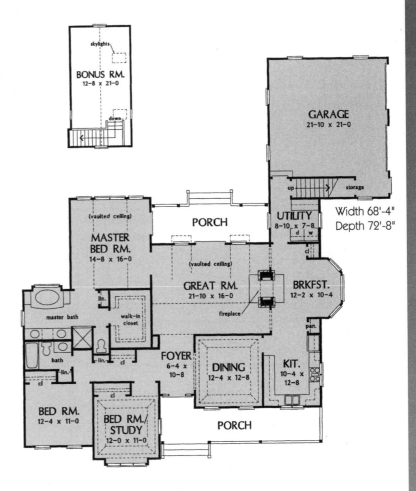

BONUS RM.
12-8 x 21-0
skylights
down

GARAGE
21-10 x 21-0

Width 68'-4"
Depth 72'-8"

PORCH

UTILITY
8-10 x 7-8

MASTER BED RM.
14-8 x 16-0
(vaulted ceiling)

GREAT RM.
21-10 x 16-0
(vaulted ceiling)

BRKFST.
12-2 x 10-4

fireplace

master bath

walk-in closet

bath

FOYER
6-4 x 10-8

DINING
12-4 x 12-8

KIT.
10-4 x 12-8

BED RM.
12-4 x 11-0

BED RM./ STUDY
12-0 x 11-0

PORCH

*T*his relaxed country home has all the extras, including front and rear covered porches, a dual-sided fireplace and a deluxe master suite. The great room, bright with natural light that streams in through two clerestory dormers, shares a fireplace with the breakfast bay. The formal dining room and front bedroom/study are dressed up with tray ceilings, while the master bedroom features a vaulted ceiling as well as access to the rear porch. Skylit bonus space over the garage provides the extra room today's families need.

Design by
Donald A. Gardner Architects, Inc.

© 1997 Donald A. Gardner Architects, Inc.

B. NATHAN

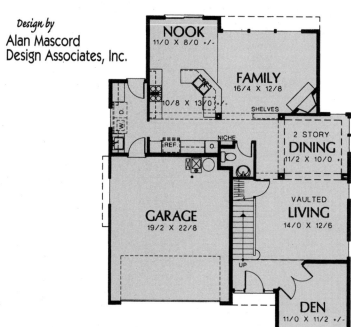

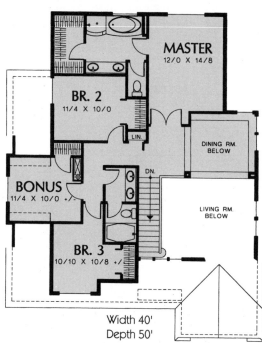

Design by
Alan Mascord
Design Associates, Inc.

NOOK
11/0 X 8/0 +/-

FAMILY
16/4 X 12/8

10/8 X 13/0 +/-

SHELVES

REF.

NICHE

2 STORY
DINING
11/2 X 10/0 +/-

GARAGE
19/2 X 22/8

VAULTED
LIVING
14/0 X 12/6

UP

DEN
11/0 X 11/2 +/-

MASTER
12/0 X 14/8

BR. 2
11/4 X 10/0

LIN.

DINING RM.
BELOW

BONUS
11/4 X 10/0 +/-

DN.

LIVING RM.
BELOW

BR. 3
10/10 X 10/8 +/-

Width 40'
Depth 50'

DESIGN 7425

First Floor:
1,174 square feet
Second Floor:
967 square feet
Total:
2,141 square feet
Bonus Room:
99 square feet

Multi-pane windows complement classic horizontal siding and asymmetrical gables and set off a gentle country flavor with this traditional design. A fabulous two-story formal dining room invites entertaining and opens through decorative columns to a vaulted living room. French doors lead to a private den with views to the front property. The second-floor sleeping quarters include a sumptuous master suite, replete with amenities such as a windowed whirlpool tub and twin vanities. Family bedrooms surround a gallery hall that leads to bonus space, and share a full bath.

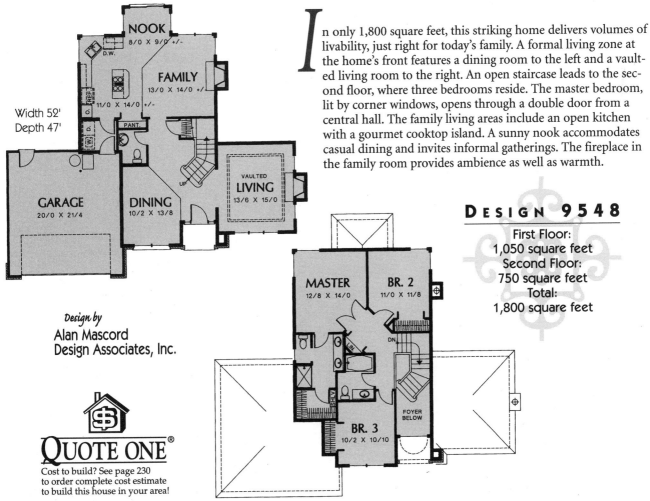

Width 52'
Depth 47'

NOOK
8/0 X 9/0 +/-

FAMILY
13/0 X 14/0 +/-

11/0 X 14/0 +/-

REF.

PANT.

W. D.

GARAGE
20/0 X 21/4

DINING
10/2 X 13/8

VAULTED
LIVING
13/6 X 15/0

UP

Design by
**Alan Mascord
Design Associates, Inc.**

MASTER
12/8 X 14/0

BR. 2
11/0 X 11/8

DN.

BR. 3
10/2 X 10/10

FOYER
BELOW

*I*n only 1,800 square feet, this striking home delivers volumes of livability, just right for today's family. A formal living zone at the home's front features a dining room to the left and a vaulted living room to the right. An open staircase leads to the second floor, where three bedrooms reside. The master bedroom, lit by corner windows, opens through a double door from a central hall. The family living areas include an open kitchen with a gourmet cooktop island. A sunny nook accommodates casual dining and invites informal gatherings. The fireplace in the family room provides ambience as well as warmth.

DESIGN 9548

First Floor:
1,050 square feet
Second Floor:
750 square feet
Total:
1,800 square feet

QUOTE ONE®

Cost to build? See page 230
to order complete cost estimate
to build this house in your area!

NOOK
9/8 X 13/8
(9' CLG.)

VAULTED
FAMILY
17/8 X 14/0

11/8 X 11/8

PANTRY

DINING
12/0 X 11/0 +
(9' CLG.)

10/2 X 12/0

UP

LIVING
13/0 X 13/8 +
(9' CLG.)

GARAGE
19/4 X 21/8

Width 44'
Depth 51'

Design by
**Alan Mascord
Design Associates, Inc.**

Tradition takes a lovely turn with this home, styled with a striking blend of stucco and classic siding. An angled staircase sets off the foyer and leads to a spectacular sleeping zone with a vaulted loft. Abundant bays and windows invite natural light throughout the stunning interior, ready for casual company as well as formal events. A focal-point fireplace warms the living room, which opens to a front patio with a privacy wall. Family members will gather in the casual living area to the rear of the plan, complete with a centered hearth of its own. The gourmet kitchen serves a breakfast nook and leads to the dining room through an ample pantry area.

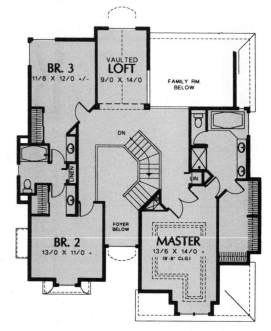

BR. 3
11/8 X 12/0 +/-

VAULTED
LOFT
9/0 X 14/0

FAMILY RM.
BELOW

DN.

LINEN

LIN.

FOYER
BELOW

BR. 2
13/0 X 11/0 +

MASTER
13/6 X 14/0
(9'-8" CLG.)

DESIGN 7408

First Floor:
1,294 square feet
Second Floor:
1,414 square feet
Total:
2,709 square feet

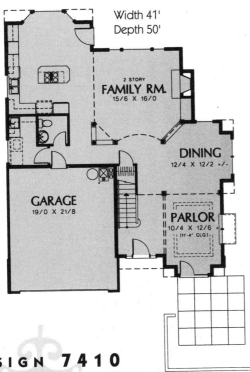

Width 41'
Depth 50'

2 STORY
FAMILY RM.
15/6 X 16/0

DINING
12/4 X 12/2 +/-

GARAGE
19/0 X 21/8

PARLOR
10/4 X 12/6
(11'-4" CLG.)

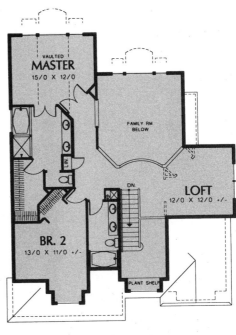

VAULTED
MASTER
15/0 X 12/0

FAMILY RM
BELOW

LOFT
12/0 X 12/0 +/-

DN.

BR. 2
13/0 X 11/0 +/-

PLANT SHELF

Design by
**Alan Mascord
Design Associates, Inc.**

DESIGN 7410

First Floor:
1,189 square feet
Second Floor:
1,030 square feet
Total:
2,219 square feet

Revival elements such as Craftsman-style transoms, classic siding and pediments call up the charm of gentler times. A well-organized and unrestrained floor plan bends but doesn't break tradition, with a formal parlor off the foyer and wide open living space at the heart of the home. The gourmet kitchen enjoys views to the outdoors through the breakfast area. Second-floor sleeping quarters include a vaulted master suite with a sizable walk-in closet, two vanities and a spa tub. An additional bedroom adjoins a hall bath.

Width 59'-4"
Depth 58'-7"

PORCH

(two story ceiling)

GREAT RM.
17-4 x 17-9

BRKFST.
11-0 x 13-10

master bath

walk-in closet

walk-in closet

fireplace

pan.

KIT.
10-4 x 13-7

MASTER BED RM.
13-0 x 13-8

pd. rm.

up

sto.

cl

storage

FOYER
10-2 x 6-1

DINING
12-4 x 12-4

UTIL.
10-4 x 6-0

d
w

PORCH

GARAGE
21-0 x 21-8

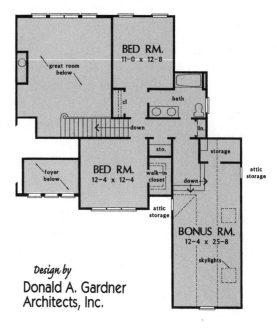

BED RM.
11-0 x 12-8

great room below

cl

bath

down

lin.

foyer below

BED RM.
12-4 x 12-4

sto.

storage

walk-in closet

down

attic storage

attic storage

BONUS RM.
12-4 x 25-8

skylights

Design by
Donald A. Gardner
Architects, Inc.

DESIGN 7644

First Floor:
1,489 square feet
Second Floor:
534 square feet
Total:
2,023 square feet
Bonus Room:
393 square feet

A smart exterior and an economical use of interior space combine to create this spacious yet practical home. The grand foyer leads to a two-story great room with a centered fireplace, a wall of windows and access to the rear porch. The breakfast room, set off by decorative columns, has its own door to the porch and shares its natural light with the kitchen. Twin walk-in closets introduce a lavish private bath in the master suite. Additional bedrooms reside on the second floor and share a full bath. A skylit bonus room offers extra storage space and the possibility of a recreation or hobby area.

The perfect blend of country and traditional, this family home would fit nicely on a narrow lot. Columns define the entry to the dining room, while the kitchen, breakfast bay and great room remain open for a casual atmosphere. A half-bath and utility room are conveniently located nearby. Upstairs, the master suite has a luxurious bath with a sunny bay. Two additional bedrooms share a skylit bath.

MASTER BED RM.
14-8 x 12-6

skylight

master bath

linen
walk-in closet

skylights   attic storage

BONUS RM.
23-0 x 13-10

cl

BED RM.
12-4 x 11-0

down

attic storage

lin.   bath

skylight

walk-in closet

BED RM.
12-4 x 11-0

Width 49'-4"
Depth 58'-10"

PORCH

GREAT RM.
14-8 x 18-2

fireplace

storage

w d   pd. rm.

UTIL.
7-6 x 7-0

cl

BRKFST.
10-8 x 9-8

pan.

KIT.
12-4 x 14-2

GARAGE
23-0 x 21-2

up

FOYER

DINING
12-4 x 13-2

PORCH

DESIGN 7642

First Floor:
1,113 square feet
Second Floor:
960 square feet
Total:
2,073 square feet
Bonus Room:
338 square feet

Design by
Donald A. Gardner
Architects, Inc.

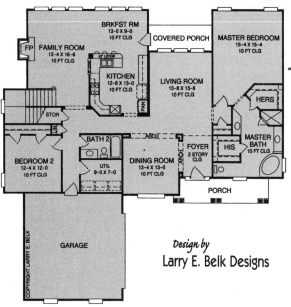

Design by
Larry E. Belk Designs

D ivided-light windows light up a country-style brick and siding exterior, while inside a family-room fireplace creates warm inglenooks for cozy gatherings. The kitchen shares a snack counter with the bright breakfast room, which leads to the rear covered porch. The formal dining room opens to the living room through columned arches, and enjoys wide open views of the outdoors. An angled master bath with His and Hers walk-in closets and two vanities sets off the homeowners' retreat, while family bedrooms enjoy a spacious game room upstairs. Please specify crawlspace or slab foundation when ordering.

DESIGN 8223

First Floor:
2,121 square feet
Second Floor:
920 square feet
Total:
3,041 square feet

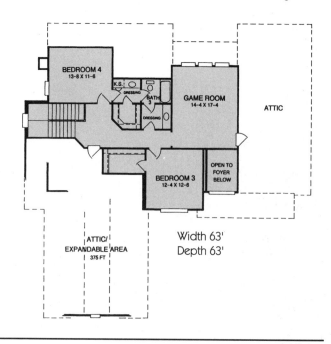

Width 63'
Depth 63'

DESIGN P280

First Floor:
1,797 square feet
Second Floor:
654 square feet
Total:
2,451 square feet

Design by
**Frank Betz
Associates, Inc.**

Capstones and brick accents add a touch of class to the charm and comfort of this American dream home. A vaulted breakfast bay brings the outdoors in and fills a sophisticated gourmet kitchen with natural light. The spacious family room enjoys radius windows and a French door to the back property, while a private formal living room opens off the foyer. A centered fireplace flanked by windows dresses up the master suite, which also features a vaulted private bath with a whirlpool tub. The second-floor bedrooms are connected by a balcony hall with overlooks to the family room and the foyer. Please specify basement or crawlspace foundation when ordering.

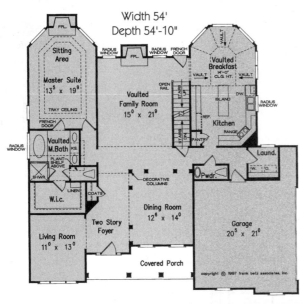

Width 54'
Depth 54'-10"

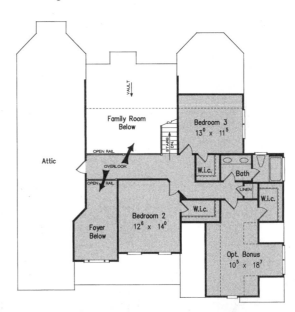

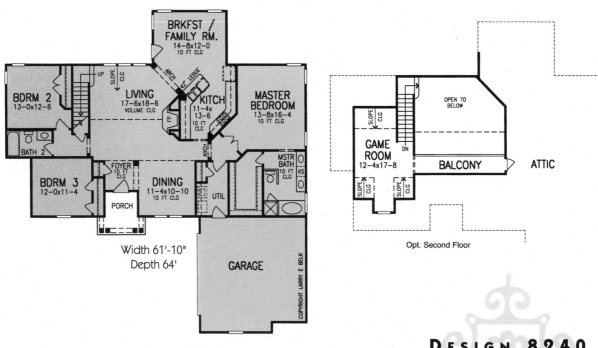

BRKFST /
FAMILY RM.
14-8x12-0
10 FT CLG

BDRM 2
13-0x12-6

UP

SLOPE CLG

LIVING
17-6x18-6
VOLUME CLG

KITCH
11-4x
13-6
10 FT
CLG

42" LEDGE

ARCH

MASTER
BEDROOM
13-8x16-4
10 FT CLG

BATH 2

FP

ARCH

MSTR
BATH
10 FT
CLG

KS

FOYER
10 FT
CLG

BDRM 3
12-0x11-4

DINING
11-4x10-10
10 FT CLG

UTIL

PORCH

Width 61'-10"
Depth 64'

GARAGE

COPYRIGHT LARRY E. BELK

GAME
ROOM
12-4x17-8

SLOPE CLG

OPEN TO
BELOW

DN

BALCONY

ATTIC

SLOPE CLG

SLOPE CLG

Opt. Second Floor

DESIGN 8240
Square Footage: 1,984

*E*nduring quality and beauty go together in this hardworking design, with an elegant country spirit. The interior blends casual, family space with formal areas—an arrangement that suits small gatherings as well as traditional occasions. French doors open to the secluded master suite, which offers a lavish bath with a spa tub and a knee-space vanity. On the opposite side of the plan, two family bedrooms share a full bath. Please specify crawlspace or slab foundation when ordering.

Design by
Larry E. Belk Designs

COPYRIGHT LARRY E. BELK

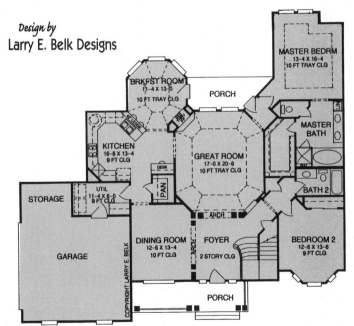

Design by
Larry E. Belk Designs

MASTER BEDRM
13-4 X 16-4
10 FT TRAY CLG

PORCH

BRKFST ROOM
11-4 X 13-0
10 FT TRAY CLG

MASTER
BATH

KITCHEN
16-6 X 13-4
9 FT CLG

GREAT ROOM
17-0 X 20-6
10 FT TRAY CLG

DESK

BATH 2

PAN

STORAGE

UTIL
11-4 X 6-0
9 FT CLG

ARCH

GARAGE

DINING ROOM
12-6 X 13-4
10 FT CLG

FOYER
2 STORY CLG

BEDROOM 2
12-6 X 13-6
9 FT CLG

COPYRIGHT LARRY E. BELK

ARCH

PORCH

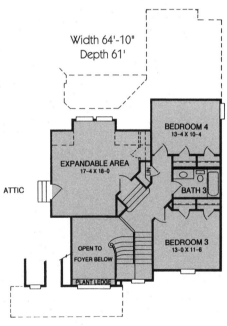

Width 64'-10"
Depth 61'

BEDROOM 4
13-4 X 10-4

EXPANDABLE AREA
17-4 X 18-0

ATTIC

BATH 3

OPEN TO
FOYER BELOW

BEDROOM 3
13-0 X 11-6

PLANT LEDGE

D ouble columns and an arch-top clerestory create an inviting entry to this fresh interpretation of traditional style. The two-story foyer features a decorative ledge perfect for displaying a tapestry. Decorative columns and arches open to the formal dining room and to the octagonal great room which has a ten-foot tray ceiling. The U-shaped kitchen looks over an angled counter to a sweet breakfast bay that brings in the outdoors and shares a through-fireplace with the great room. A sitting area and a lavish bath set off the secluded master suite. A nearby secondary bedroom with its own bath could be used as a guest suite, while, upstairs, two family bedrooms share a full bath and a hall that leads to an expandable area. Please specify crawlspace or slab foundation when ordering.

DESIGN 8161

First Floor:
2,028 square feet
Second Floor:
558 square feet
Total:
2,586 square feet

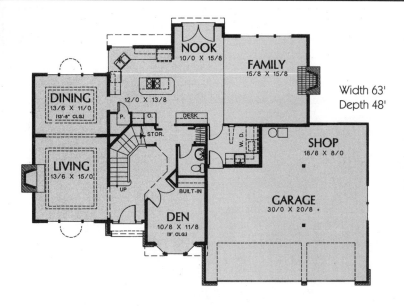

NOOK
10/0 X 15/8

FAMILY
15/8 X 15/8

DINING
13/6 X 11/0
(13'-8" CLG.)

12/0 X 13/8

DESK

LIVING
13/6 X 15/0

STOR.

P.

O.

W. D.

SHOP
18/8 X 8/0

UP

BUILT-IN

DEN
10/8 X 11/8
(9' CLG.)

GARAGE
30/0 X 20/8 +

Width 63'
Depth 48'

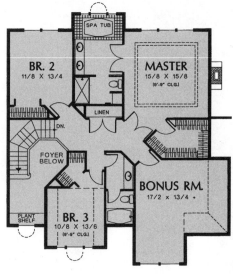

SPA TUB

BR. 2
11/8 X 13/4

MASTER
15/8 X 15/8
(9'-9" CLG.)

LINEN

DN.

FOYER
BELOW

BONUS RM.
17/2 x 13/4 +

PLANT
SHELF

BR. 3
10/8 X 13/6
(9'-9" CLG.)

Design by
Alan Mascord
Design Associates, Inc.

Here's traditional style at its best! A den with a beautiful bay window is positioned to the front of the plan, making it ideal for use as an office or home-based business. Formal rooms enjoy their own wing for privacy, and each room has a triple arch-top window for views and light. The gourmet kitchen features a sunlit corner sink, a cooktop island counter and a built-in planning desk. Second-floor sleeping quarters include a master suite with a relaxing spa tub, a separate shower and a sizable walk-in closet. Two family bedrooms share a hall bath, and the central upstairs hall leads to a sizable bonus room.

DESIGN 9542

First Floor:
1,465 square feet
Second Floor:
1,103 square feet
Total:
2,568 square feet

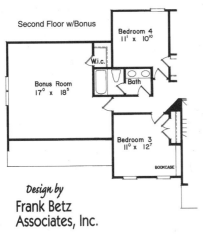

Second Floor w/Bonus

Bedroom 4
11' x 10¹⁰

W.i.c.

Bath

Bonus Room
17⁰ x 18⁵

Bedroom 3
11⁰ x 12⁷

BOOKCASE

Design by

**Frank Betz
Associates, Inc.**

DESIGN P195

First Floor:
1,290 square feet
Second Floor:
1,108 square feet
Total:
2,398 square feet

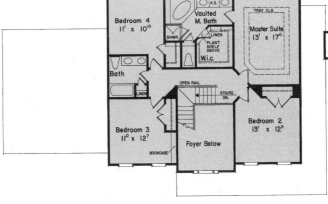

Garage
20⁹ x 23⁵

Kitchen
RANGE
ISLAND
Breakfast

FRENCH DOOR

Family Room
22' x 15⁰

FPL

REF.
W.
PWDR.
COATS
PANTRY
ARCHED OPENING

Laundry
W.
D.

STAIRS DN.
OPEN RAIL
Living Room
13' x 13³

FRENCH DOOR

Dining Room
13⁵ x 11⁰

STAIRS UP
Two Story Foyer

Covered Porch

copyright © 1993 frank betz associates, inc.

Width 67'-4"
Depth 38'-6"

Bedroom 4
11' x 10¹⁰

Vaulted M. Bath
K.S.
TRAY CLG

Master Suite
13' x 17⁰

SHWR
LINEN
PLANT SHELF ABOVE
W.i.c.

Bath

LINEN

OPEN RAIL
STAIRS DN.

Bedroom 3
11⁰ x 12⁷

Foyer Below

Bedroom 2
13' x 12⁵

BOOKCASE

A symmetrical gables and tall, arch-top windows accent a comfortably elegant exterior that blends American tradition with European grace. A centered fireplace framed by windows, and a French door to the rear covered porch redraw the open space of the family room to cozier dimensions. Upstairs, the master suite offers a windowed whirlpool tub, twin lavatories with a knee-space vanity and a sizable walk-in closet. Three additional bedrooms share a central hall with an open rail staircase to the foyer. Please specify basement or crawlspace foundation when ordering.

Arch-top windows reflect the charm and character of this country home, and complement a quaint covered entry. The two-story foyer opens through decorative columns to the formal dining room and to the living area, which boasts a vaulted ceiling. The U-shaped kitchen overlooks the family room, which offers an extended-hearth fireplace and a cathedral ceiling. A secluded master suite offers a private bath with a bumped-out spa tub and twin vanities. Upstairs, three family bedrooms share two full baths.

DESIGN 7617

First Floor:
1,847 square feet
Second Floor:
964 square feet
Total:
2,811 square feet

Design by
Donald A. Gardner
Architects, Inc.

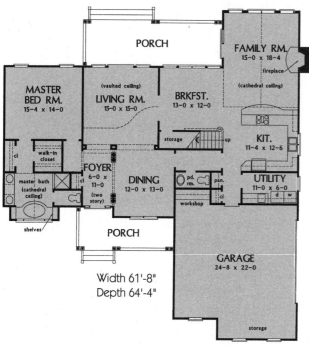

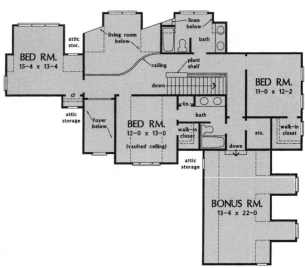

Width 61'-8"
Depth 64'-4"

B. NATHAN.

*D*oric columns and an arched pediment announce a home designed with a casually elegant style. A quiet foyer with an L-shaped staircase leads to a formal dining room and to casual living space, which offers a cathedral ceiling and a rounded-hearth fireplace. The great room opens to the outdoors and lets in the views through three windows, while the cozy breakfast nook enjoys a private entry to the rear patio, flanked by columns. Sleeping quarters include a lavish first-floor master suite and two family bedrooms upstairs.

DESIGN 7606

First Floor:
1,577 square feet
Second Floor:
613 square feet
Total:
2,190 square feet

Design by
Donald A. Gardner
Architects, Inc.

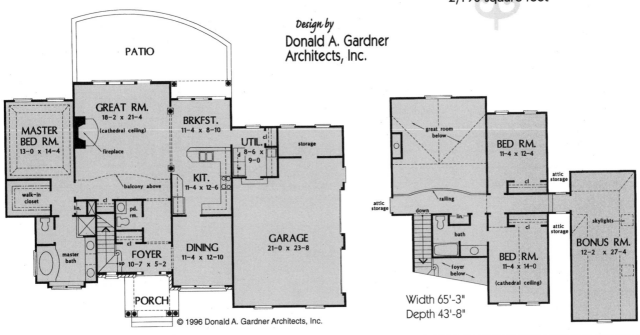

© 1996 Donald A. Gardner Architects, Inc.

Width 65'-3"
Depth 43'-8"

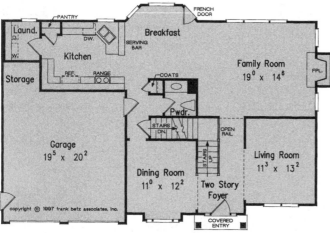

Width 52'-10"
Depth 34'-6"

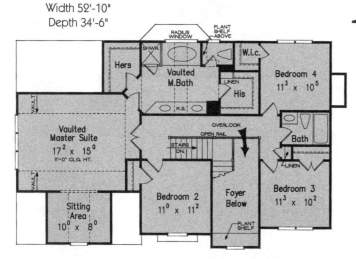

DESIGN P273

First Floor:
1,127 square feet
Second Floor:
1,218 square feet
Total:
2,345 square feet

Keystone arches and double-hung windows decorate a comfortably elegant elevation and introduce an interior designed for today's family. Open living space creates harmony with a bayed breakfast nook, well lit with two windows and a French door to the back property. A vaulted ceiling and a secluded sitting area highlight the master bedroom, while its private bath enjoys lavish amenities such as a whirlpool tub with its own radius window. Three additional bedrooms share a balcony hall with an overlook to the foyer. Please specify basement or crawlspace foundation when ordering.

Design by
Frank Betz
Associates, Inc.

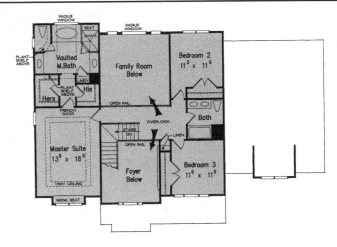

Width 61'
Depth 41'

C lapboard siding enjoys a partnership with classic brick accents on this new traditional design. The foyer opens to the formal rooms and leads to an expansive, two-story family room made cozy by an extended-hearth fireplace and French doors to the back property. The second-floor master suite has a box-bay window with a seat, and an interior French door that leads to a lavish vaulted bath with a windowed spa tub, separate vanities and a windowed whirlpool tub. A balcony hall overlooks the family room and the foyer. Please specify crawlspace or basement foundation when ordering.

DESIGN **P267**

First Floor:
1,428 square feet
Second Floor:
1,000 square feet
Total:
2,428 square feet
Bonus Room:
509 square feet

Design by
Frank Betz
Associates, Inc.

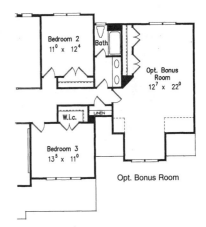

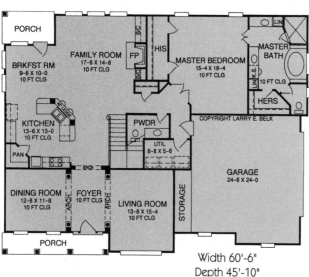

PORCH

BRKFST RM
9-6 X 10-0
10 FT CLG

FAMILY ROOM
17-6 X 14-8
10 FT CLG

HIS

MASTER BEDROOM
15-4 X 18-4
10 FT CLG

MASTER BATH

LIN

FP

B/C

HERS

KITCHEN
13-6 X 13-0
10 FT CLG

PWDR

PAN

UTIL
8-8 X 5-6

COPYRIGHT LARRY E. BELK

DINING ROOM
12-8 X 11-8
10 FT CLG

FOYER
10 FT CLG

LIVING ROOM
13-6 X 15-4
10 FT CLG

STORAGE

GARAGE
24-6 X 24-0

PORCH

Width 60'-6"
Depth 45'-10"

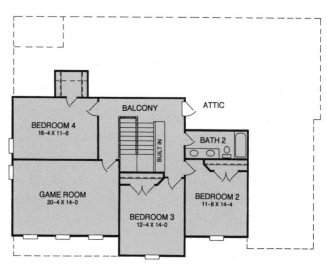

BEDROOM 4
16-4 X 11-6

BALCONY

ATTIC

BUILT IN

BATH 2

GAME ROOM
20-4 X 14-0

BEDROOM 3
12-4 X 14-0

BEDROOM 2
11-8 X 14-4

Here's an elegant home with a warm country spirit. A box-paneled door opens to a grand foyer, adorned with columned archways, which leads to the formal living and dining rooms. Casual living space includes a spacious family room with triple-window views to the outdoors, an extended-hearth fireplace and built-in bookshelves. The first-floor master suite offers a whirlpool bath with a knee-space vanity and opens through double doors from a private hall. Upstairs, three family bedrooms share a full bath with two vanities, and open to a balcony hall that leads to a sizable game room. Please specify crawlspace or slab foundation when ordering.

DESIGN 8226

First Floor:
1,935 square feet
Second Floor:
1,170 square feet
Total:
3,105 square feet

Design by
Larry E. Belk Designs

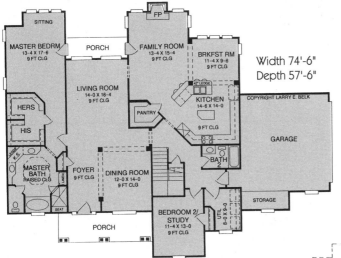

Width 74'-6"
Depth 57'-6"

DESIGN 8228

First Floor:
2,346 square feet
Second Floor:
972 square feet
Total:
3,318 square feet

Design by
Larry E. Belk Designs

Graceful arches, multi-pane windows, and asymmetrical gables accent the exterior of this traditional home. The foyer opens to an expansive formal living area and to a dining room, set off by decorative columns. The gourmet kitchen enjoys a roomy walk-in pantry and a snack counter. A delightful sitting area highlights the master bedroom on the first floor, while second-floor family bedrooms open to a spacious game room. Please specify crawlspace or slab foundation when ordering.

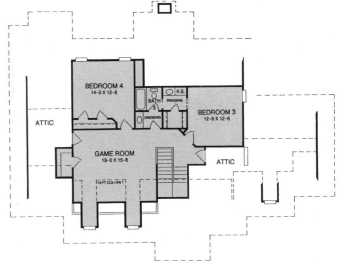

*T*his traditional home's stunning exterior is set off by an arched entry and brick accents with a gentle European flavor. A dazzling interior sparkles with space and style, with an unrestrained floor plan designed for the needs of the modern family. The formal living room, or study, features exposed beams, a warming fireplace and a lovely bay window. The two-story family room boasts its own hearth plus wide views of the outdoors. A walk-in pantry and a centered food preparation counter highlight the gourmet kitchen. The master suite features a tray ceiling, access to the rear porch and a lavish bath. Three bedrooms, each with a walk-in closet, and two full baths are upstairs.

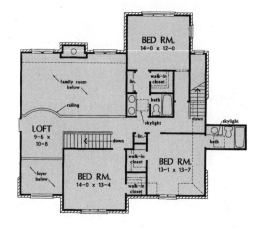

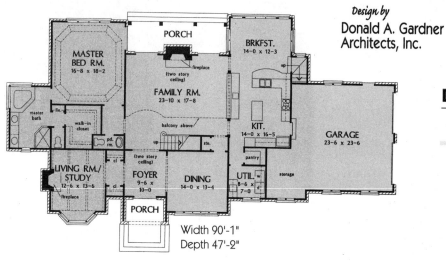

Design by
Donald A. Gardner
Architects, Inc.

DESIGN 7646

First Floor:
2,330 square feet
Second Floor:
1,187 square feet
Total:
3,517 square feet

Width 90'-1"
Depth 47'-2"

© 1997 Donald A. Gardner Architects, Inc.

© 1996 Donald A. Gardner Architects, Inc.

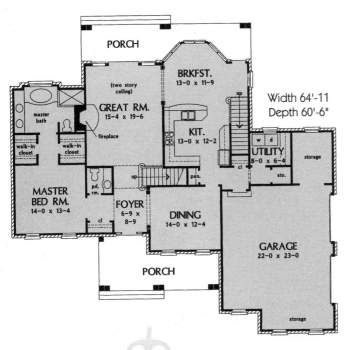

PORCH

BRKFST.
13-0 x 11-9

(two story ceiling)

GREAT RM.
15-4 x 19-6

master bath

fireplace

walk-in closet

walk-in closet

KIT.
13-0 x 12-2

UTILITY
8-0 x 6-4

storage

Width 64'-11
Depth 60'-6"

MASTER BED RM.
14-0 x 13-4

pd. rm.

up

FOYER
6-9 x 8-9

DINING
14-0 x 12-4

cl

pan.

sto.

GARAGE
22-0 x 23-0

storage

PORCH

DESIGN 7638

First Floor:
1,719 square feet
Second Floor:
632 square feet
Total:
2,351 square feet

Design by
Donald A. Gardner Architects, Inc.

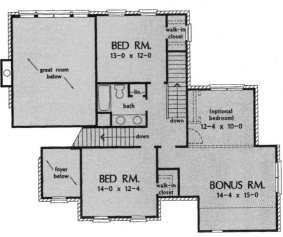

great room below

BED RM.
13-0 x 12-0

walk-in closet

bath

lin.

(optional bedroom)
12-4 x 10-0

down

foyer below

BED RM.
14-0 x 12-4

walk-in closet

down

BONUS RM.
14-4 x 15-0

Traditional homes are known to be warm and inviting, and this home is a perfect example. The stately brick exterior, set off with a finely detailed balustrade, presents a new look for the comfortably elegant home. Inside, a contemporary floor plan provides open space as a perfect complement to well-defined, formal rooms. The expansive vaulted great room opens to the bayed breakfast nook, which leads outside to the back covered porch. A private master suite features two walk-in closets, twin vanities and a compartmented toilet. Second-floor family bedrooms share a full bath and a hall that leads to a sizable bonus room.

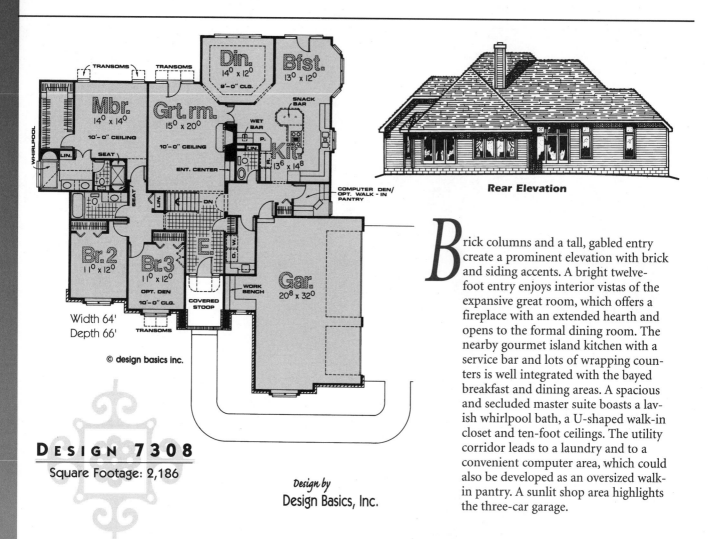

Din.
14⁰ x 12⁰
9'-0" CLG.

Bfst.
13⁰ x 12⁰

TRANSOMS   TRANSOMS

Mbr.
14⁰ x 14⁰

10'-0" CEILING

WHIRLPOOL

LIN.   SEAT

Grt. rm.
15⁰ x 20⁰

10'-0" CEILING

ENT. CENTER

SNACK BAR

WET BAR

P.

Kit.
13⁶ x 14⁸

LIN.

SEAT

DN

LIN.

COMPUTER DEN/
OPT. WALK - IN
PANTRY

Br. 2
11⁰ x 12⁰

Br. 3
11⁰ x 12⁰

OPT. DEN

10'-0" CLG.

E.

D.W.

WORK BENCH

Gar.
20⁸ x 32⁰

COVERED STOOP

TRANSOMS

Width 64'
Depth 66'

© design basics inc.

Rear Elevation

DESIGN 7308
Square Footage: 2,186

Design by
Design Basics, Inc.

*B*rick columns and a tall, gabled entry create a prominent elevation with brick and siding accents. A bright twelve-foot entry enjoys interior vistas of the expansive great room, which offers a fireplace with an extended hearth and opens to the formal dining room. The nearby gourmet island kitchen with a service bar and lots of wrapping counters is well integrated with the bayed breakfast and dining areas. A spacious and secluded master suite boasts a lavish whirlpool bath, a U-shaped walk-in closet and ten-foot ceilings. The utility corridor leads to a laundry and to a convenient computer area, which could also be developed as an oversized walk-in pantry. A sunlit shop area highlights the three-car garage.

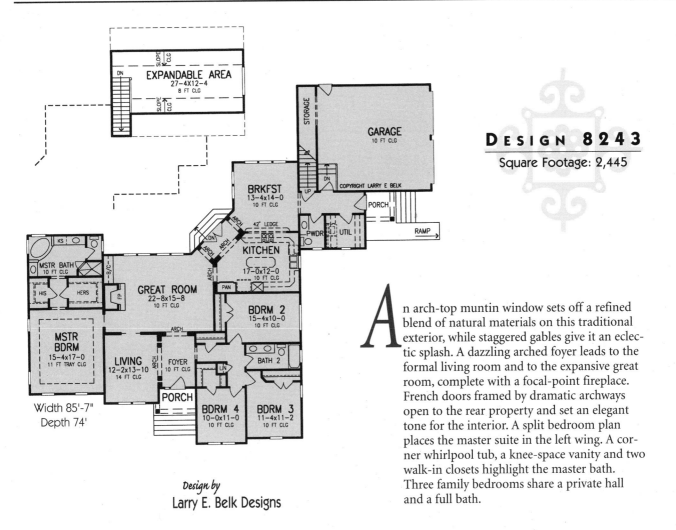

EXPANDABLE AREA
27-4x12-4
8 FT CLG

GARAGE
10 FT CLG

STORAGE

COPYRIGHT LARRY E BELK

BRKFST
13-4x14-0
10 FT CLG

PORCH

UP   DN

42" LEDGE

PWDR   UTIL

RAMP

KITCHEN
17-0x12-0
10 FT CLG

MSTR BATH
10 FT CLG

KS

HIS   HERS

GREAT ROOM
22-8x15-8
10 FT CLG

PAN

BDRM 2
15-4x10-0
10 FT CLG

MSTR
BDRM
15-4x17-0
11 FT TRAY CLG

LIVING
12-2x13-10
14 FT CLG

ARCH

FOYER
10 FT CLG

BATH 2

Width 85'-7"
Depth 74'

PORCH

BDRM 4
10-0x11-0
10 FT CLG

BDRM 3
11-4x11-2
10 FT CLG

Design by
Larry E. Belk Designs

DESIGN 8243

Square Footage: 2,445

An arch-top muntin window sets off a refined blend of natural materials on this traditional exterior, while staggered gables give it an eclectic splash. A dazzling arched foyer leads to the formal living room and to the expansive great room, complete with a focal-point fireplace. French doors framed by dramatic archways open to the rear property and set an elegant tone for the interior. A split bedroom plan places the master suite in the left wing. A corner whirlpool tub, a knee-space vanity and two walk-in closets highlight the master bath. Three family bedrooms share a private hall and a full bath.

COPYRIGHT LARRY E. BELK

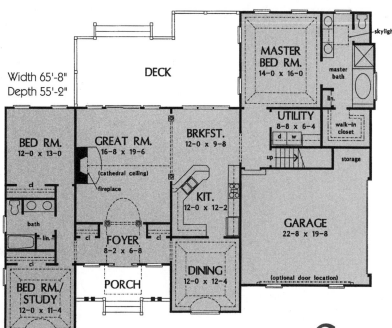

Width 65'-8"
Depth 55'-2"

DECK

BED RM.
12-0 x 13-0

GREAT RM.
16-8 x 19-6

(cathedral ceiling)

fireplace

BRKFST.
12-0 x 9-8

MASTER
BED RM.
14-0 x 16-0

skylight

master bath

lin.

UTILITY
8-8 x 6-4

d   w

up

walk-in closet

storage

KIT.
12-0 x 12-2

bath

lin.

FOYER
8-2 x 6-8

cl

cl

cl

GARAGE
22-8 x 19-8

BED RM./
STUDY
12-0 x 11-4

PORCH

DINING
12-0 x 12-4

(optional door location)

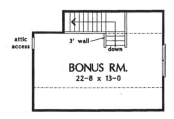

attic access

3' wall

down

BONUS RM.
22-8 x 13-0

Design by
Donald A. Gardner
Architects, Inc.

DESIGN 7637

Square Footage: 1,959
Bonus Room:
385 square feet

Square columns with chamfered corners set off classic clapboard siding and complement a country-style dormer and twin pediments. The vaulted great room has a focal-point fireplace and access to the rear deck. The well-appointed kitchen opens to a bright breakfast area and enjoys its natural light. The dining room, front bedroom/study and master bedroom feature tray ceilings. The private master suite also includes a skylit bath. Please specify basement or crawlspace foundation when ordering.

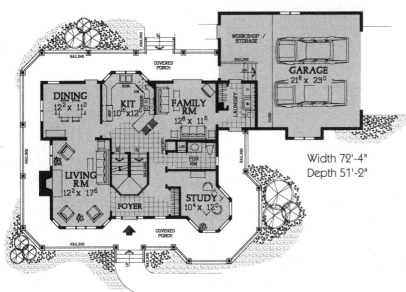

Design by
Home Planners

Width 72'-4"
Depth 51'-2"

DESIGN 3805

First Floor:
1,186 square feet
Second Floor:
988 square feet
Total:
2,174 square feet

L **D**

A bounty of beautiful windows offsets vintage ornaments and invites sunlight to pour into the interior of this well-appointed Victorian home. The tiled entry opens to quiet, formal rooms and leads past a convenient powder room to the family's casual living space. On the first floor, a bay window harbors a private study, or home office. Upstairs, a U-shaped walk-in closet and dressing area introduce a lavish master bath with a garden tub, a separate shower and an enclosed toilet. The homeowner's bedroom boasts a warming fireplace with an extended hearth. Three family bedrooms share a full bath, while one of these room bathes in the light of the second-floor bay window.

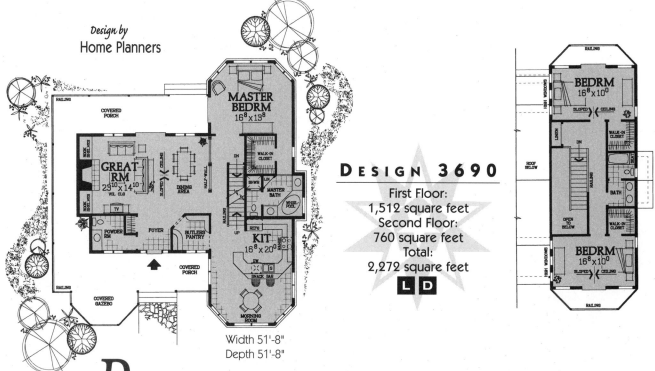

Design by
Home Planners

GREAT RM
23¹⁰ x 14¹⁰

MASTER BEDRM
16⁸ x 13⁸

KIT
16⁸ x 20⁰

DESIGN 3690

First Floor:
1,512 square feet
Second Floor:
760 square feet
Total:
2,272 square feet

L **D**

Width 51'-8"
Depth 51'-8"

BEDRM
16⁸ x 10⁰

BEDRM
16⁸ x 10⁰

Balustrades and brackets, dual balconies and a quaint wraparound porch set off by a stylish gazebo lend a dash of Victoriana, and volumes of charm, to this country-style exterior. An aura of hospitality prevails throughout the well-planned interior, starting with a tiled foyer that opens to an expansive great room rich with natural light and enhanced by a fireplace with tiled hearth. A sunny, bayed morning room invites casual dining and shares its light with a well-appointed U-shaped kitchen, which offers a snack counter. A spacious master suite contained in the opposite bay offers a sumptuous bath with corner whirlpool, dual lavatories, walk-in closet and dressing area. Upstairs, two family bedrooms, each with a private balcony and a walk-in closet, share a full bath with twin vanities.

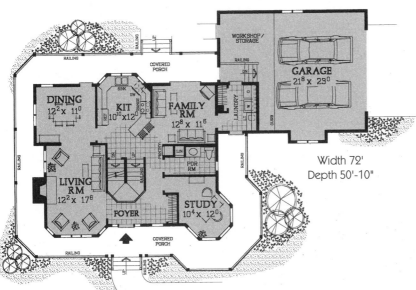

DINING
12² x 11⁰

KIT
10¹⁰ x 12⁰

FAMILY RM
12⁸ x 11⁶

WORKSHOP/ STORAGE

GARAGE
21⁸ x 23⁰

LIVING RM
12² x 17⁶

FOYER

STUDY
10⁴ x 12⁰

COVERED PORCH

Width 72'
Depth 50'-10"

GARDEN TUB

MASTER BATH

BEDRM
10⁴ x 10⁰

BEDRM
11⁴ x 9⁰

WALK-IN CLOSET

BATH

MASTER BEDRM
12² x 13⁴

BEDRM
10⁰ x 11²

OPEN TO FOYER

Design by
Home Planners

A Palladian window, fishscale shingles, and turret-style bays set off this country-style Victorian exterior. Muntin windows and a quintessential wraparound porch introduce an unrestrained floor plan with plenty of bays and niches. An impressive tiled entry opens to the formal rooms, which nestle to the side of the plan and enjoy natural light from an abundance of windows. A focal-point fireplace with an extended hearth lends more than heat to this area—it gives warmth. More than just a pretty face, the turret houses a secluded study on the first floor and provides a sunny bay window for a family bedroom upstairs. The second-floor master suite boasts its own fireplace, a dressing area with a walk-in closet, and a lavish bath with a garden tub and twin vanities. The two-car garage offers space for a workshop or extra storage, and leads to a service entrance to the walk-through utility room.

DESIGN 3696

First Floor:
1,186 square feet
Second Floor:
988 square feet
Total:
2,174 square feet

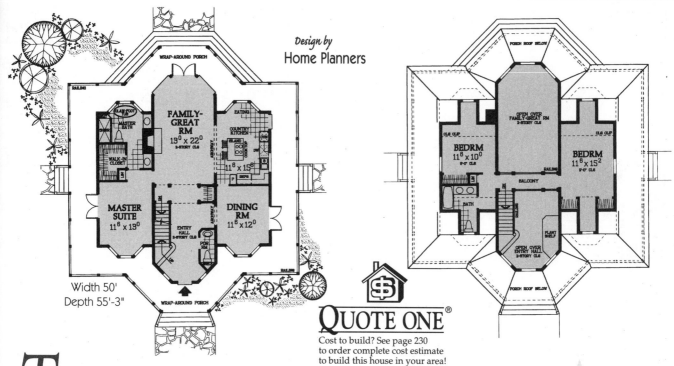

Design by
Home Planners

FAMILY-GREAT RM
13⁰ x 22⁰
2-STORY CLG

MASTER SUITE
11⁶ x 13⁰

DINING RM
11⁶ x 12⁰

EATING

COUNTRY KITCHEN
11⁶ x 15⁸

ENTRY HALL
2-STORY CLG

MASTER BATH

WRAP-AROUND PORCH

Width 50'
Depth 55'-3"

BEDRM
11⁶ x 10⁰

BEDRM
11⁶ x 15²

OPEN OVER FAMILY-GREAT RM
2-STORY CLG

BALCONY

BATH

OPEN OVER ENTRY HALL
2-STORY CLG

QUOTE ONE®

Cost to build? See page 230
to order complete cost estimate
to build this house in your area!

This Southern country farmhouse extends a warm welcome with a wraparound porch and a bayed entry. An unrestrained floor plan, replete with soaring, open space as well as sunny bays and charming niches, invites traditional festivities and cozy family gatherings. Colonial columns introduce the two-story great room which boasts an extended-hearth fireplace and French doors to the wraparound porch, and opens through a wide arch to the tiled country kitchen with cooktop island counter and snack bar. The first-floor master suite enjoys its own bay window, private access to the wraparound porch, and a sumptuous bath with a claw-foot tub and separate vanities. Upstairs, two family bedrooms share a full bath and a balcony hall that overlooks the great room and the entry.

DESIGN 3620

First Floor:
1,295 square feet
Second Floor:
600 square feet
Total:
1,895 square feet

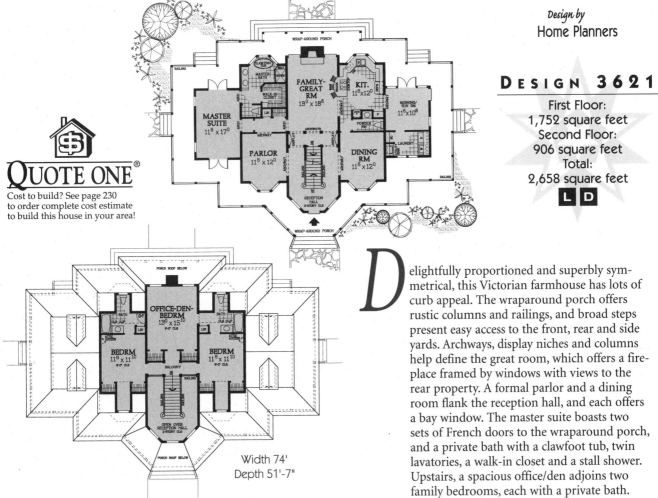

Design by
Home Planners

DESIGN 3621

First Floor:
1,752 square feet
Second Floor:
906 square feet
Total:
2,658 square feet

L D

Width 74'
Depth 51'-7"

*D*elightfully proportioned and superbly symmetrical, this Victorian farmhouse has lots of
curb appeal. The wraparound porch offers
rustic columns and railings, and broad steps
present easy access to the front, rear and side
yards. Archways, display niches and columns
help define the great room, which offers a fireplace framed by windows with views to the
rear property. A formal parlor and a dining
room flank the reception hall, and each offers
a bay window. The master suite boasts two
sets of French doors to the wraparound porch,
and a private bath with a clawfoot tub, twin
lavatories, a walk-in closet and a stall shower.
Upstairs, a spacious office/den adjoins two
family bedrooms, each with a private bath.

DESIGN 3309

First Floor:
1,375 square feet
Second Floor:
1,016 square feet
Total:
2,391 square feet

L

QUOTE ONE®

Cost to build? See page 230
to order complete cost estimate
to build this house in your area!

Design by
Home Planners

Covered porches, front and back, are a fine preview to the livable nature of this Victorian. Living areas are defined in a family room with a fireplace, formal living and dining rooms and a kitchen with a breakfast room. An ample laundry room, a garage with storage area, and a powder room round out the first floor. Three second-floor bedrooms are joined by a study and two full baths. The master suite on this floor has two closets, including an ample walk-in, as well as a relaxing bath with a tile-rimmed whirlpool tub and a separate shower with a seat.

This home, as shown in the photograph, may differ from the actual blueprints.
For more detailed information, please check the floor plans carefully.

Width 62'-7"
Depth 54'

Photo by Bob Greenspan

Sunbursts, simple balusters and a stylish turret set off this Victorian exterior, complete with two finely detailed covered porches. An unrestrained floor plan offers bays and nooks, open spaces and cozy niches—a proper combination for an active family. Formal living and dining areas invite gatherings, whether large or small, planned or casual—but the heart of the home is the family area. A wide bay window and a fireplace with an extended hearth warm up both the family room and the breakfast area, while the nearby kitchen offers a snack counter for easy meals. The second floor includes three family bedrooms and a lavish master suite with an oversized whirlpool spa and twin walk-in closets.

Design by
Home Planners

D E S I G N   2 9 7 3

First Floor:
1,269 square feet
Second Floor:
1,227 square feet
Total:
2,496 square feet

L

QUOTE ONE®

Cost to build? See page 230
to order complete cost estimate
to build this house in your area!

Width 70'
Depth 44'-5"

This home, as shown in the photograph, may differ from the actual blueprints. For more detailed information, please check the floor plans carefully.

Photo by Andrew D. Lautman

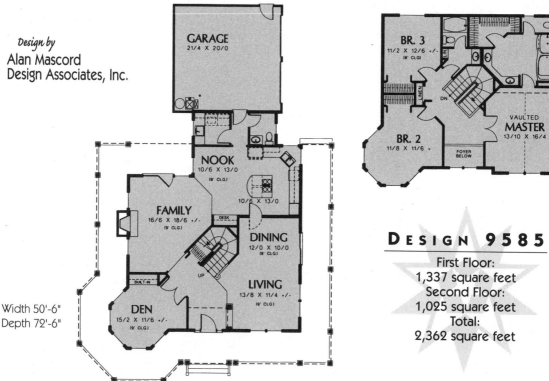

Design by
**Alan Mascord
Design Associates, Inc.**

GARAGE
21/4 X 20/0

NOOK
10/6 X 13/0
(9' CLG.)

10/6 X 13/0

FAMILY
16/6 X 18/6 +/-
(9' CLG.)

DESK

DINING
12/0 X 10/0
(9' CLG.)

UP

BUILT-IN

LIVING
13/8 X 11/4 +/-
(9' CLG.)

DEN
15/2 X 11/6 +/-
(9' CLG.)

Width 50'-6"
Depth 72'-6"

BR. 3
11/2 X 12/6 +/-
(8' CLG)

BR. 2
11/8 X 11/6 +/-

LINEN

DN

FOYER
BELOW

**VAULTED
MASTER**
13/10 X 16/4

DESIGN 9585

First Floor:
1,337 square feet
Second Floor:
1,025 square feet
Total:
2,362 square feet

An octagonal tower, fishscale shingles and a wraparound porch lend a true Victorian flavor to this impressive plan. More than just a pretty face, the turret houses a spacious den with built-in cabinetry on the first floor, and provides a sunny bay window for a family bedroom upstairs. Just off the foyer, the formal living and dining rooms provide an elegant open space for enter-taining, while a focal-point fireplace with an extended hearth warms up a spacious family area. The cooktop island kitchen and morning nook lead to a powder room and laundry area, and to the garage. Two second-floor bedrooms share a full bath, while the master suite offers a private bath with an oversized whirlpool tub, twin vanities and a U-shaped walk-in closet.

QUOTE ONE®

Cost to build? See page 230
to order complete cost estimate
to build this house in your area!

Victorian houses are well known for their orientation on narrow building sites. At only 38 feet wide, this home is still highly livable. From the covered front porch, the foyer directs traffic all the way to the back of the plan where the open living and dining rooms reside. The U-shaped kitchen conveniently serves both the dining room and the front breakfast room. The veranda and the screen porch, both at the rear of the home, extend an invitation to enjoy the outdoors. Three bedrooms, including the master bedroom, and two baths fill the second floor. The attic provides ample storage space.

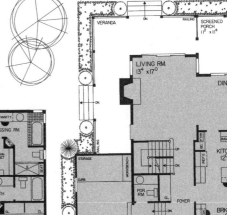

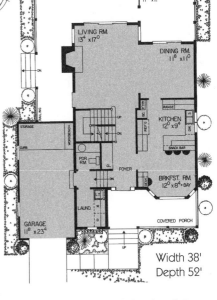

DESIGN 2974

First Floor:
911 square feet
Second Floor:
861 square feet
Total:
1,772 square feet

L

Design by
Home Planners

Width 38'
Depth 52'

This home, as shown in the photograph, may differ from the actual blueprints. For more detailed information, please check the floor plans carefully.

Photo by Bob Greenspan

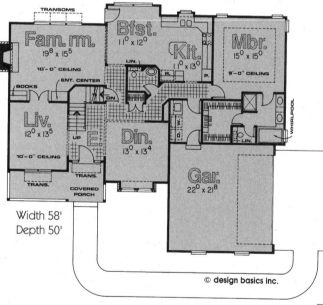

TRANSOMS

Fam. rm.
19⁸ x 15⁵

10'-0" CEILING

BOOKS

Liv.
12⁰ x 13⁵

10'-0" CEILING

ENT. CENTER

UP

TRANS.

TRANS.

COVERED PORCH

Bfst.
11⁰ x 12⁰

LIN.

DN

Kit.
11⁰ x 13⁰

Din.
13⁰ x 13⁴

D. W.

Mbr.
15⁰ x 15⁰

9'-0" CEILING

P.

LIN.

WHIRLPOOL

Gar.
22⁰ x 21⁸

© design basics inc.

Width 58'
Depth 50'

DESIGN 7327

First Floor:
1,722 square feet
Second Floor:
710 square feet
Total:
2,432 square feet

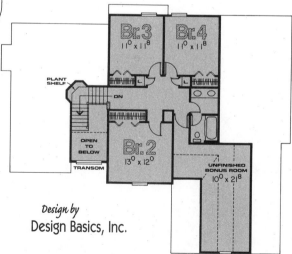

PLANT SHELF

DN

Br. 3
11⁰ x 11⁸

Br. 4
11⁰ x 11⁸

OPEN TO BELOW

Br. 2
13⁰ x 12⁰

TRANSOM

UNFINISHED BONUS ROOM
10⁰ x 21⁸

Design by
Design Basics, Inc.

Classic and modern elements come together in striking harmony in this Revival style, which calls up the past but lives in the future. Ceramic tile runs through a central hall that connects the living areas, starting with the formal rooms. An interesting design scheme places French doors between the living and family rooms—an invitation for guests to linger by the cozy hearth. The first-floor master suite features a tray ceiling and a lavish bath with a whirlpool tub and an enclosed toilet. Upstairs, three family bedrooms share a full bath and a hall that leads to sizable bonus space.

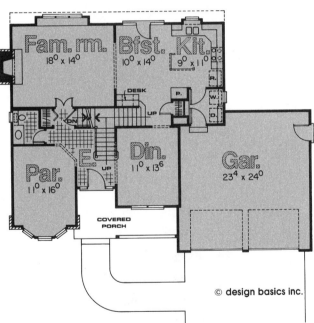

© design basics inc.

DESIGN 7312

First Floor:
1,134 square feet
Second Floor:
1,149 square feet
Total:
2,283 square feet

Design by
Design Basics, Inc.

Width 53'-4"
Depth 42'

A two-story bay window and a covered front porch combine to give this home plenty of curb appeal. Inside, formal areas await, with the dining room on the right and a bayed parlor on the left. At the back of the house, informal living takes place with the spacious island kitchen and sunny breakfast room playing counterpoint to the attractive family room which is further enhanced by a warming fireplace. Upstairs, the sleeping quarters offer a lavish master suite with an expansive, U-shaped walk-in closet, as well as three family bedrooms and a hall bath with twin vanities.

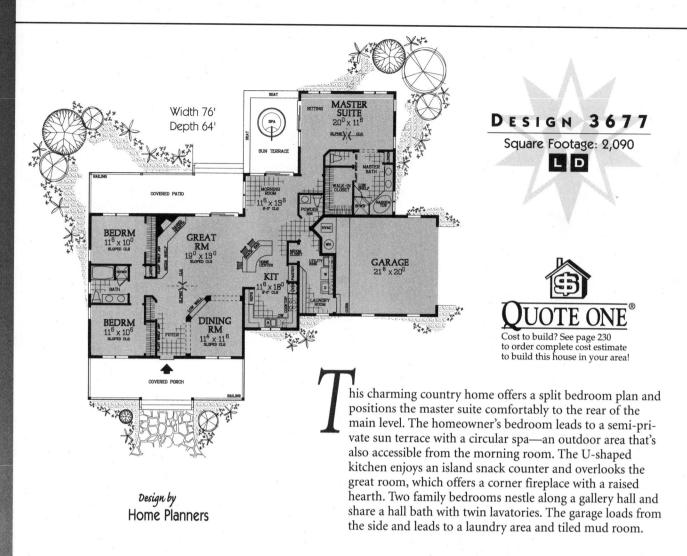

Width 76'
Depth 64'

SEAT

SEAT

SPA

SUN TERRACE

MASTER SUITE
20'0 x 11'8
SLOPE CLG

SITTING

RAILING

COVERED PATIO

MORNING ROOM
11'8 x 13'8
9'-0" CLG

MASTER BATH

WALK-IN CLOSET

POWDER RM

BEDRM
11'8 x 10'0
SLOPED CLG

GREAT RM
19'0 x 13'0
SLOPED CLG

HOME CENTER

HVAC

WH

BROOM CLOSET

UTILITY BANK

GARAGE
21'8 x 20'

BATH

KIT
11'8 x 18'0
9'-0" CLG

PANTRY

BEDRM
11'8 x 10'8
SLOPED CLG

FOYER

DINING RM
11'8 x 11'8
SLOPED CLG

LAUNDRY ROOM

COVERED PORCH

RAILING

Design by
Home Planners

DESIGN 3677
Square Footage: 2,090
L D

This charming country home offers a split bedroom plan and positions the master suite comfortably to the rear of the main level. The homeowner's bedroom leads to a semi-private sun terrace with a circular spa—an outdoor area that's also accessible from the morning room. The U-shaped kitchen enjoys an island snack counter and overlooks the great room, which offers a corner fireplace with a raised hearth. Two family bedrooms nestle along a gallery hall and share a hall bath with twin lavatories. The garage loads from the side and leads to a laundry area and tiled mud room.

From the covered front porch to the three shuttered dormers, this design offers appealing details. Inside, the foyer presents a formal dining room, defined by two elegant pillars. The great room features a raised-hearth fireplace, a media wall, and access to the rear covered patio. A U-shaped kitchen efficiently serves this room as well as the dining room. On the first floor, the sleeping zone consists of two bedrooms sharing a deluxe bath with separate shower and garden tub. Located upstairs for privacy, the master suite offers a large walk-in closet, a plant shelf, twin vanities, a separate shower and a whirlpool tub.

Design by
Home Planners

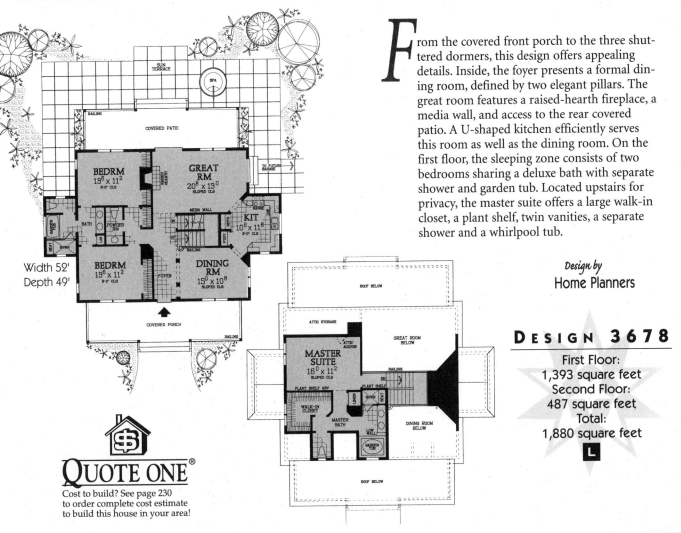

Width 52'
Depth 49'

QUOTE ONE®

Cost to build? See page 230
to order complete cost estimate
to build this house in your area!

DESIGN 3678

First Floor:
1,393 square feet
Second Floor:
487 square feet
Total:
1,880 square feet

L

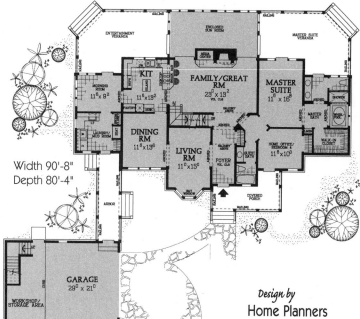

Width 90'-8"
Depth 80'-4"

Design by
Home Planners

DESIGN 3606

First Floor:
1,969 square feet
Second Floor:
660 square feet
Total:
2,629 square feet
Bonus Room:
360 square feet

L D

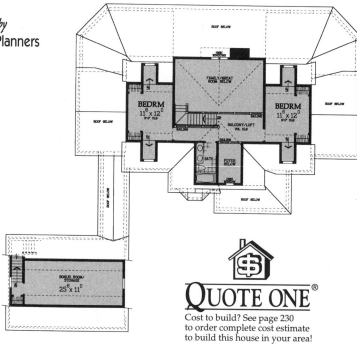

QUOTE ONE ®
Cost to build? See page 230
to order complete cost estimate
to build this house in your area!

Shake siding and simple dormers lend a rustic appeal, while details like the side arbor and the quaint front covered porch give a sense of serenity to this farmhouse design. Inside, traditional formality meets casual family living with defined rooms as well as open spaces. The foyer opens through a graceful archway to formal areas. A gourmet kitchen serves the dining room as well as a sunlit morning room which opens to an entertainment veranda. The fireplace in the great room is framed by twin doors to an enclosed sun room. The secluded master suite enjoys a private veranda and a sumptuous bath with a windowed whirlpool tub. Two family bedrooms share a balcony hall and a full bath on the second floor.

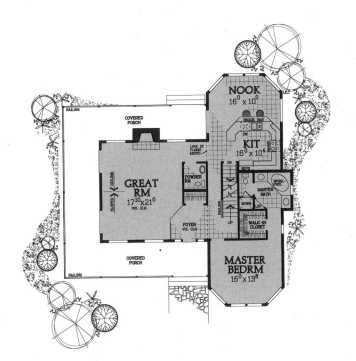

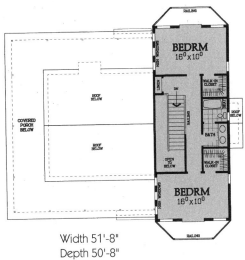

Width 51'-8"
Depth 50'-8"

alustrades and brackets, dual balconies and a wraparound porch create a country-style exterior meant for soft summer evenings. An aura of hospitality pervades the well-planned interior, starting with a tiled foyer that opens to an expansive two-story great room filled with light from six windows, a fireplace with tiled hearth, and a sloped ceiling. The sunny, bayed nook invites casual dining and shares its natural light with a snack counter and a well-appointed U-shaped kitchen. A spacious master suite occupies the bay on the opposite side of the plan and offers a sumptuous bath with corner whirlpool, dual lavatories and walk-in closet. On the second floor, two family bedrooms, each with a private balcony and a walk-in closet, share a full bath.

DESIGN 3687

First Floor:
1,374 square feet
Second Floor:
600 square feet
Total:
1,974 square feet

L D

Width 86'-7"
Depth 54'

PORTE
COCHERE

BEDRM
12⁸ x 9⁶

OPEN TO
GREAT
ROOM
BELOW

HALF WALL

BEDRM
12⁸ x 9⁶

BATH

Design by
Home Planners

COVERED
PORCH

NOOK
14⁴ x 14⁴

GREAT
RM
20⁰ x 15⁸

WALK-IN
CLOSET

MASTER
BATH

LINEN

LAUNDRY

SNACK BAR

KIT
14⁴ x12⁰

PANTRY

POWDER
ROOM

SITTING
/STUDY
/NURSERY

MASTER
BEDRM
11⁸ x 16³

FOYER

DINING
14⁴ x 10¹⁰

COVERED
PORCH

PLANTER

C ountry's not a place but a state of mind, and you can enjoy life's simple pleasures anywhere with this stylish country charmer. Rustic rafter tails and double columns highlight the front covered porch of this slightly rugged exterior, but sophisticated amenities abound inside and out—starting with the unique porte cochere and quiet side entrance to the home. To the left of the foyer, a formal dining room is bathed in natural light from two sets of triple windows. This area is easily served by a well-appointed kitchen with a built-in desk and a snack bar. A secluded master suite is replete with popular amenities: a garden tub with separate shower, knee-space vanity, dual lavatories and an adjoining study or sitting room. Upstairs, a balcony hall connects two additional bedrooms and a full bath—there's even space for a library or study area!

DESIGN 3499

First Floor:
1,836 square feet
Second Floor:
600 square feet
Total:
2,436 square feet

L D

QUOTE ONE®
Cost to build? See page 230
to order complete cost estimate
to build this house in your area!

DESIGN 9557

First Floor:
1,371 square feet
Second Floor:
916 square feet
Total:
2,287 square feet

Design by
Alan Mascord
Design Associates, Inc.

Classic columns and balusters decorate a charming wrap-around porch on this comfortable home. A secluded den on the first floor offers a through-fireplace to the family room, which opens to the outdoors. The morning nook and L-shaped kitchen, with a cooktop island counter and a built-in writing desk, open through columns to an elegant formal dining room. The second-floor master suite opens through French doors and offers a spacious bath. Two family bedrooms share a full bath.

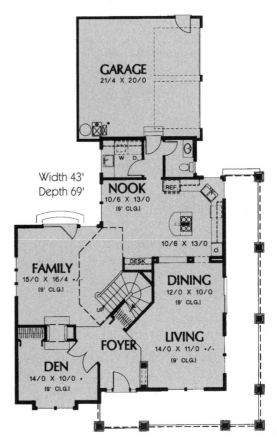

Width 43'
Depth 69'

GARAGE
21/4 X 20/0

NOOK
10/6 X 13/0
(9' CLG.)

10/6 X 13/0

FAMILY
15/0 X 16/4 +/-
(9' CLG.)

DESK

DINING
12/0 X 10/0
(9' CLG.)

FOYER

LIVING
14/0 X 11/0 +/-
(9' CLG.)

DEN
14/0 X 10/0 +/-
(9' CLG.)

QUOTE ONE®
Cost to build? See page 230
to order complete cost estimate
to build this house in your area!

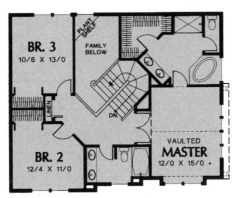

BR. 3
10/6 X 13/0

PLANT SHELF

FAMILY BELOW

LINEN

DN.

BR. 2
12/4 X 11/0

VAULTED
MASTER
12/0 X 15/0 +

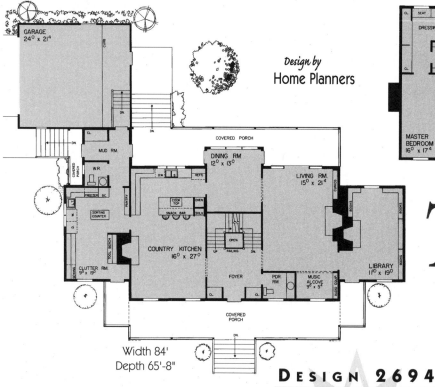

GARAGE
24⁰ x 21⁴

MUD RM.

W.R.

COVERED PORCH

FREEZER

SORTING COUNTER

CLUTTER RM.
9⁰ x 19⁰

COVERED PORCH

DINING RM.
12⁰ x 13⁰

D.W.

REF'G

PANTRY

COOK TOP

OVEN

SNACK BAR

COUNTRY KITCHEN
16⁰ x 27⁰

OPEN RAILING

FOYER

PDR. RM.

MUSIC ALCOVE
9⁰ x 5⁵

CL.

LIVING RM.
15⁰ x 21⁴

BOOKS

LIBRARY
11⁰ x 19⁰

BOOKS

COVERED PORCH

Design by
Home Planners

CL.   SEAT   SEAT   CL.

DRESSING RM.   BATH   WHIRLPOOL

BEDROOM
16⁰ x 13⁴

WALK-IN CLOSET

CL.

OPEN RAILING

MASTER BEDROOM
16⁰ x 17⁴

LINEN

BATH

BEDROOM
12⁰ x 15⁰

Width 84'
Depth 65'-8"

DESIGN 2694

First Floor:
2,026 square feet
Second Floor:
1,386 square feet
Total:
3,412 square feet

L

This two-story design faithfully recalls the 18th-Century homestead of Secretary of Foreign Affairs John Jay. Classic siding and shutters work to create a classic exterior which will blend beautifully into pedigree neighborhoods, Arcadian farmland or casual countryside. A discreet library offers a place for books and curios. The living room features a grand fireplace, a music alcove and an expansive back porch—perfect for outdoor entertaining. The formal dining room offers a bay bathed in sunlight, with great views of the rear grounds. Upstairs, a plush master suite with a two-vanity bath shares a balcony hall with two sizable family bedrooms and a bath.

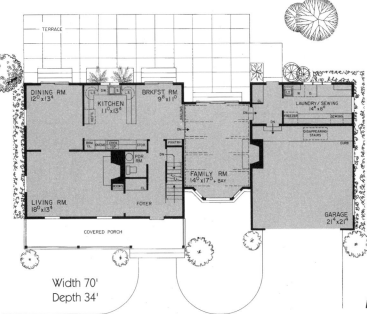

Width 70'
Depth 34'

Design by
Home Planners

DESIGN 2908

First Floor:
1,427 square feet
Second Floor:
1,153 square feet
Total:
2,580 square feet
L D

*T*his Early American offers plenty of modern comfort with its covered front porch with pillars and rails, double chimneys, spacious rooms and large country kitchen with breakfast room. A step-down family room features a fireplace, as does the formal living room. Upstairs, three family bedrooms share a full hall bath. The master suite is complete with a dual vanity and a compartmented bath with dressing room. Special features of this home include a laundry/sewing room with freezer and washer/dryer space, a large rear terrace and an entry-hall powder room.

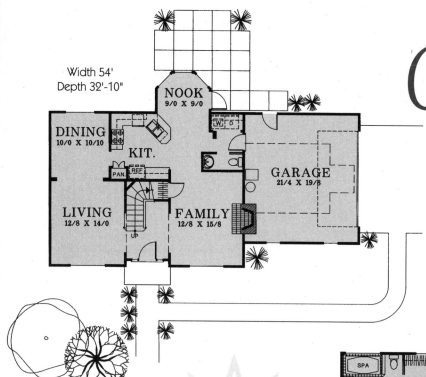

Width 54'
Depth 32'-10"

NOOK
9/0 X 9/0

DINING
10/0 X 10/10

KIT.

PAN. REF

LIVING
12/8 X 14/0

FAMILY
12/8 X 15/8

W D

GARAGE
21/4 X 19/8

UP

*C*olonial styling gives an efficient form to this popular design. The dramatic two-story foyer with an angled stairway forms the circulation hub for this comfortable family home. The formal living room and adjacent dining room have easy access to the kitchen—perfect for entertaining. The cook-friendly kitchen overlooks the bay-window breakfast nook and has easy access to the service entrance and the family room. Upstairs is the master bedroom with spa tub, large shower, double vanity and walk-in closet. Two additional bedrooms are provided, along with a bonus room over the garage, which could be the fourth bedroom.

DESIGN 9462

First Floor:
935 square feet
Second Floor:
772 square feet
Total:
1,707 square feet

Design by
Alan Mascord
Design Associates, Inc.

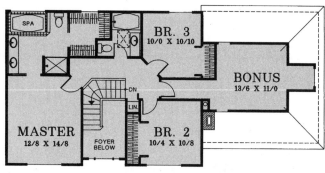

SPA

BR. 3
10/0 X 10/10

BONUS
13/6 X 11/0

DN

LIN.

MASTER
12/8 X 14/8

FOYER
BELOW

BR. 2
10/4 X 10/8

Width 40'
Depth 40'

DESIGN 3510

First Floor:
1,120 square feet
Second Floor:
1,083 square feet
Total:
2,203 square feet

Sweeping front and rear raised covered porches, delicately detailed railings and an abundance of fireplaces give this farmhouse its character. Designed to accommodate a relatively narrow building site, the efficient floor plan delivers outstanding livability. Both the formal living and dining rooms have corner fireplaces, as does the family room. The large tiled country kitchen has lots of workspace, a planning desk and easy access to the utility room. On the second floor, the master retreat boasts its own fireplace. Optional space on the third floor adds 597 square feet when developed.

Design by
Home Planners

QUOTE ONE®

Cost to build? See page 230
to order complete cost estimate
to build this house in your area!

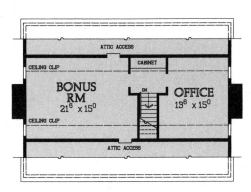

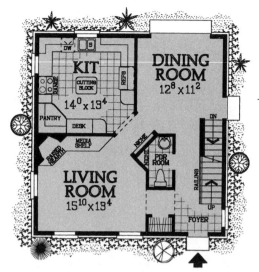

KIT
14⁰ x 13⁴

DINING ROOM
12⁸ x 11²

PANTRY

DESK

MEDIA SHELF

RAISED HEARTH

LIVING ROOM
15¹⁰ x 13⁴

NICHE

PDR ROOM

RAILING

DN

UP

FOYER

Width 28'-8"
Depth 28'-8"

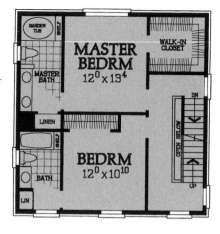

GARDEN TUB

MASTER BATH

MASTER BEDRM
12⁰ x 13⁴

WALK-IN CLOSET

LINEN

SHELF

OPEN RAILING

DN

BATH

LIN

BEDRM
12⁰ x 10¹⁰

UP

DESIGN 3524

First Floor:
822 square feet
Second Floor:
766 square feet
Total:
1,588 square feet
Bonus/Bedroom:
405 square feet

L

Design by
Home Planners

BONUS/ BEDROOM
22⁴ x 15⁰

OPT BATH

OPEN RAILING

DN

*C*lassic simplicity and symmetry call up a sense of America's early history with this simply grand Colonial exterior, while the roomy interior steps out in well-heeled style. The tiled foyer opens to comfortably elegant living space, complete with a raised-hearth fireplace and a media shelf. A spacious dining room serves planned events as well as family meals, easily served by the gourmet kitchen, which offers a cutting block center island, a corner pantry and a ceramic tile floor. The second floor holds a spacious master suite with a tiled bath and a U-shaped walk-in closet, as well as an additional bedroom with its own bath. Bonus space on the third floor offers the possibility of a third bedroom and full bath.

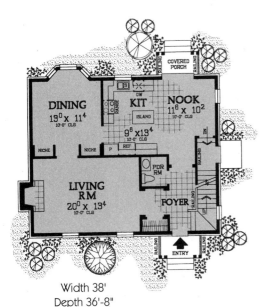

DINING
18⁰ x 11⁴
10'-0" CLG

KIT
9⁶ x13⁴
10'-0" CLG

NOOK
11⁶ x 10²
10'-0" CLG

COVERED PORCH

NICHE   NICHE

LIVING RM
20⁰ x 13⁴
10'-0" CLG

PDR RM

FOYER

DN

UP

ENTRY

Width 38'
Depth 36'-8"

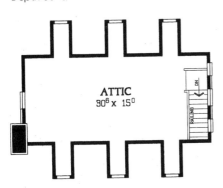

ATTIC
30⁶ x 15⁰

DN

MASTER BATH

LIN   SHWR   BEDRM
10⁰ x 9¹⁰
9'-0" CLG

LIN   BATH

WALK-IN CLOSET

MASTER BEDRM
19⁰ x 18¹⁰
9'-0" CLG

BEDRM
11⁶ x 10⁰
9'-0" CLG

DN

UP

DESIGN 3526

First Floor:
1,056 square feet
Second Floor:
960 square feet
Total:
2,016 square feet
Attic: 659 square feet

L D

Design by
Home Planners

A symmetrical facade and steeply pitched roof call up the past with this Williamsburg Colonial home. A pedimented entry leads to a tiled foyer with an L-shaped staircase to the second-floor sleeping quarters. The formal living room opens to the dining room and shares natural light from its bay window—one of many modern touches in this Early American design. The gourmet kitchen serves planned events and casual gatherings with ease, and adjoins a spacious breakfast nook with access to a private covered porch. The second-floor master suite enjoys a tiled bath with a knee-space vanity and two lavatories, while two family bedrooms share a sizable hall bath. Third-floor attic space is available for later development.

© Design Traditions

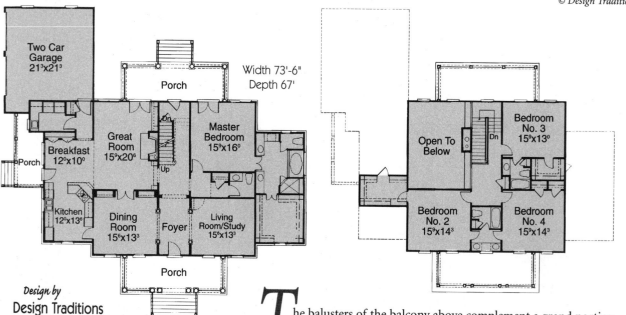

Two Car
Garage
21³x21³

Porch

Width 73'-6"
Depth 67'

Breakfast
12⁰x10⁰

Great
Room
15⁹x20⁶

Master
Bedroom
15⁹x16⁰

Dn

Up

Porch

Kitchen
12⁰x13⁶

Dining
Room
15⁶x13³

Foyer

Living
Room/Study
15⁹x13³

Porch

Open To
Below

Dn

Bedroom
No. 3
15⁹x13⁰

Bedroom
No. 2
15⁹x14³

Bedroom
No. 4
15⁹x14³

Design by
Design Traditions

DESIGN 9982

First Floor:
2,174 square feet
Second Floor:
1,113 square feet
Total:
3,287 square feet

The balusters of the balcony above complement a grand portico, which highlights the exterior of this Colonial-style home. Formal rooms flank a two-story foyer that leads to a gallery hall central to all living areas—and to a rear porch. Two-story windows in the great room allow soaring vistas and add an abundance of natural light in the heart of the plan. The kitchen adjoins a cozy breakfast area with access to a private porch. French doors open the master suite to the rear porch and let in a feeling of nature. An expansive walk-in closet and a lavish private bath with a whirlpool tub help to create a relaxing retreat for the homeowner. Three second-floor family bedrooms enjoy a balcony overlook to the great room. This home is designed with a basement foundation.

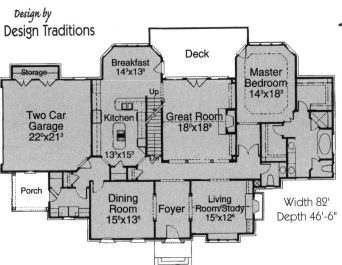

Bedroom No. 4
13⁰x12⁰

Bedroom No. 3
13⁹x14³

Bedroom No. 2
15⁶x13⁹

Attic Storage

Dn

Design by
Design Traditions

Storage

Breakfast
14³x13⁰

Deck

Master Bedroom
14³x18³

Up

Kitchen

Two Car Garage
22⁰x21³

Great Room
18⁰x18⁹

13⁹x15³

Dn

Porch

Dining Room
15⁶x13⁶

Foyer

Living Room/Study
15³x12⁶

Width 82'
Depth 46'-6"

DESIGN 9986

First Floor:
2,336 square feet
Second Floor:
1,089 square feet
Total:
3,425 square feet

Keystones and shutters offset a high-pitched roof and lend a romantic spirit to this Colonial-style exterior. This home says cozy on the outside but lives well and enjoys open space inside. Formal living areas host an elegant theme of quiet symmetry and walls of windows invite natural light. At the heart of this home is a great room open to a gallery hall through columns and arches, and French doors that let in a feeling of the outdoors. A rear deck opens to a bayed breakfast nook which shares its light with an L-shaped gourmet kitchen. The master wing offers two walk-in closets, a garden tub and an angled shower, as well as private access to the deck. Upstairs, three family bedrooms and two full baths share a gallery hall that leads to attic storage space. This home is designed with a basement foundation.

© *Design Traditions*

© *Design Traditions*

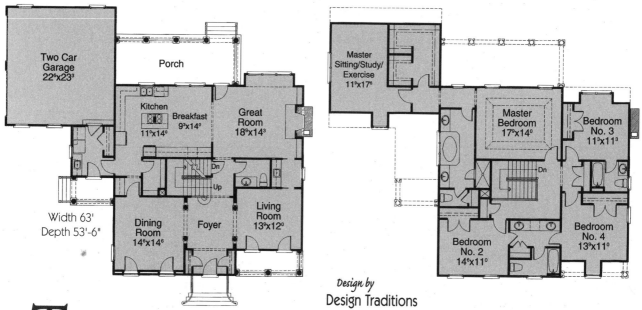

Two Car Garage 22⁶x23³

Porch

Kitchen
Breakfast 9³x14⁰

Great Room 18⁹x14³

Width 63'
Depth 53'-6"

Dining Room 14⁶x14⁶

Foyer

Living Room 13⁹x12⁰

Dn

Up

Master Sitting/Study/Exercise 11⁹x17⁶

Master Bedroom 17⁹x14⁰

Bedroom No. 3 11³x11³

Dn

Bedroom No. 2 14⁶x11⁰

Bedroom No. 4 13⁹x11⁰

Design by
Design Traditions

This New England-style design offers classic simplicity and symmetry on the outside, and well-heeled style on the inside. The foyer opens to quiet formal rooms defined by columns—the living room boasts a private covered porch. Casual space is wide open to the rear of the plan, made cozy by an extended-hearth fireplace in the great room. The breakfast area enjoys access to the outdoors and shares light with the island kitchen. A second-floor master suite has a boxed ceiling and a lavish bath, and adjoins a spacious study—which could also be used as an exercise room. Two family bedrooms share a full bath, while an additional bedroom, or guest suite, offers a private bath. This home is designed with a basement foundation.

DESIGN 9967

First Floor:
1,567 square feet
Second Floor:
1,895 square feet
Total:
3,462 square feet

Width 50'
Depth 63'

Design by
Home Planners

DESIGN 3503

First Floor:
1,748 square feet
Second Floor:
1,748 square feet
Third Floor:
1,100 square feet
Total:
4,596 square feet

L D

This Early American brick exterior serves as a lovely introduction to a thoroughly modern floor plan. The tiled foyer opens through decorative columns to the formal living room, which offers a fireplace framed by built-in cabinetry. The convenient island kitchen offers a snack bar and opens to a conversation room with a bay window and a hearth. Second-floor sleeping quarters offer a master suite with its own fireplace, a bumped-out bay window and a lavish bath with a whirlpool tub. Two family bedrooms share a full bath with a double-bowl vanity. A sumptuous guest suites shares the third floor with a library or playroom.

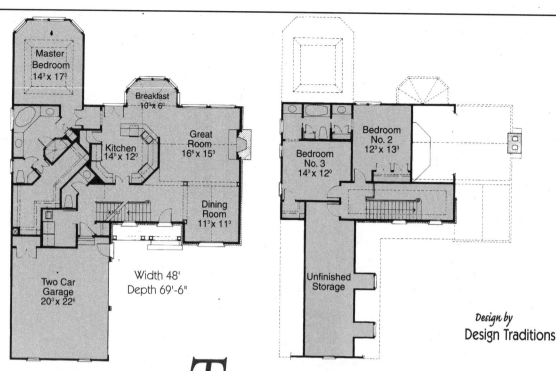

Master
Bedroom
14³ x 17³

Breakfast
10³ x 6⁰

Great
Room
16⁶ x 15³

Kitchen
14⁰ x 12⁰

Dining
Room
11³ x 11³

Two Car
Garage
20³ x 22⁶

Width 48'
Depth 69'-6"

Bedroom
No. 2
12³ x 13³

Bedroom
No. 3
14³ x 12⁰

Unfinished
Storage

Design by
Design Traditions

DESIGN 7819

First Floor:
1,580 square feet
Second Floor:
595 square feet
Total:
2,175 square feet

Today's tastes are more eclectic and household arrangements come in new flavors, so a flexible floor plan is key. Traditional formality asks for well-defined rooms, while the demands of sophisticated lifestyles call for wide open spaces that bend to patterns of living. This plan marries the best of both casual and elegant elements, for a home that breathes with individual style. The formal dining room opens through decorative pillars to the two-story great room, which features a fireplace. French doors lead from the bayed breakfast area to the private master suite, a retreat with a lavish bath with an angled whirlpool tub, a glass-enclosed shower, twin vanities and a rambling walk-in closet. Two family bedrooms share a bath upstairs. This home is designed with a basement foundation.

© *Design Traditions*

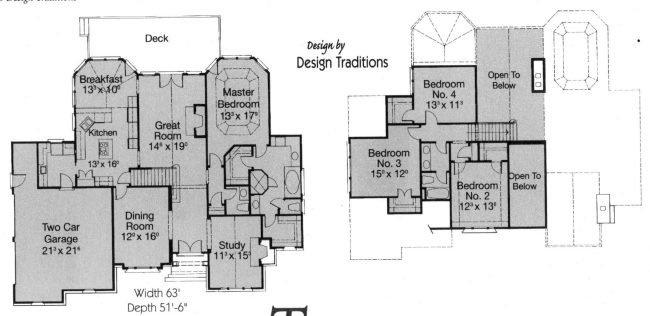

Deck

Breakfast
13³ x 10⁰

Kitchen
13³ x 16⁰

Great
Room
14⁶ x 19⁰

Master
Bedroom
13³ x 17⁹

Design by
Design Traditions

Bedroom
No. 4
13³ x 11³

Open To
Below

Bedroom
No. 3
15⁰ x 12⁰

Bedroom
No. 2
12³ x 13⁶

Open To
Below

Two Car
Garage
21³ x 21⁶

Dining
Room
12⁰ x 16⁰

Study
11³ x 15³

Width 63'
Depth 51'-6"

DESIGN 7802

First Floor:
1,932 square feet
Second Floor:
807 square feet
Total:
2,739 square feet

This sensational country Colonial exterior is set off by a cozy covered porch, just right for enjoying cool evenings outside. A two-story foyer opens to a quiet study with a centered fireplace, and to the formal dining room with views to the front property. The gourmet kitchen features an island cooktop counter and a charming bayed breakfast nook. The great room soars two stories high but is made cozy with a fireplace. Two walk-in closets, a garden tub and a separate shower highlight the master bath, while a coffered ceiling decorates the homeowner's bedroom. Three family bedrooms, each with a walk-in closet, share a full bath upstairs. This home is designed with a basement foundation.

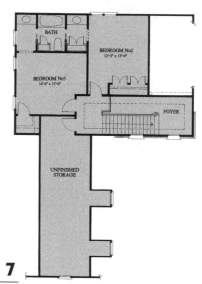

MASTER BEDROOM
14'-6" x 17'-2"

BREAKFAST
10'-6" x 6'-6"

GREAT ROOM
16'-6" x 15'-2"

M.BATH
12'-6" x 12'-6"

KITCHEN
14'-6" x 12'-6"

FOYER

DINING ROOM
11'-4" x 13'-6"

LAUNDRY
7'-6" x 7'-6"

TWO-CAR GARAGE
20'-4" x 22'-6"

BATH

BEDROOM No2
12'-2" x 13'-6"

BEDROOM No3
14'-4" x 12'-6"

FOYER

UNFINISHED STORAGE

Width 48'-6"
Depth 70'-11"

Design by
Design Traditions

DESIGN 9817

First Floor:
1,580 square feet
Second Floor:
595 square feet
Total:
2,175 square feet

QUOTE ONE®
Cost to build? See page 230
to order complete cost estimate
to build this house in your area!

W hite trim, multi-pane windows and ink-black shutters stand out against the rich brick and gray clapboard backdrop. Inside, the spacious foyer leads directly to a large vaulted great room with its handsome fireplace. The dining room to the right of the foyer features a dramatic vaulted ceiling. The spacious kitchen offers both storage and large work areas that open to the breakfast room. In the privacy and quiet of the rear of the home is the master suite with its luxury bath, double vanities and oversized walk-in closet. The second floor provides two additional bedrooms with a shared bath and balcony overlook to the foyer below. Extended storage space or a fourth bedroom may be developed over the garage. This home is designed with a basement foundation.

This home, as shown in the photograph, may differ from the actual blueprints. For more detailed information, please check the floor plans carefully.

Photo by Dave Dawson

© *Design Traditions*

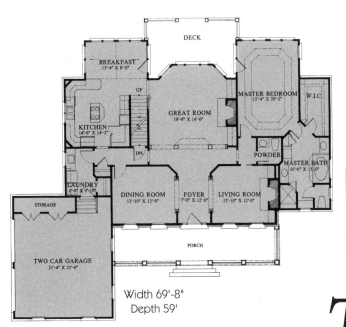

DECK

BREAKFAST
13'-4" X 8'-0"

UP

GREAT ROOM
19'-0" X 14'-0"

MASTER BEDROOM
13'-4" X 20'-2"

W.I.C.

KITCHEN
14'-0" X 14'-2"

DN

POWDER

MASTER BATH
10'-0" X 15'-0"

LAUNDRY
6'-0" X 9'-10"

STORAGE

DINING ROOM
13'-10" X 12'-0"

FOYER
7'-0" X 12'-0"

LIVING ROOM
13'-10" X 12'-0"

TWO CAR GARAGE
21'-4" X 22'-0"

PORCH

Width 69'-8"
Depth 59'

BEDROOM NO.2
14'-0" X 11'-0"

OPEN TO BELOW

UNFINISHED STORAGE
7'-10" X 12'-2"

BATH

BATH

BEDROOM NO.3
13'-10" X 12'-0"

BEDROOM NO.4
12'-4" X 12'-0"

Design by
Design Traditions

QUOTE ONE®

Cost to build? See page 230
to order complete cost estimate
to build this house in your area!

DESIGN 9850

First Floor:
1,960 square feet
Second Floor:
905 square feet
Total:
2,865 square feet

This Georgian country-style home displays an impressive appearance. The front porch and columns frame the elegant, elliptical entrance. Georgian symmetry balances the living room and dining room off the foyer. The first floor continues into the two-story great room, which offers built-in cabinetry, a fireplace and a large bay window that overlooks the rear deck. A dramatic tray ceiling, a wall of glass and access to the rear deck complete the master bedroom. The master bath features separate vanities and a large walk-in closet. To the left of the great room, a large kitchen opens to a breakfast area with walls of windows. Upstairs, each of three family bedrooms features ample closet space as well as direct access to a bathroom. This home is designed with a basement foundation.

© Design Traditions

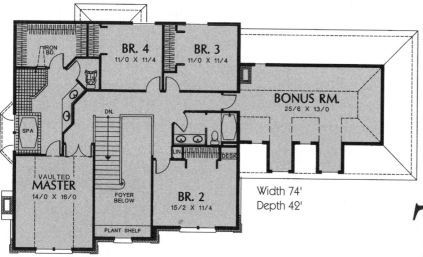

NOOK
10/4 X 11/0
(9' CLG.)

12/0 X 13/8

FAMILY
18/0 X 15/8
(9' CLG.)

GARAGE
30/8 X 23/4

PANTRY

DINING
16/0 X 10/0
(9' CLG.)

D. W.

PARLOR
14/0 X 15/0
(9' CLG.)

DEN
12/10 X 10/0
(9' CLG.)

UP

Design by
**Alan Mascord
Design Associates, Inc.**

BR. 4
11/0 X 11/4

BR. 3
11/0 X 11/4

BONUS RM.
25/6 X 13/0

DN.

SPA

VAULTED
MASTER
14/0 X 16/0

FOYER
BELOW

BR. 2
15/2 X 11/4

LIN.

DESK

PLANT SHELF

Width 74'
Depth 42'

DESIGN 9511

First Floor:
1,575 square feet
Second Floor:
1,329 square feet
Total:
2,904 square feet

This elegant four-bedroom home is designed to accommodate a growing family. Second-floor sleeping quarters include three sizable family bedrooms, which share a full bath, as well as an expansive bonus room with twin dormer windows. The vaulted master suite, also on this floor, features a rambling bath with a tiled-rim spa tub, two vanities and a U-shaped walk-in closet. The first floor offers a formal parlor with a focal-point fireplace. The elegant dining room is served by a well-appointed gourmet kitchen, complete with a cooktop island counter and a walk-in pantry. A secluded den to the front of the plan enjoys a nearby full bath, making it an ideal optional bedroom for guests.

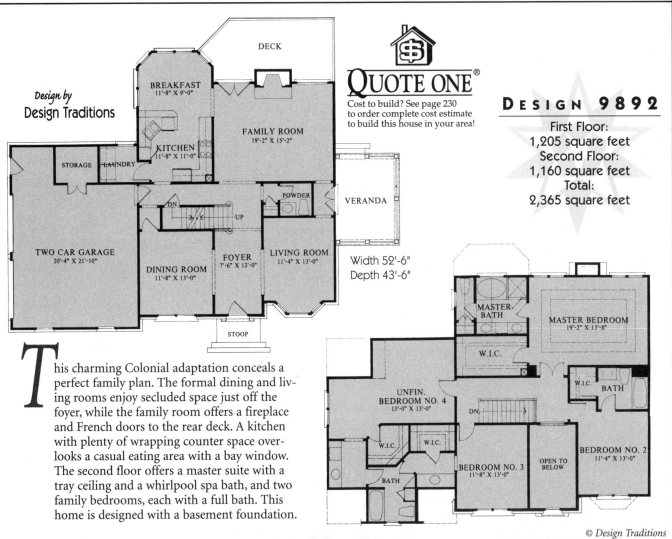

Design by
Design Traditions

DECK

BREAKFAST
11'-8" X 9'-0"

FAMILY ROOM
19'-2" X 15'-2"

KITCHEN
11'-8" X 11'-0"

STORAGE   LAUNDRY

DN   UP

POWDER

VERANDA

TWO CAR GARAGE
20'-4" X 21'-10"

DINING ROOM
11'-8" X 13'-0"

FOYER
7'-6" X 13'-0"

LIVING ROOM
11'-4" X 13'-0"

STOOP

QUOTE ONE®
Cost to build? See page 230
to order complete cost estimate
to build this house in your area!

DESIGN 9892
First Floor:
1,205 square feet
Second Floor:
1,160 square feet
Total:
2,365 square feet

Width 52'-6"
Depth 43'-6"

MASTER
BATH

MASTER BEDROOM
19'-2" X 13'-8"

W.I.C.

W.I.C.   BATH

UNFIN.
BEDROOM NO. 4
13'-0" X 13'-0"

DN

W.I.C.   W.I.C.

BATH

BEDROOM NO. 3
11'-8" X 13'-0"

OPEN TO
BELOW

BEDROOM NO. 2
11'-4" X 13'-0"

© Design Traditions

This charming Colonial adaptation conceals a perfect family plan. The formal dining and living rooms enjoy secluded space just off the foyer, while the family room offers a fireplace and French doors to the rear deck. A kitchen with plenty of wrapping counter space overlooks a casual eating area with a bay window. The second floor offers a master suite with a tray ceiling and a whirlpool spa bath, and two family bedrooms, each with a full bath. This home is designed with a basement foundation.

DESIGN P115

Square Footage: 1,856

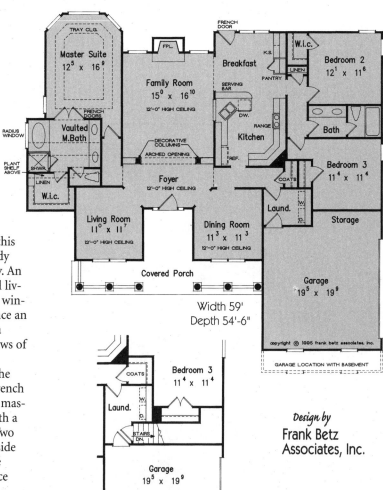

TRAY CLG.

Master Suite
12⁵ x 16⁹

FPL.

Family Room
15⁰ x 16¹⁰
12'-0" HIGH CEILING

FRENCH DOOR

Breakfast

K.S.

W.i.c.

LINEN

PANTRY

Bedroom 2
12¹ x 11⁶

RADIUS WINDOW

Vaulted
M.Bath

FRENCH DOORS

SERVING BAR

DW.

Kitchen

RANGE

Bath

PLANT SHELF ABOVE

SHWR.

LINEN

DECORATIVE COLUMNS

ARCHED OPENING

REF.

Bedroom 3
11⁴ x 11⁴

W.i.c.

Foyer
12'-0" HIGH CEILING

COATS

Living Room
11⁰ x 11⁷
12'-0" HIGH CEILING

Dining Room
11³ x 11³
12'-0" HIGH CEILING

Laund.

Storage

Covered Porch

Garage
19⁵ x 19⁹

Width 59'
Depth 54'-6"

copyright © 1995 frank betz associates, inc.

GARAGE LOCATION WITH BASEMENT

COATS

Bedroom 3
11⁴ x 11⁴

Laund.

W. D.

STAIRS DN.

Garage
19⁵ x 19⁹

Opt. Basement Stair Location

Design by
Frank Betz
Associates, Inc.

Southern charm is written all over this country home, starting with a shady front porch with an arch-top entry. An open foyer is framed by the formal living and dining rooms, bright with windows. Decorative columns announce an expansive family room, set off by a focal-point fireplace framed by views of the outdoors. The well-appointed kitchen shares a serving bar with the breakfast area, which provides a French door to the rear property. A lavish master suite features a vaulted bath with a radius window and a plant shelf. Two family bedrooms on the opposite side of the plan share a full bath. Please specify basement, slab or crawlspace foundation when ordering.

DESIGN 8143

Square Footage: 2,648

Design by
Larry E. Belk Designs

This Southern-raised elevation looks cozy but lives large, with an interior layout and amenities preferred by today's homeowners. Inside, twelve-foot ceilings and graceful columns and arches lend an aura of hospitality throughout the formal rooms and the family's living space, the great room. Double doors open to the gourmet kitchen, which offers a built-in desk, a snack counter for easy meals and a breakfast room with a picture window. The secluded master suite features His and Hers walk-in closets, a whirlpool tub and a knee-space vanity. Each of two family bedrooms enjoys separate access to a shared bath and a private vanity. Please specify crawlspace or slab foundation when ordering.

Width 68'-10"
Depth 77'-10"

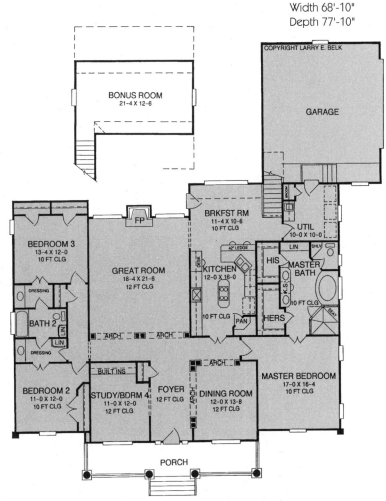

DESIGN 3525

Square Footage: 2,195

Design by
Home Planners

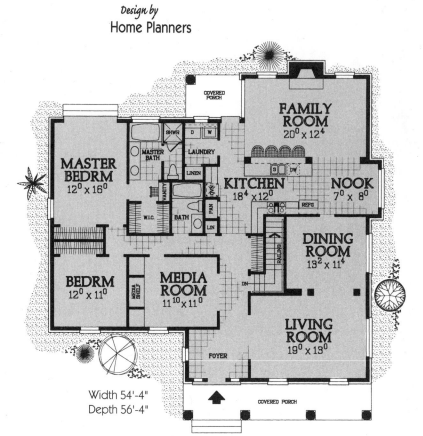

Doric columns and a pedimented porch introduce a sensational design and an unrestrained floor plan with plenty of bays and niches. A tiled foyer opens to the formal living and dining rooms, and leads back to a well-appointed kitchen with a snack bar that it shares with the family room. The sleeping wing offers a master suite with a private bath, and a family bedroom which shares a hall bath with the media room or guest bedroom. Good indoor/outdoor relationships are enhanced by a rear covered porch.

COVERED PORCH

FAMILY ROOM
$20^0 \times 12^4$

MASTER BEDRM
$12^0 \times 16^0$

SHWR D W

MASTER BATH

LAUNDRY

LINEN

KITCHEN
$18^4 \times 12^0$

NOOK
$7^0 \times 8^0$

S DW

REFG

VANITY

W.I.C.

BATH

PAN OVN

LIN

DINING ROOM
$13^2 \times 11^4$

RAILING

BEDRM
$12^0 \times 11^0$

MEDIA SHELF

MEDIA ROOM
$11^{10} \times 11^0$

DN

LIVING ROOM
$19^0 \times 13^0$

FOYER

COVERED PORCH

Width 54'-4"
Depth 56'-4"

E. REINKE

Width 64'
Depth 46'

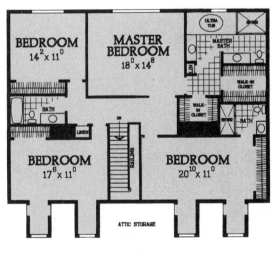

Design by
Home Planners

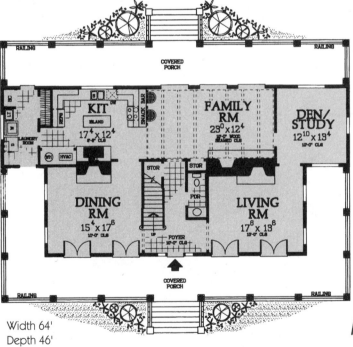
DESIGN 3515

First Floor:
1,669 square feet
Second Floor:
1,627 square feet
Total:
3,296 square feet

L **D**

*T*wo sets of twin dormers set off a signature hip roof and classic columns on this Southern home. An elegant tiled foyer opens to formal areas on each side, and leads to a rustic family area designed to allow generous views. Lovely French doors create a striking ambience in the formal areas—and each of these rooms offers a warming fireplace. A rambling wraparound porch invites good indoor/outdoor flow. The second-floor sleeping zone offers three family bedrooms, a hall bath and a master suite with two walk-in closets, dual lavatories and a whirlpool tub.

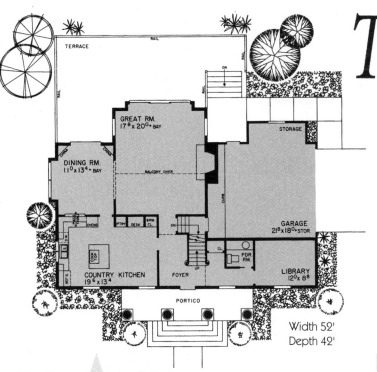

TERRACE

GREAT RM.
17⁸ x 20⁰⁺ BAY

STORAGE

DINING RM.
11⁰ x 13⁴⁺ BAY

BALCONY OVER

GARAGE
21⁸ x 18⁰⁺ STOR.

OVENS

PTRY DESK

BRM.
CL.

PDR
RM.

COOK
TOP

REF'G

COUNTRY KITCHEN
19⁶ x 13⁴

FOYER

UP

LIBRARY
12⁰ x 8⁸

PORTICO

Width 52'
Depth 42'

DESIGN 2668

First Floor:
1,206 square feet
Second Floor:
1,254 square feet
Total:
2,460 square feet

L

This elegant Southern Colonial home is just as livable inside as the facade is grand outside, with every bit of space put to good use focusing on family living. The front country kitchen is efficiently planned with an island cooktop and pass-through to the dining room. The impressive great room is highlighted with a full two stories of pane windows—it will definitely be the center of all family activities. A secluded library in the front of the plan provides a relaxing retreat. A balcony lounge overlooks the grand windows of the great room from the second-floor landing. Three family bedrooms share a full hall bath. The master suite has a lush bath and features a balcony open to the two-story foyer below.

Design by
Home Planners

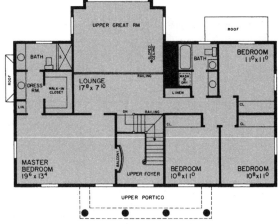

UPPER GREAT RM.

ROOF

BATH

BATH

BEDROOM
11⁰ x 11⁰

ROOF

DRESS
RM.

WALK-IN
CLOSET

LOUNGE
17⁸ x 7¹⁰

RAILING

WASH
& DRY

LINEN

LIN

DN

RAILING

CL

CL

CL

MASTER
BEDROOM
19⁶ x 13⁴

BALCONY

UPPER FOYER

BEDROOM
10⁸ x 11⁰

BEDROOM
10⁸ x 11⁰

UPPER PORTICO

$ QUOTE ONE®

Cost to build? See page 230
to order complete cost estimate
to build this house in your area!

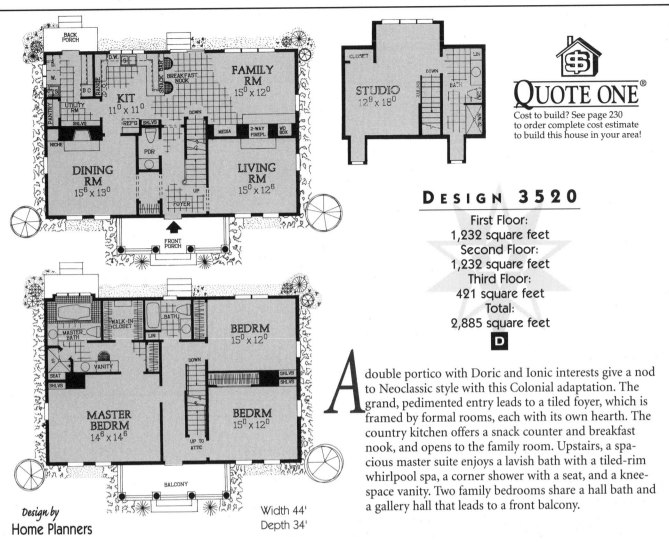

FAMILY RM
15⁰ x 12⁰

KIT
11⁰ x 11⁰

DINING RM
15⁶ x 13⁰

LIVING RM
15⁰ x 12⁶

STUDIO
12⁹ x 18⁰

BACK PORCH

FRONT PORCH

MASTER BEDRM
14⁶ x 14⁶

BEDRM
15⁰ x 12⁰

BEDRM
15⁰ x 12⁰

BALCONY

Design by
Home Planners

Width 44'
Depth 34'

QUOTE ONE®
Cost to build? See page 230
to order complete cost estimate
to build this house in your area!

DESIGN 3520

First Floor:
1,232 square feet
Second Floor:
1,232 square feet
Third Floor:
421 square feet
Total:
2,885 square feet

D

A double portico with Doric and Ionic interests give a nod to Neoclassic style with this Colonial adaptation. The grand, pedimented entry leads to a tiled foyer, which is framed by formal rooms, each with its own hearth. The country kitchen offers a snack counter and breakfast nook, and opens to the family room. Upstairs, a spacious master suite enjoys a lavish bath with a tiled-rim whirlpool spa, a corner shower with a seat, and a knee-space vanity. Two family bedrooms share a hall bath and a gallery hall that leads to a front balcony.

Varying hip roof planes complement a glass-paneled entry and divided-light transoms that reflect a well-articulated style and make a bold statement. The tiled foyer opens to formal and casual living areas, defined by arched colonnades and set off by an extended-hearth fireplace in the family room. The gourmet kitchen boasts a food preparation island, an angled snack bar and a walk-in pantry. A guest suite, or study, resides just off the living area. The secluded master suite enjoys a private patio with a spa, as well as a spacious bath with a box-bay whirlpool tub, twin lavatories and a knee-space vanity. A home office or den with a separate entry and porch, and two family bedrooms with a full bath complete the plan.

DESIGN 3612

Square Footage: 2,946

L

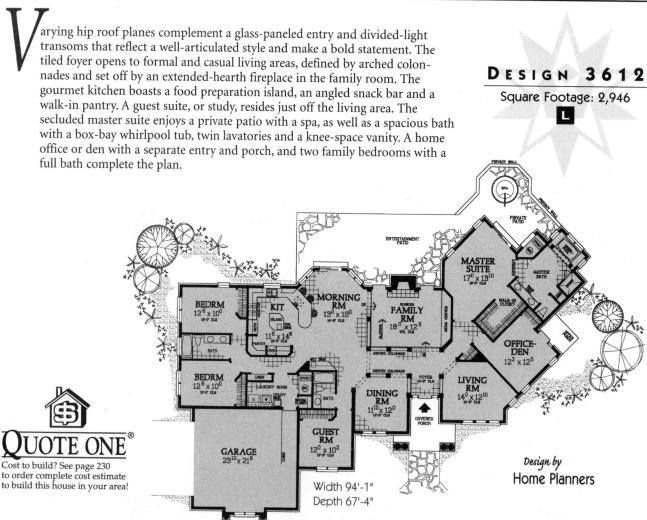

Width 94'-1"
Depth 67'-4"

Design by
Home Planners

MASTER SUITE TERRACE

COVERED TERRACE

NOOK
9⁴ x 12⁸
11'-4" CLG.

FAMILY RM
13⁰ x 19⁴
11'-4" CLG.

CABANA BATH

MASTER BEDRM
15⁰ x 18⁴

SLPB CLG.

RAISED OPENING

KIT
13⁸ x 15²

SNACK BAR

PANTRY

OVEN

PLANT SHELF ABOVE

LIVING RM
22⁰ x 14¹⁰
9'-0" CLG.

RAISED HEARTH

BEDRM
11⁹ x 12⁰

BATH

WALK-IN CLOSET

STORAGE

LINEN

WH

NICHE

VANITY

MECH

FURN WH

FOYER

DINING RM
13¹⁰ x 12¹⁰
9'-0" CLG.

LAUNDRY

FURN

WH

LY

BEDRM
12⁸ x 11⁶

MASTER BATH

GARDEN TUB

SHOWER

PDR

WET BAR

COVERED PORCH

GARDEN AREA

GARDEN PATIO

DEN/STUDY
11⁸ x 19¹⁰

SLPG CLG.

GARAGE
24⁸ x 24⁸

Width 84'-4"
Depth 75'-4"

DESIGN 3634

Square Footage: 3,264

L

Design by
Home Planners

QUOTE ONE®

Cost to build? See page 230
to order complete cost estimate
to build this house in your area!

T hree pediments, Doric columns and keystone arches set off the casually elegant exterior of this distinctive transitional home. Inside, a formal living room, angled for interest, warmly greets friends and provides a perfect complement to the nearby dining room. The island kitchen overlooks the covered entertainment terrace and easily serves planned and casual occasions, while the morning nook and family room invite cozy gatherings. The master suite enjoys the seclusion of its own wing, and offers a private step-down terrace and wide views of the outdoors. A dressing area leads to the master bath, which features an angled walk-in closet, a garden tub and twin lavatories. Two family bed-rooms, one with a full cabana bath, complete the plan.

This home, as shown in the photograph, may differ from the actual blueprints. For more detailed information, please check the floor plans carefully.

Photo by Andrew D. Lautman

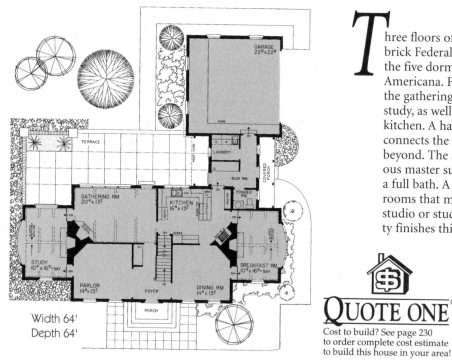

Width 64'
Depth 64'

Three floors of livability are available in this stately brick Federal design. From the two chimney stacks to the five dormer windows, the appeal is pure Americana. First-floor features include fireplaces in the gathering room, the breakfast room and the study, as well as a built-in barbecue in the gourmet kitchen. A handy mud room with a powder room connects the kitchen to the laundry and to the garage beyond. The second floor is dominated by a sumptuous master suite and two family bedrooms that share a full bath. A third floor holds two additional bedrooms that might serve well as guest rooms or as a studio or study space. A full bath with a double vanity finishes this floor.

QUOTE ONE®
Cost to build? See page 230 to order complete cost estimate to build this house in your area!

Design by
Home Planners

DESIGN 2662

First Floor:
1,735 square feet
Second Floor:
1,075 square feet
Third Floor:
746 square feet
Total:
3,556 square feet

L

This home, as shown in the photograph, may differ from the actual blueprints.
For more detailed information, please check the floor plans carefully.

Photo by Andrew D. Lautman

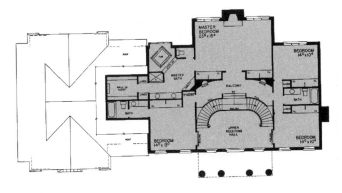

Width 90'-4"
Depth 44'-8"

Cost to build? See page 230

Design by
Home Planners

This classic Georgian design offers outstanding features, inside and out: a pediment gable with cornice work and dentils, quoins, and Doric columns. The interior steps out in contemporary style with spacious formal areas off the two-story receiving hall. The gathering room with a raised-hearth fireplace framed by floor-to-ceiling windows offers a place to spread out—or throw a bash on the entertainment terrace. A nearby study allows private access to the outdoors. Upstairs, an extension over the garage permits an oversized walk-in closet in the master suite, which also includes an angled bath with a corner windowed tub and twin vanities.

DESIGN 2889

First Floor:
2,349 square feet
Second Floor:
1,918 square feet
Total:
4,267 square feet

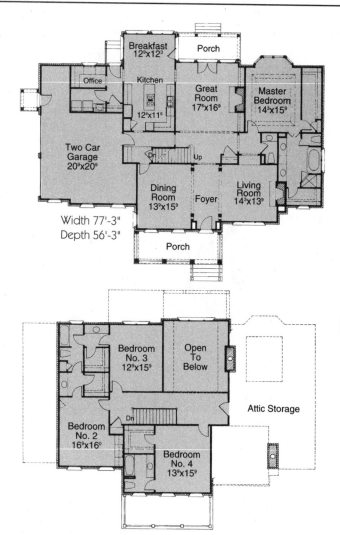

First floor:

Breakfast
12⁹x12³

Porch

Office

Kitchen
12⁹x11⁶

Great Room
17⁶x16⁹

Master Bedroom
14³x15⁹

Two Car Garage
20⁹x20⁹

Dn

Up

Dining Room
13⁹x15⁹

Foyer

Living Room
14³x13⁹

Width 77'-3"
Depth 56'-3"

Porch

Second floor:

Bedroom No. 3
12⁹x15⁹

Open To Below

Attic Storage

Bedroom No. 2
16⁹x16⁹

Dn

Bedroom No. 4
13⁹x15⁹

Design by
Design Traditions

DESIGN 9985

First Floor:
2,191 square feet
Second Floor:
1,228 square feet
Total:
3,419 square feet

Simplicity and symmetry create classic appeal with this Colonial adaptation, while Doric columns and white balustrades dress up a casual appearance. A central great room opens to a covered porch, also accessed from a windowed breakfast nook. The family chef will appreciate the gourmet features of this cooktop island kitchen, which leads to a home office and to the great room, set off by a centered fireplace. Two walk-in closets and a gently bayed window highlight the first-floor master suite. Upstairs, three family bedrooms cluster around a central hall that leads to sizable attic space. This home is designed with a basement foundation.

© Design Traditions

© Design Traditions

Design by
Design Traditions

Deck

Solaruim
11⁹x12⁶

Screened
Porch
10⁰x12⁶

Family
Room
15⁹x15³

Kitchen
16⁶x13⁰

Two Car
Garage
20⁹x25³

Living
Room
13⁹x12⁰

Foyer

Dn

Up

Dining
Room
14⁶x12⁶

Width 61'-6"
Depth 51'

Master
Bedroom
16⁶x13⁰

Bedroom
No. 4
15⁹x120³

Bedroom
No. 2
13⁹x12⁰

Dn

Open
To
Below

Bedroom
No. 3
14⁶x12⁰

DESIGN 9979

First Floor:
1,698 square feet
Second Floor:
1,542 square feet
Total:
3,240 square feet

This Colonial-style traditional really makes its mark with an elegant brick exterior that conceals a thoroughly modern floor plan. Well-defined formal rooms complement casual family areas on the first floor, while a gourmet kitchen, a solarium, a screened porch and a deck invite informal gatherings. The second-floor sleeping quarters include an expansive master suite with a luxurious private bath that features a garden tub and an ample walk-in closet. Also on this floor, Bedrooms 3 and 4 share a full bath, while Bedroom 2 enjoys a bath of its own. This home is designed with a basement foundation.

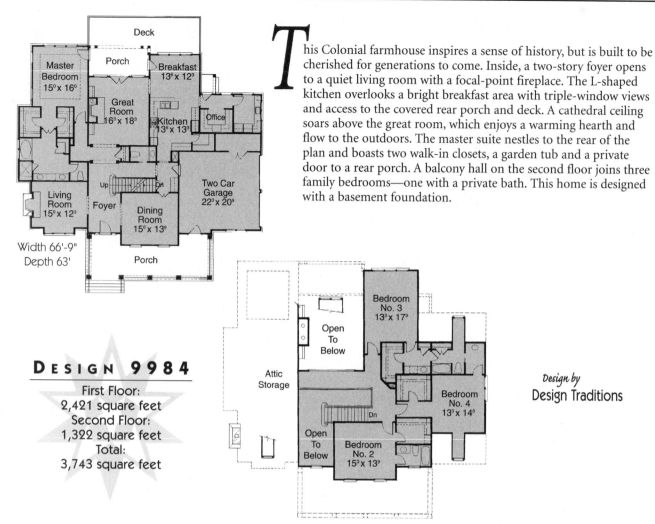

This Colonial farmhouse inspires a sense of history, but is built to be cherished for generations to come. Inside, a two-story foyer opens to a quiet living room with a focal-point fireplace. The L-shaped kitchen overlooks a bright breakfast area with triple-window views and access to the covered rear porch and deck. A cathedral ceiling soars above the great room, which enjoys a warming hearth and flow to the outdoors. The master suite nestles to the rear of the plan and boasts two walk-in closets, a garden tub and a private door to a rear porch. A balcony hall on the second floor joins three family bedrooms—one with a private bath. This home is designed with a basement foundation.

Width 66'-9"
Depth 63'

DESIGN 9984

First Floor:
2,421 square feet
Second Floor:
1,322 square feet
Total:
3,743 square feet

Design by
Design Traditions

© Design Traditions

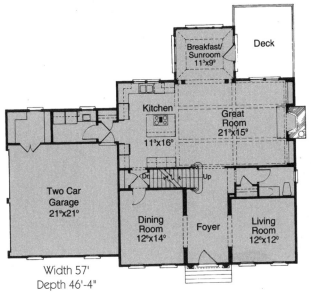

Width 57'
Depth 46'-4"

The semi-circular fanlight in the low-pitched gable echoes the one over the door, furthering the symmetry that dignifies the exterior of this impressive traditional home. Formal living areas are entered from the foyer—to the right is the living room and to the left, the dining room. A butler's pantry links the dining room to the island kitchen. The second floor holds a spacious master suite, three family bedrooms—Bedroom 4 enjoys its own private bath—and three full baths. This home is designed with a basement foundation.

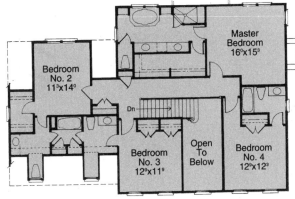

DESIGN 9980

First Floor:
1,448 square feet
Second Floor:
1,491 square feet
Total:
2,939 square feet

Design by
Design Traditions

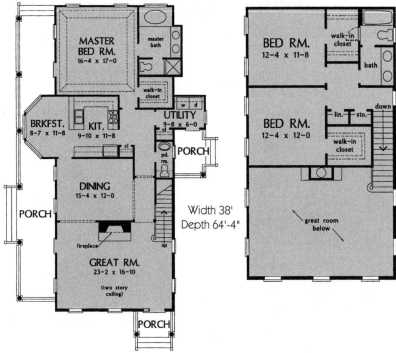

MASTER BED RM.
16-4 x 17-0

master bath

walk-in closet

w d

UTILITY
9-8 x 6-0

BRKFST.
8-7 x 11-8

KIT.
9-10 x 11-8

cl

pd. rm.

PORCH

DINING
15-4 x 12-0

PORCH

fireplace

up

GREAT RM.
23-2 x 16-10

(two story ceiling)

PORCH

Width 38'
Depth 64'-4"

BED RM.
12-4 x 11-8

walk-in closet

bath

BED RM.
12-4 x 12-0

lin. sto.

down

walk-in closet

great room below

Design by
Donald A. Gardner Architects, Inc.

GARAGE
22-4 x 25-4

DESIGN 7647

First Floor:
1,545 square feet
Second Floor:
560 square feet
Total:
2,105 square feet

This graceful country home with New South charm offers a sleek design that would work very well on a narrow lot. An impressive two-story great room welcomes family and guests with a warming fireplace. A well-appointed U-shaped kitchen serves the formal dining room as well as a bayed breakfast nook. The first-floor master suite is carefully positioned for privacy and features an elegant tray ceiling, a walk-in closet and a private bath. Upstairs, two family bedrooms, each with a walk-in closet, share a full bath and extra linen storage.

DESIGN 7640

First Floor:
1,939 square feet
Second Floor:
657 square feet
Total:
2,596 square feet

This country farmhouse offers an inviting wraparound porch for comfort and three gabled dormers for style. The foyer leads to a generous great room with an extended-hearth fireplace, a cathedral ceiling and access to the back covered porch. The first-floor master suite enjoys a sunny bay window and features a private bath with a cathedral ceiling, twin vanities and a windowed whirlpool tub. Upstairs, two family bedrooms share an elegant bath with a cathedral ceiling.

Design by
Donald A. Gardner
Architects, Inc.

Width 80'-10"
Depth 55'-8"

BONUS RM.
21-0 x 19-3

attic storage

SCREEN PORCH
16-10 x 14-0

PORCH

storage

MASTER BED RM.
12-8 x 19-0

master bath

(cathedral ceiling)

lin.

walk-in closet

walk-in closet

BED RM./STUDY
12-8 x 11-10

(vaulted ceiling)

GREAT RM.
15-4 x 20-4

fireplace

balcony above

storage

FOYER
11-7 x 9-8

up

bath

BRKFST.
12-8 x 11-0

KIT.
12-8 x 11-10

DINING
12-8 x 13-4

cl

UTIL.
7-6 x 8-0

up

storage

GARAGE
21-0 x 24-0

PORCH

optional bedroom wall location

attic storage

great room below

railing

optional bedroom wall location

attic storage

BED RM.
12-8 x 12-4

cl

down

sto.

lin.

bath

(cathedral ceiling)

BED RM.
12-8 x 12-4

cl

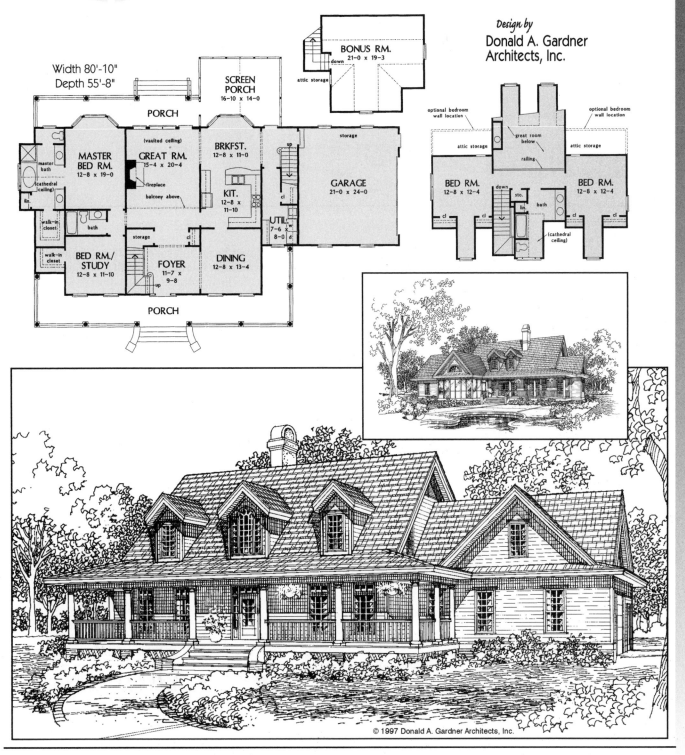

© 1997 Donald A. Gardner Architects, Inc.

DESIGN 3461

First Floor:
1,391 square feet
Second Floor:
611 square feet
Total:
2,002 square feet

L

Muntin windows, shutters and flower boxes add charm to this well-designed family farmhouse. The impressive foyer boasts a high ceiling and opens through decorative columns to the living room. Casual living takes off in the family room, with its own fireplace, and the open gourmet kitchen, which offers space for gathering. The first-floor master bedroom provides a sunny bay window, while the master bath offers a large walk-in closet, a knee-space vanity and a tiled-rim whirlpool tub. Three family bedrooms share an ample full bath upstairs.

Design by
Home Planners

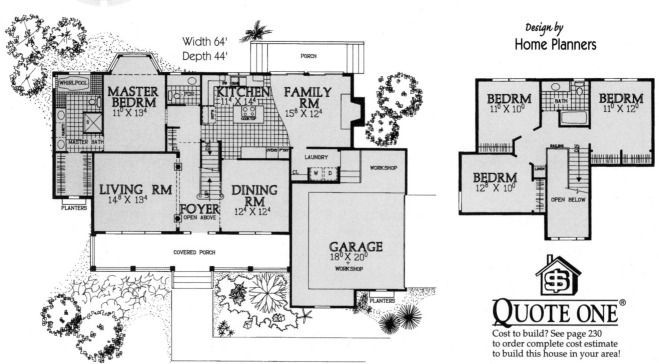

Width 64'
Depth 44'

Quote One®

Cost to build? See page 230 to order complete cost estimate to build this house in your area!

DESIGN 9645

First Floor:
1,356 square feet
Second Floor:
542 square feet
Total:
1,898 square feet

Design by
**Donald A. Gardner
Architects, Inc.**

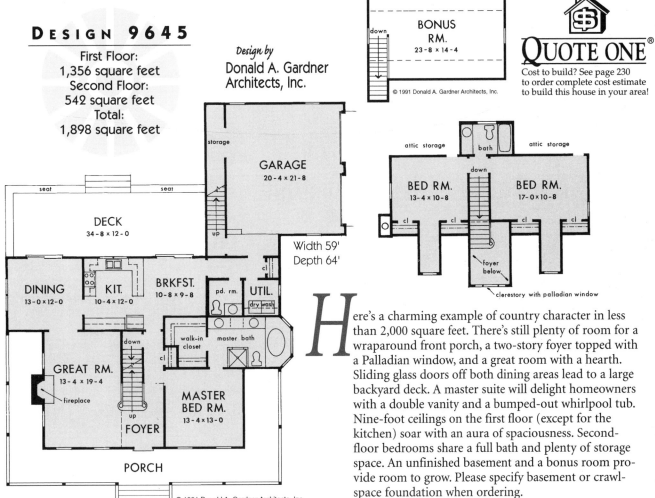

BONUS
RM.
23-8 × 14-4

down

© 1991 Donald A. Gardner Architects, Inc.

$\$$ **QUOTE ONE**®

Cost to build? See page 230
to order complete cost estimate
to build this house in your area!

GARAGE
20-4 × 21-8

storage

Width 59'
Depth 64'

DECK
34-8 × 12-0

seat   seat

up

DINING
13-0 × 12-0

KIT.
10-4 × 12-0

BRKFST.
10-8 × 9-8

pd. rm.

UTIL.
dry wash

cl

walk-in
closet

master bath

GREAT RM.
13-4 × 19-4

fireplace

down

cl

up

FOYER

**MASTER
BED RM.**
13-4 × 13-0

PORCH

© 1991 Donald A. Gardner Architects, Inc.

attic storage   bath   attic storage

down

BED RM.
13-4 × 10-8

BED RM.
17-0 × 10-8

cl   cl   cl   cl

foyer
below

clerestory with palladian window

*H*ere's a charming example of country character in less than 2,000 square feet. There's still plenty of room for a wraparound front porch, a two-story foyer topped with a Palladian window, and a great room with a hearth. Sliding glass doors off both dining areas lead to a large backyard deck. A master suite will delight homeowners with a double vanity and a bumped-out whirlpool tub. Nine-foot ceilings on the first floor (except for the kitchen) soar with an aura of spaciousness. Second-floor bedrooms share a full bath and plenty of storage space. An unfinished basement and a bonus room provide room to grow. Please specify basement or crawl-space foundation when ordering.

DESIGN 9792

First Floor:
1,480 square feet
Second Floor:
511 square feet
Total:
1,991 square feet

A quaint covered porch, dormers and arch-top windows stir memories of gentler times with this country home, but an idea-packed interior is designed for active lifestyles in a busy world. The foyer opens to a formal dining room with a bay window, and leads to a two-story great room with a fireplace and views to the outdoors. The first-floor master suite opens to a rear deck and spa and offers a whirlpool bath with a windowed walk-in closet. Two family bedrooms share a full bath and a balcony hall upstairs.

Design by
Donald A. Gardner Architects, Inc.

BONUS RM.
12-8 x 25-8

skylights

attic storage

down

attic storage

Deck

DECK

spa

GREAT RM.
15-4 x 19-2

BRKFST.
11-4 x 9-0

storage

UTILITY
9-8 x 7-5

w   d

GARAGE
20-4 x 25-8

MASTER BED RM.
14-4 x 16-2

fireplace
(cathedral ceiling)

balcony above

KIT.
11-4 x 12-2

up   cl

storage

master bath

cl

pd. rm.

DINING
11-4 x 13-4

FOYER
9-8 x 8-0

up

walk-in closet

PORCH

storage

great room below

attic storage   attic storage

railing

BED RM.
11-4 x 12-6

down

BED RM.
11-4 x 12-6

bath

cl   cl

foyer below

cl   cl

© 1995 Donald A. Gardner Architects, Inc.

Width 73'
Depth 51'-10"

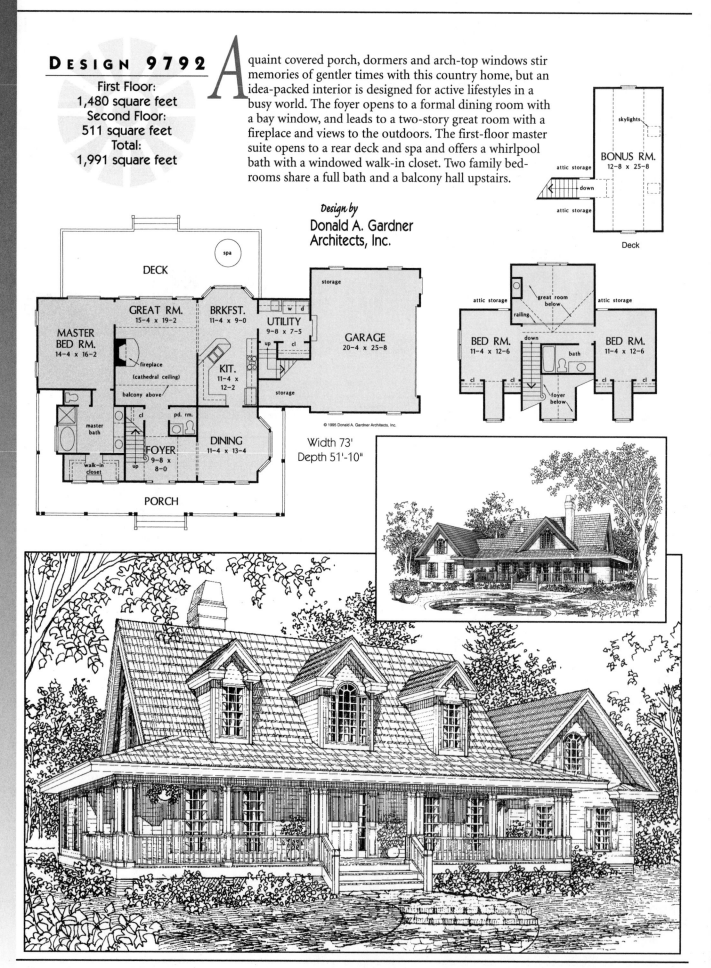

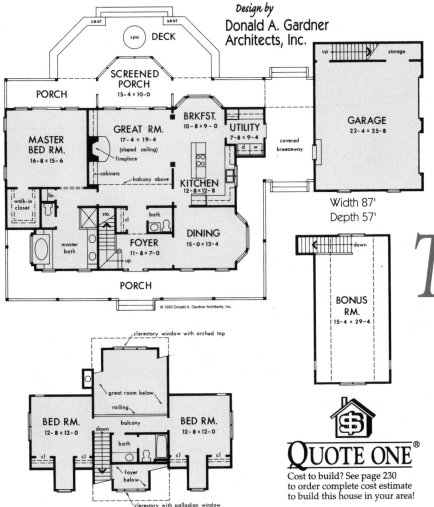

Design by
Donald A. Gardner
Architects, Inc.

seat • seat

spa DECK

SCREENED
PORCH
15-4 × 10-0

up storage

PORCH

GARAGE
22-4 × 25-8

MASTER
BED RM.
16-8 × 15-6

GREAT RM.
17-4 × 19-4
(sloped ceiling)
fireplace

BRKFST.
10-8 × 9-0

UTILITY
7-8 × 9-4

d w

covered
breezeway

cabinets

balcony above

walk-in
closet

lin.

KITCHEN
12-8 × 12-8

master
bath

sto.

cl

bath

DINING
15-0 × 12-4

FOYER
11-8 × 7-0

up

PORCH

© 1993 Donald A. Gardner Architects, Inc.

Width 87'
Depth 57'

DESIGN 9702

First Floor:
1,618 square feet
Second Floor:
570 square feet
Total:
2,188 square feet

down

BONUS
RM.
15-4 × 29-4

clerestory window with arched top

great room below

railing

balcony

BED RM.
12-8 × 12-0

down

BED RM.
12-8 × 12-0

bath

cl

cl

cl

cl

foyer
below

clerestory with palladian window

QUOTE ONE®
$

Cost to build? See page 230
to order complete cost estimate
to build this house in your area!

*T*he entrance foyer and great room
enjoy Palladian window clerestories
to allow natural light to enter the
well-planned interior of this country
home. The spacious great room
boasts a fireplace, built-in cabinets
and an overlook from the second-
floor balcony. The kitchen has a
cooktop island counter and is placed
conveniently between the breakfast
room and the formal dining room. A
generous first-floor master suite has
plenty of closet space and a lavish
bath with a windowed whirlpool tub.
Upstairs, two family bedrooms share
a full bath. Bonus space over the
garage awaits later development.

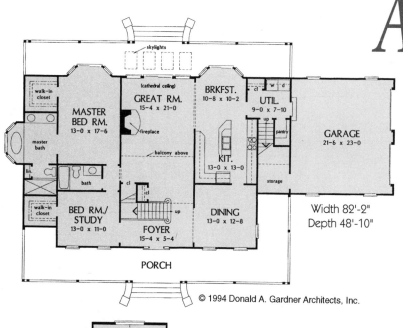

skylights

(cathedral ceiling)

walk-in closet

MASTER BED RM.
13-0 x 17-6

master bath

GREAT RM.
15-4 x 21-0

fireplace

balcony above

BRKFST.
10-8 x 10-2

UTIL.
9-0 x 7-10

up

a w d

pantry

GARAGE
21-6 x 23-0

KIT.
13-0 x 13-0

storage

lin.

bath

cl

cl

walk-in closet

BED RM./
STUDY
13-0 x 11-0

FOYER
15-4 x 5-4

up

DINING
13-0 x 12-8

Width 82'-2"
Depth 48'-10"

PORCH

© 1994 Donald A. Gardner Architects, Inc.

great room below

attic storage

attic storage

attic storage

BONUS RM.
21-6 x 14-0

railing

up

down

attic storage

BED RM.
12-8 x 12-0

down

bath

BED RM.
12-8 x 12-0

cl

cl

cl

cl

foyer below

attic storage

Design by
**Donald A. Gardner
Architects, Inc.**

A clerestory window and a quaint covered porch unite to give this upscale home a cottage feel. An inviting glass-paneled entry leads to the grand, two-story foyer, which opens to a formal dining room bright with windows. This home shows its character at the heart of the plan—in the great room, where a cathedral ceiling soars above a generous fireplace with an extended hearth, and sliding glass doors lead out to a covered porch with skylights. In the kitchen, oodles of counter and cabinet space along with a cooktop island bring out the joy of cooking. The breakfast nook boasts a bumped-out bay that calls in the outdoors, and an abundance of natural light. The master bedroom suite features a private bath with a bay-window whirlpool tub and an adjoining study with its own walk-in closet. Upstairs, two family bedrooms enjoy a balcony overlook to the great room. A bonus room over the garage awaits future expansion.

DESIGN 9767

First Floor:
1,829 square feet
Second Floor:
584 square feet
Total:
2,413 square feet

T his fetching four-bedroom country home, with porches and dormers at both front and rear, offers a welcoming touch to an open floor plan. The spacious great room enjoys a large fireplace, a cathedral ceiling and a clerestory with an arched window. The expansive first-floor master suite features a generous walk-in closet and includes a luxurious master bath which boasts a bumped-out whirlpool tub, twin vanities and a separate shower. A second bedroom just off the foyer may be used as a study if desired. Upstairs, two family bedrooms share a full bath.

D E S I G N 9 7 3 3

First Floor:
1,871 square feet
Second Floor:
731 square feet
Total:
2,602 square feet

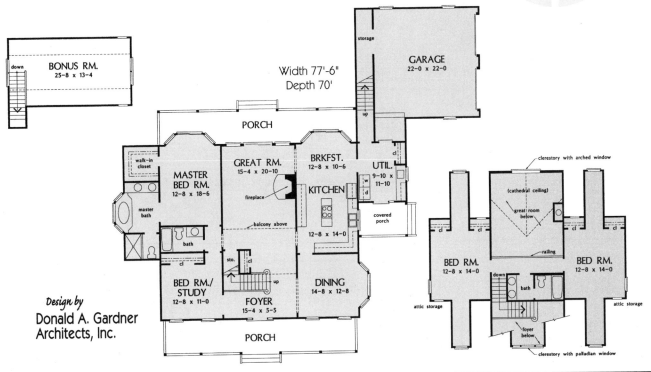

BONUS RM.
25-8 x 13-4

down

Width 77'-6"
Depth 70'

storage

GARAGE
22-0 x 22-0

up

PORCH

walk-in closet

MASTER BED RM.
12-8 x 18-6

master bath

bath

cl

BED RM./ STUDY
12-8 x 11-0

sto. cl

FOYER
15-4 x 5-5

GREAT RM.
15-4 x 20-10

fireplace

balcony above

up

BRKFST.
12-8 x 10-6

KITCHEN

12-8 x 14-0

DINING
14-8 x 12-8

UTIL.
9-10 x 11-10

w
d

cl

covered porch

PORCH

clerestory with arched window

(cathedral ceiling)

great room below

railing

BED RM.
12-8 x 14-0

BED RM.
12-8 x 14-0

cl

cl

down

bath

attic storage

attic storage

foyer below

clerestory with palladian window

Design by
Donald A. Gardner
Architects, Inc.

B. NATHAN

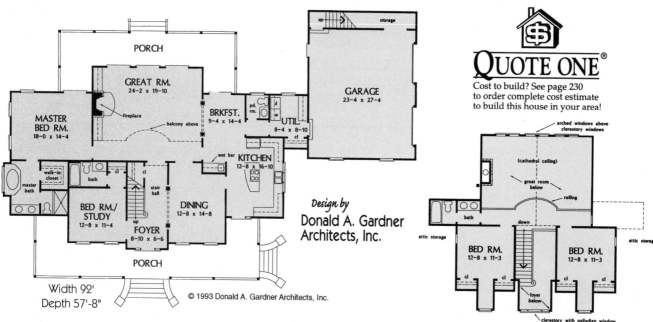

PORCH

GREAT RM.
24-2 x 19-10

fireplace

balcony above

MASTER
BED RM.
18-0 x 14-4

BRKFST.
9-4 x 14-4

pd.
rm.

UTIL.
8-4 x 8-10

GARAGE
23-4 x 27-4

up   storage

master
bath

walk-in
closet

bath

cl

cl

wet bar

KITCHEN
12-8 x 16-10

BED RM./
STUDY
12-8 x 11-4

stair
hall

DINING
12-8 x 14-8

up

FOYER
8-10 x 6-6

PORCH

Width 92'
Depth 57'-8"

© 1993 Donald A. Gardner Architects, Inc.

Design by
**Donald A. Gardner
Architects, Inc.**

QUOTE ONE®

Cost to build? See page 230
to order complete cost estimate
to build this house in your area!

arched windows above
clerestory windows

(cathedral ceiling)

great room
below

railing

bath

attic storage

BED RM.
12-8 x 11-3

down

BED RM.
12-8 x 11-3

attic storage

cl   cl

cl   cl

foyer
below

clerestory with palladian window

A rustic balustrade sets off the grand country exterior of this charming plan. The foyer enjoys natural light from a Palladian clerestory window, and leads to a living area crowned with a cathedral ceiling that allows great views to the outdoors. The gourmet kitchen includes a morning room with private access to the rear covered porch. The secluded master suite boasts a windowed garden tub and access to a private area of the wraparound porch. Two family bedrooms upstairs share a balcony hall with an overlook to the great room.

DESIGN 9723
First Floor:
2,064 square feet
Second Floor:
594 square feet
Total:
2,658 square feet

down

BONUS RM.
27-4 x 14-0

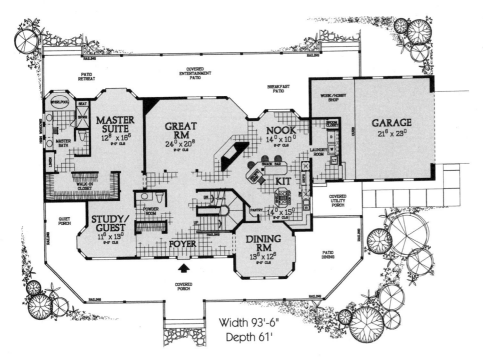

DESIGN 3608

First Floor:
2,347 square feet
Second Floor:
1,087 square feet
Total:
3,434 square feet

L

QUOTE ONE®

Cost to build? See page 230
to order complete cost estimate
to build this house in your area!

Design by
Home Planners

Varied rooflines and sunburst trim provide an extra measure of style with this new farmhouse. The sunburst is repeated on a clerestory window, which lets sunlight into the foyer. Traditional elegance is splashed with contemporary style in the formal dining room. A centered hearth warms casual living and dining areas, which open to an outdoor entertainment patio. A secluded master suite offers a bumped-out bay with wide views to the rear property, and private access to the patio. Each of the three second-floor bedrooms as well as the loft has a dormer window. A full bath with twin vanities and a separate shower with a seat complete the plan.

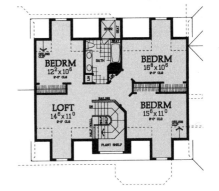

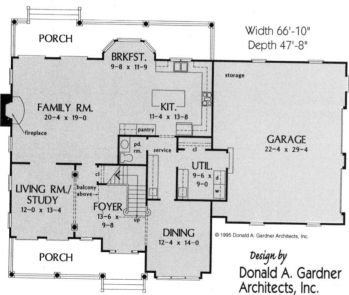

PORCH

BRKFST.
9-8 x 11-9

Width 66'-10"
Depth 47'-8"

storage

FAMILY RM.
20-4 x 19-0

KIT.
11-4 x 13-8

fireplace

pantry

GARAGE
22-4 x 29-4

pd.
rm.

service

cl

UTIL.
9-6 x
9-0

d

w

LIVING RM./
STUDY
12-0 x 13-4

balcony
above

cl

FOYER
13-6 x
9-8

up

DINING
12-4 x 14-0

© 1995 Donald A. Gardner Architects, Inc.

PORCH

Design by
**Donald A. Gardner
Architects, Inc.**

This country home displays a quaint rural character outside and a savvy sophistication within. The foyer opens on either side to elegant formal areas, beautifully lit with natural light from multi-pane windows. A casual living area opens to the U-shaped kitchen and bayed breakfast nook, and features a focal-point fireplace. The master suite offers a sumptuous bath with a bumped-out whirlpool tub, twin vanities and a generous walk-in closet. Three family bedrooms share a gallery hall that leads to a spacious bonus room.

DESIGN 9798

First Floor:
1,483 square feet
Second Floor:
1,349 square feet
Total:
2,832 square feet

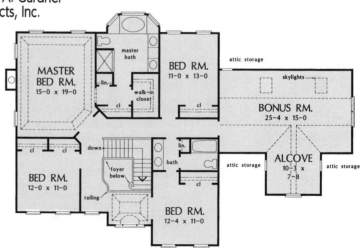

master bath

MASTER
BED RM.
15-0 x 19-0

lin.

BED RM.
11-0 x 13-0

attic storage

skylights

walk-in
closet

cl

cl

BONUS RM.
25-4 x 15-0

cl

cl

down

lin.

bath

cl

attic storage

ALCOVE
10-3 x
7-8

attic storage

BED RM.
12-0 x 11-0

foyer
below

railing

BED RM.
12-4 x 11-0

© 1992 Donald A. Gardner Architects, Inc.

DESIGN 9667

First Floor:
1,357 square feet
Second Floor:
1,204 square feet
Total:
2,561 square feet

Width 80'
Depth 57'

This elegant four-bedroom farmhouse catches the eye with a delicate Palladian clerestory window, double-gabled roof, and intricate detailing on the entry and wraparound porch. The foyer opens on either side to formal areas. A gourmet kitchen features a cooktop island, counter space galore, a double sink, and views to the property. The nearby breakfast room allows outdoor access through a bumped-out bay and enjoys an abundance of natural light. The second-floor master suite boasts a bay-windowed whirlpool tub, twin lavatories, and a walk-in closet with window. Three additional bedrooms share a full bath.

Design by
Donald A. Gardner
Architects, Inc.

QUOTE ONE®

Cost to build? See page 230 to order complete cost estimate to build this house in your area!

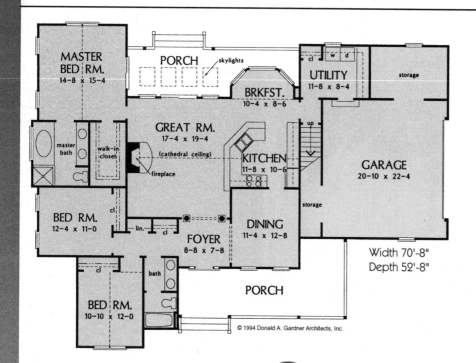

MASTER BED RM.
14-8 x 15-4

PORCH

skylights

master bath

walk-in closet

fireplace

GREAT RM.
17-4 x 19-4

(cathedral ceiling)

BRKFST.
10-4 x 8-6

UTILITY
11-8 x 8-4

storage

cl w d

up

KITCHEN
11-8 x 10-6

BED RM.
12-4 x 11-0

cl

lin.

cl

FOYER
8-8 x 7-8

DINING
11-4 x 12-8

GARAGE
20-10 x 22-4

storage

cl

bath

BED RM.
10-10 x 12-0

PORCH

Width 70'-8"
Depth 52'-8"

© 1994 Donald A. Gardner Architects, Inc.

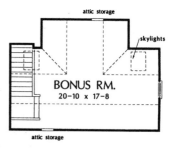

attic storage

skylights

BONUS RM.
20-10 x 17-8

attic storage

**Design by
Donald A. Gardner
Architects, Inc.**

DESIGN 9763

Square Footage: 1,807

Countrified and comfortable, this one-story home is smaller in square footage but large on livability. The covered front porch leads directly to a columned foyer. Turn right and enter the formal dining room. Pass through the columns and experience the open great room. There, a fireplace warms in winter and sliding glass doors admit cool summer breezes from the covered rear porch. A breakfast nook nearby accommodates casual dining. The master suite also opens to the rear porch and is appointed with a walk-in closet and stupendous bath. Family bedrooms share a full bath with double lavatories.

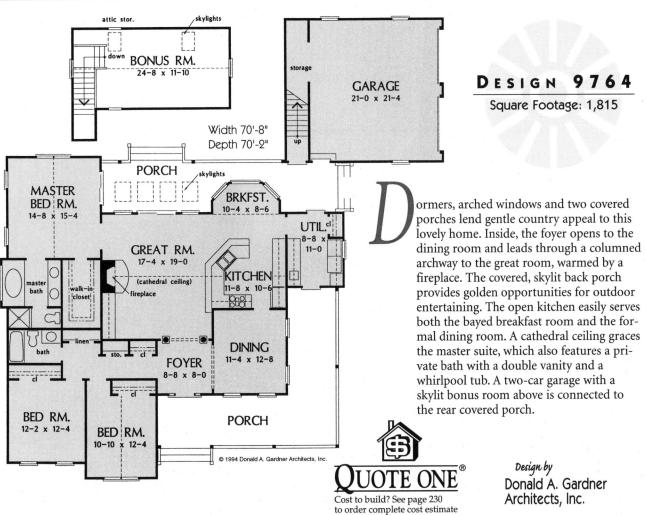

attic stor.   skylights

down

BONUS RM.
24-8 x 11-10

storage

GARAGE
21-0 x 21-4

up

Width 70'-8"
Depth 70'-2"

PORCH

skylights

DESIGN 9764

Square Footage: 1,815

MASTER BED RM.
14-8 x 15-4

BRKFST.
10-4 x 8-6

UTIL. cl.
8-8 x 11-0

master bath

walk-in closet

GREAT RM.
17-4 x 19-0

(cathedral ceiling)
fireplace

KITCHEN
11-8 x 10-6

linen

bath

sto.   cl

FOYER
8-8 x 8-0

DINING
11-4 x 12-8

cl

cl

BED RM.
12-2 x 12-4

BED RM.
10-10 x 12-4

PORCH

© 1994 Donald A. Gardner Architects, Inc.

*D*ormers, arched windows and two covered porches lend gentle country appeal to this lovely home. Inside, the foyer opens to the dining room and leads through a columned archway to the great room, warmed by a fireplace. The covered, skylit back porch provides golden opportunities for outdoor entertaining. The open kitchen easily serves both the bayed breakfast room and the formal dining room. A cathedral ceiling graces the master suite, which also features a private bath with a double vanity and a whirlpool tub. A two-car garage with a skylit bonus room above is connected to the rear covered porch.

Design by
**Donald A. Gardner
Architects, Inc.**

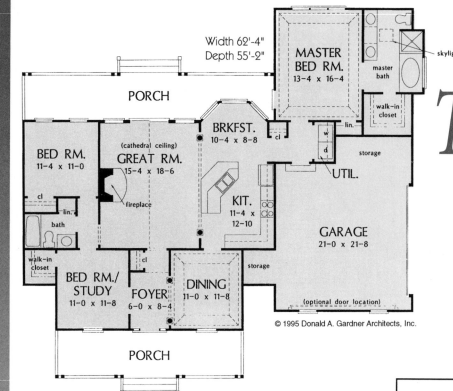

Width 62'-4"
Depth 55'-2"

MASTER BED RM.
13-4 x 16-4

master bath

skylight

walk-in closet

PORCH

BRKFST.
10-4 x 8-8

cl

lin.

w
d

storage

UTIL.

BED RM.
11-4 x 11-0

(cathedral ceiling)
GREAT RM.
15-4 x 18-6

fireplace

cl

lin.

bath

KIT.
11-4 x 12-10

walk-in closet

GARAGE
21-0 x 21-8

BED RM./ STUDY
11-0 x 11-8

FOYER
6-0 x 8-4

cl

DINING
11-0 x 11-8

storage

(optional door location)

© 1995 Donald A. Gardner Architects, Inc.

PORCH

*T*his country home has more than just elegance, style and a host of amenities—it has heart. A cathedral ceiling highlights the great room, while a clerestory window and sliding glass doors really let in the light. Broad windows in the breakfast bay splash the L-shaped kitchen with natural light. The private master suite, with a tray ceiling and a walk-in closet, boasts luxurious amenities in the skylit master bath: a windowed whirlpool tub complements a separate shower. Two additional bedrooms share a full bath. The front bedroom features a walk-in closet and could also double as a study.

Design by
Donald A. Gardner Architects, Inc.

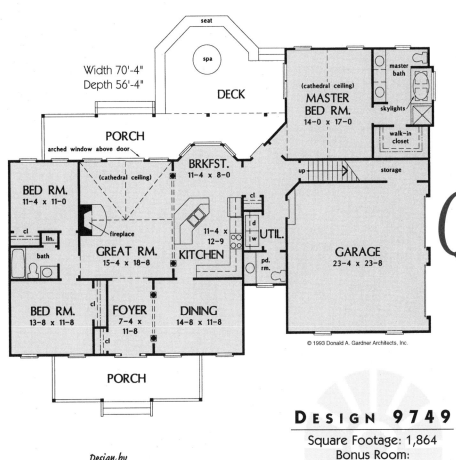

Width 70'-4"
Depth 56'-4"

DECK

seat

spa

PORCH

arched window above door

BED RM.
11-4 x 11-0

(cathedral ceiling)

fireplace

cl

lin.

bath

BRKFST.
11-4 x 8-0

KITCHEN

11-4 x
12-9

cl

d
w

UTIL.

pd.
rm.

GREAT RM.
15-4 x 18-8

MASTER BED RM.
14-0 x 17-0

(cathedral ceiling)

master bath

skylights

walk-in closet

up

storage

GARAGE
23-4 x 23-8

© 1993 Donald A. Gardner Architects, Inc.

BED RM.
13-8 x 11-8

cl

FOYER
7-4 x
11-8

cl

DINING
14-8 x 11-8

PORCH

Design by
**Donald A. Gardner
Architects, Inc.**

BONUS RM.
14-4 x 23-8

down

skylights

DESIGN 9749

Square Footage: 1,864
Bonus Room:
420 square feet

Quaint and cozy on the outside with front and rear porches, this three-bedroom country home surprises with an open floor plan featuring a large great room with a cathedral ceiling. Nine-foot ceilings add volume throughout the home. A central kitchen with an angled counter opens to the breakfast and great rooms for easy entertaining. The master bedroom is carefully positioned for privacy and offers a cathedral ceiling, garden tub with skylights, roomy walk-in closet and access to the rear deck. Two secondary bedrooms share a full hall bath. A bonus room with skylights may be developed later. Please specify basement or crawlspace foundation when ordering.

B. NATHAN

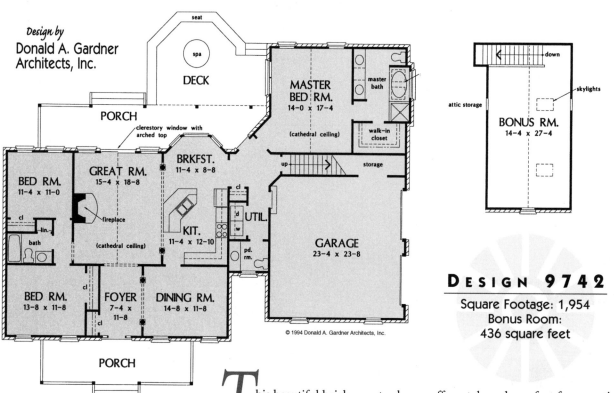

Design by
Donald A. Gardner
Architects, Inc.

seat

spa

DECK

PORCH

clerestory window with
arched top

BED RM.
11-4 x 11-0

cl

lin.

bath

GREAT RM.
15-4 x 18-8

fireplace

(cathedral ceiling)

BRKFST.
11-4 x 8-8

cl

KIT.
11-4 x 12-10

d
w

UTIL.

pd.
rm.

MASTER
BED RM.
14-0 x 17-4

(cathedral ceiling)

master
bath

walk-in
closet

up

storage

GARAGE
23-4 x 23-8

BED RM.
13-8 x 11-8

cl

FOYER
7-4 x
11-8

cl

DINING RM.
14-8 x 11-8

PORCH

down

attic storage

skylights

BONUS RM.
14-4 x 27-4

© 1994 Donald A. Gardner Architects, Inc.

DESIGN 9742

Square Footage: 1,954
Bonus Room:
436 square feet

Width 71'-3"
Depth 62'-6"

*T*his beautiful brick country home offers style and comfort for an active family. Two covered porches and a rear deck with spa invite enjoyment of the outdoors, while a well-defined interior provides places to gather and entertain. A cathedral ceiling soars above the central great room, warmed by an extended-hearth fireplace and by sunlight through an arch-top clerestory window. A splendid master suite enjoys its own secluded wing, and offers a skylit whirlpool bath, a cathedral ceiling and private access to the deck. Two family bedrooms share a full bath on the opposite side of the plan.

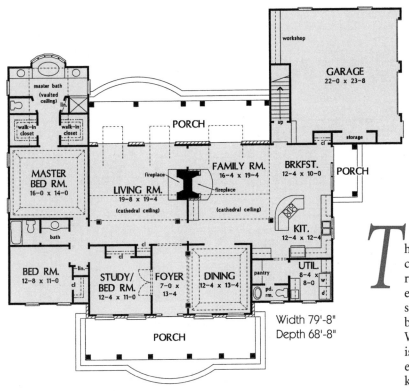

master bath
(vaulted
ceiling)

walk-in
closet

walk-in
closet

MASTER
BED RM.
16-0 x 14-0

bath

BED RM.
12-8 x 11-0

STUDY/
BED RM.
12-4 x 11-0

FOYER
7-0 x
13-4

DINING
12-4 x 13-4

pantry

pd.
rm.

UTIL.
8-4 x
8-0

w.
d.

KIT.
12-4 x 12-4

BRKFST.
12-4 x 10-0

FAMILY RM.
16-4 x 19-4

LIVING RM.
19-8 x 19-4
(cathedral ceiling)

fireplace

fireplace

(cathedral ceiling)

PORCH

workshop

GARAGE
22-0 x 23-8

up

storage

PORCH

PORCH

Width 79'-8"
Depth 68'-8"

BONUS RM.
22-0 x 14-8

down

Design by
**Donald A. Gardner
Architects, Inc.**

DESIGN 7616

Square Footage: 2,450
Bonus Room:
647 square feet

*T*his elegant home's understated Early American country theme introduces an interior plan that represents the height of style—but never at the expense of comfort. The foyer opens on either side to quiet formal rooms—or make one a bedroom—and leads to a central gallery hall. Wide open living space with a cathedral ceiling is defined by a double fireplace, with an extended hearth on each side. An L-shaped kitchen enjoys views of the outdoors and interior vistas of the family room over a centered island counter. The nearby breakfast room leads to a private porch and to the two-car garage, which offers a workshop and additional storage. Twin walk-in closets, a dressing area and a bumped-out tub highlight the master bath, which also features a vaulted ceiling. A secondary bedroom shares access to linen storage and offers its own bath.

B. NATHAN

© 1995 Donald A. Gardner Architects, Inc.

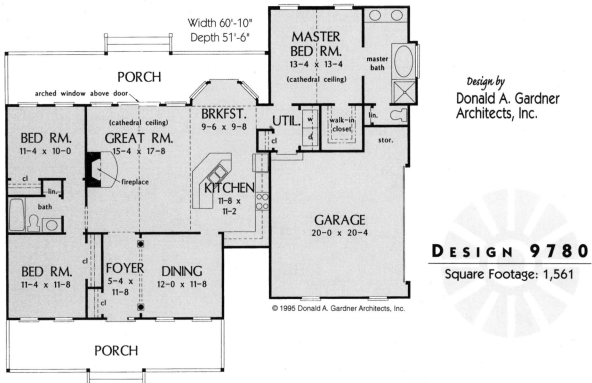

Width 60'-10"
Depth 51'-6"

PORCH

arched window above door

MASTER
BED RM.
13-4 x 13-4
(cathedral ceiling)

master
bath

BRKFST.
9-6 x 9-8

UTIL.

w
d

walk-in
closet

lin.

(cathedral ceiling)

BED RM.
11-4 x 10-0

GREAT RM.
15-4 x 17-8

fireplace

cl

stor.

cl

lin.

bath

KITCHEN
11-8 x
11-2

GARAGE
20-0 x 20-4

BED RM.
11-4 x 11-8

FOYER
5-4 x
11-8

DINING
12-0 x 11-8

cl

cl

PORCH

Design by
Donald A. Gardner
Architects, Inc.

DESIGN 9780
Square Footage: 1,561

© 1995 Donald A. Gardner Architects, Inc.

Combining quaint country details with stunning modern elements, this lovely one-story home can really stretch a modest budget. The foyer opens to a formal dining room defined by columns, and leads to the great room which boasts a cathedral ceiling and a focal-point fireplace. The kitchen and breakfast room are open to the living area and offer access to the rear porch through the windowed bay. A quiet master suite nestles to the rear of the plan and includes a lavish bath with a garden tub and separate shower. Two family bedrooms share a full bath that opens from a gallery hall. The two-car garage adds space for storage.

© 1994 Donald A. Gardner Architects, Inc.

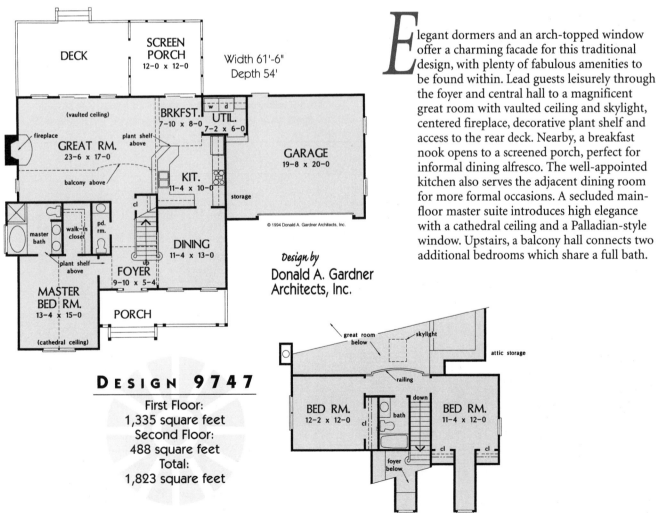

DECK

SCREEN PORCH
12-0 x 12-0

Width 61'-6"
Depth 54'

(vaulted ceiling)

fireplace

GREAT RM.
23-6 x 17-0

plant shelf above

balcony above

BRKFST.
7-10 x 8-0

UTIL.
7-2 x 6-0

w d

GARAGE
19-8 x 20-0

KIT.
11-4 x 10-0

storage

© 1994 Donald A. Gardner Architects, Inc.

master bath

walk-in closet

pd. rm.

cl

plant shelf above

MASTER BED RM.
13-4 x 15-0

FOYER
9-10 x 5-4

DINING
11-4 x 13-0

PORCH

up

(cathedral ceiling)

Design by
**Donald A. Gardner
Architects, Inc.**

DESIGN 9747

First Floor:
1,335 square feet
Second Floor:
488 square feet
Total:
1,823 square feet

great room below

skylight

attic storage

railing

BED RM.
12-2 x 12-0

cl

bath

down

BED RM.
11-4 x 12-0

cl   cl

foyer below

*E*legant dormers and an arch-topped window offer a charming facade for this traditional design, with plenty of fabulous amenities to be found within. Lead guests leisurely through the foyer and central hall to a magnificent great room with vaulted ceiling and skylight, centered fireplace, decorative plant shelf and access to the rear deck. Nearby, a breakfast nook opens to a screened porch, perfect for informal dining alfresco. The well-appointed kitchen also serves the adjacent dining room for more formal occasions. A secluded main-floor master suite introduces high elegance with a cathedral ceiling and a Palladian-style window. Upstairs, a balcony hall connects two additional bedrooms which share a full bath.

DESIGN 9662

First Floor:
1,025 square feet
Second Floor:
911 square feet
Total:
1,936 square feet

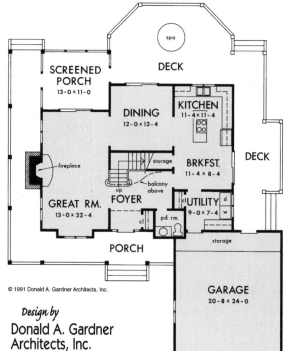

SCREENED PORCH
13-0 × 11-0

DECK

spa

DINING
12-0 × 12-4

KITCHEN
11-4 × 11-4

DECK

fireplace

storage

BRKFST.
11-4 × 8-4

GREAT RM.
13-0 × 22-4

FOYER

up

balcony above

UTILITY
9-0 × 7-4

d

w

cl

pd. rm.

PORCH

storage

© 1991 Donald A. Gardner Architects, Inc.

Design by
Donald A. Gardner Architects, Inc.

GARAGE
20-8 × 24-0

QUOTE ONE®

Cost to build? See page 230 to order complete cost estimate to build this house in your area!

master bath

closet

closet

cl

BED RM.
11-0 × 12-4

BED RM.
10-0 × 12-4

down

walk-in closet

sto.

storage

MASTER BED RM.
13-0 × 14-4

balcony

foyer below

bath

sto.

Width 53'-8"
Depth 67'-8"

BONUS RM.
12-4 × 24-0

*T*he exterior of this three-bedroom country-style home is enhanced by its many gables, arched windows and wraparound porch. A large great room with an impressive fireplace leads to both the dining room and screened porch. Sized for entertaining, the deck wraps to provide room for a spa and outdoor dining space adjacent to the dining room and the informal breakfast area. An open kitchen offers a country atmosphere. The second-floor master suite has two walk-in closets and an impressive bath enhanced with a spa tub in a bumped-out bay. Two family bedrooms share a full bath and plenty of storage. Bonus space over the garage can be developed for future use.

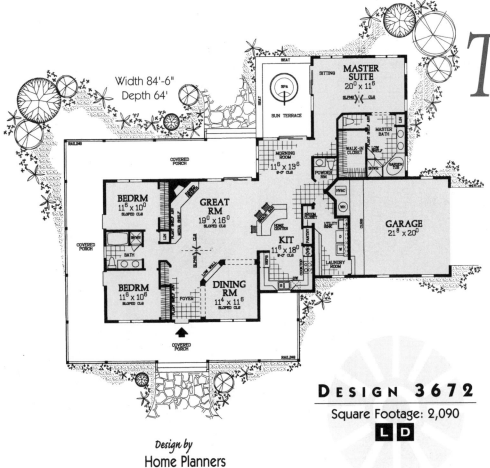

Width 84'-6"
Depth 64'

DESIGN 3672
Square Footage: 2,090
L D

Design by
Home Planners

*T*his classic farmhouse enjoys a wraparound porch that's perfect for enjoyment of the outdoors. To the rear of the plan, a sun terrace with a spa opens from the master suite and the morning room. A grand great room offers a sloped ceiling and a corner fireplace with a raised hearth. The formal dining room is defined by a low wall and by graceful archways set off by decorative columns. The tiled kitchen has a centered island counter with a snack bar and adjoins a laundry area. Two family bedrooms reside to the side of the plan, and each enjoys private access to the covered porch. A secluded master suite nestles in its own wing and features a sitting area with access to the rear terrace and spa.

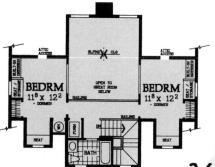

BEDRM 11⁸ x 12²

BEDRM 11⁸ x 12²

OPEN TO GREAT ROOM BELOW

BATH

Design 3674

DESIGN 3673/3674

First Floor: 1,086 square feet
Second Floor: 554 square feet
Total: 1,640 square feet

L **D**

Design by
Home Planners

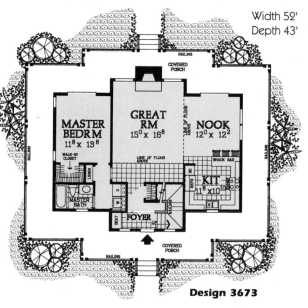

Width 52'
Depth 43'

MASTER BEDRM 11⁸ x 13⁸

GREAT RM 15⁰ x 16⁸

NOOK 12⁰ x 12²

MASTER BATH

KIT 11⁸ x10⁰

FOYER

Design 3673

QUOTE ONE®

Cost to build? See page 230
to order complete cost estimate
to build this house in your area!

A touch of tradition (Design 3674) and a charming Victorian vogue (Design 3673) provide alternate exterior styles with this delightful farmhouse. A welcoming entry and a tiled foyer lead to a thoughtful floor plan, starting with a built-in seat with shoe storage. The two-story great room is the heart of the plan and offers an extended-hearth fireplace framed by grand picture windows. The adjacent nook and efficient kitchen create a spacious area for formal and informal gatherings. The secluded first-floor master suite features private access to the wraparound porch, and leads to a gallery hall with a laundry niche. Skylights brighten the balcony hall which connects the two second-floor family bedrooms and a full bath.

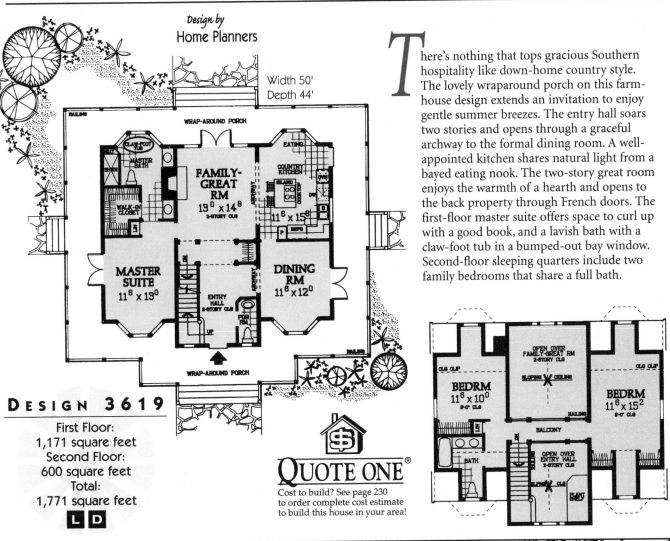

Design by
Home Planners

Width 50'
Depth 44'

WRAP-AROUND PORCH

RAILING

CLAW-FOOT TUB
MASTER BATH

FAMILY-GREAT RM
13⁰ x 14⁸
2-STORY CLG

EATING

COUNTRY KITCHEN
11⁶ x 15⁶

ISLAND
COOKTOP

OVN

DW

WALK-IN CLOSET

ARCHWAY

REFRIG

P

MASTER SUITE
11⁸ x 13⁰

ARCHWAY

DINING RM
11⁸ x 12⁰

ENTRY HALL
2-STORY CLG

POR RM

UP

RAILING

WRAP-AROUND PORCH

DESIGN 3619

First Floor:
1,171 square feet
Second Floor:
600 square feet
Total:
1,771 square feet

L **D**

There's nothing that tops gracious Southern hospitality like down-home country style. The lovely wraparound porch on this farmhouse design extends an invitation to enjoy gentle summer breezes. The entry hall soars two stories and opens through a graceful archway to the formal dining room. A well-appointed kitchen shares natural light from a bayed eating nook. The two-story great room enjoys the warmth of a hearth and opens to the back property through French doors. The first-floor master suite offers space to curl up with a good book, and a lavish bath with a claw-foot tub in a bumped-out bay window. Second-floor sleeping quarters include two family bedrooms that share a full bath.

QUOTE ONE®
Cost to build? See page 230 to order complete cost estimate to build this house in your area!

OPEN OVER FAMILY-GREAT RM
2-STORY CLG

SLOPING CEILING

CLG CLP

CLG CLP

BEDRM
11⁶ x 10⁰
8'-0" CLG

BEDRM
11⁸ x 15²
8'-0" CLG

RAILING

BALCONY

BATH

LIN

OPEN OVER ENTRY HALL
2-STORY CLG

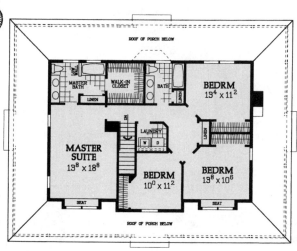

Symmetrical gables and clapboard siding lend a Midwestern style to this prairies-and-plains farmhouse. A spacious foyer opens to formal rooms and leads to a casual living area with a tiled-hearth fireplace and a breakfast bay. The U-shaped kitchen enjoys an easy-care ceramic tile floor and a walk-in pantry. The second-floor sleeping quarters include a generous master suite with a window-seat dormer and a private bath with a whirlpool tub, a walk-in closet, twin vanities and linen storage. Three family bedrooms share a full bath and a central hall which leads to additional storage and a laundry.

Design by
Home Planners

Width 56'
Depth 42'

QUOTE ONE®

Cost to build? See page 230 to order complete cost estimate to build this house in your area!

DESIGN 3653

First Floor:
1,216 square feet
Second Floor:
1,191 square feet
Total:
2,407 square feet

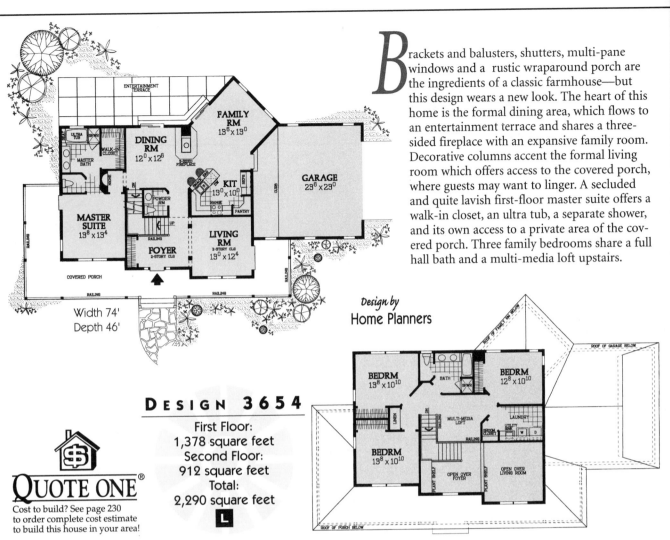

Brackets and balusters, shutters, multi-pane windows and a rustic wraparound porch are the ingredients of a classic farmhouse—but this design wears a new look. The heart of this home is the formal dining area, which flows to an entertainment terrace and shares a three-sided fireplace with an expansive family room. Decorative columns accent the formal living room which offers access to the covered porch, where guests may want to linger. A secluded and quite lavish first-floor master suite offers a walk-in closet, an ultra tub, a separate shower, and its own access to a private area of the covered porch. Three family bedrooms share a full hall bath and a multi-media loft upstairs.

Width 74'
Depth 46'

Design by
Home Planners

DESIGN 3654

First Floor:
1,378 square feet
Second Floor:
912 square feet
Total:
2,290 square feet

L

QUOTE ONE®

Cost to build? See page 230
to order complete cost estimate
to build this house in your area!

Width 76'-4"
Depth 73'-4"

Design by
Home Planners

Quote One®

Cost to build? See page 230
to order complete cost estimate
to build this house in your area!

DESIGN 3662
Square Footage: 1,937

L

Gables, dormers and an old-fashioned covered porch create a winsome, country look for this transitional exterior but, inside, it delivers an upscale, educated floor plan. The great room offers a sloped ceiling, a fireplace with extended hearth, access to a patio deck and built-in shelves for an entertainment center. The kitchen offers an angled desk set against a curved half-wall with a display shelf below. Gourmet features in the kitchen include a cooktop island counter, easy care ceramic tile flooring and a divided sink. Triple windows grace the morning nook with an abundance of natural light. A split bedroom plan allows a separate wing for the master suite, which features a private sitting area as well as a relaxing bath with a windowed garden tub and two vanities—one with knee space.

Width 68'-6"
Depth 66'-5"

Design by
Home Planners

DESIGN 3663

First Floor:
1,655 square feet
Second Floor:
515 square feet
Total:
2,170 square feet

L D

An arched clerestory, multi-pane windows and a balustered porch splash this classic country exterior with an extraordinary new spirit. Inside, the two-story foyer is flanked by the sunny formal dining room and an elegant stairway. The great room offers a fireplace with a tiled hearth, a built-in media center, and a snack bar that it shares with the large island kitchen and breakfast room. Ceramic tiles dress up the L-shaped kitchen, which boasts a built-in desk, extra closet space and double ovens. The first floor master suite is appointed with a sitting area and enjoys private access to the rear covered porch, while the master bath boasts an angled whirlpool tub and twin lavatories. Upstairs, two secondary bedrooms—each with its own balcony—share a full bath with ample linen storage.

_T_his charming country home gives a nod to the past but speaks to the future as well, with an interior designed for family living. A sloped ceiling lends a sense of spaciousness to the living room, which also features a corner hearth and a door to the outside. The U-shaped kitchen serves a convenient dining area, well lit by a bay window. A hall bath serves two family bedrooms, while a generous master suite has a private bath with a compartmented vanity and a walk-in closet. The two-car garage provides addtional storage space and a service entrance that leads to the kitchen. Please specify crawlspace or slab foundation when ordering.

Design by
Larry E. Belk Designs

DESIGN 8246
Square Footage: 1,170

Width 51'-10"
Depth 53'-6"

GARAGE

MSTR BDRM
11-0x13-8
10 FT CLG

LIVING
13-0x17-8
10 FT CLG

DINING
11-0x
9-2

STORAGE

MSTR BATH

DESK

KITCH
11-6x
8-0

BATH 2

STOR

FOYER

LIN

BDRM 3
10-10x11-6

COVERED PORCH

BDRM 2
10-4x10-2

COPYRIGHT LARRY E. BELK

Rear Elevation

DESIGN 8241

Square Footage: 1,993
Unfinished Loft:
307 square feet

Design by
Larry E. Belk Designs

A gabled roof, flanked by attractive dormers, tops the welcoming covered front porch of this country charmer. Inside, a formal dining room opens directly off the foyer, announced by decorative columns. The nearby living room offers a warming fireplace and access to the rear covered porch. Angled counters in the kitchen contribute to easy food preparation, while a snack counter accommodates quick meals. Nestled in its own wing, the master suite opens through double doors from a private vestibule and offers a relaxing retreat for the homeowner. On the other side of the plan, two family bedrooms share a full hall bath. Please specify crawl-space or slab foundation when ordering.

Width 66'-10
Depth 71'-5"

Arch-top windows and a front covered porch with a balustrade add charm to this country-style exterior. Inside, the formal parlor offers a ten-foot ceiling and a dining room option. The tiled entry opens through French doors to a well-lit breakfast area with a patio door to a covered deck. The gourmet kitchen offers a food preparation island counter, a wrapping pantry and convenient access to the large family room, which boasts a fireplace. Upstairs, two secondary bedrooms each feature a built-in desk and open to a gallery hall that leads to a full bath. The sun-filled master suite, also on this floor, boasts a private dressing area set off by French doors.

DESIGN 7253
First Floor:
976 square feet
Second Floor:
823 square feet
Total:
1,799 square feet

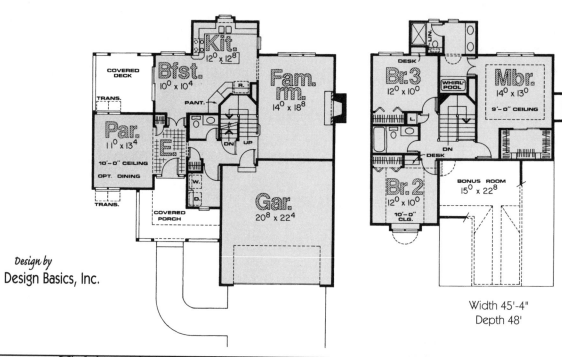

COVERED DECK

TRANS.

Par.
11⁰ x 13⁴
10'-0" CEILING
OPT. DINING

TRANS.

Bfst.
10⁰ x 10⁴

PANT.

Kit.
12⁰ x 12⁸

Fam. rm.
14⁰ x 18⁸

DN   UP

W.
D.

COVERED PORCH

Gar.
20⁸ x 22⁴

Br. 3
12⁰ x 10⁰

DESK

WHIRL-POOL

Mbr.
14⁰ x 13⁰
9'-0" CEILING

DN

DESK

Br. 2
12⁰ x 10⁰
10'-0" CLG.

BONUS ROOM
15⁰ x 22⁸

Design by
Design Basics, Inc.

Width 45'-4"
Depth 48'

G. McDONALD

Rear Elevation

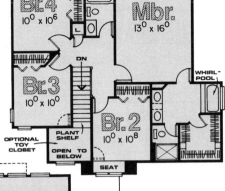

Design by
Design Basics, Inc.

Width 39'-4"
Depth 46'

E stablished tradition meets new style with this country exterior—an old fashioned covered porch complements sunbursts and asymmetrical gables. The tiled entry leads to a formal dining room or parlor and to casual living space, which includes a centered fireplace and views through three windows to the rear property. An L-shaped kitchen offers a snack bar, wide wrapping counters and a breakfast area with doors to the patio. A second-floor master suite hosts a roomy walk-in closet, a windowed whirlpool tub, a compartmented toilet and a double-bowl vanity. A nearby secondary bedroom, with a window seat and an ample wardrobe, could be used as a study. Two additional bedrooms share a full bath.

DESIGN 7316
First Floor:
866 square feet
Second Floor:
905 square feet
Total:
1,771 square feet

DESIGN 9242

First Floor:
1,322 square feet
Second Floor:
1,272 square feet
Total:
2,594 square feet

Quote One®

Cost to build? See page 230 to order complete cost estimate to build this house in your area!

Design by
Design Basics, Inc.

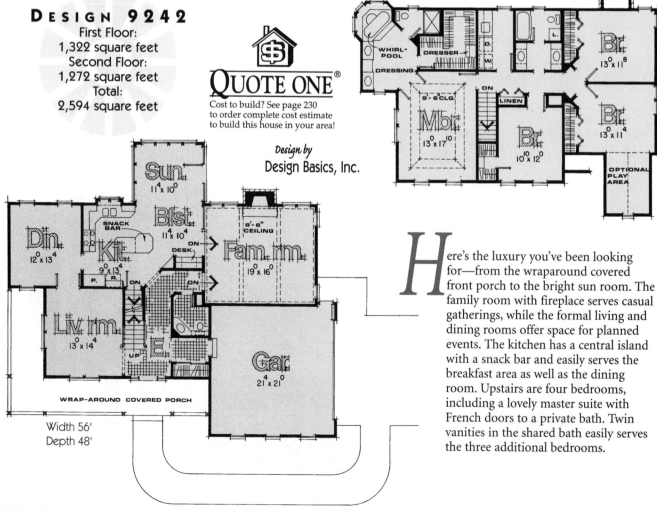

Width 56'
Depth 48'

*H*ere's the luxury you've been looking for—from the wraparound covered front porch to the bright sun room. The family room with fireplace serves casual gatherings, while the formal living and dining rooms offer space for planned events. The kitchen has a central island with a snack bar and easily serves the breakfast area as well as the dining room. Upstairs are four bedrooms, including a lovely master suite with French doors to a private bath. Twin vanities in the shared bath easily serves the three additional bedrooms.

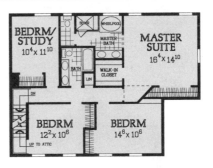

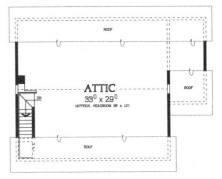

Width 63'-6"
Depth 48'

QUOTE ONE®

Cost to build? See page 230
to order complete cost estimate
to build this house in your area!

Design by
Home Planners

Horizontal clapboard siding, varying roof planes and finely detailed window treatments set a delightful tone for this farmhouse favorite. A tiled foyer leads past a convenient powder room to a spacious central morning room with an exposed beam ceiling and a wide door to the entertainment terrace. The U-shaped island kitchen offers service to the formal dining room, which enjoys a bay window and leads to an expansive living room. Upstairs, a gallery hall connects three family bedrooms and a hall bath.

DESIGN 3325

First Floor:
1,595 square feet
Second Floor:
1,112 square feet
Total:
2,707 square feet

L **D**

© Design Traditions

The winsome lines of New England's Colonial seacoast homes inspired this new traditional design, with details to satisfy a homeowner's dreams. Shingles, shutters and vertical siding lend country cottage appeal to this home, which will build in any region. The foyer leads to family living space, featuring a great room with a spider-beam ceiling, a bumped-out bay window and a focal-point fireplace. Open space includes a morning room with French doors to the rear veranda and deck. A guest bedroom, which could also serve as a library or study, enjoys a compartmented vanity and full bath. Upstairs, an L-shaped hall connects a lavish master suite, which offers a private spa bath and a walk-in closet, and two family bedrooms that share a full bath with compartmented vanities. This home is designed with a basement foundation.

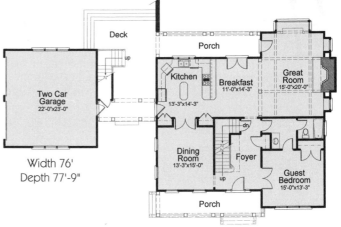

Width 76'
Depth 77'-9"

Design by
Design Traditions

DESIGN 9998

First Floor:
1,578 square feet
Second Floor:
1,324 square feet
Total:
2,902 square feet

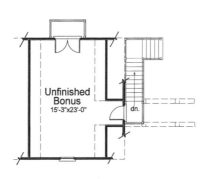

© Design Traditions

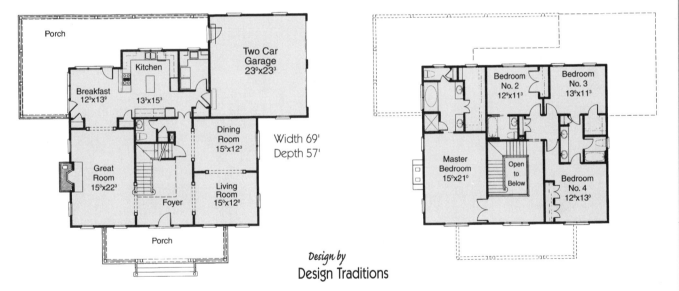

Porch

Kitchen
13³x15³

Breakfast
12³x13⁹

Two Car
Garage
23⁰x23³

Dining
Room
15⁰x12³

Width 69'
Depth 57'

Great
Room
15⁰x22³

Foyer

Living
Room
15⁰x12⁰

Porch

Master
Bedroom
15⁰x21⁰

Bedroom
No. 2
12⁶x11³

Bedroom
No. 3
13⁶x11³

Open
to
Below

Bedroom
No. 4
12⁶x13⁰

Design by
Design Traditions

*T*his new design wears the ageless appeal of classic country style, but gives it a fresh face. A low-pitched roof complements the columns and balusters of the front covered porch and creates a sense of shelter. Formal areas inside are secluded to one side of the plan, while the family room, the gourmet kitchen, and a sunny breakfast area enjoy open interior space and views to the rear property. A plush master suite on the second floor boasts a windowed whirlpool tub and twin lavatories. Each of two secondary bedrooms enjoys private access to a shared bath, while an additional bedroom offers its own full bath. This home is designed with a basement foundation.

DESIGN 9997

First Floor:
1,613 square feet
Second Floor:
1,546 square feet
Total:
3,159 square feet

DESIGN 9999

Square Footage: 2,721

Porch

Breakfast
16'-3"x11'-0"

Bedroom No. 3
15'-3"x14'-3"

Great Room
21'-0"x18'-0"

Kitchen
16'-3"x12'-9"

Master Bedroom
13'-3"x18'-0"

dn.

Foyer

Dining Room
15'-0"x12'-0"

up

Bedroom No. 2
15'-3"x16'-0"

Porch

Width 69'-3"
Depth 79'-3"

Two Car Garage
22'-3"x24'-9"

A satisfying blend of shingles and wood trim complements a box-bay window and a Palladian-style clerestory on this stylish farmhouse. A formal dining room invites planned events, but the grand great room, with a focal-point fireplace, built-in cabinetry and double doors to the rear porch, welcomes any occasion. A split bedroom plan affords seclusion to the master suite, which offers a spacious private bath and a wall of windows for natural light. On the opposite side of the plan, two family bedrooms share a gallery hall and a full bath. This home is designed with a basement foundation.

Design by
Design Traditions

© Design Traditions

© *Design Traditions*

This traditional home features board-and-batten and cedar shingles in a well-proportioned exterior. The foyer opens to the dining room and leads to the great room, which offers French doors to the rear columned porch. An additional bedroom, or study, shares a full bath with a family bedroom, while the lavish master suite enjoys a private bath with two walk-in closets, two vanities, a whirlpool tub and a compartmented toilet. The kitchen overlooks a bayed breakfast area and shares views of the outdoors with the great room. A fourth bedroom, home office or guest suite nestles to the rear of the plan and is handy to the laundry. This home is designed with a basement foundation.

Design by
Design Traditions

DESIGN 9853

Square Footage: 2,090

QUOTE ONE®

Cost to build? See page 230
to order complete cost estimate
to build this house in your area!

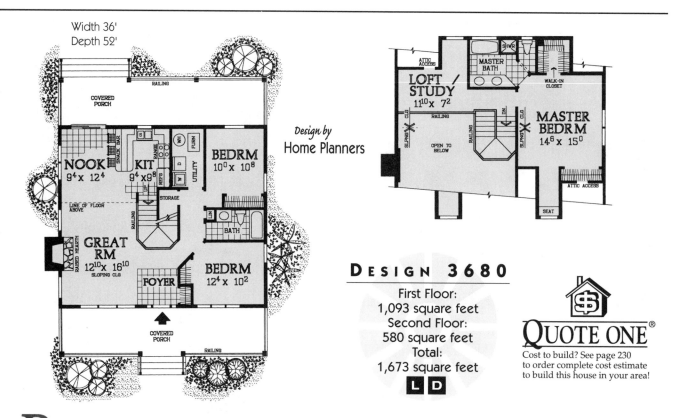

Width 36'
Depth 52'

COVERED PORCH

NOOK
9⁴ x 12⁴

KIT
9⁴ x 9⁸

BEDRM
10⁰ x 10⁸

RANGE
FURN
WH

SNACK BAR

LINE OF FLOOR ABOVE

STORAGE

UTILITY

GREAT RM
12¹⁰ x 16¹⁰
SLOPING CLG

RAISED HEARTH

BATH

FOYER

BEDRM
12⁴ x 10²

COVERED PORCH

RAILING

Design by
Home Planners

LOFT STUDY
11¹⁰ x 7²

ATTIC ACCESS

MASTER BATH

SHWR

WALK-IN CLOSET

RAILING

OPEN TO BELOW

MASTER BEDRM
14⁶ x 15⁰

ATTIC ACCESS

SEAT

DESIGN 3680

First Floor:
1,093 square feet
Second Floor:
580 square feet
Total:
1,673 square feet

L D

QUOTE ONE®

Cost to build? See page 230
to order complete cost estimate
to build this house in your area!

Brackets and balustrades on front and rear covered porches spell old fashioned country charm on this rustic retreat. Warm evenings will invite family and guests outdoors for watching sunsets and stars. In cooler weather, the raised-hearth fireplace will make the great room a cozy place to gather. The nearby well-appointed kitchen serves both snack bar and breakfast nook. Two family bedrooms and a full bath complete the main level. Upstairs, a master bedroom with sloped ceiling offers a secluded window seat and a complete bath with garden tub, separate shower and twin lavatories. The adjacent loft/study overlooks the great room and shares the glow of the fireplace.

Here's a great country farmhouse with a lot of appeal—Palladian and arch topped windows make a sweet complement to a classic wraparound porch. If you prefer the rustic look of a log home, select Design 3683. Or Design 3681 provides a more traditional option. The generous use of windows—including two sets of triple muntin windows in the front—adds exciting visual elements to the exterior as well as plenty of natural light to the interior. An impressive tiled entry opens to a two-story great room with a raised hearth and views to the front and side grounds. The U-shaped kitchen offers a snack counter in addition to a casual dining nook with rear porch access. The family bedrooms reside on the main floor, while an expansive master suite with adjacent study creates a resplendent retreat upstairs, complete with a private balcony, walk-in closet and pampering bath.

Width 52'
Depth 46'

Design by
Home Planners

Design 3681

QUOTE ONE®

Cost to build? See page 230 to order complete cost estimate to build this house in your area!

D E S I G N
3 6 8 1 / 3 6 8 3

First Floor:
1,039/1,139 square feet
Second Floor:
576 square feet
Total:
1,669/1,715 square feet

L **D**

Design 3683

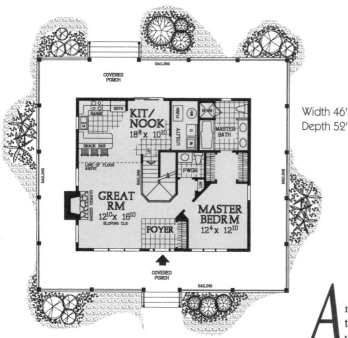

Width 46'
Depth 52'

Quote One®

Cost to build? See page 230
to order complete cost estimate
to build this house in your area!

DESIGN 3682

First Floor:
1,093 square feet
Second Floor:
603 square feet
Total:
1,696 square feet

Design by
Home Planners

A rustic country style combined with contemporary livability set this plan apart from the rest. Arch-topped dormer windows and a wraparound porch with a balustrade create a welcoming exterior, but the real charm begins within. A tiled foyer opens to a two-story great room with sloped ceiling, raised-hearth fireplace and views of the front property through triple windows. The tiled kitchen and windowed eating nook offer a snack bar, open to the great room, and access to the rear covered porch. An impressive master suite with a walk-in closet, garden tub and separate shower, is snugly tucked away to the side of the first-floor plan. Upstairs, two additional bedrooms and a loft/study with dormer window seat share a full bath as well as the view below to the great room.

This lovely home wears a gently European flavored exterior, dressed to impress with a stone-and-stucco blend and a columned entry. The great room features a cathedral ceiling and adjoins a sunny breakfast room with a private porch. The kitchen provides plenty of wrapping counter space, a pantry and a cooktop peninsula that overlooks the casual eating area. A separate utility room has built-in cabinets and a countertop with a laundry sink. Double doors lead into the first-floor master suite, which offers a box-bay window, two walk-in closets and a lavish bath. Two family bedrooms are located upstairs with a full bath, linen storage and a skylit bonus room.

DESIGN 7643

First Floor:
1,572 square feet
Second Floor:
549 square feet
Total:
2,121 square feet

Width 59'-4"
Depth 53'-11"

Design by
Donald A. Gardner
Architects, Inc.

© 1997 Donald A. Gardner Architects, Inc.

© 1996 Donald A. Gardner Architects, Inc.

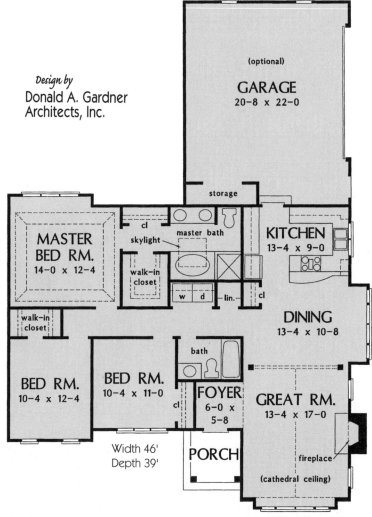

Three box-bay windows dress up a hip roof on this stunning stucco exterior. A contemporary floor plan offers an open, airy feel with a cathedral ceiling and a colonnaded opening in the great room. A fireplace warms this common area, designed for family gatherings as well as planned events. The master suite boasts a U-shaped walk-in closet, a dressing area and a sensational private bath with a whirlpool tub and a skylight. A hall bath serves two family bedrooms, one with its own walk-in closet. The side-entry garage offers a service entrance to the kitchen and additional storage space.

Design by
Donald A. Gardner
Architects, Inc.

GARAGE
20-8 x 22-0
(optional)

storage

master bath
cl
skylight

KITCHEN
13-4 x 9-0

MASTER
BED RM.
14-0 x 12-4

walk-in
closet

w   d   lin.   cl

DINING
13-4 x 10-8

walk-in
closet

bath

BED RM.
10-4 x 12-4

BED RM.
10-4 x 11-0

FOYER
6-0 x
5-8

cl

GREAT RM.
13-4 x 17-0

fireplace

DESIGN 7635
Square Footage: 1,417

Width 46'
Depth 39'

PORCH

(cathedral ceiling)

© 1996 Donald A. Gardner Architects, Inc.

B. NATHAN

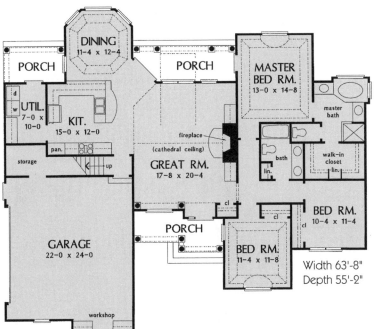

PORCH

DINING
11-4 x 12-4

PORCH

MASTER
BED RM.
13-0 x 14-8

master
bath

UTIL.
7-0 x
10-0

KIT.
15-0 x 12-0

fireplace

(cathedral ceiling)

walk-in
closet

pan.

storage

up

GREAT RM.
17-8 x 20-4

bath

lin.

BED RM.
10-4 x 11-4

cl

GARAGE
22-0 x 24-0

PORCH

cl

BED RM.
11-4 x 11-8

Width 63'-8"
Depth 55'-2"

workshop

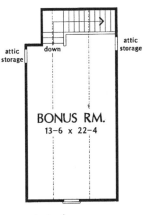

attic
storage

down

attic
storage

BONUS RM.
13-6 x 22-4

Design by
Donald A. Gardner
Architects, Inc.

Keystone arches, asymmetrical gables and a stunning stucco exterior lend European sophistication to this great plan. The interior starts with an expansive great room, which features an extended-hearth fireplace and views to the outdoors. The U-shaped kitchen serves a spectacular dining room, with bay-window views that feast the soul. A private master suite nestles to the rear of the plan and offers a tray ceiling and a lavish bath with a garden tub, twin vanities and a corner whirlpool tub. Two additional bedrooms share a full bath nearby, while upstairs bonus space is available for future development.

DESIGN 7634

Square Footage: 1,699
Bonus Room:
386 square feet

DESIGN 3664

Square Footage: 2,471

L

Width 86'-4"
Depth 80'-2"

Capstones, quoins and gentle arches lend an unpretentious spirit to this European-style plan. A vaulted entry introduces an unrestrained floor plan designed for comfort. The tiled gallery opens to a sizable great room that invites casual entertaining and features a handsome fireplace with an extended hearth, framed with decorative niches. The kitchen features a cooktop island and a built-in desk, and opens to a windowed breakfast bay which lets in natural light. For formal occasions, a great dining room permits quiet, unhurried evening meals. Relaxation awaits the homeowner in a sensational master suite, with an inner retreat and a private patio. Two family bedrooms share a private bath, and one room opens to a covered patio. A golf cart will easily fit into a side garage, which adjoins a roomy two-car garage that loads from the opposite side.

QUOTE ONE®

Cost to build? See page 230
to order complete cost estimate
to build this house in your area!

Design by
Home Planners

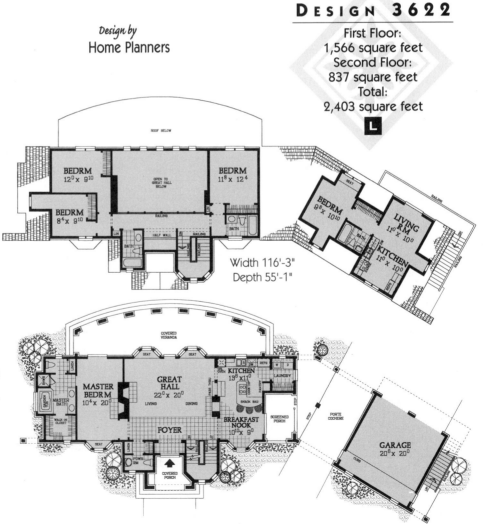

Brick detailing, corner quoins and graceful arches all work to create a European-style exterior that's simply elegant. A tiled foyer opens to a two-story great hall which offers a fireplace that warms living and dining areas, and two window seats that enjoy views to the rear property. Distinctive details coveted in older homes highlight the interior—such as the extended-hearth fireplace and the bayed window seat in the master suite. Three second-level family bedrooms share two full baths and a balcony overlook to the great hall. This plan offers an optional apartment, which might be used as income property, a guest suite, or separate lodging for relatives.

Design by
Home Planners

DESIGN 3622

First Floor:
1,566 square feet
Second Floor:
837 square feet
Total:
2,403 square feet

L

Width 116'-3"
Depth 55'-1"

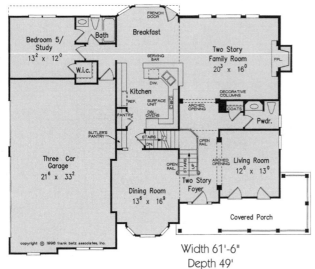

Bedroom 5/ Study
13² x 12⁰

Bath

Breakfast

FRENCH DOOR

W.i.c.

SERVING BAR

Two Story Family Room
20³ x 16⁰

FPL

DW.

Kitchen

SURFACE UNIT

REF.

DECORATIVE COLUMNS

ARCHED OPENING

DBL. OVENS

PANTRY

COATS

Pwdr.

BUTLER'S PANTRY

STAIRS DN.

OPEN RAIL

Three Car Garage
21⁶ x 33²

OPEN RAIL

STAIRS

ARCHED OPENING

Living Room
12⁰ x 13⁰

Dining Room
13⁶ x 16⁹

Two Story Foyer

Covered Porch

copyright © 1998 frank betz associates, inc.

Width 61'-6"
Depth 49'

DESIGN P249

First Floor:
1,615 square feet
Second Floor:
1,763 square feet
Total:
3,378 square feet

Design by
**Frank Betz
Associates, Inc.**

Asymmetrical gables set off a fresh blend of shingles and siding on this Victorian adaptation. An up-to-date interior offers amenities that draw on the future, starting with a balcony bridge that overlooks both the foyer and the family room. The second-floor master bedroom features a sitting area with French doors to a lavish bath. An additional bedroom, or guest suite, offers a private bath, while two family bedrooms share a full bath. Please specify basement or crawlspace foundation when ordering.

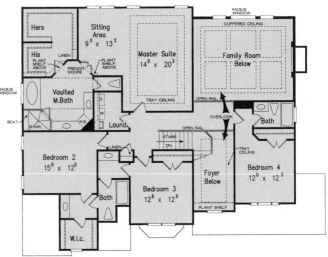

Hers

Sitting Area
9⁰ x 13²

RADIUS WINDOW

COFFERED CEILING

His

LINEN

PLANT SHELF ABOVE

FRENCH DOORS

PLANT SHELF ABOVE

Master Suite
14⁰ x 20³

Family Room Below

RADIUS WINDOW

Vaulted M.Bath

D.

W.

TRAY CEILING

OPEN RAIL

SEAT

SHWR.

K.S.

Laund.

OVERLOOK

Bath

Bedroom 2
15⁰ x 12⁰

LINEN

OPEN RAIL

STAIRS DN.

OPEN RAIL

Bedroom 4
12⁰ x 12³

TRAY CEILING

Bath

Bedroom 3
12⁶ x 12⁰

Foyer Below

PLANT SHELF

W.i.c.

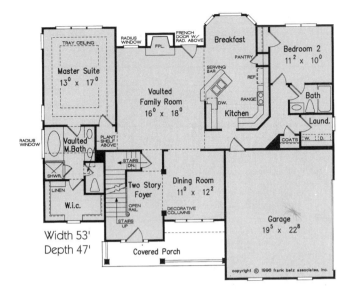

Master Suite
13⁰ x 17⁰

Width 53'
Depth 47'

Breakfast

Bedroom 2
11² x 10⁰

Vaulted Family Room
16⁰ x 18⁰

Bath

Laund.

Vaulted M.Bath

Two Story Foyer

Dining Room
11⁰ x 12²

Garage
19⁵ x 22⁸

Covered Porch

copyright © 1996 frank betz associates, inc.

DESIGN P184

First Floor:
1,583 square feet
Second Floor:
543 square feet
Total:
2,126 square feet

Design by
Frank Betz Associates, Inc.

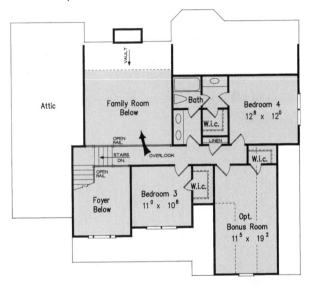

Attic

Family Room Below

Bath

Bedroom 4
12⁸ x 12⁰

Foyer Below

Bedroom 3
11⁰ x 10⁸

Opt. Bonus Room
11⁵ x 19²

*H*ere's a new country home with a fresh face and a dash of Victoriana. Inside, decorative columns help define an elegant dining room, but the heart of the home is the vaulted family room with a radius window and a French door to the rear property. The first-floor master suite features a private bath with a vaulted ceiling and a whirlpool tub. On the opposite side of the plan, an additional bedroom or guest suite offers its own full bath. Upstairs, two family bedrooms share a full bath and a gallery hall with a balcony overlook to the family room. Please specify basement or crawlspace foundation when ordering.

© Design Traditions

Design by
Design Traditions

DESIGN 9884
Square Footage: 2,120

Graceful arches accent this traditional facade and announce a floor plan that's just a little different than the rest. The foyer, formal dining room and an expansive family room, with a centered fireplace flanked by picture windows, are open to one another through columned archways. The master suite offers a coffered ceiling and a plush bath with a dressing area, as well as a private den. An island kitchen and breakfast room enjoy views through the spectacular sun room. This home is designed with a basement foundation.

QUOTE ONE®
Cost to build? See page 230
to order complete cost estimate
to build this house in your area!

DESIGN 9894

Square Footage: 1,733

DECK

Width 55'-6"
Depth 57'-6"

BREAKFAST
11'-4" X 8'-6"

BEDROOM NO. 3
11'-6" X 11'-0"

GREAT ROOM
14'-0" X 17'-6"

KITCHEN
11'-4" X 10'-0"

MASTER
BEDROOM
12'-4" X 15'-6"

BATH

FOYER
6'-6" X 6'-6"

DN

HIS

MASTER
BATH

BEDROOM NO. 2
11'-0" X 14'-8"

DINING ROOM
11'-4" X 10'-6"

PWDR.

HERS

LAUNDRY

TWO-CAR GARAGE
20'-4" X 19'-4"

*D*elightfully different, this brick one-story home has everything for the active family. The foyer opens to a formal dining room accented with decorative columns, and to a great room with warming fireplace and lovely French doors to the rear deck. The efficient kitchen adjoins a light-filled breakfast nook. A split bedroom plan offers a secluded master suite with coffered ceiling, His and Hers walk-in closets, double vanity and garden tub. Two family bedrooms, or one and a study, have separate access to a full bath on the left side of the plan. This home is designed with a basement foundation.

Design by
Design Traditions

QUOTE ONE®

Cost to build? See page 230 to order complete cost estimate to build this house in your area!

© *Design Traditions*

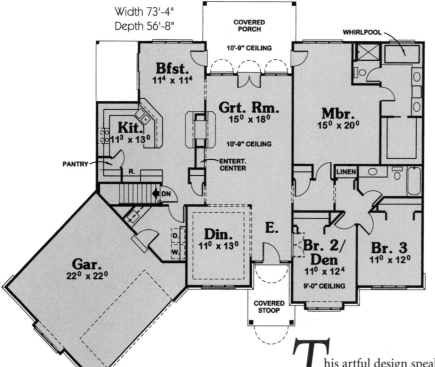

Width 73'-4"
Depth 56'-8"

COVERED PORCH
10'-9" CEILING

WHIRLPOOL

Bfst.
11⁴ x 11⁴

Grt. Rm.
15⁰ x 18⁰

10'-9" CEILING

Mbr.
15⁰ x 20⁰

Kit.
11³ x 13⁰

PANTRY

ENTERT. CENTER

R.

DN

LINEN

D.
W.

Din.
11⁰ x 13⁰

E.

Br. 2/
Den
11⁰ x 12⁴

9'-0" CEILING

Br. 3
11⁰ x 12⁰

Gar.
22⁰ x 22⁰

COVERED STOOP

DESIGN 7320

Square Footage: 2,057

Design by
Design Basics, Inc.

This artful design speaks volumes about European charm, with a stucco veneer and an arch-top entry. A central great room features French doors to the back covered porch and a see-through fireplace it shares with the kitchen, which boasts a walk-in pantry. An elegant formal dining room opens to the great room and enjoys easy access from the kitchen. The master suite provides a whirlpool bath and private access to the back covered porch. One of two additional bedrooms to the front of the plan offers the option of a den, which would expand the living space of the home.

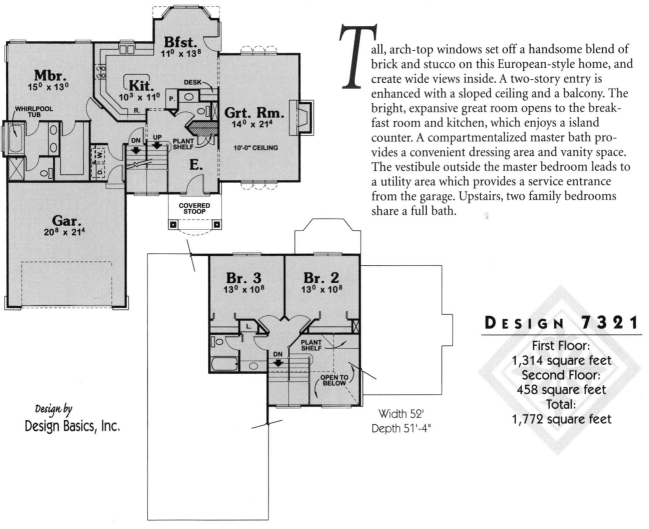

Bfst.
11⁰ x 13⁸

Mbr.
15⁰ x 13⁰

WHIRLPOOL
TUB

Kit.
10³ x 11⁰

DESK

P.

R.

Grt. Rm.
14⁰ x 21⁴

10'-0" CEILING

DN   UP

PLANT
SHELF

E.

D. W.

Gar.
20⁸ x 21⁴

COVERED
STOOP

*T*all, arch-top windows set off a handsome blend of brick and stucco on this European-style home, and create wide views inside. A two-story entry is enhanced with a sloped ceiling and a balcony. The bright, expansive great room opens to the breakfast room and kitchen, which enjoys a island counter. A compartmentalized master bath provides a convenient dressing area and vanity space. The vestibule outside the master bedroom leads to a utility area which provides a service entrance from the garage. Upstairs, two family bedrooms share a full bath.

Br. 3
13⁰ x 10⁸

Br. 2
13⁰ x 10⁸

L.

PLANT
SHELF

DN

OPEN TO
BELOW

Width 52'
Depth 51'-4"

Design by
Design Basics, Inc.

DESIGN 7321

First Floor:
1,314 square feet
Second Floor:
458 square feet
Total:
1,772 square feet

DESIGN 8048

First Floor:
2,469 square feet
Second Floor:
1,025 square feet
Total:
3,494 square feet

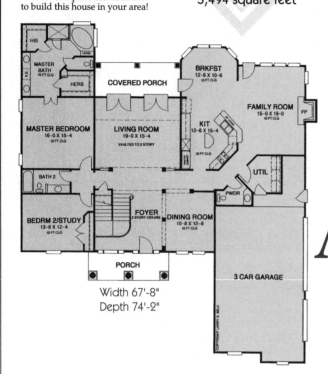

Width 67'-8"
Depth 74'-2"

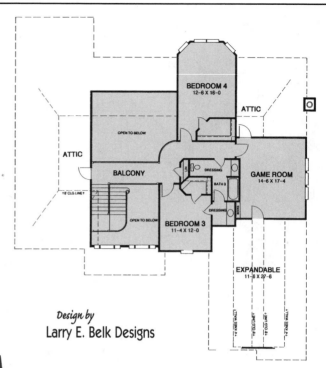

Design by
Larry E. Belk Designs

A double arch gives this European-style home a commanding presence. Inside, elegant square columns define the formal dining room and lend a spacious feeling to the formal area. An island kitchen and bayed breakfast room overlook the family room, which offers a focal-point fireplace and an array of windows that let in natural light. The master suite features two walk-in closets, a corner garden tub and a separate shower. A second bedroom—which could double as a nursery or study—and a full bath are nearby. Upstairs, two bedrooms and a bath with two dressing areas share a gallery hall that leads to an expansive game room. Please specify crawlspace or slab foundation when ordering.

COPYRIGHT 1993 LARRY E. BELK

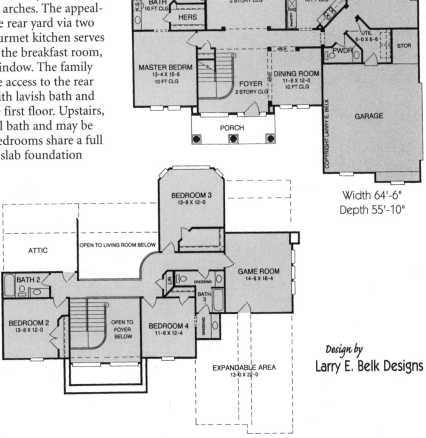

An entry framed by Doric columns and elegant arches topped off with capstones creates a warm welcome to this contemporary European-style home. Inside, the formal dining room to the right of the foyer is defined by yet another set of columns and arches. The appealing living room offers access to the rear yard via two sets of double French doors. A gourmet kitchen serves the formal dining room as well as the breakfast room, which offers a bumped-out bay window. The family room offers a fireplace and private access to the rear porch. The deluxe master suite, with lavish bath and two walk-in closets, completes the first floor. Upstairs, a large bedroom offers its own full bath and may be used as a guest suite. Two other bedrooms share a full bath. Please specify crawlspace or slab foundation when ordering.

Width 64'-6"
Depth 55'-10"

DESIGN 8186

First Floor:
1,919 square feet
Second Floor:
1,190 square feet
Total:
3,109 square feet

Design by
Larry E. Belk Designs

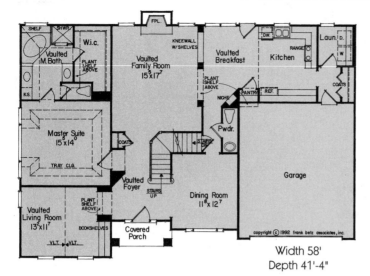

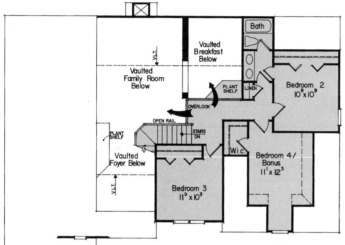

Width 58'
Depth 41'-4"

DESIGN P112

First Floor:
1,637 square feet
Second Floor:
671 square feet
Total:
2,308 square feet

Varied rooflines, keystones and arches set off a stucco exterior that's highlighted by stone accents. Inside, the vaulted living room enjoys built-in bookshelves, while the formal dining room is well lit by an arch-top transom window. The foyer leads to the family room with a centered fireplace flanked by windows that offer wide views of the outdoors. Sleeping quarters include a first-floor master suite with a vaulted bath. Please specify basement or crawl-space foundation when ordering.

Design by
**Frank Betz
Associates, Inc.**

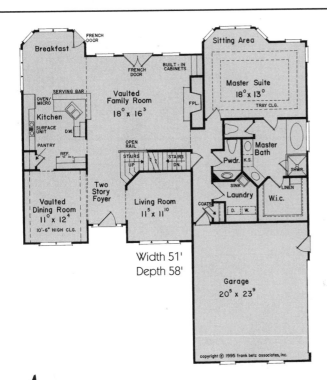

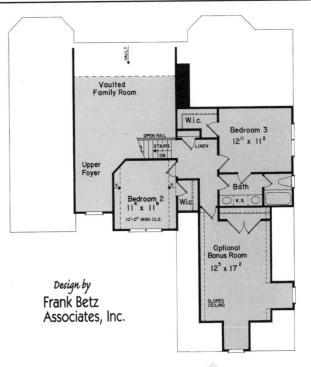

Design by
Frank Betz Associates, Inc.

Width 51'
Depth 58'

A charming stone-and-stucco facade lends a European flavor to this country home. The two-story foyer opens to the formal rooms and leads to an expansive, vaulted family room made cozy by an extended-hearth fireplace and French doors to the rear property. The first-floor master suite has a bayed sitting area and a private bath with a windowed tub and separate shower. The kitchen shares a serving bar with the breakfast room, which offers wide views through a plentitude of windows. Two second-floor family bedrooms share a full bath. Please specify basement or crawlspace foundation when ordering.

DESIGN P263

First Floor:
1,682 square feet
Second Floor:
516 square feet
Total:
2,198 square feet

© Design Traditions

Design by
Design Traditions

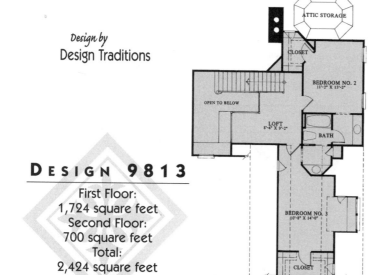

DESIGN 9813

First Floor:
1,724 square feet
Second Floor:
700 square feet
Total:
2,424 square feet

Width 47'-10"
Depth 63'-10"

Quote One®

Cost to build? See page 230
to order complete cost estimate
to build this house in your area!

This cozy English home might be found hidden away in a European garden. Gables, stonework and multi-level rooflines create a charming exterior. Inside, a sunlit dining room is highlighted by a dramatic tray ceiling and transom windows. Formal areas flow into one another to create a perfect open area for entertaining. The gourmet kitchen offers a work island, oversize pantry and a bright octagonal breakfast room. The great room features a pass-through wet bar, a fireplace and built-in cabinetry. The first-floor master suite enjoys privacy nestled to the rear of the plan. An open-rail loft above the foyer leads to additional bedrooms with walk-in closets, private vanities and a shared bath. This home is designed with a basement foundation.

DESIGN 9816

First Floor:
1,900 square feet
Second Floor:
800 square feet
Total:
2,700 square feet

Width 63'
Depth 51'

QUOTE ONE®

Cost to build? See page 230
to order complete cost estimate
to build this house in your area!

BEDROOM NO. 4
13'-4" X 11'-4"

OPEN TO BELOW

BEDROOM NO. 3
15'-0" X 12'-0"

BATH

BEDROOM NO. 2
12'-4" X 13'-6"

OPEN TO BELOW

Design by
Design Traditions

BREAKFAST
13'-6" X 10'-0"

KITCHEN
13'-4" X 16'-0"

GREAT ROOM
14'-6" X 15'-0"

MASTER BEDROOM
13'-4" X 17'-10"

LAUNDRY
8'-0" X 9'-0"

MASTER BATH
10'-8" X 16'-4"

W.I.C.

TWO CAR GARAGE
21'-4" X 21'-6"

DINING ROOM
12'-0" X 16'-0"

FOYER
7'-0" X 13'-0"

STUDY
11'-4" X 15'-2"

W.I.C.

A perfect blend of stucco and stacked stone sets off keystones, transoms and arches in this French country facade to inspire an elegant spirit. The foyer is flanked by the spacious dining room and study, accented by a vaulted ceiling and a fireplace. A great room with a full wall of glass connects the interior with the outdoors. A first-floor master suite offers both style and intimacy with a coffered ceiling and a secluded bath. Upstairs, three family bedrooms share a hall bath. This home is designed with a basement foundation.

© *Design Traditions*

© Design Traditions

Deck

Width 76'-6"
Depth 51'-6"

Breakfast
14⁶x10⁰

Office

Great Room
21³x17⁶

Master
Bedroom
14⁶x17⁰

Kitchen
14⁶x12⁰

Dn   Up

Two Car
Garage
21³x21⁰

Dining
Room
13⁰x15³

Foyer

Study
14³x13⁹

Design by
Design Traditions

DESIGN 9976

First Floor:
2,387 square feet
Second Floor:
1,518 square feet
Total:
3,905 square feet

T his impressive translation of European country style blends bright divided-light windows with Old World gables and cornices. Inside, a formal dining room and a study, or parlor, flank the elegant foyer, which leads to a casual living area. The great room opens through French doors to a rear deck that's also accessible from the breakfast nook. A first-floor secluded master suite enjoys luxurious amenities, while three family bedrooms share a balcony hall upstairs. This home is designed with a basement foundation.

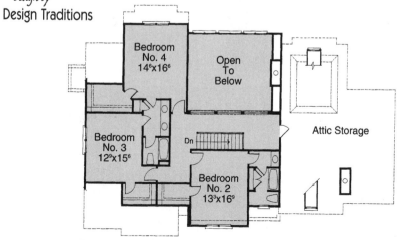

Bedroom
No. 4
14⁶x16⁶

Open
To
Below

Bedroom
No. 3
12⁹x15⁶

Dn

Attic Storage

Bedroom
No. 2
13³x16⁹

© Design Traditions

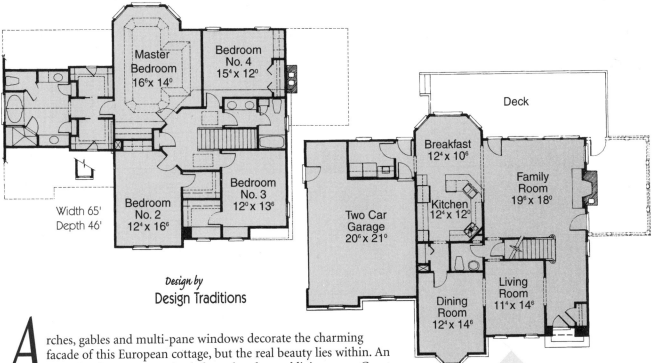

Master
Bedroom
16⁶ x 14⁰

Bedroom
No. 4
15⁴ x 12⁰

Bedroom
No. 2
12⁴ x 16⁶

Bedroom
No. 3
12⁰ x 13⁶

Width 65'
Depth 46'

Design by
Design Traditions

Deck

Breakfast
12⁴ x 10⁶

Family
Room
19⁶ x 18⁰

Kitchen
12⁴ x 12⁰

Two Car
Garage
20⁶ x 21⁰

Living
Room
11⁴ x 14⁶

Dining
Room
12⁴ x 14⁶

Arches, gables and multi-pane windows decorate the charming facade of this European cottage, but the real beauty lies within. An extensive foyer opens to both formal and casual living areas. Guests may want to linger in the stylish bayed dining room, but coax them back to a more comfortable space near the fireplace in the family room. The nearby kitchen offers an angled counter and a breakfast nook which promises a warm bath of sunshine in the morning. A split bedroom plan upstairs affords privacy to the master suite—a comfortable retreat for the homeowner, with His and Hers walk-in closets, dual vanities and whirlpool tub. Three family bedrooms share a generous hall bath. This home is designed with a basement foundation.

DESIGN 7815

First Floor:
1,383 square feet
Second Floor:
1,576 square feet
Total:
2,959 square feet

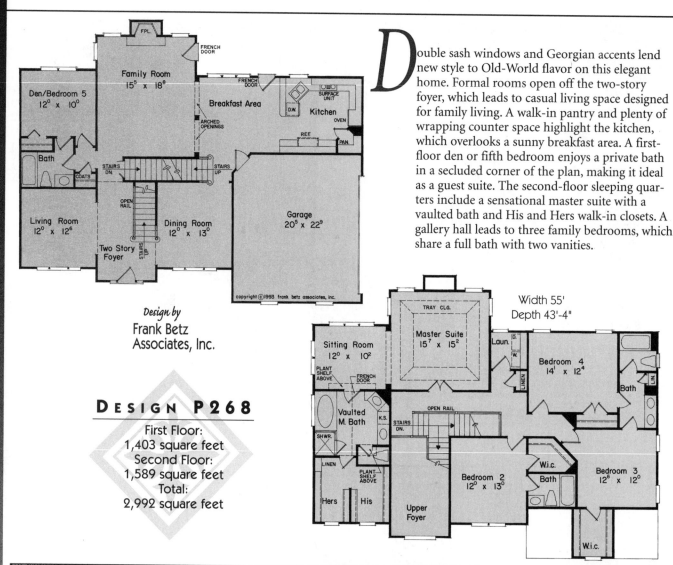

Family Room
15⁵ x 18⁸

FPL.

FRENCH DOOR

FRENCH DOOR

Den/Bedroom 5
12⁰ x 10⁰

Breakfast Area

SURFACE UNIT

D.W.

Kitchen

OVEN

Bath

ARCHED OPENINGS

REF.

PAN.

STAIRS DN.

STAIRS UP

COATS

OPEN RAIL

Living Room
12⁰ x 12⁶

Garage
20⁵ x 22⁹

Dining Room
12⁰ x 13⁰

Two Story Foyer

STAIRS UP

copyright © 1993 frank betz associates, inc.

Design by

Frank Betz
Associates, Inc.

DESIGN P268

First Floor:
1,403 square feet
Second Floor:
1,589 square feet
Total:
2,992 square feet

TRAY CLG.

Master Suite
15⁷ x 15²

Width 55'
Depth 43'-4"

Sitting Room
12⁰ x 10²

Laun.

Bedroom 4
14¹ x 12⁴

PLANT SHELF ABOVE

FRENCH DOOR

LINEN

Bath

LIN.

Vaulted M. Bath

K.S.

OPEN RAIL

SHWR.

STAIRS DN.

LINEN

PLANT SHELF ABOVE

W.i.c.

Bedroom 3
12⁶ x 12⁰

Hers

His

Bedroom 2
12⁶ x 13⁰

Bath

Upper Foyer

W.i.c.

*D*ouble sash windows and Georgian accents lend new style to Old-World flavor on this elegant home. Formal rooms open off the two-story foyer, which leads to casual living space designed for family living. A walk-in pantry and plenty of wrapping counter space highlight the kitchen, which overlooks a sunny breakfast area. A first-floor den or fifth bedroom enjoys a private bath in a secluded corner of the plan, making it ideal as a guest suite. The second-floor sleeping quarters include a sensational master suite with a vaulted bath and His and Hers walk-in closets. A gallery hall leads to three family bedrooms, which share a full bath with two vanities.

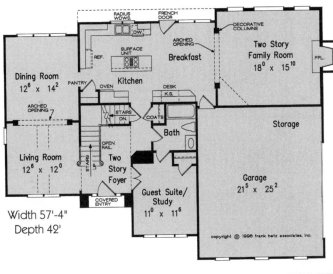

Width 57'-4"
Depth 42'

RADIUS WDWS.
FRENCH DOOR
DECORATIVE COLUMNS
DW.
ARCHED OPENING
Two Story Family Room 18⁰ x 15¹⁰
REF.
SURFACE UNIT
Breakfast
FPL.
Dining Room 12⁶ x 14²
PANTRY
OVEN
Kitchen
DESK
K.S.
ARCHED OPENING
STAIRS DN.
COATS
Storage
OPEN RAIL
Bath
Living Room 12⁶ x 12⁰
STAIRS UP
Two Story Foyer
Garage 21⁵ x 25²
Guest Suite/Study 11⁰ x 11⁶
COVERED ENTRY

copyright © 1996 frank betz associates, inc.

D E S I G N P 2 2 9

First Floor:
1,374 square feet
Second Floor:
1,311 square feet
Total:
2,685 square feet

Design by
Frank Betz Associates, Inc.

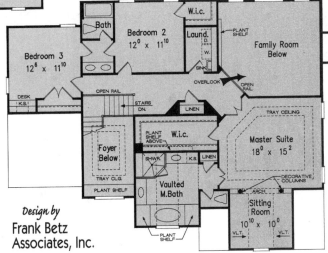

RADIUS WINDOW
W.i.c.
Bath
Bedroom 2 12⁰ x 11¹⁰
Laund.
PLANT SHELF
Family Room Below
Bedroom 3 12⁶ x 11¹⁰
SINK
OVERLOOK
DESK
K.S.
OPEN RAIL
STAIRS DN.
LINEN
OPEN RAIL
TRAY CEILING
PLANT SHELF ABOVE
W.i.c.
Foyer Below
SHWR.
K.S.
LINEN
Master Suite 18⁰ x 15²
TRAY CLG.
PLANT SHELF
Vaulted M.Bath
DECORATIVE COLUMNS
ARCH.
PLANT SHELF
Sitting Room 10¹⁰ x 10⁰
VLT.
VLT.

*C*harming French accents create an inviting facade on this country home. An arched opening set off by decorative columns introduces a two-story family room with a fireplace and a radius window. The gourmet kitchen features an island cooktop counter, a planning desk and a roomy breakfast area with a French door to the back property. The second-floor master suite offers a secluded sitting room, a tray ceiling in the bedroom and a lavish bath with an oversized corner shower. Two family bedrooms share a gallery hall with a balcony overlook to the family room. Please specify basement or crawlspace foundation when ordering.

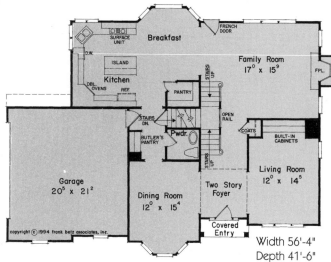

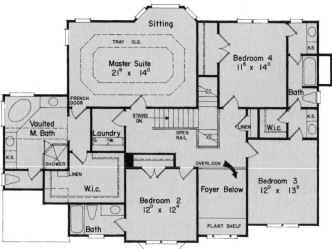

DESIGN P269

First Floor:
1,335 square feet
Second Floor:
1,585 square feet
Total:
2,920 square feet

Design by
**Frank Betz
Associates, Inc.**

Width 56'-4"
Depth 41'-6"

Here's a lovely European-style design with room for a growing family. Second-floor sleeping quarters include a sumptuous master suite with a sitting bay and a lavish vaulted bath with a corner tub and an angled shower. Three sizable secondary bedrooms, one with a private bath, share a hall with a balcony overlook to the foyer. The first floor places formal rooms to the front of the plan. An elegant dining room is served through a butler's pantry by a gourmet kitchen with an island counter. A fireplace and a French door to the back property highlight the family room, while the living room features built-in cabinets.

DESIGN P245

First Floor:
1,267 square feet
Second Floor:
1,568 square feet
Total:
2,835 square feet

Design by
**Frank Betz
Associates, Inc.**

Decorative cornices and capstones splash this New-World home with a taste of Old-World flavor. Inside, a two-story foyer opens to the formal dining room and the living room, which features French doors to the family's living space. This area is highlighted by a centered fireplace flanked by windows. The two-story breakfast room offers a bayed nook and opens to the gourmet kitchen, which features a serving bar and a radius window above the double sink. A spacious sitting area, a garden tub and a sizable walk-in closet make the master suite a relaxing retreat. A full bath with two lavatories serves two family bedrooms, while an additional bedroom provides a private bath. Please specify basement, slab or crawlspace foundation when ordering.

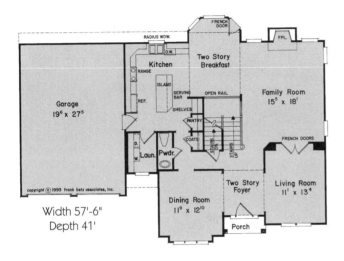

Width 57'-6"
Depth 41'

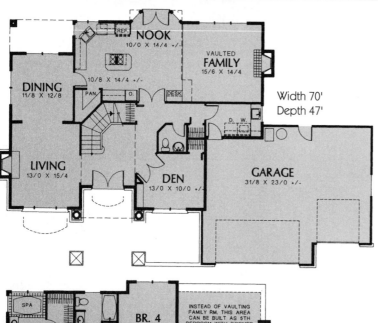

NOOK
10/0 X 14/4 +/-

VAULTED
FAMILY
15/6 X 14/4

DINING
11/8 X 12/8

10/8 X 14/4 +/-

DESK

LIVING
13/0 X 15/4

DEN
13/0 X 10/0 +/-

GARAGE
31/8 X 23/0 +/-

Width 70'
Depth 47'

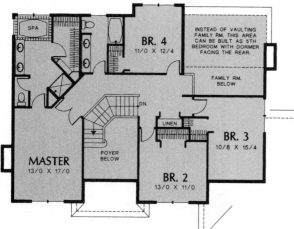

SPA

BR. 4
11/0 X 12/4

INSTEAD OF VAULTING
FAMILY RM. THIS AREA
CAN BE BUILT AS 5TH
BEDROOM WITH DORMER
FACING THE REAR.

FAMILY RM.
BELOW

LINEN

BR. 3
10/8 X 15/4

MASTER
13/0 X 17/0

FOYER
BELOW

DN.

BR. 2
13/0 X 11/0

Design by
**Alan Mascord
Design Associates, Inc.**

DESIGN 9597

First Floor:
1,470 square feet
Second Floor:
1,269 square feet
Total:
2,739 square feet

Multi-pane glass windows, double French doors and an arched pediment with columns create a spectacular stucco exterior with this blue-ribbon European design. A two-story foyer opens to formal areas and through French doors to a secluded den with built-in cabinetry. Casual living space is defined by interior French doors that open to the morning nook and kitchen. The vaulted family room offers a fireplace with an extended tile hearth and sliding-glass door access to the rear property. Second-floor sleeping quarters include a master suite with a tile-rimmed spa tub, twin vanities and a walk-in closet, and three family bedrooms which share a full bath and a gallery hall with a balcony overlook. This plan offers the option of replacing the family room's vaulted ceiling with a fifth bedroom above.

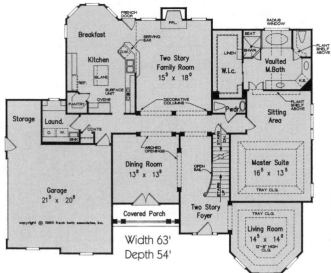

DESIGN P118

First Floor:
2,044 square feet
Second Floor:
896 square feet
Total:
2,940 square feet

Design by
Frank Betz
Associates, Inc.

Width 63'
Depth 54'

Varied rooflines, keystones and arches set off a stucco exterior that's highlighted by a turret with three divided-light windows. Inside, the formal living room enjoys a tray ceiling and floor-to-ceiling light from the turret's windows. The formal dining room leads to a private covered porch for after-dinner conversation on pleasant evenings. Sleeping quarters include a first-floor master suite with a vaulted bath and a sitting area with a plant shelf, and three second-floor family bedrooms which share a balcony overlook. Please specify basement or crawl-space foundation when ordering.

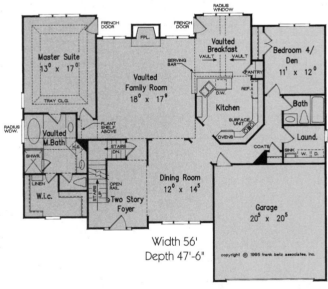

French Door
French Door
RADIUS WINDOW
FPL.
Master Suite 13⁰ x 17⁰
Vaulted Breakfast
VAULT
VAULT
SERVING BAR
Bedroom 4/ Den 11' x 12⁰
TRAY CLG.
Vaulted Family Room 18⁰ x 17⁹
D.W.
PANTRY
REF.
Kitchen
Bath
RADIUS WDW.
Vaulted M.Bath
PLANT SHELF ABOVE
SURFACE UNIT
OVENS
Laund.
SHWR.
STAIRS DN.
LINEN
COATS
SINK
W. D.
W.i.c.
OPEN RAIL
Dining Room 12⁰ x 14⁵
Two Story Foyer
Garage 20⁵ x 20⁵

Width 56'
Depth 47'-6"

copyright © 1995 frank betz associates, inc.

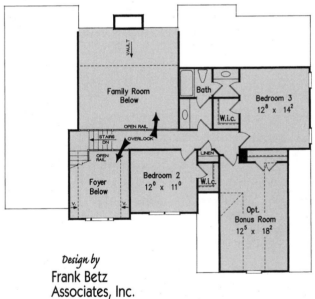

VAULT
Family Room Below
Bath
Bedroom 3 12⁸ x 14²
W.i.c.
OPEN RAIL
OVERLOOK
STAIRS DN
OPEN RAIL
Foyer Below
Bedroom 2 12⁰ x 11⁰
LINEN
W.i.c.
Opt. Bonus Room 12⁵ x 18²

Design by
**Frank Betz
Associates, Inc.**

Quoins and keystones complement arch-top windows and a glass-paneled entry on this European-style design. The heart of the home is a spacious family room with a centered fireplace flanked by windows. The nearby kitchen offers a serving bar that it shares with a vaulted breakfast room that features a radius window and a French door to the back property. A first-floor master suite with a vaulted bath features a tray ceiling and its own French door to the outside. Upstairs, two family bedrooms share a full bath and a gallery hall with overlooks to the family room and the foyer. Please specify basement or crawlspace foundation when ordering.

DESIGN P132
First Floor:
1,761 square feet
Second Floor:
580 square feet
Total:
2,341 square feet

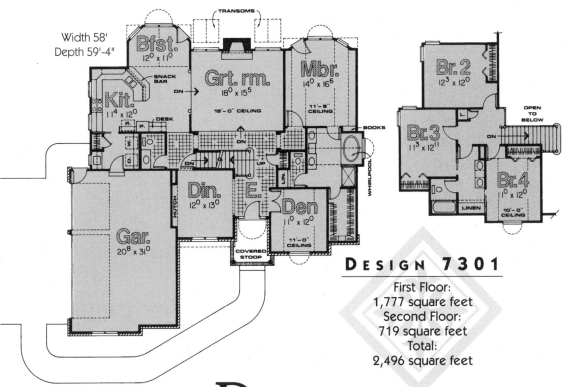

Width 58'
Depth 59'-4"

TRANSOMS

Bfst.
12⁰ x 11⁰

Grt. rm.
18⁰ x 15⁵
18'-0" CEILING

Mbr.
14⁰ x 16⁶
11'-8" CEILING

SNACK BAR

Kit.
11⁴ x 12⁰

DESK

BOOKS

WHIRLPOOL

Dom.
12⁰ x 13⁰

Den
11⁰ x 12⁰
11'-0" CEILING

Gar.
20⁸ x 31⁰

COVERED STOOP

Br. 2
12³ x 12⁰

OPEN TO BELOW

Br. 3
11³ x 12¹¹

Br. 4
11⁰ x 12⁰
10'-0" CEILING

LINEN

DESIGN 7301

First Floor:
1,777 square feet
Second Floor:
719 square feet
Total:
2,496 square feet

Design by
Design Basics, Inc.

Dramatic rooflines complement an arched pediment and columns, set off by a stunning, glass-paneled entry which highlights this traditional exterior. The tiled entry overlooks the formal dining room and opens to the den through French doors. The great room is down one step from the well-appointed kitchen and bayed breakfast area. A volume ceiling and a bay window highlight the master suite, and a central hall connects three family bedrooms upstairs.

DESIGN 7314

Design by
Design Basics, Inc.

First Floor:
2,041 square feet
Second Floor:
809 square feet
Total:
2,850 square feet

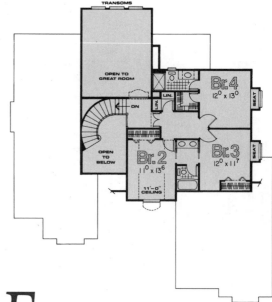

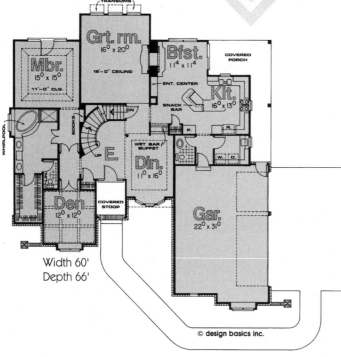

Width 60'
Depth 66'

© design basics inc.

*E*xquisite paneling, muntin windows and an arched entry create a classic exterior for this Tudor adaptation. Inside, an elegant curved staircase decorates the entry, which opens to the formal dining room. The great room features a through-fireplace shared with the breakfast area and kitchen. The master suite features a sumptuous bath with an angled whirlpool, a walk-in closet and a tiled, compartmented toilet. A gallery hall leads to a nearby den with a paneled ceiling. The second floor offers three additional bedrooms, one with a private bath.

This home, as shown in the photograph, may differ from the actual blueprints. For more detailed information, please check the floor plans carefully.

Photo by Bob Greenspan

DESIGN 9410

First Floor:
1,484 square feet
Second Floor:
1,402 square feet
Total:
2,886 square feet
Bonus Room:
430 square feet

Design by
Alan Mascord
Design Associates, Inc.

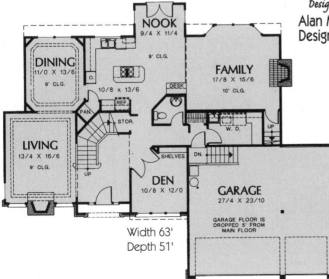

Width 63'
Depth 51'

This impressive Tudor is designed for lots that slope up slightly from the street—the garage is five feet below the main level. Just to the right of the entry, the den is arranged to work well as an office. Formal living areas include a living room with a fireplace and an elegant dining room. The family room also offers a fireplace and is close to the bumped-out nook. On the upper level, all the bedrooms are generously sized, and the master suite features a tray ceiling and a huge walk-in closet. A large vaulted bonus room is provided with convenient access from both the family room and the garage. Three family bedrooms and a full bath complete the upper level.

DESIGN 7266

First Floor:
1,631 square feet
Second Floor:
1,426 square feet
Total:
3,057 square feet

Stucco accents and graceful window treatments enhance this charming elevation. Off a tiled foyer, French doors open to a private den with a bright, bayed window. A spacious living room provides natural light through two sets of transom windows, and opens to a vestibule with French doors to an expansive screened veranda. The gourmet kitchen enjoys a bayed breakfast nook and offers a snack bar for easy meals. Upstairs, a fabulous master suite features a beautiful bay window, a dressing area with a built-in dresser, and a lavish bath with a corner whirlpool tub. Bedroom 2 enjoys a private bath, while Bedrooms 3 and 4 share a full bath with compartmented vanities.

Design by
Design Basics, Inc.

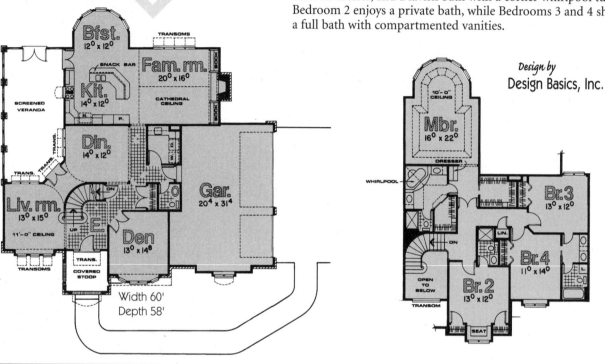

Width 60'
Depth 58'

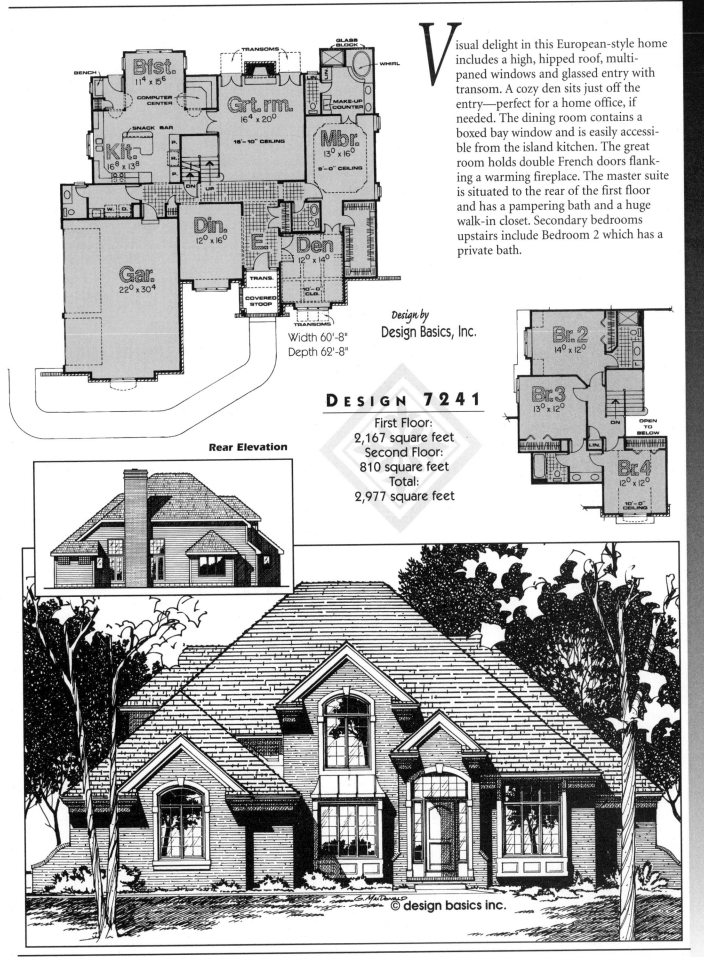

Bfst.
11⁴ x 15⁶

BENCH

COMPUTER
CENTER

SNACK BAR

Kit.
16⁸ x 13⁸

W.D.

Gar.
22⁰ x 30⁴

TRANSOMS

P.
R.
P.

DN   UP

Din.
12⁰ x 16⁰

E.

Grt. rm.
16⁴ x 20⁰

18'-10" CEILING

TRANS.

COVERED
STOOP

TRANSOMS

Den
12⁰ x 14⁰

10'-0"
CLG.

GLASS
BLOCK

WHIRL

LIN. LIN.

MAKE-UP
COUNTER

Mbr.
13⁰ x 16⁰

9'-0" CEILING

Width 60'-8"
Depth 62'-8"

Design by
Design Basics, Inc.

Br. 2
14⁰ x 12⁰

Br. 3
13⁰ x 12⁰

DN

OPEN
TO
BELOW

LIN.

Br. 4
12⁰ x 12⁰

10'-0"
CEILING

DESIGN 7241

First Floor:
2,167 square feet
Second Floor:
810 square feet
Total:
2,977 square feet

Visual delight in this European-style home includes a high, hipped roof, multi-paned windows and glassed entry with transom. A cozy den sits just off the entry—perfect for a home office, if needed. The dining room contains a boxed bay window and is easily accessible from the island kitchen. The great room holds double French doors flanking a warming fireplace. The master suite is situated to the rear of the first floor and has a pampering bath and a huge walk-in closet. Secondary bedrooms upstairs include Bedroom 2 which has a private bath.

Rear Elevation

© design basics inc.

Copyright 1992 Stephen S. Full

© Design Traditions

OPEN TO BELOW

BEDROOM NO. 3
11'-4" X 14'-0"

BATH

FUTURE BEDROOM NO. 4
10'-6" X 14'-0"

DN.

W.I.C.

W.I.C.

OPEN TO BELOW

BEDROOM NO. 2
11'-4" X 14'-0"

BATH

FUTURE W.I.C.

DESIGN 9877

First Floor:
1,660 square feet
Second Floor:
665 square feet
Total:
2,325 square feet

Design by
Design Traditions

QUOTE ONE®

Cost to build? See page 230 to order complete cost estimate to build this house in your area!

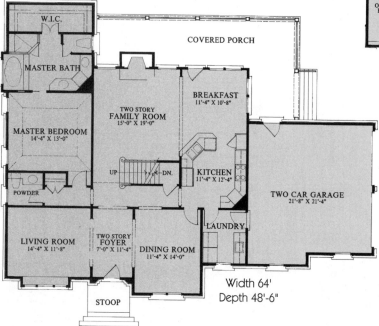

W.I.C.

MASTER BATH

MASTER BEDROOM
14'-4" X 13'-0"

POWDER

LIVING ROOM
14'-4" X 11'-8"

COVERED PORCH

TWO STORY FAMILY ROOM
15'-0" X 19'-0"

BREAKFAST
11'-4" X 10'-8"

UP ––– DN.

KITCHEN
11'-4" X 12'-4"

TWO CAR GARAGE
21'-8" X 21'-4"

TWO STORY FOYER
7'-0" X 11'-4"

DINING ROOM
11'-4" X 14'-0"

LAUNDRY

STOOP

Width 64'
Depth 48'-6"

Stately brick and jack-arch detailing create an exterior that may look established but this floor plan offers 21st-Century livability. A dramatic two-story entry is framed by formal living and dining areas. The family room ceiling soars above a cozy fireplace flanked by sensational views to the rear grounds. Nearby, the cheery breakfast nook allows rear covered porch access and opens to a kitchen loaded with modern amenities and positioned near the laundry room and garage. A coffered ceiling, sumptuous bath, His and Hers vanities and a walk-in closet highlight the master suite. Upstairs, two additional bedrooms, an optional fourth bedroom and two baths complete the plan. This home is designed with a basement foundation.

Width 50'
Depth 50'-6"

DECK

GUEST ROOM
13'-6" x 12'-0"

BREAKFAST
9'-4" x 10'-0"

FAMILY ROOM
19'-8" x 15'-4"

KITCHEN
15'-0" x 11'-8"

LAUNDRY
9'-8" x 5'-10"

PANTRY

DINING ROOM
14'-9" x 10'-9"

UP

DN

FOYER
6'-6" x 18'-8"

LIVING ROOM
12'-4" x 12'-7"

TWO-CAR GARAGE
21'-4" x 23'-4"

POWDER

STOOP

VLT.CLG.

BEDROOM No.4
13'-6" x 13'-0"

MASTER BATH
12'-8" x 10'-7"

MASTER SUITE
19'-8" x 15'-4"

BATH

HERS

HIS

STUDY
12'-4" x 11'-3"

DN

BEDROOM No.3
13'-6" x 12'-10"

CLOSET

DESIGN 9819

First Floor:
1,678 square feet
Second Floor:
1,677 square feet
Total:
3,355 square feet

Design by
Design Traditions

This English Manor home features a dramatic brick-and-stucco exterior accented by a gabled roofline and artful half-timbering. Inside, the foyer opens to the formal living room, accented with a vaulted ceiling and boxed bay window. The dining room features its own angled bay window. The family room will be the center of activity with its centered hearth flanked by windows and French-door access to the rear deck. A secluded guest suite offers privacy to the left of the plan. Two family bedrooms and a spacious master suite with a sizable adjoining study reside upstairs. A coffered ceiling, garden tub and cozy fireplace highlight the homeowner's retreat. This home is designed with a basement foundation.

© Design Traditions

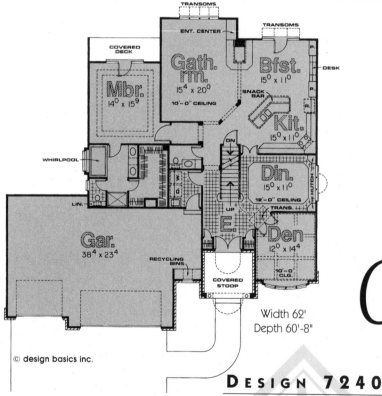

COVERED DECK

Mbr.
14⁰ x 15⁹

WHIRLPOOL

LIN.

Gar.
38⁴ x 23⁴

RECYCLING BINS

COVERED STOOP

© design basics inc.

TRANSOMS

ENT. CENTER

Gath. rm.
15⁴ x 20⁰

10'-0" CEILING

SNACK BAR

DN

TRANSOMS

Bfst.
15⁰ x 11⁰

DESK

Kit.
15⁰ x 11⁰

Din.
15⁰ x 11⁰

12'-0" CEILING

TRANS.

Den
12⁰ x 14⁴

10'-0" CLG.

Width 62'
Depth 60'-8"

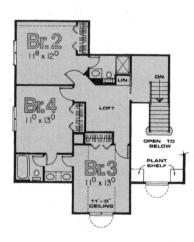

Br. 2
11⁸ x 12⁰

LIN.

DN

Br. 4
11⁰ x 13⁰

LOFT

OPEN TO BELOW

Br. 3
11⁰ x 13⁰

11'-0" CEILING

PLANT SHELF

Design by
Design Basics, Inc.

DESIGN 7240

First Floor:
1,800 square feet
Second Floor:
803 square feet
Total:
2,603 square feet

Columns and double doors at the entry create a dash of European flavor for this fine two-story home. The tiled entry opens to a dining area with a twelve-foot ceiling and a cozy den with spider-beams and a bowed window. French doors in the dining room allow entry to the island kitchen. The adjacent breakfast area shares a three-sided fireplace with the gathering room. The secluded master suite boasts a private covered deck, whirlpool bath and large walk-in closet. Bedroom 2 has a private bath, while Bedrooms 3 and 4 share a compartmented bath. A popular three-car garage includes a recycling center and convenient laundry room access.

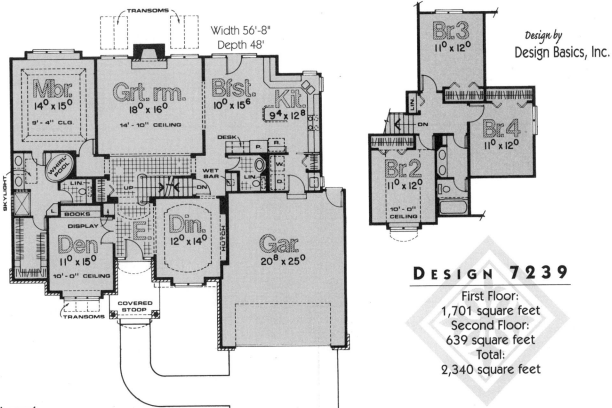

Width 56'-8"
Depth 48'

Design by
Design Basics, Inc.

DESIGN 7239

First Floor:
1,701 square feet
Second Floor:
639 square feet
Total:
2,340 square feet

The impressive entry into this graceful 1½-story home boasts a high ceiling and a built-in curio cabinet. To the left, French doors provide an elegant entrance to a den with built-in cabinets. To the right, the formal dining room presents dramatic ceiling detail and space for a buffet or hutch. To the rear, the great room takes center stage, featuring a raised-hearth fireplace flanked on either side by floor-to-ceiling windows. The private, first-floor master suite is highlighted with vaulted ceilings, a master bath with a tunneled skylight above an oval whirlpool tub and a walk-in closet. The second floor includes three family bedrooms and a full bath.

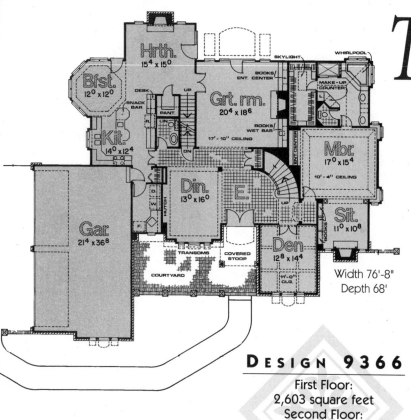

This exceptional European-style facade conceals a spectacular floor plan designed for comfort with a masterful use of space. The glorious great room, open dining room and private den—with a spider-beam ceiling-make up the heart of the home. A cozy hearth room with a fireplace rounds out the kitchen and breakfast areas. The master bedroom opens to a private sitting room with its own fireplace. Three family bedrooms occupy the second floor, each with a private bath.

QUOTE ONE®

Cost to build? See page 230
to order complete cost estimate
to build this house in your area!

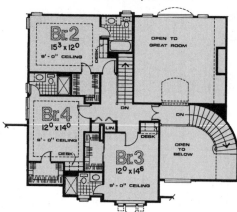

DESIGN 9366

First Floor:
2,603 square feet
Second Floor:
1,020 square feet
Total:
3,623 square feet

Design by
Design Basics, Inc.

This home, as shown in the photograph, may differ from the actual blueprints.
For more detailed information, please check the floor plans carefully.

Photo by Bob Greenspan

The magnificent entry of this elegant traditional home makes a grand impression. The soaring ceiling of the foyer looks over a curved staircase that leads to secondary sleeping quarters. The first-floor master suite offers an expansive retreat for the homeowner, with mitered windows and a see-through fireplace shared with the spacious, spa-style bath. Formal rooms open from the foyer, while a gallery hall leads to the casual living area, with a two-story family room and French doors to the outside. The three-car garage offers wardrobe space for cloaks.

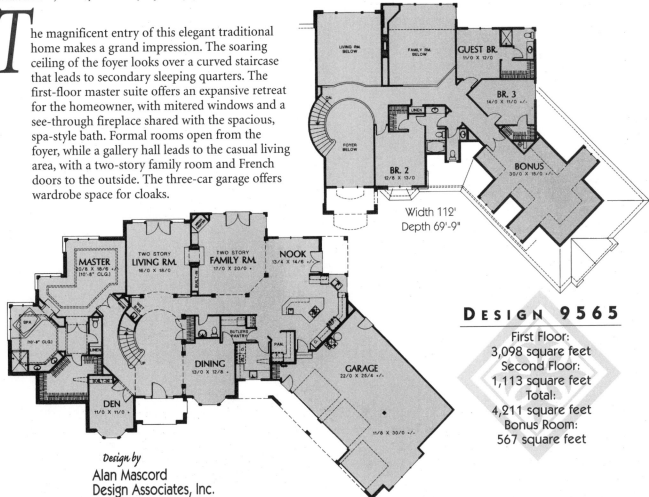

Width 112'
Depth 69'-9"

DESIGN 9565

First Floor:
3,098 square feet
Second Floor:
1,113 square feet
Total:
4,211 square feet
Bonus Room:
567 square feet

Design by
Alan Mascord
Design Associates, Inc.

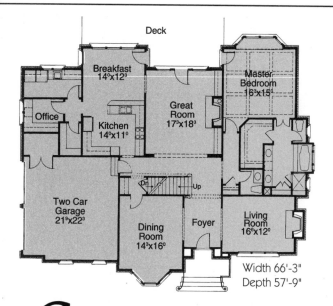

Deck

Breakfast
14⁶x12³

Office

Kitchen
14⁰x11⁰

Great
Room
17⁹x18³

Master
Bedroom
16³x15⁴

Two Car
Garage
21⁹x22³

Dining
Room
14³x16⁹

Foyer

Living
Room
16⁶x12⁰

Dn   Up

Bedroom
No. 4
14⁰x15⁹

Open
To
Below

Attic Storage

Bedroom
No. 3
15⁹x13³

Dn

Bedroom
No. 2
14³x15⁹

Open
To
Below

Open
To
Below

Width 66'-3"
Depth 57'-9"

Design by
Design Traditions

G ently arched cornices and capstones call up a sense of history with this country home. Formal rooms flank the two-story foyer, which leads to comfortably elegant living space with an extended-hearth fireplace. A sizable kitchen serves the formal dining room through a butler's pantry and overlooks the breakfast room, with wide views of the outdoors. A secluded home office is a quiet place for business conversations. The master suite nestles to the rear of the plan and offers a spider-beam ceiling, a sizable walk-in closet and a private bath with a garden tub and twin vanities. Upstairs, Bedrooms 3 and 4 share a full bath with two lavatories, while Bedroom 2 enjoys a private bath. This home is designed with a basement foundation.

DESIGN 9983

First Floor:
2,302 square feet
Second Floor:
1,177 square feet
Total:
3,479 square feet

© *Design Traditions*

DESIGN 9831

Square Footage: 2,150

QUOTE ONE®

Cost to build? See page 230
to order complete cost estimate
to build this house in your area!

Design by
Design Traditions

Width 64'
Depth 64'-4"

© Design Traditions

This home draws its inspiration from both French and English country homes. From the foyer and across the spacious great-room, French doors give a generous view of the covered rear porch. The adjoining dining room is subtly defined by the use of columns and a large triple window. The kitchen offers a large work island and adjoins the breakfast area and keeping room, which features a fireplace. The study to the front of the first floor could be a guest room. It shares a bath with the bedroom beside it. A secluded master suite with a coffered ceiling, angled bath and generous walk-in closet completes the plan. This home is designed with a basement foundation.

© Design Traditions

DECK

BREAKFAST
9'-4" X 10'-6"

TWO STORY
GREAT ROOM
16'-8" X 15'-4"

MEDIA ROOM
12'-0" X 12'-0"

KITCHEN
15'-8" X 14'-0"

STORAGE

LAUNDRY
6'-2" X 7'-6"

UP   DN.

POWDER   WET BAR

TWO-CAR GARAGE
21'-4" X 21'-4"

DINING ROOM
12'-0" X 13'-0"

UP

TWO STORY
FOYER
10'-6" X 13'-0"

LIVING ROOM
12'-0" X 12'-2"

PORCH

Design by
Design Traditions

Q uaint keystones and shutters offer charming accents to the stucco-and stone exterior of this stately English country home. The two-story foyer opens through decorative columns to the formal living room, which offers a service bar. The nearby media room shares a through-fireplace with the two-story great room; double doors lead to the rear deck. A bumped-out bay holds a breakfast area that shares its light with an expansive gourmet kitchen with an angled cooktop counter. This area opens to the formal dining room through a convenient butler's pantry. One wing of the second floor is dedicated to the rambling master suite, which boasts unusual amenities: the bedroom features angled walls, a tray ceiling, and a bumped-out bay with a sitting area. This home is designed with a basement foundation.

SITTING

MASTER
BEDROOM
16'-0" X 13'-0"

OPEN TO BELOW

BEDROOM NO. 2
12'-0" X 11'-4"

BALCONY

DN.

DN.

BATH

MASTER
BATH

BATH

OPEN TO
BELOW

BEDROOM NO. 3
12'-0" X 11'-4"

W.I.C.

BEDROOM NO. 4
11'-2" X 12'-0"

SECRET
ROOM

Width 57'-6"
Depth 46'-6"

DESIGN 9869

First Floor:
1,475 square feet
Second Floor:
1,460 square feet
Total:
2,935 square feet

QUOTE ONE®

Cost to build? See page 230
to order complete cost estimate
to build this house in your area!

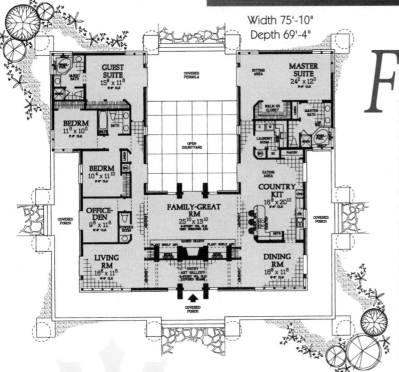

Width 75'-10"
Depth 69'-4"

*F*orm follows function as dual gallery halls lead from formal areas to split sleeping quarters in this Prairie adaptation, inspired by Frank Lloyd Wright. At the heart of the plan, the grand-scale great room offers a raised-hearth fireplace framed by built-in cabinetry and plant shelves. Traditional, formal rooms blend into more open, casual living areas through classic archways. Open planning combines the country kitchen with an informal dining space, and adds an island counter with snack bar. A lavish master suite, secluded to the rear of the plan, harbors a sitting area with private access to the covered pergola. The secondary sleeping wing includes a spacious guest suite with an angled whirlpool tub and twin lavatories. A fifth bedroom or home office offers its own door to the wraparound porch. Plans for a detached garage with an optional guest suite are included with the blueprints.

DESIGN 3637
Square Footage: 3,278

L

Design by
Home Planners

QUOTE ONE®
Cost to build? See page 230
to order complete cost estimate
to build this house in your area!

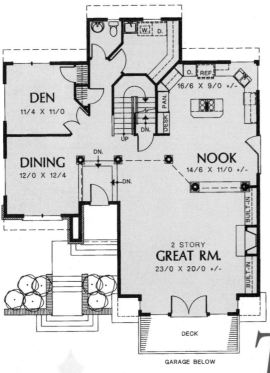

BR. 2
12/6 X 10/8

BR. 3
12/6 X 10/8

SPA

LINEN

SCISSOR VAULT
MASTER
12/0 X 16/0

SKYLITE

LINEN

GREAT RM.
BELOW

Width 43'
Depth 50'

DEN
11/4 X 11/0

DINING
12/0 X 12/4

O. REF.

16/6 X 9/0 +/-

DESK PAN.

UP
DN.

DN.

DN.

NOOK
14/6 X 11/0 +/-

BUILT-IN

BUILT-IN

2 STORY
GREAT RM.
23/0 X 20/0 +/-

DECK

GARAGE BELOW

Design 9538

First Floor:
1,538 square feet
Second Floor:
1,089 square feet
Total:
2,627 square feet

Design by
**Alan Mascord
Design Associates, Inc.**

This attractive two-story home will fit a sloping lot and fulfill seaside views. The foyer opens to interior vistas through decorative columns, while the two-story great room boasts lovely French doors to a front deck. The gourmet kitchen features an island cooktop counter, a sunny corner sink and a nook with a pass-through to the great room. A formal dining room, a secluded den and a sizable laundry complete the first floor. The second-floor master suite employs a scissor-vault ceiling and a divided light window for style, and a relaxing bath with a spa tub for comfort. Two family bedrooms, each with a private lavatory, share a full bath on this floor.

Design by
Alan Mascord Design Associates, Inc.

DINING
11/0 X 14/0

NOOK
10/0 X 10/0

14/0 X 14/0

BR.

UP DN

WET BAR

PAN

DN.

SUNKEN
FAMILY
13/8 X 14/8

DEN
13/8 X 12/4

TWO STORY
LIVING
13/2 X 16/10

DN

DECK

GARAGE
UNDER

Width 50'
Depth 35'

DESIGN 9573

First Floor:
1,502 square feet
Second Floor:
954 square feet
Total:
2,456 square feet

*C*ome home to spectacular views as well as stylish comfort with this dazzling hillside home. Inside, a carefully designed floor plan provides livability with a touch of luxury. The living room features a soaring two story ceiling and shares a see-through fireplace with the formal dining room. A secluded den offers a quiet place to study or read, as well as access to a private deck through double doors. The sunken family room also enjoys a fireplace and is near the kitchen which has a cooktop island and breakfast nook. Upstairs, a master suite with vaulted ceiling enjoys privacy, away from the two secondary bedrooms, and offers a bath with whirlpool spa, twin lavatories and walk-in closet. The family bedrooms share a full bath.

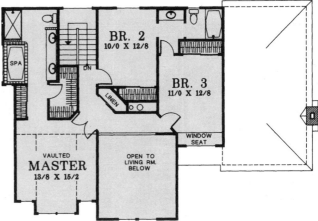

SPA

BR. 2
10/0 X 12/8

DN

BR. 3
11/0 X 12/8

LINEN

WINDOW
SEAT

VAULTED
MASTER
13/8 X 15/2

OPEN TO
LIVING RM.
BELOW

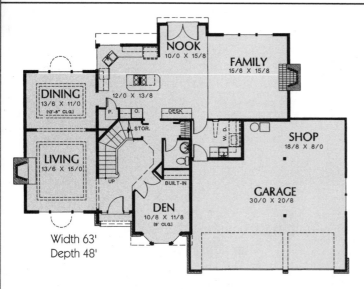

DESIGN 9504

First Floor:
1,465 square feet
Second Floor:
1,103 square feet
Total:
2,568 square feet

Design by
Alan Mascord
Design Associates, Inc.

Width 63'
Depth 48'

With a plan that boasts excellent traffic patterns, this home will accommodate the modern family well. Formal dining and living rooms remain to one side of the house and create an elegant atmosphere for entertaining. Highlights of the front den include a bay window and built-in bookshelves. The gourmet kitchen opens into a nook and a family room. Two second-floor family bedrooms share a large hall bath along with a bonus room that's perfect for a game room. The spacious master suite has a walk-in closet and luxurious spa bath.

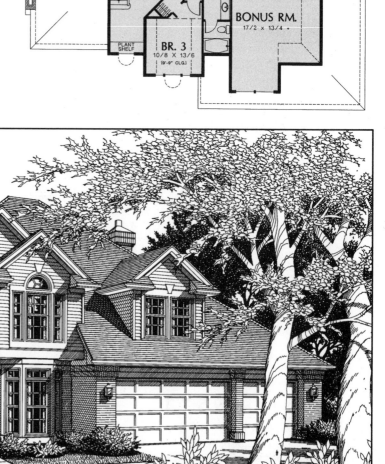

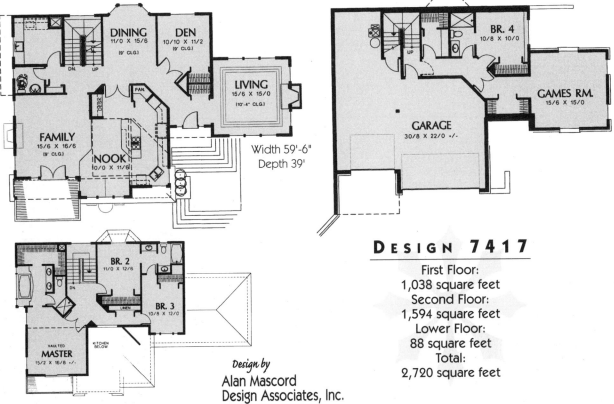

Width 59'-6"
Depth 39'

DESIGN 7417

First Floor:
1,038 square feet
Second Floor:
1,594 square feet
Lower Floor:
88 square feet
Total:
2,720 square feet

Design by
**Alan Mascord
Design Associates, Inc.**

This contemporary design calls for ocean views, and would be a stunning seaside villa, with arch-top transoms and tall, divided-light windows. The foyer opens to a handsome living room with an elegant tray ceiling and a focal-point fireplace. The formal dining room features a bay window and is near the den, secluded through French doors for quiet conversation. The first-floor family area enjoys its own balcony—placed above street level for privacy. Sleeping quarters reside on the second floor and include a spacious master suite with a private bath and two family bedrooms which share a full bath.

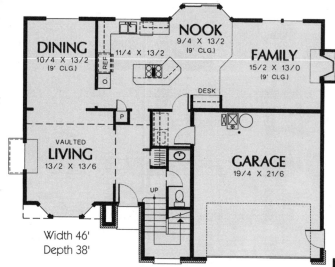

DINING
10/4 X 13/2
(9' CLG.)

NOOK
9/4 X 13/2
(9' CLG.)

11/4 X 13/2

FAMILY
15/2 X 13/0
(9' CLG.)

DESK

REF.

P

VAULTED
LIVING
13/2 X 13/6

GARAGE
19/4 X 21/6

UP

Width 46'
Depth 38'

DESIGN 7416

First Floor:
1,102 square feet
Second Floor:
1,092 square feet
Total:
2,194 square feet

Design by
Alan Mascord
Design Associates, Inc.

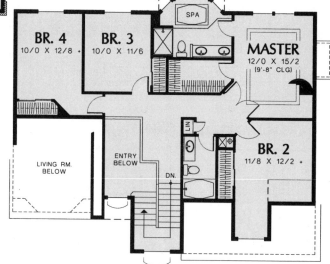

BR. 4
10/0 X 12/8

BR. 3
10/0 X 11/6

SPA

MASTER
12/0 X 15/2
(9'-8" CLG)

LIVING RM.
BELOW

ENTRY
BELOW

LIN

DN.

BR. 2
11/8 X 12/2

Brick, siding and stucco are blended on this contemporary facade to create a stunning new look. Well-defined formal rooms complement casual family space to the back of the plan. The gourmet kitchen serves both dining room and bayed breakfast nook. On the second floor, a classic tray ceiling decorates the master bedroom, which leads to a private bath with lavish amenities, such as a whirlpool spa-style tub. A gallery hall connects three additional bedrooms.

DESIGN 7405

First Floor:
1,632 square feet
Second Floor:
1,334 square feet
Total:
2,968 square feet

Design by

Alan Mascord
Design Associates, Inc.

MASTER
14/10 X 18/2 +
(9'-1" CLG.)

SPA

IRON
BD.

DN.

BR. 2
12/6 X 10/6

LINEN

FOYER
BELOW

PLANT SHELVES

LIN.

BR. 3
11/4 X 10/0 +

BR. 4
11/4 X 12/4

Width 61'
Depth 61'

NOOK
10/0 X 12/0

FAMILY
17/0 X 16/2
(9' CLG.)

12/4 X 17/2

REF.

LIVING
14/6 X 13/0
(10'-1" CLG.)

WET
BAR

PANTRY

STOR.

DINING
14/6 X 11/0
(10'-1" CLG.)

W.C.

UP

BUILT-IN

GARAGE
23/8 X 23/8

DEN
14/6 X 12/4
(10'-1" CLG.)

12/8 X 25/4

A grand arched entry highlights the perfect blend of brick and stucco on this contemporary exterior. Well-defined formal rooms share the right wing of the plan with a private den, which opens off the foyer through French doors. A gourmet kitchen with a cooktop island counter serves a sunny breakfast nook, as well as the formal dining room. A luxurious homeowner's retreat is found in an expansive master suite on the second floor. The lavish bath features a tile-rimmed, spa-style tub and a generous walk-in closet. The central staircase leads to a gallery hall that connects the family sleeping quarters and a full bath.

This home, as shown in the photograph, may differ from the actual blueprints.
For more detailed information, please check the floor plans carefully.

Photos by Bob Greenspan

DESIGN 3558

First Floor:
2,328 square feet
Second Floor:
603 square feet
Total:
2,931 square feet

L D

Width 69'-4"
Depth 66'

Design by
Home Planners

This contemporary home wraps traditional formality with an avant-garde spirit to create the perfect blend of old elegance and new style. The foyer opens to the formal living room, which offers broad views of the rear property, and to a gallery hall that leads to casual family areas. The first-floor master suite offers a sumptuous bath with a corner whirlpool tub. A coffered ceiling highlights the master bedroom, which leads out to a private patio. Two family bedrooms share a full bath on the second floor.

QUOTE ONE®

Cost to build? See page 230
to order complete cost estimate
to build this house in your area!

Width 63'
Depth 48'

Design by

**Alan Mascord
Design Associates, Inc.**

Balconies and feature windows are as useful as they are luxurious in this roomy home. Inside, a see-through fireplace warms the formal living room and den. Both living spaces open onto a balcony that's convenient for relaxing after dinner in the formal dining room. Second-floor sleeping quarters include two bedrooms that share a corner bath. Beyond a set of double doors, the master suite an extended-hearth fireplace and a private balcony. The lower floor accommodates a shop and a bonus room for future development.

DESIGN 9554

First Floor:
1,989 square feet
Second Floor:
1,349 square feet
Total:
3,338 square feet
Lower Floor:
592 square feet

QUOTE ONE®

Cost to build? See page 230
to order complete cost estimate
to build this house in your area!

This home, as shown in the photograph, may differ from the actual blueprints. For more detailed information, please check the floor plans carefully.

Photo by Bob Greenspan

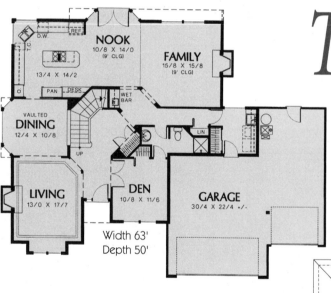

NOOK
10/8 X 14/0
(9' CLG)

FAMILY
15/8 X 15/8
(9' CLG)

D.W.

REF

13/4 X 14/2

PAN DESK

WET BAR

VAULTED
DINING
12/4 X 10/8

UP

LIN

LIVING
13/0 X 17/7

DEN
10/8 X 11/6

GARAGE
30/4 X 22/4 +/-

Width 63'
Depth 50'

Design by
Alan Mascord
Design Associates, Inc.

DESIGN 7414

First Floor:
1,580 square feet
Second Floor:
943 square feet
Total:
2,523 square feet

*T*all windows dress up a new look in contemporary stucco exteriors, and afford wide views inside. The formal living room features floor-to-ceiling windows and opens to the dining room. A gourmet island counter with a cooktop serves planned events as well as casual meals in the adjoining nook. A wet bar nestles off the family room, which has a warming fireplace. The spacious master suite defines the second-floor sleeping quarters, which include two additional bedrooms and a full bath with two vanities. A sizable bonus room is available for later development.

SPA

MASTER
14/10 X 15/10
(9'-9" CLG)

DN

DINING RM
BELOW

BONUS
11/2 X 13/0 +

LN

FOYER
BELOW

BR. 3
10/8 X 11/8

BR. 2
10/0 X 12/0

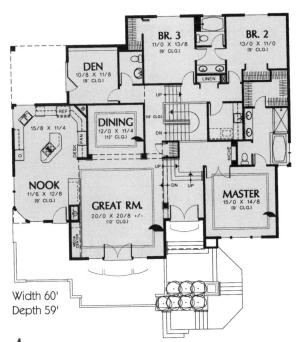

BR. 3
11/0 X 13/8
(9' CLG.)

BR. 2
13/0 X 11/0
(9' CLG.)

DEN
10/8 X 11/8
(9' CLG.)

LINEN

DINING
12/0 X 11/4
(12' CLG.)

15/8 X 11/4

REF

DESK PAN.

UP

DN

UP

DN UP

NOOK
11/6 X 12/8
(9' CLG.)

GREAT RM.
20/0 X 20/8 +/-
(12' CLG.)

MEDIA CENTER

MASTER
15/0 X 14/8
(9' CLG.)

NICHE

Width 60'
Depth 59'

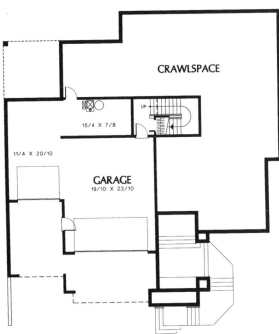

CRAWLSPACE

15/4 X 7/8

UP

11/4 X 20/10

GARAGE
19/10 X 23/10

A grand great room sets the tone for this fabulous floor plan, with an elegant tray ceiling and French doors to a private front balcony. With windows and glass panels to take in the view, this design would make an exquisite seaside resort. The formal dining room is off the center of the plan for privacy, and is served by a nearby gourmet kitchen. Three steps up from the foyer, the sleeping level includes a spacious master suite with a sizable private bath. Each of two additional bedrooms has private access to a shared bath with two vanities.

DESIGN 7412

Square Footage: 2,412
Lower Floor:
130 square feet

Design by
**Alan Mascord
Design Associates, Inc.**

NOOK
8/6 X 10/6
(11'-6" CLG.)

TWO STORY
GREAT RM.
18/0 X 17/6

MASTER
12/8 X 16/0
(10'-8" CLG.)

LINEN

DINING
11/6 X 12/6
(11'-6" CLG.)

UP

PANTRY

DEN
11/0 X 13/2
(9' CLG.)

GARAGE
19/8 X 22/0   10/0 X 20/4

Width 60'
Depth 53'

DESIGN 7419

First Floor:
1,818 square feet
Second Floor:
698 square feet
Total:
2,516 square feet

Design by
Alan Mascord
Design Associates, Inc.

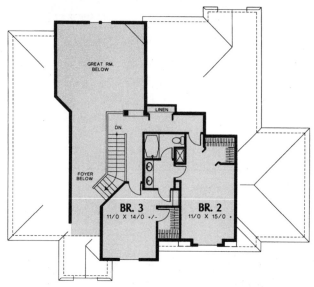

GREAT RM.
BELOW

LINEN

DN.

FOYER
BELOW

BR. 3
11/0 X 14/0 +/-

BR. 2
11/0 X 15/0

An inviting pedimented entry introduces a gallery foyer that opens to formal rooms and leads to a two-story great room. The master suite opens from a central hall through French doors, and enjoys a private bath with a windowed whirlpool tub. A walk-in pantry highlights a well-appointed kitchen that adjoins a bright nook with outdoor access. On the second floor, two family bedrooms share a full bath. Plans for an optional two-car garage are included.

MASTER
12/6 X 16/2
(9' CLG.)

GREAT RM.
16/6 X 18/6 +/-
(11'-6" CLG.)

NOOK
12/6 X 12/0 +/-
(9' CLG.)

DESK

PANTRY

12/4 X 13/0

GARAGE
22/0 X 19/0

11/0 X 19/0

DINING
12/0 X 12/6
(11'-6" CLG.)

Width 60'
Depth 54'

BR. 4
11/2 X 10/2

BR. 3
10/6 X 13/10

DEN
8/8 X 8/8

DN

LINEN

BR. 2
16/6 X 11/10 +/-

Design by
**Alan Mascord
Design Associates, Inc.**

*H*ere's a bright exterior that blends stately gables with the warmth of stucco. The formal dining room opens off the foyer and is served by a well-organized gourmet kitchen. A flexible floor plan offers the option of a fireplace and an additional window in the great room. French doors open to the first-floor master suite, while double doors to the lavish master bath echo this theme. Upstairs, three additional bedrooms share a full bath and a central hall that leads to a quiet den. Plans for an optional two-car garage are included.

DESIGN 7415

First Floor:
1,655 square feet
Second Floor:
830 square feet
Total:
2,485 square feet

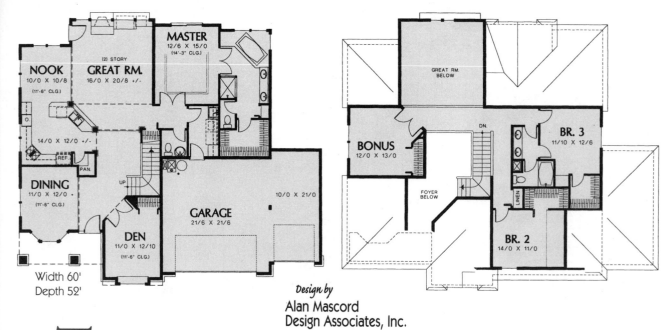

NOOK
10/0 X 10/8
(11'-6" CLG.)

(2) STORY
GREAT RM.
16/0 X 20/8 +/-

MASTER
12/6 X 15/0
(14'-3" CLG.)

14/0 X 12/0 +/-

REF.

PAN.

DINING
11/0 X 12/0 +
(11'-6" CLG.)

UP

GARAGE
21/6 X 21/6

10/0 X 21/0

DEN
11/0 X 12/10
(11'-6" CLG.)

Width 60'
Depth 52'

GREAT RM.
BELOW

BONUS
12/0 X 13/0

DN.

BR. 3
11/10 X 12/6

FOYER
BELOW

LINEN

BR. 2
14/0 X 11/0

Design by
**Alan Mascord
Design Associates, Inc.**

The interior of this Contemporary is drenched with natural light from an abundance of windows plus a skylight. A corner master suite makes elegant use of interior space with a sizable bath that opens through French doors from the bedroom. The two-story great room offers an optional fireplace and provides access to the outdoors. Stunning floor-to ceiling windows dress up the front elevation and provide great views from the dining room. Second-floor sleeping quarters include two family bedrooms, a full bath and a gallery hall that leads to bonus space. Plans for an optional two-car garage are included.

DESIGN 7418

First Floor:
1,786 square feet
Second Floor:
690 square feet
Total:
2,476 square feet

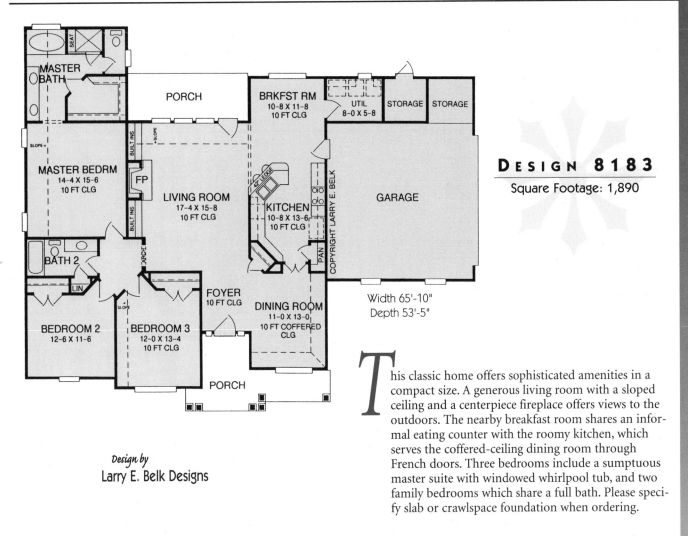

MASTER
BATH

PORCH

BRKFST RM
10-8 X 11-8
10 FT CLG

UTIL
8-0 X 5-8

STORAGE

STORAGE

MASTER BEDRM
14-4 X 15-6
10 FT CLG

SLOPE →

FP

LIVING ROOM
17-4 X 15-8
10 FT CLG

KITCHEN
10-8 X 13-6
10 FT CLG

GARAGE

COPYRIGHT LARRY E. BELK

DESIGN 8183

Square Footage: 1,890

BATH 2

LIN

BEDROOM 2
12-6 X 11-6

BEDROOM 3
12-0 X 13-4
10 FT CLG

FOYER
10 FT CLG

DINING ROOM
11-0 X 13-0
10 FT COFFERED
CLG

Width 65'-10"
Depth 53'-5"

PORCH

Design by
Larry E. Belk Designs

*T*his classic home offers sophisticated amenities in a compact size. A generous living room with a sloped ceiling and a centerpiece fireplace offers views to the outdoors. The nearby breakfast room shares an informal eating counter with the roomy kitchen, which serves the coffered-ceiling dining room through French doors. Three bedrooms include a sumptuous master suite with windowed whirlpool tub, and two family bedrooms which share a full bath. Please specify slab or crawlspace foundation when ordering.

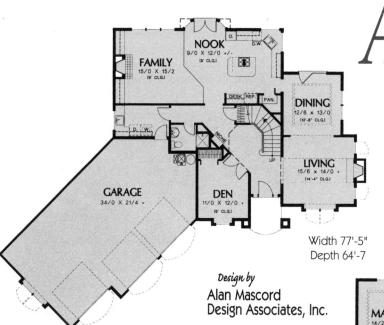

Width 77'-5"
Depth 64'-7

Design by
**Alan Mascord
Design Associates, Inc.**

A grand arched entry announces this spectacular Sun Country home, with a floor plan suited for active families. The foyer opens through French doors to a secluded den with cloak or wardrobe space and a convenient powder room nearby. Casual living space includes a well-appointed kitchen with a cooktop island counter and a built-in planning desk. The bright breakfast nook features angled windows as well as French doors to the outside. A focal-point fireplace with an extended tile hearth is positioned between flanking built-in shelves, perfect for a library or entertainment center.

DESIGN 9560

First Floor:
1,592 square feet
Second Floor:
1,178 square feet
Total:
2,770 square feet

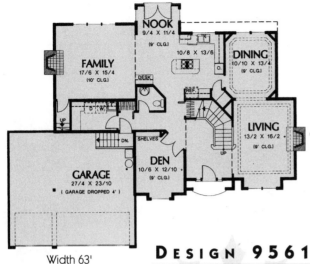

NOOK
9/4 X 11/4
(9' CLG.)

10/8 X 13/6

DINING
10/10 X 13/4
(9' CLG.)

FAMILY
17/6 X 15/4
(10' CLG.)

DESK

REF.

LIVING
13/2 X 16/2
(9' CLG.)

SHELVES

GARAGE
27/4 X 23/10
(GARAGE DROPPED 4')

UP

DN.

SHELVES

DEN
10/6 X 12/10
(9' CLG.)

UP

Width 63'
Depth 51'

D E S I G N 9 5 6 1

First Floor:
1,564 square feet
Second Floor:
1,422 square feet
Total:
2,986 square feet
Bonus Room:
430 square feet

Design by
**Alan Mascord
Design Associates, Inc.**

SPA

MASTER
17/8 X 15/6

LINEN

BR. 2
12/0 X 13/2

UP

DN.

BR. 4
13/4 X 15/0

DN.

BONUS
19/4 X 13/4 +/-

BR. 3
10/8 X 13/0

**FOYER
BELOW**

K eystones, stucco and dramatic rooflines create a stately exterior for this traditional home. The formal living and dining rooms invite elegant occasions, while the clustered family room, breakfast nook and gourmet kitchen take care of casual gatherings. A quiet den with built-in shelves opens off the foyer—perfect for a library or home office. The second-floor master suite, a few steps up from the central hall, features a coffered ceiling and a divided walk-in closet. The master bedroom opens to the spa bath through French doors. Three family bedrooms share a full bath. Unfinished bonus space above the garage can be developed into a hobby or study room.

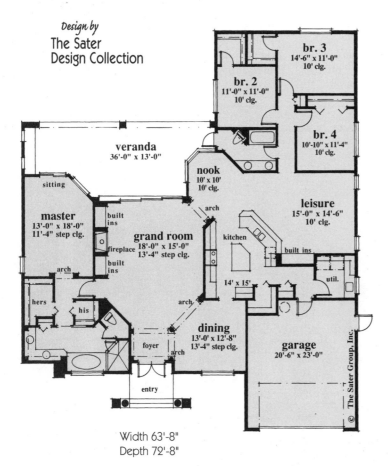

Design by
**The Sater
Design Collection**

veranda
36'-0" x 13'-0"

sitting

master
13'-0" x 18'-0"
11'-4" step clg.

built ins

fireplace

built ins

grand room
18'-0" x 15'-0"
13'-4" step clg.

arch

arch

hers

his

arch

nook
10' x 10'
10' clg.

kitchen

14' x 15'

arch

dining
13'-0" x 12'-8"
13'-4" step clg.

foyer

arch

entry

br. 3
14'-6" x 11'-0"
10' clg.

br. 2
11'-0" x 11'-0"
10' clg.

br. 4
10'-10" x 11'-4"
10' clg.

leisure
15'-0" x 14'-6"
10' clg.

built ins

util.

garage
20'-6" x 23'-0"

© The Sater Group, Inc.

Width 63'-8"
Depth 72'-8"

DESIGN 6659
Square Footage: 2,659

Varied roof lines, multi-pane windows and elegant pillars combine to present a fine traditional family home. Through double entry doors, columns frame the foyer, creating arches that lead to the formal dining room and grand room. The central living area boasts a wall of sliding glass doors to the rear veranda, a fireplace and built-ins. Off the leisure room, three family bedrooms—each with ample closet space—share a full bath with twin vanities, while the deluxe master suite nestles in a private wing of the plan.

© The Sater Group, Inc.

This home is designed to be a homeowner's dream come true. A formal living area opens from the gallery foyer through graceful arches and looks out to the veranda, which hosts an outdoor grill and service counter. The leisure room offers a private veranda and a cabana bath just off the gourmet kitchen. The master suite opens to the rear property through French doors, and boasts a lavish bath with a corner whirlpool tub that overlooks a private garden.

DESIGN 6663

Square Footage: 2,978

Design by
The Sater
Design Collection

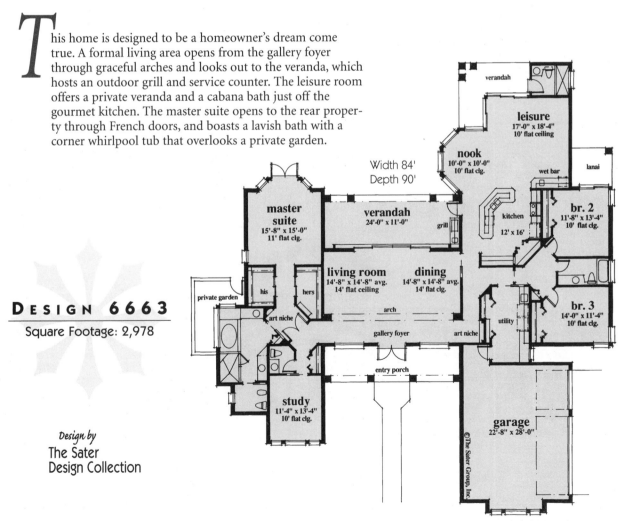

Width 84'
Depth 90'

Design 3632

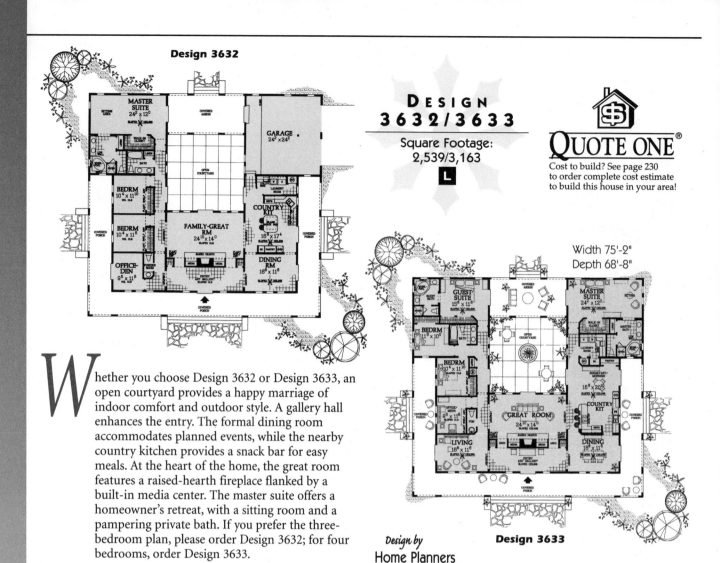

DESIGN
3632/3633

Square Footage:
2,539/3,163

L

QUOTE ONE®
Cost to build? See page 230
to order complete cost estimate
to build this house in your area!

Width 75'-2"
Depth 68'-8"

Whether you choose Design 3632 or Design 3633, an open courtyard provides a happy marriage of indoor comfort and outdoor style. A gallery hall enhances the entry. The formal dining room accommodates planned events, while the nearby country kitchen provides a snack bar for easy meals. At the heart of the home, the great room features a raised-hearth fireplace flanked by a built-in media center. The master suite offers a homeowner's retreat, with a sitting room and a pampering private bath. If you prefer the three-bedroom plan, please order Design 3632; for four bedrooms, order Design 3633.

Design by
Home Planners

Design 3633

An historic Spanish-style elevation with an arched portico and twin turrets introduces an up-to-date interior that marries traditional comfort with 21st-Century style. The formal rooms flank a tiled foyer set off by a stunning fountain. Casual living space offers a tiled-hearth fireplace and opens to the columned, covered porch with an outdoor grill and deck with spa. A pampering master suite includes a bayed reading nook, a private fireplace, a spacious bath and exercise area, and a study or home office with its own entry and porch. Three secondary bedrooms—one with a bay window— share a gallery hall that leads to a laundry and a three-car garage.

Design by
Home Planners

Design 3631
Square Footage: 2,831

L

Quote One®
Cost to build? See page 230 to order complete cost estimate to build this house in your area!

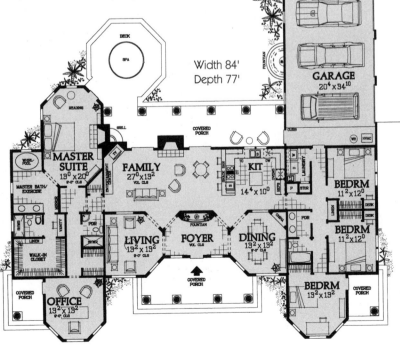

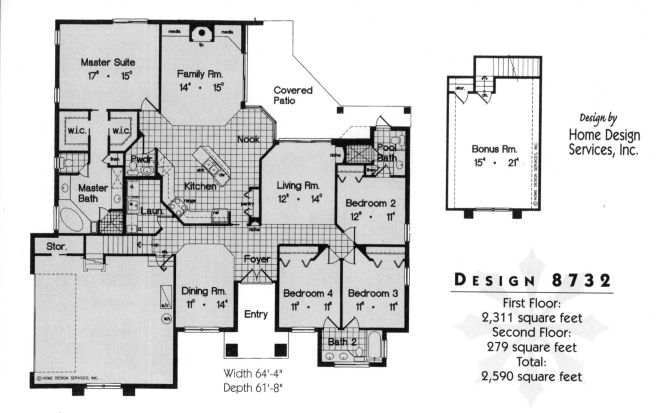

Master Suite
17⁸ · 15⁰

Family Rm.
14⁴ · 15⁰

Covered
Patio

w.i.c.   w.i.c.

Pwdr.

Nook

Pool
Bath

Master
Bath

Kitchen

Living Rm.
12⁸ · 14⁰

Bedroom 2
12⁶ · 11⁴

Laun.

Stor.

Foyer

Dining Rm.
11⁰ · 14⁴

Bedroom 4
11² · 11⁸

Bedroom 3
11⁸ · 11⁴

Entry

Bath 2

Width 64'-4"
Depth 61'-8"

Bonus Rm.
15⁴ · 21⁴

Design by
**Home Design
Services, Inc.**

DESIGN 8732

First Floor:
2,311 square feet
Second Floor:
279 square feet
Total:
2,590 square feet

A niche becomes the focal point as the tiled foyer flows to the heart of the home. The gourmet kitchen invites all occasions—planned events and casual gatherings—with an island counter, a sizable pantry and angled counters. A wall of sliding glass doors in the living room offers wide views of the back prop-erty. Two walk-in closets introduce a spacious bath in the master suite. Tucked out of the way near the master suite's entry vestibule is a convenient powder room. Three family bedrooms are placed at the opposite end of the plan, with a full bath. A cabana bath serves traffic from the back covered patio.

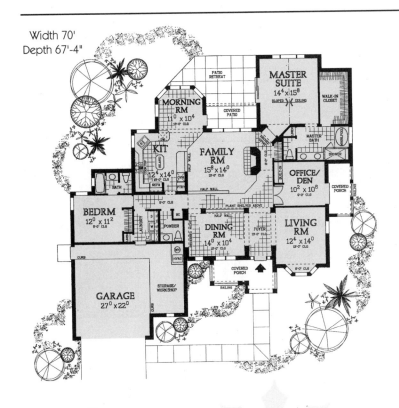

Width 70'
Depth 67'-4"

Sunbursts and multi-pane windows decorate the delicate facade of this contemporary home. Outdoor living areas like the patio retreat and the front covered porch make this plan an all-time favorite. A central formal dining room, set off by decorative columns and a plant shelf, invites planned occasions but hosts family dinners as well. The bayed morning room enjoys access to the patio and retreat, and shares sunlight with the gourmet kitchen with food preparation island. A sloped ceiling adds volume and contrast to the master bedroom, while ceramic tiles and a whirlpool tub enhance a relaxing retreat for the homeowner. A family bedroom or guest suite adjoins a full bath.

Design by
Home Planners

DESIGN 3602
Square Footage: 2,312

L

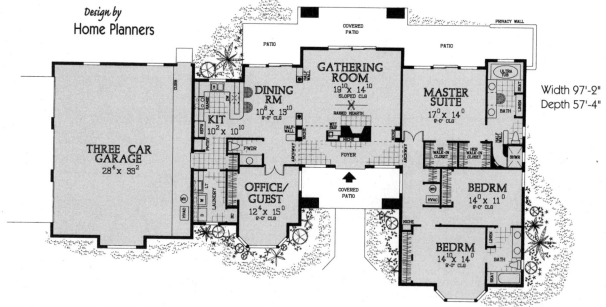

Design by
Home Planners

Width 97'-2"
Depth 57'-4"

DESIGN 3657

Square Footage: 2,319

he grand style of this new design is reflected in divided-light windows and sunburst transoms that create a dazzling entry for this Mission-style country home. A Spanish-tile roof splashes the stately exterior with casual elegance, while the foyer lends dignity to a floor plan designed for active families. The heart of the home is the gathering room, with a raised-hearth fireplace, a wet bar and sliding-glass doors to the entertainment patio. The formal dining room opens to a U-shaped kitchen, which offers a snack bar and leads to a tiled laundry. A home office or guest suite enjoys a nearby powder room. The right wing houses the family sleeping quarters which include a luxurious master suite with two walk in closets, twin lavatories, a spa bath and doors to the covered patio. Two spacious secondary bedrooms share a private bath.

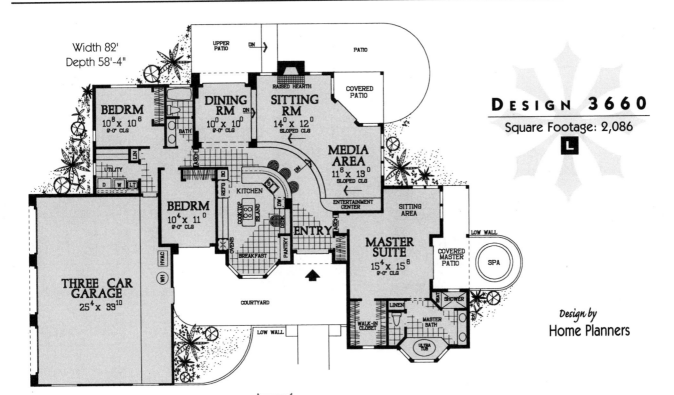

Width 82'
Depth 58'-4"

BEDRM
10⁸ x 10⁸
9'-0" CLG

DINING RM
10⁰ x 10⁰
9'-0" CLG

SITTING RM
14⁰ x 12⁰
SLOPED CLG

UPPER PATIO

PATIO

RAISED HEARTH

COVERED PATIO

MEDIA AREA
11⁶ x 13⁰
SLOPED CLG

UTILITY

D   W   LT

HVAC

WH

THREE CAR GARAGE
25⁴ x 33¹⁰

KITCHEN

BEDRM
10⁴ x 11⁰
9'-0" CLG

OVENS

BREAKFAST

PANTRY

ENTRY

ENTERTAINMENT CENTER

SITTING AREA

MASTER SUITE
15⁴ x 15⁶
9'-0" CLG

COVERED MASTER PATIO

SPA

LOW WALL

COURTYARD

LOW WALL

WALK-IN CLOSET

LINEN

MASTER BATH

SHOWER

ULTRA TUB

DESIGN 3660
Square Footage: 2,086
L

Design by
Home Planners

QUOTE ONE®

Cost to build? See page 230
to order complete cost estimate
to build this house in your area!

*T*his home exhibits wonderful dual-use space in the sunken living room and media area. Anchoring each end of this spacious living zone is the raised-hearth fireplace and the entertainment center. The outstanding kitchen has an informal breakfast bay and looks over the snack bar to the family area. Through a graceful archway, a gallery hall leads to two family bedrooms. At the opposite end of the plan, a master suite features a sitting area filled with natural light, and French doors to the covered patio.

Width 76'-6"
Depth 77'-4"

Design by
Home Planners

Design 3661

Design 3665

QUOTE ONE®
Cost to build? See page 230
to order complete cost estimate
to build this house in your area!

DESIGN
3661/3665

Square Footage:
2,385/2,678

L

A vaulted entry and tall muntin windows complement a classic stucco exterior on this Floridian-style home, which offers a choice of two floor plans. Design 3665 replaces the golf-cart garage offered in Design 3661 with a fifth bedroom and full bath. In both plans, an entry gallery opens to the great room, with generous views to the rear property and columned access to a patio retreat. Niches, built-ins and half-walls decorate and help define this area. The island kitchen serves a convenient snack bar, while the nearby formal dining room offers privacy and natural light from a bay window. A secluded master wing soothes the homeowner with a sumptuous bath, a walk-in closet and an inner retreat with access to a covered patio.

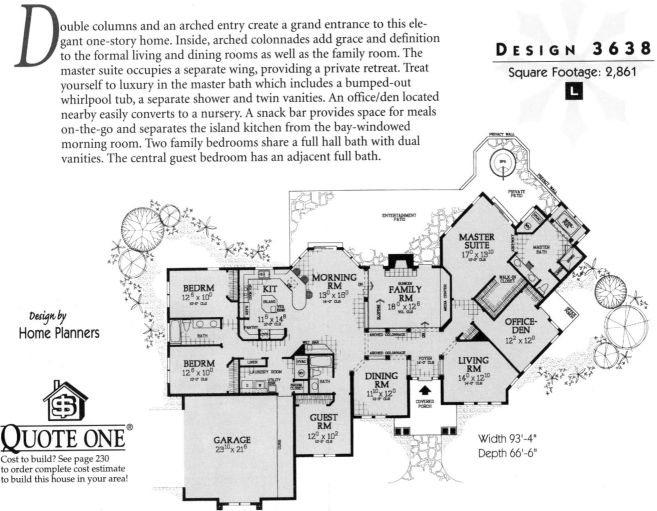

*D*ouble columns and an arched entry create a grand entrance to this elegant one-story home. Inside, arched colonnades add grace and definition to the formal living and dining rooms as well as the family room. The master suite occupies a separate wing, providing a private retreat. Treat yourself to luxury in the master bath which includes a bumped-out whirlpool tub, a separate shower and twin vanities. An office/den located nearby easily converts to a nursery. A snack bar provides space for meals on-the-go and separates the island kitchen from the bay-windowed morning room. Two family bedrooms share a full hall bath with dual vanities. The central guest bedroom has an adjacent full bath.

DESIGN 3638
Square Footage: 2,861

L

Design by
Home Planners

QUOTE ONE®
Cost to build? See page 230
to order complete cost estimate
to build this house in your area!

Width 93'-4"
Depth 66'-6"

A grand entry enhances the exterior of this elegant stucco home. The foyer leads to an open formal area that will invite planned occasions. The corner kitchen with bayed breakfast area serves casual meals with a snack bar counter, and more traditional and festive events with the formal dining room, defined by a decorative half-wall. The private master suite boasts an indoor retreat by a cozy fireplace, as well as access to a private patio with a spa, secluded by a privacy wall. Two family bedrooms on the opposite side of the plan share a full bath and a gallery hall that leads to the casual living area and to a media room.

DESIGN 3630

Square Footage: 3,034

L

QUOTE ONE®

Cost to build? See page 230 to order complete cost estimate to build this house in your area!

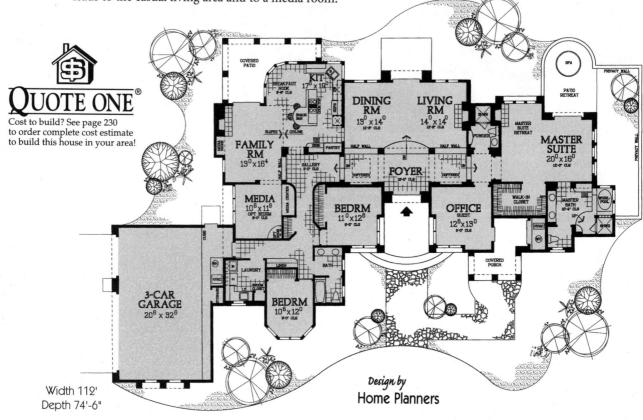

Width 112'
Depth 74'-6"

Design by
Home Planners

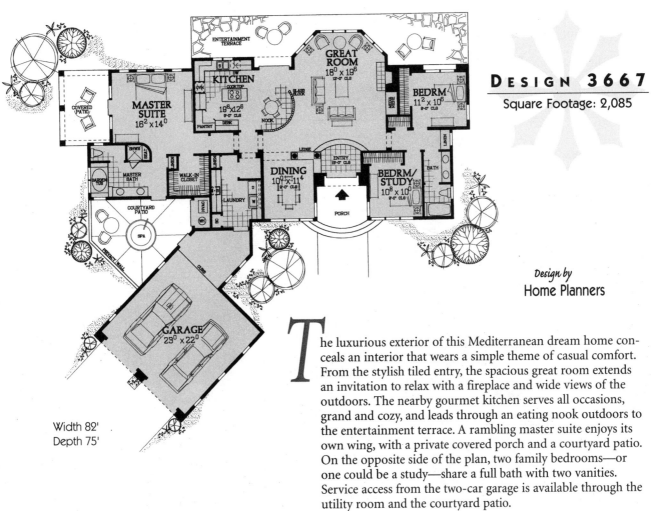

DESIGN 3667

Square Footage: 2,085

Design by
Home Planners

Width 82'
Depth 75'

Teh luxurious exterior of this Mediterranean dream home conceals an interior that wears a simple theme of casual comfort. From the stylish tiled entry, the spacious great room extends an invitation to relax with a fireplace and wide views of the outdoors. The nearby gourmet kitchen serves all occasions, grand and cozy, and leads through an eating nook outdoors to the entertainment terrace. A rambling master suite enjoys its own wing, with a private covered porch and a courtyard patio. On the opposite side of the plan, two family bedrooms—or one could be a study—share a full bath with two vanities. Service access from the two-car garage is available through the utility room and the courtyard patio.

DESIGN 8736

Square Footage: 3,448

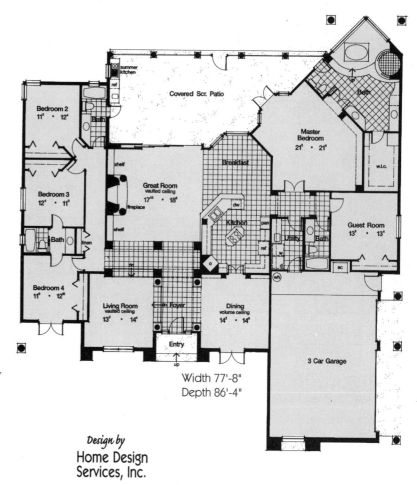

This Contemporary design makes a grand entrance with a vaulted foyer, set off with decorative columns. Striking architectural elements such as the columned hearth in the open great room offset more practical devices like the 12-foot sliding glass door to the back patio. A bay window brightens the tiled breakfast nook and kitchen. The master suite leads out to the patio through French doors and provides a spectacular bath with a circular glass-walled shower and a curved soaking tub. Three family bedrooms have a private wing with two full baths.

Width 77'-8"
Depth 86'-4"

Design by
Home Design Services, Inc.

Design by
**Home Design
Services, Inc.**

Width 63'-8"
Depth 64'-4"

DESIGN 8733

Square Footage:
2,718 square feet

**Master
Bedroom**
14⁸ · 17⁴

Bath

Covered Patio
volume ceiling

Bath

Bedroom 3
volume ceiling
11⁰ · 11⁸

Breakfast
volume ceiling

Bedroom 4
volume ceiling
16⁰ · 11⁸

Family Room
volume ceiling
13⁸ · 22⁰

Kitchen

desk

w.i.c.

fireplace

Bedroom 5
volume ceiling
13⁴ · 12⁰

pantry

Bath

Utility

Dining
volume ceiling
11⁰ · 12⁸

Living Room
volume ceiling
12⁰ · 13⁴

Foyer

Guest / Den
volume ceiling
10⁸ · 10⁴

Entry

ac

Double Garage

© HOME DESIGN SERVICES, INC.

Here's an exciting Contemporary that's more than just a pretty face. A tiled foyer leads to an open family room with a volume ceiling and a wall of glass that brings in a sense of the outdoors. The master wing provides a guest suite, complete with its own full bath. An oversize spa-style tub highlights the homeowner's retreat, which includes a generous walk-in closet, a soaking tub enclosed in a curved wall of glass block, and a tray ceiling in the bedroom. The kitchen features a walk-in pantry and a mitered-glass nook for casual meals. Three secondary bedrooms share a cabana bath, which opens to the covered patio.

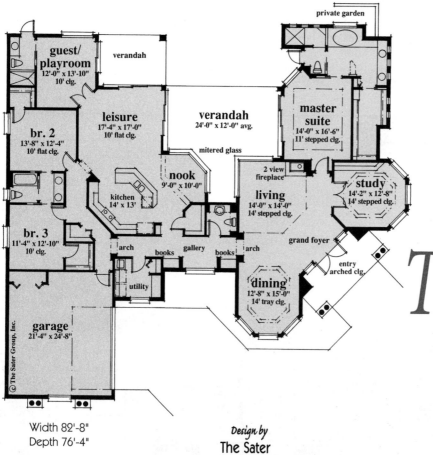

guest/
playroom
12'-0" x 13'-10"
10' clg.

verandah

private garden

master
suite
14'-0" x 16'-6"
11' stepped clg.

leisure
17'-4" x 17'-0"
10' flat clg.

verandah
24'-0" x 12'-0" avg.

DESIGN 6633

Square Footage: 2,986

br. 2
13'-8" x 12'-4"
10' flat clg.

mitered glass

nook
9'-0" x 10'-0"

2 view
fireplace

kitchen
14' x 13'

living
14'-0" x 14'-0"
14' stepped clg.

study
14'-2" x 12'-8"
14' stepped clg.

br. 3
11'-4" x 12'-10"
10' clg.

arch

books

gallery

books

arch

grand foyer

entry
arched clg.

utility

dining
12'-8" x 15'-0"
14' tray clg.

© The Sater Group, Inc.

garage
21'-4" x 24'-8"

Width 82'-8"
Depth 76'-4"

Design by
The Sater
Design Collection

*T*radition takes a bold step up with this Sun Country exterior—a bright introduction to the grand, unrestrained floor plan. Double doors lead to the formal rooms, which include an open living room with a two-view fireplace, a bayed dining room and a parlor or study with its own bay window. A secluded master suite with a compartmented bath complements family sleeping quarters, zoned for privacy.

DESIGN 6635

First Floor:
4,760 square feet
Second Floor:
1,552 square feet
Total:
6,312 square feet

*T*his beautiful home features a blend of spectacular arch-top transoms, French doors and bay windows. Two-story ceilings add an aura of spaciousness throughout the interior, while an unrestrained floor plan offers plenty of private space as well as places to gather. The living room opens to the back property through three sets of French doors, while a nearby study leads out to a lanai shared only with the master suite. A grand gourmet kitchen serves an elegant formal dining room as well as a bayed eating nook that offers a wet bar and opens to a spacious leisure room. A second-floor gallery loft connects three spacious guest suites.

Design by
The Sater
Design Collection

Width 98'
Depth 103'-8"

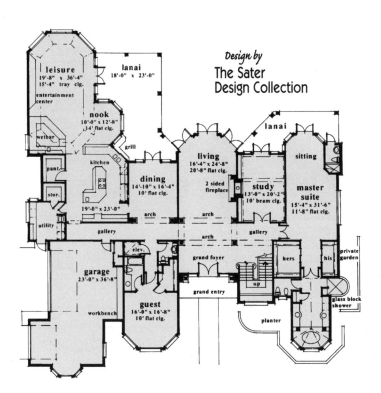

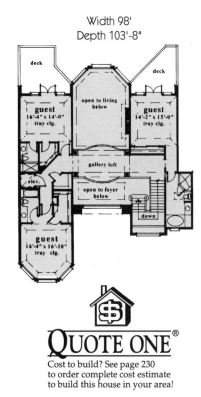

QUOTE ONE®

Cost to build? See page 230
to order complete cost estimate
to build this house in your area!

This home, as shown in the photograph, may differ from the actual blueprints. For more detailed information, please check the floor plans carefully.

Photo by Oscar Thompson

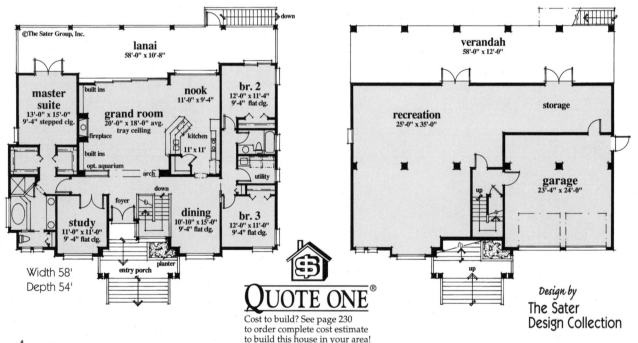

©The Sater Group, Inc.

lanai
58'-0" x 10'-8"

master suite
13'-0" x 15'-0"
9'-4" stepped clg.

built ins

nook
11'-0" x 9'-4"

br. 2
12'-0" x 11'-4"
9'-4" flat clg.

grand room
20'-0" x 18'-0" avg.
tray ceiling

fireplace

built ins

opt. aquarium

kitchen
11' x 11'

arch

down

study
11'-0" x 11'-0"
9'-4" flat clg.

foyer

dining
10'-10" x 15'-0"
9'-4" flat clg.

br. 3
12'-0" x 11'-0"
9'-4" flat clg.

utility

entry porch

planter

Width 58'
Depth 54'

verandah
58'-0" x 12'-0"

recreation
25'-0" x 35'-0"

storage

up

garage
23'-4" x 24'-0"

up

down

QUOTE ONE®
Cost to build? See page 230
to order complete cost estimate
to build this house in your area!

Design by
The Sater Design Collection

A strikingly simple staircase leads to the dramatic entry of this Contemporary design. The foyer opens to an expansive grand room with a fireplace and a built-in entertainment center. An expansive lanai opens from the living area and offers good inside/outside relationships. For more traditional occasions and planned events, a front-facing dining room offers a place for quiet, elegant entertaining. The master suite features a lavish bath with two sizable walk-in closets, a windowed whirlpool tub, twin lavatories and a compartmented toilet. Double doors open from the gallery hall to a secluded study that is convenient to the master bedroom. Two additional bedrooms share a private hall and a full bath on the opposite side of the plan.

DESIGN 6622
Square Footage: 2,190

This home, as shown in the photograph, may differ from the actual blueprints.
For more detailed information, please check the floor plans carefully.

Photo by Oscar Thompson

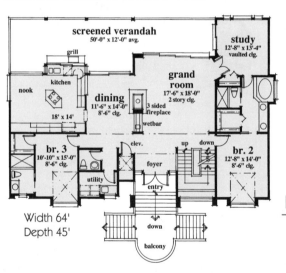

Width 64'
Depth 45'

*T*his striking Floridian plan is designed for entertaining. A large, open floor plan offers soaring, sparkling space for planned gatherings. The foyer leads to the grand room, highlighted by a glass fireplace, a wet bar and wide views of the outdoors. Both the grand room and the formal dining room open to a screened veranda. The first floor includes two spacious family bedrooms and a secluded study which opens from the grand room. The second-floor master suite offers sumptuous amenities, including a private deck and spa, a three-sided fireplace, a sizable walk-in closet and a gallery hall with an overlook to the grand room.

DESIGN 6620

First Floor:
2,066 square feet
Second Floor:
810 square feet
Total:
2,876 square feet
Lower Level:
1,260 square feet

Design by
The Sater
Design Collection

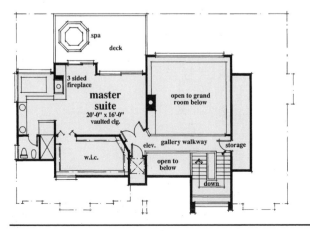

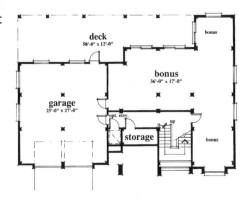

When You're Ready To Order . . .

Let Us Show You Our Home Blueprint Package.

Building a home? Planning a home? Our Blueprint Package has nearly everything you need to get the job done right, whether you're working on your own or with help from an architect, designer, builder or subcontractors. Each Blueprint Package is the result of many hours of work by licensed architects or professional designers.

QUALITY

Hundreds of hours of painstaking effort have gone into the development of your blueprint set. Each home has been quality-checked by professionals to insure accuracy and buildability.

VALUE

Because we sell in volume, you can buy professional-quality blueprints at a fraction of their development cost. With our plans, your dream home design costs only a few hundred dollars, not the thousands of dollars that custom architects charge.

SERVICE

Once you've chosen your favorite home plan, you'll receive fast, efficient service whether you choose to mail or fax your order to us or call us toll free at 1-800-521-6797.

SATISFACTION

Over 50 years of service to satisfied home plan buyers provide us unparalleled experience and knowledge in producing quality blueprints. What this means to you is satisfaction with our product and performance.

ORDER TOLL FREE 1-800-521-6797

After you've looked over our Blueprint Package and Important Extras on the following pages, simply mail the order form on page 237 or call toll free on our Blueprint Hotline: 1-800-521-6797. We're ready and eager to serve you.

Each set of blueprints is an interrelated collection of detail sheets which includes components such as floor plans, interior and exterior elevations, dimensions, cross-sections, diagrams and notations. These sheets show exactly how your house is to be built.

Among the sheets included may be:

Frontal Sheet
This artist's sketch of the exterior of the house gives you an idea of how the house will look when built and landscaped. Large ink-line floor plans show all levels of the house and provide an overview of your new home's livability, as well as a handy reference for deciding on furniture placement.

Foundation Plan
This sheet shows the foundation layout includ-

SAMPLE PACKAGE

ing support walls, excavated and unexcavated areas, if any, and foundation notes. If slab construction rather than basement, the plan shows footings and details for a monolithic slab. This page, or another in the set, may include a sample plot plan for locating your house on a building site.

Detailed Floor Plans
These plans show the layout of each floor of the house. Rooms and interior spaces are carefully dimensioned and keys are given for cross-section details provided later in the plans. The positions of electrical outlets and switches are shown.

House Cross-Sections
Large-scale views show sections or cut-aways of the foundation, interior walls, exterior walls, floors, stairways and roof details. Additional cross-sections may show important changes in

floor, ceiling or roof heights or the relationship of one level to another. Extremely valuable for construction, these sections show exactly how the various parts of the house fit together.

Interior Elevations
Many of our drawings show the design and placement of kitchen and bathroom cabinets, laundry areas, fireplaces, bookcases and other built-ins. Little "extras," such as mantelpiece and wainscoting drawings, plus moulding sections, provide details that give your home that custom touch.

Exterior Elevations
These drawings show the front, rear and sides of your house and give necessary notes on exterior materials and finishes. Particular attention is given to cornice detail, brick and stone accents or other finish items that make your home unique.

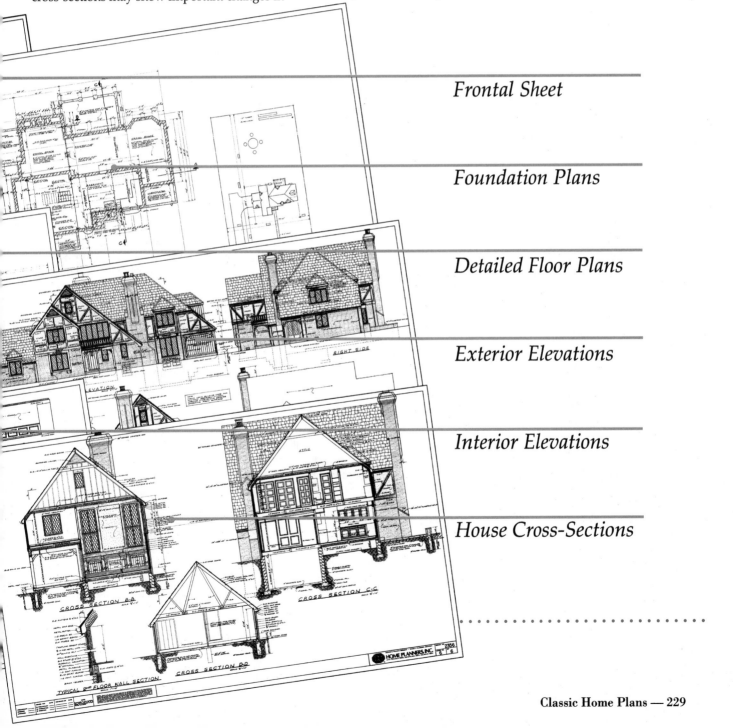

Frontal Sheet

Foundation Plans

Detailed Floor Plans

Exterior Elevations

Interior Elevations

House Cross-Sections

Important Extras To Do The Job Right!

Introducing eight important planning and construction aids developed by our professionals to help you succeed in your home-building project.

MATERIALS LIST

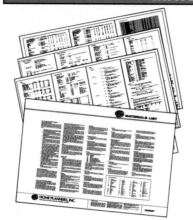

For many of the designs in our portfolio, we offer a customized materials take-off that is invaluable in planning and estimating the cost of your new home. This Materials List outlines the quantity, type and size of materials needed to build your house (with the exception of mechanical system items). Included are framing lumber, windows and doors, kitchen and bath cabinetry, rough and finish hardware, and much more. This handy list helps you or your builder cost out materials and serves as a reference sheet when you're compiling bids.

(Note: Because of the diversity of local building codes, our Materials List does not include mechanical materials.)

SPECIFICATION OUTLINE

This valuable 16-page document is critical to building your house correctly. Designed to be filled in by you or your builder, this book lists 166 stages or items crucial to the building process. It provides a comprehensive review of the construction process and helps in making choices of materials. When combined with the blueprints, a signed contract, and a schedule, it becomes a legal document and record for the building of your home.

QUOTE ONE®

Summary Cost Report / Materials Cost Report

A new service for estimating the cost of building select designs, the Quote One® system is available in two separate stages: The Summary Cost Report and the Materials Cost Report.

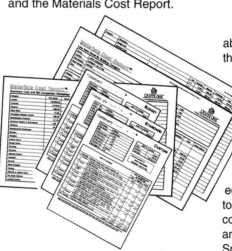

Make even more informed decisions about your home-building project with the second phase of our package, our Materials Cost Report. This tool is invaluable in planning and estimating the cost of your new home. The material and installation (labor and equipment) cost is shown for each of over 1,000 line items provided in the Materials List (Standard grade) which is included when you purchase this estimating tool. It allows you to determine building costs for your specific zip-code area and for your chosen home design. Space is allowed for additional estimates from contractors and subcontractors, such as for mechanical materials, which are not included in our packages. This invaluable tool is available for a price of $110 ($120 for a Schedule E plan) which includes a Materials List.

The Summary Cost Report is the first stage in the package and shows the total cost per square foot for your chosen home in your zip-code area and then breaks that cost down into ten categories showing the costs for building materials, labor and installation. The total cost for the report (which includes three grades: Budget, Standard and Custom) is just $19.95 for one home, and additionals are only $14.95. These reports allow you to evaluate your building budget and compare the costs of building a variety of homes in your area.

The Quote One® program is continually updated with new plans. If you are interested in a plan that is not indicated as Quote One®, please call and ask our sales reps, they will be happy to verify the status for you. To order these invaluable reports, use the order form on page 237 or call 1-800-521-6797.

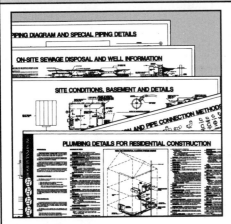

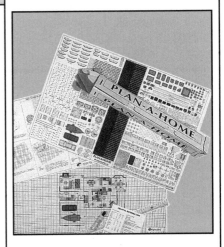
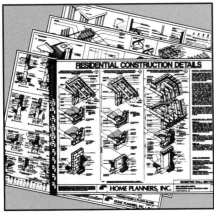

D The Deck Blueprint Package

Many of the homes in this book can be enhanced with a professionally designed Home Planners' Deck Plan. Those home plans highlighted with a D have a matching or corresponding deck plan available which includes a Deck Plan Frontal Sheet, Deck Framing and Floor Plans, Deck Elevations and a Deck Materials List. A Standard Deck Details Package, also available, provides all the how-to information necessary for building *any* deck. Our Complete Deck Building Package contains 1 set of Custom Deck Plans of your choice, plus 1 set of Standard Deck Building Details all for one low price. Our plans and details are carefully prepared in an easy-to-understand format that will guide you through every stage of your deck-building project. This page contains a sampling of 12 of the 25 different Deck layouts to match your favorite house. See page 234 for prices and ordering information.

SPLIT-LEVEL SUN DECK
Deck Plan D100

BI-LEVEL DECK WITH COVERED DINING
Deck Plan D101

WRAP-AROUND FAMILY DECK
Deck Plan D104

DECK FOR DINING AND VIEWS
Deck Plan D107

TREND SETTER DECK
Deck Plan D110

TURN-OF-THE-CENTURY DECK
Deck Plan D111

WEEKEND ENTERTAINER DECK
Deck Plan D112

CENTER-VIEW DECK
Deck Plan D114

KITCHEN-EXTENDER DECK
Deck Plan D115

SPLIT-LEVEL ACTIVITY DECK
Deck Plan D117

TRI-LEVEL DECK WITH GRILL
Deck Plan D119

CONTEMPORARY LEISURE DECK
Deck Plan D120

L *The Landscape Blueprint Package*

For the homes marked with an L in this book, Home Planners has created a front-yard landscape plan that matches or is complementary in design to the house plan. These comprehensive blueprint packages include a Frontal Sheet, Plan View, Regionalized Plant & Materials List, a sheet on Planting and Maintaining Your Landscape, Zone Maps and Plant Size and Description Guide. These plans will help you achieve professional results, adding value and enjoyment to your property for years to come. Each set of blueprints is a full 18" x 24" in size with clear, complete instructions and easy-to-read type. Six of the forty front yard Landscape Plans to match your favorite house are shown below.

Regional Order Map

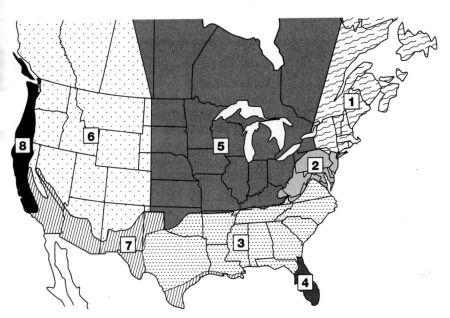

Most of the Landscape Plans shown on these pages are available with a Plant & Materials List adapted by horticultural experts to 8 different regions of the country. Please specify Geographic Region when ordering your plan. See page 234 for prices, ordering information and regional availability.

Region	1	Northeast
Region	2	Mid-Atlantic
Region	3	Deep South
Region	4	Florida & Gulf Coast
Region	5	Midwest
Region	6	Rocky Mountains
Region	7	Southern California & Desert Southwest
Region	8	Northern California & Pacific Northwest

CAPE COD COTTAGE
Landscape Plan L202

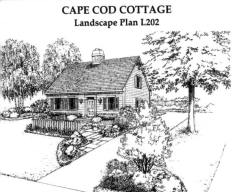

GAMBREL-ROOF COLONIAL
Landscape Plan L203

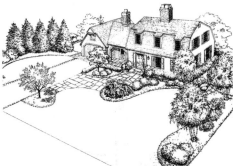

CENTER-HALL COLONIAL
Landscape Plan L204

CLASSIC NEW ENGLAND COLONIAL
Landscape Plan L205

COUNTRY-STYLE FARMHOUSE
Landscape Plan L207

TRADITIONAL SPLIT-LEVEL
Landscape Plan L228

Price Schedule & Plans Index

House Blueprint Price Schedule
(Prices guaranteed through December 31, 1998)

Tier	1-set Study Package	4-set Building Package	8-set Building Package	1-set Reproducible Sepias	Home Customizer® Package
A	$350	$395	$455	$555	$605
B	$390	$435	$495	$615	$665
C	$430	$475	$535	$675	$725
D	$470	$515	$575	$735	$785
E	$590	$635	$695	$795	$845

Prices for 4- or 8-set Building Packages honored only at time of original order.
Additional Identical Blueprints in same order ....$50 per set
Reverse Blueprints (mirror image) ....$50 per set
Specification Outlines ....$10 each
Materials Lists (available only from those designers listed below):

▲ Home Planners Designs..$50
● The Sater Design Collection $50
✳ Alan Mascord Designs...$50
† Design Basics Designs..$75
◆ Donald Gardner Designs..$50
≠ Larry E. Belk Designs...$50
■ Design Traditions..$50

Materials Lists for "E" price plans are an additional $10.

Deck Plans Price Schedule

CUSTOM DECK PLANS

Price Group	Q	R	S
1 Set Custom Plans	$25	$30	$35

Additional identical sets $10 each
Reverse sets (mirror image) $10 each

STANDARD DECK DETAILS
1 Set Generic Construction Details ....$14.95 each

COMPLETE DECK BUILDING PACKAGE

Price Group	Q	R	S
1 Set Custom Plans, plus			
1 Set Standard Deck Details $35		$40	$45

Landscape Plans Price Schedule

Price Group	X	Y	Z
1 set	$35	$45	$55
3 sets	$50	$60	$70
6 sets	$65	$75	$85

Additional Identical Sets..................................$10 each
Reverse Sets (mirror image)..............................$10 each

Index

To use the Index below, refer to the design number listed in numerical order (a helpful page reference is also given). Note the price index letter and refer to the House Blueprint Price Schedule above for the cost of one, four or eight sets of blueprints or the cost of a reproducible sepia. Additional prices are shown for identical and reverse blueprint sets, as well as a very useful Materials List for some of the plans. Also note in the Index below those plans that have matching or complementary Deck Plans or Landscape Plans. Refer to the schedules above for prices of these plans. All Home Planners' plans can be customized with Home Planners' Home Customizer® Package. These plans are indicated below with this symbol: ♠. See page 237 for information. Some plans are also part of our Quote One® estimating service and are indicated by this symbol: 🏠. See page 230 for more information.

To Order: Fill in and send the order form on page 237—or call toll free 1-800-521-6797 or 520-297-8200.

DESIGN	PRICE	PAGE	CUSTOMIZABLE	QUOTE ONE®	DECK	DECK PRICE	LANDSCAPE	LANDSCAPE PRICE	REGIONS
▲2571	A	7	♠		D114	R	L202	X	1-3,5,6,8
▲2662	C	106	♠	🏠			L216	Y	1-3,5,6,8
▲2668	B	102	♠	🏠			L214	Z	1-3,5,6,8
▲2682	A	6	♠		D115	Q	L200	X	1-3,5,6,8
▲2694	C	82	♠	🏠			L209	Y	1-6,8
▲2774	B	9	♠	🏠	D100	Q	L207	Z	1-6,8
▲2826	B	14	♠	🏠	D116	R			
▲2878	B	19	♠	🏠	D112	R	L200	X	1-3,5,6,8
▲2889	D	107	♠	🏠	D107	S	L215	Z	1-6,8
▲2908	B	83	♠	🏠	D117	S	L205	Y	1-3,5,6,8
▲2927	B	16	♠	🏠	D100	Q			
▲2946	C	8	♠	🏠	D114	R	L207	Z	1-6,8
▲2947	B	17	♠	🏠	D112	R	L200	X	1-3,5,6,8
▲2973	B	71	♠	🏠			L223	Z	1-3,5,6,8
▲2974	A	73	♠	🏠			L223	Z	1-3,5,6,8
▲3309	B	70	♠	🏠			L209	Y	1-6,8
▲3325	C	145	♠	🏠	D100	Q	L238	Y	3,4,7,8
▲3332	B	24	♠	🏠			L200	X	1-3,5,6,8
▲3348	C	25	♠	🏠			L200	X	1-3,5,6,8
▲3461	B	114	♠	🏠			L204	Y	1-3,5,6,8
▲3471	E	15	♠	🏠			L236	Z	3,4,7
▲3487	B	21	♠	🏠			L209	Y	1-6,8
▲3499	B	80		🏠	D111	S	L283	X	1-8
▲3503	E	91	♠	🏠	D108	R	L210	Y	1-3,5,6,8
▲3510	C	85	♠						
▲3515	D	101	♠	🏠	D111	S	L214	Z	1-3,5,6,8
▲3520	C	103		🏠	D115	Q			
▲3524	B	86	♠	🏠			L202	X	1-3,5,6,8
▲3525	B	100	♠	🏠					
▲3526	B	87	♠	🏠	D110	R	L202	X	1-3,5,6,8
▲3558	C	200	♠	🏠	D105	R	L203	Y	1-3,5,6,8
▲3602	C	215	♠	🏠			L220	Y	1-3,5,6,8
▲3606	C	78	♠	🏠	D110	R	L224	Y	1-3,5,6,8
▲3608	D	121	♠	🏠			L223	Z	1-3,5,6,8
▲3609	C	29	♠	🏠	D100	Q	L224	Y	1-3,5,6,8
▲3612	C	104	♠	🏠			L206	Z	1-6,8
▲3619	B	135	♠	🏠	D111	S	L207	Z	1-6,8
▲3620	B	68	♠	🏠					
▲3621	C	69	♠	🏠	D111	S	L223	Z	1-3,5,6,8
▲3622	C	157	♠	🏠			L224	Y	1-3,5,6,8
▲3630	C	220	♠	🏠			L209	Y	1-6,8
▲3631	C	213	♠	🏠			L214	Z	1-3,5,6,8
▲3632	C	212	♠	🏠			L237	Y	7
▲3633	C	212	♠	🏠			L237	Y	7
▲3634	D	105	♠	🏠			L224	Y	1-3,5,6,8
▲3635	C	27	♠	🏠			L283	X	1-8
▲3637	D	193	♠	🏠			L235	Z	1-3,5,6,8
▲3638	C	219	♠	🏠			L215	Z	1-6,8
▲3651	C	20	♠	🏠	D112	R	L235	Z	1-3,5,6,8
▲3652	B	22	♠	🏠	D105	R	L220	Y	1-3,5,6,8
▲3653	C	136	♠	🏠	D111	S	L209	Y	1-6,8
▲3654	C	137	♠	🏠			L292	X	1-8

Before You Order . . .

Before filling out the coupon at right or calling us on our Toll-Free Blueprint Hotline, you may want to learn more about our services and products. Here's some information you will find helpful.

Quick Turnaround

We process and ship every blueprint order from our office within 48 hours. Because of this quick turnaround, we won't send a formal notice acknowledging receipt of your order.

Our Exchange Policy

Since blueprints are printed in response to your order, we cannot honor requests for refunds. However, we will exchange your entire first order for an equal number of blueprints at a price of $50 for the first set and $10 for each additional set; $70 total exchange fee for 4 sets; $100 total exchange fee for 8 sets . . . *plus* the difference in cost if exchanging for a design in a higher price bracket or *less* the difference in cost if exchanging for a design in lower price bracket. One exchange is allowed within a year of purchase date. **(Sepias are not exchangeable.)** All sets from the first order must be returned before the exchange can take place. Please add $18 for postage and handling via ground service; $30 via Second Day Air; $40 via Next Day Air.

About Reverse Blueprints

If you want to build in reverse of the plan as shown, we will include an extra set of reverse blueprints (mirror image) for an additional fee of $50. Although lettering and dimensions will appear backward, reverses will be a useful aid if you decide to flop the plan.

Revising, Modifying and Customizing Plans

The wide variety of designs available in this publication allows you to select ideas and concepts for a home to fit your building site and match your family's needs, wants and budget. Like many homeowners who buy these plans, you and your builder, architect or engineer may want to make changes to them. Some minor changes may be made by your builder, but we recommend that most changes be made by a licensed architect or engineer. If you need to make alterations to a design that is customizable, you need only order our Home Customizer® Package to get you started. As set forth below, we cannot assume any responsibility for blueprints which have been changed, whether by you, your builder or by professionals selected by you or referred to you by us, because such individuals are outside our supervision and control.

Architectural and Engineering Seals

Some cities and states are now requiring that a licensed architect or engineer review and "seal" a blueprint, or officially approve it, prior to construction due to concerns over energy costs, safety and other factors. Prior to application for a building permit or the start of actual construction, we strongly advise that you consult your local building official who can tell you if such a review is required.

About the Designers

The architects and designers whose work appears in this publication are among America's leading residential designers. Each plan was designed to meet the requirements of a nationally recognized model building code in effect at the time and place the plan was drawn. Because national building codes change from time to time, plans may not comply with any such code at the time they are sold to a customer. In addition, building officials may not accept these plans as final construction documents of record as the plans may need to be modified and additional drawings and details added to suit local conditions and requirements. We strongly advise that purchasers consult a licensed architect or engineer, and their local building official, before starting any construction related to these plans.

Local Building Codes and Zoning Requirements

At the time of creation, our plans are drawn to specifications published by the Building Officials and Code Administrators (BOCA) International, Inc.; the Southern Building Code Congress (SBCCI) International, Inc.; the International Conference of Building Officials; or the Council of American Building Officials (CABO). Our plans are designed to meet or exceed national building standards. Because of the great differences in geography and climate throughout the United States and Canada, each state, county and municipality has its own building codes, zone requirements, ordinances and building regulations. Your plan may need to be modified to comply with local requirements regarding snow loads, energy codes, soil and seismic conditions and a wide range of other matters. In addition, you may need to obtain permits or inspections from local governments before and in the course of construction. Prior to using blueprints ordered from us, we strongly advise that you consult a licensed architect or engineer—and speak with your local building official—before applying for any permit or beginning construction. We authorize the use of our blueprints on the express condition that you strictly comply with all local building codes, zoning requirements and other applicable laws, regulations, ordinances and requirements. **Notice:** Plans for homes to be built in Nevada must be re-drawn by a Nevada-registered professional. Consult your building official for more information on this subject.

Foundation and Exterior Wall Changes

Most of our plans are drawn with either a full or partial basement foundation. Depending on your specific climate or regional building practices, you may wish to change this basement to a slab or crawlspace. Most professional contractors and builders can easily adapt your plans to alternate foundation types. Likewise, most can easily change 2x4 wall construction to 2x6, or vice versa.

Disclaimer

We and the designers we work with have put substantial care and effort into the creation of our blueprints. However, because we cannot provide on-site consultation, supervision and control over actual construction, and because of the great variance in local building requirements, building practices and soil, seismic, weather and other conditions, WE CANNOT MAKE ANY WARRANTY, EXPRESS OR IMPLIED, WITH RESPECT TO THE CONTENT OR USE OF OUR BLUEPRINTS, INCLUDING BUT NOT LIMITED TO ANY WARRANTY OF MERCHANTABILITY OR OF FITNESS FOR A PARTICULAR PURPOSE.

Terms and Conditions

These designs are protected under the terms of United States Copyright Law and may not be copied or reproduced in any way, by any means, unless you have purchased Sepias or Reproducibles which clearly indicate your right to copy or reproduce. We authorize the use of your chosen design as an aid in the construction of one single-family home only. You may not use this design to build a second or multiple dwellings without purchasing another blueprint or blueprints or paying additional design fees.

How Many Blueprints Do You Need?

A single set of blueprints is sufficient to study a home in greater detail. However, if you are planning to obtain cost estimates from a contractor or subcontractors—or if you are planning to build immediately—you will need more sets. Because additional sets are cheaper when ordered in quantity with the original order, make sure you order enough blueprints to satisfy all requirements. The following checklist will help you determine how many you need:

____ Owner

____ Builder (generally requires at least three sets; one as a legal document, one to use during inspections, and at least one to give to subcontractors)

____ Local Building Department (often requires two sets)

____ Mortgage Lender (usually one set for a conventional loan; three sets for FHA or VA loans)

____ TOTAL NUMBER OF SETS

The Home Customizer®

"This house is perfect...if only the family room were two feet wider." Sound familiar? In response to the numerous requests for this type of modification, Home Planners has developed **The Home Customizer® Package**. This exclusive package offers our top-of-the-line materials to make it easy for anyone, anywhere to customize any Home Planners design to fit their needs. Check the index on pages 234-235 for those plans which are customizable.

Some of the changes you can make to any of our plans include:

- exterior elevation changes
- kitchen and bath modifications
- roof, wall and foundation changes
- room additions and more!

The Home Customizer® Package includes everything you'll need to make the necessary changes to your favorite Home Planners design. The package includes:

- instruction book with examples
- architectural scale and clear work film
- erasable red marker and removable correction tape
- ¼"-scale furniture cutouts
- 1 set reproducible, erasable Sepias
- 1 set study blueprints for communicating changes to your design professional
- a copyright release letter so you can make copies as you need them
- referral letter with the name, address and telephone number of the professional in your region who is trained in modifying Home Planners designs efficiently and inexpensively.

The price of the **Home Customizer® Package** ranges from $605 to $845, depending on the price schedule of the design you have chosen. **The Home Customizer® Package** will not only save you 25% to 75% of the cost of drawing the plans from scratch with a custom architect or engineer, it will also give you the flexibility to have your changes and modifications made by our referral network or by the professional of your choice. Now it's even easier and more affordable to have the custom home you've always wanted.

 For information about any of our services or to order call 1-800-521-6797. Plus, browse our website: www.homeplanners.com

---
BLUEPRINTS ARE NOT RETURNABLE

ORDER FORM

HOME PLANNERS, A Division of Hanley-Wood, Inc.
3275 WEST INA ROAD, SUITE 110
TUCSON, ARIZONA 85741

THE BASIC BLUEPRINT PACKAGE
Rush me the following (please refer to the Plans Index and Price Schedule in this section):

_____ Set(s) of blueprints for plan number(s) _____.	$_____
_____ Set(s) of sepias for plan number(s) _____.	$_____
_____ Home Customizer® Package for plan(s) _____	$_____
_____ Additional identical blueprints in same order @ $50 per set.	$_____
_____ Reverse blueprints @ $50 per set.	$_____

IMPORTANT EXTRAS
Rush me the following:

_____ Materials List: $50
$75 Design Basics. Add $10 for a Schedule E plan Materials List. $_____
_____ **Quote One®** Summary Cost Report @ $19.95 for 1, $14.95 for each additional, for plans _____ $_____
Building location: City _____ Zip Code _____
_____ **Quote One®** Materials Cost Report @ $110 Schedule A-D; $120 Schedule E for plan _____ $_____
(Must be purchased with Blueprints set; Materials List included)
Building location: City _____ Zip Code _____
_____ Specification Outlines @ $10 each. $_____
_____ Detail Sets @ $14.95 each; any two for $22.95; any three for $29.95; all four for $39.95 (save $19.85). $_____
❏ Plumbing ❏ Electrical ❏ Construction ❏ Mechanical
(These helpful details provide general construction advice and are not specific to any single plan.)
_____ Plan-A-Home® @ $29.95 each. $_____

DECK BLUEPRINTS
_____ Set(s) of Deck Plan _____. $_____
_____ Additional identical blueprints in same order @ $10 per set. $_____
_____ Reverse blueprints @ $10 per set. $_____
_____ Set of Standard Deck Details @ $14.95 per set. $_____
_____ Set of Complete Building Package (Best Buy!)
Includes Custom Deck Plan _____.
(See Index and Price Schedule)
Plus Standard Deck Details $_____

LANDSCAPE BLUEPRINTS
_____ Set(s) of Landscape Plan _____ $_____
_____ Additional identical blueprints in same order @ $10 per set. $_____
_____ Reverse blueprints @ $10 per set. $_____

Please indicate the appropriate region of the country for
Plant & Material List. (See Map on page 233): Region _____

POSTAGE AND HANDLING	1-3 sets	4+ sets
DELIVERY (Requires street address - No P.O. Boxes)		
•Regular Service (Allow 7-10 days delivery)	❏ $15.00	❏ $18.00
•Priority (Allow 4-5 days delivery)	❏ $20.00	❏ $30.00
•Express (Allow 3 days delivery)	❏ $30.00	❏ $40.00
CERTIFIED MAIL (Requires signature)	❏ $20.00	❏ $30.00
If no street address available. (Allow 7-10 days delivery)		
OVERSEAS DELIVERY		
Note: All delivery times are from date Blueprint Package is shipped.	fax, phone or mail for quote	

POSTAGE (From box above) $_____
SUB-TOTAL $_____
SALES TAX (AZ , CA, DC, IL, MI, MN, NY & WA residents, please add appropriate state and local sales tax.) $_____
TOTAL (Sub-total and tax) $_____

YOUR ADDRESS (please print)
Name _____
Street _____
City _____ State _____ Zip _____
Daytime telephone number (_____) _____

FOR CREDIT CARD ORDERS ONLY
Please fill in the information below:
Credit card number _____
Exp. Date: Month / Year _____
Check one ❏ Visa ❏ MasterCard ❏ Discover Card

Signature _____
Please check appropriate box: ❏ Licensed Builder-Contractor
❏ Homeowner

ORDER TOLL FREE!
1-800-521-6797 or 520-297-8200

Order Form Key
TB55

Helpful Books & Software

Home Planners wants your building experience to be as pleasant and trouble-free as possible. That's why we've expanded our library of Do-It-Yourself titles to help you along. In addition to our beautiful plans books, we've added books to guide you through specific projects as well as the construction process. In fact, these are titles that will be as useful after your dream home is built as they are right now.

ONE-STORY

1 448 designs for all lifestyles. 860 to 5,400 square feet. 384 pages $9.95

TWO-STORY

2 460 designs for one-and-a-half and two stories. 1,245 to 7,275 square feet. 384 pages $9.95

VACATION

3 345 designs for recreation, retirement and leisure. 312 pages $8.95

MULTI-LEVEL

4 312 designs for split-levels, bi-levels, multi-levels and walkouts. 224 pages $8.95

COUNTRY

5 200 country designs from classic to contemporary by 7 winning designers. 224 pages $8.95

MOVE-UP

6 200 stylish designs for today's growing families from 9 hot designers. 224 pages $8.95

NARROW-LOT

7 200 unique homes less than 60' wide from 7 designers. Up to 3,000 square feet. 224 pages $8.95

SMALL HOUSE

8 200 beautiful designs chosen for versatility and affordability. 224 pages $8.95

BUDGET-SMART

9 200 efficient plans from 7 top designers, that you can really afford to build! 224 pages $8.95

EXPANDABLES

10 200 flexible plans that expand with your needs from 7 top designers. 240 pages $8.95

ENCYCLOPEDIA

11 500 exceptional plans for all styles and budgets—the best book of its kind! 352 pages $9.95

AFFORDABLE

12 Completely revised and updated, featuring 300 designs for modest budgets. 256 pages $9.95

ENCYCLOPEDIA 2

13 500 Completely new plans. Spacious and stylish designs for every budget and taste. 352 pages $9.95

VICTORIAN

14 160 striking Victorian and Farmhouse designs from three leading designers. 192 pages $12.95

EASY-LIVING

15 216 Efficient and sophisticated plans that are small in size, but big on livability. 224 pages $8.95

LUXURY

16 154 fine luxury plans-loaded with luscious amenities! 192 pages $14.95

LIGHT-FILLED

17 223 great designs that make the most of natural sunlight. 240 pages $8.95

BEST SELLERS

18 Our 50th Anniversary book with 200 of our very best designs in full color! 224 pages $12.95

SPECIAL COLLECTION

19 70 Romantic house plans that capture the classic tradition of home design. 160 pages $17.95

COUNTRY HOUSES

20 208 Unique home plans that combine traditional style and modern livability. 224 pages $9.95

TRADITIONAL

21 403 designs of classic beauty and elegance. 304 pages $9.95

MODERN & CLASSIC

22 341 impressive homes featuring the latest in contemporary design. 304 pages $9.95

NEW ENGLAND

23 260 of the best in Colonial home design. Special interior design sections, too. 384 pages $14.95

SOUTHERN

24 207 homes rich in Southern styling and comfort. 240 pages $8.95

SUNBELT
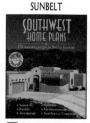
25 215 Designs that capture the spirit of the Southwest. 208 pages $10.95

WESTERN

26 215 designs that capture the spirit and diversity of the Western lifestyle. 208 pages $9.95

Landscape Designs

EASY CARE

27 41 special landscapes designed for beauty and low maintenance. 160 pages $14.95

FRONT & BACK

28 The first book of do-it-yourself landscapes. 40 front, 15 backyards. 208 pages $14.95

BACKYARDS

29 40 designs focused solely on creating your own specially themed backyard oasis. 160 pages $14.95

Outdoor Projects

OUTDOOR

30 42 unique outdoor projects. Gazebos, strombellas, bridges, sheds, playsets and more! 96 pages $7.95

GARAGES & MORE

31 101 Multi-use garages and outdoor structures to enhance any home. 96 pages $7.95

DECKS

32 25 outstanding single-, double- and multi-level decks you can build. 112 pages $7.95

Design Software

| BOOK & CD ROM | 3D DESIGN SUITE | ENERGY GUIDE | BATHROOMS | KITCHENS | HOUSE CONTRACTING | WINDOWS & DOORS | CONTRACTING GUIDE |

33 Both the Home Planners Gold book and matching Windows™ CD ROM with 3D floorplans. $24.95

34 Home design made easy! View designs in 3D, take a virtual reality tour, add decorating details and more. $59.95

35 The most comprehensive energy efficiency and conservation guide available. 280 pages $35.00

36 An innovative guide to organizing, remodeling and decorating your bathroom. 96 pages $8.95

37 An imaginative guide to designing the perfect kitchen. Chock full of bright ideas to make your job easier. 176 pages $14.95

38 Everything you need to know to act as your own general contractor...and save up to 25% off building costs. 134 pages $12.95

39 Installation techniques and tips that make your project easier and more professional looking. 80 pages $7.95

40 Loaded with information to make you more confident in dealing with contractors and subcontractors. 287 pages $18.95

| ROOFING | FRAMING | VISUAL HANDBOOK | BASIC WIRING | PATIOS & WALKS | TILE | PLUMBING | TRIM & MOLDING |

   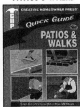   

41 Information on the latest tools, materials and techniques for roof installation or repair. 80 pages $7.95

42 For those who want to take a more-hands on approach to their dream. 319 pages $19.95

43 A plain-talk guide to the construction process; financing to final walk-through, this book covers it all. 498 pages $19.95

44 A straight forward guide to one of the most misunderstood systems in the home. 160 pages $12.95

45 Clear step-by-step instructions take you from the basic design stages to the finished project. 80 pages $7.95

46 Every kind of tile for every kind of application. Includes tips on use installation and repair. 176 pages $12.95

47 Tackle any plumbing installation or repair as quickly and efficiently as a professional. 160 pages $12.95

48 Step-by-step instructions for installing baseboards, window and door casings and more. 80 pages $7.95

Additional Books Order Form

To order your books, just check the box of the book numbered below and complete the coupon. We will process your order and ship it from our office within 48 hours. Send coupon and check (in U.S. funds).

YES! Please send me the books I've indicated:

☐ 1:VO	$9.95	☐ 25:SW	$10.95
☐ 2:VT	$9.95	☐ 26:WH	$9.95
☐ 3:VH	$8.95	☐ 27:ECL	$14.95
☐ 4:VS	$8.95	☐ 28:HL	$14.95
☐ 5:FH	$8.95	☐ 29:BYL	$14.95
☐ 6:MU	$8.95	☐ 30:YG	$7.95
☐ 7:NL	$8.95	☐ 31:GG	$7.95
☐ 8:SM	$8.95	☐ 32:DP	$7.95
☐ 9:BS	$8.95	☐ 33:HPGC	$24.95
☐ 10:EX	$8.95	☐ 34:PLANSUITE	$59.95
☐ 11:EN	$9.95	☐ 35:RES	$35.00
☐ 12:AF	$9.95	☐ 36:CDB	$8.95
☐ 13:E2	$9.95	☐ 37:CKI	$14.95
☐ 14:VDH	$12.95	☐ 38:SBC	$12.95
☐ 15:EL	$8.95	☐ 39:CGD	$7.95
☐ 16:LD2	$14.95	☐ 40:BCC	$18.95
☐ 17:NA	$8.95	☐ 41:CGR	$7.95
☐ 18:HPG	$12.95	☐ 42:SRF	$19.95
☐ 19:WEP	$17.95	☐ 43:RVH	$19.95
☐ 20:CN	$9.95	☐ 44:CBW	$12.95
☐ 21:ET	$9.95	☐ 45:CGW	$7.95
☐ 22:EC	$9.95	☐ 46:CWT	$12.95
☐ 23:NES	$14.95	☐ 47:CMP	$12.95
☐ 24:SH	$8.95	☐ 48:CGT	$7.95

Canadian Customers
Order Toll-Free 1-800-561-4169

Additional Books Sub-Total .... $_____
ADD Postage and Handling .... $ 3.00
Sales Tax: (AZ, CA, DC, IL, MI, MN, NY & WA residents, please add appropriate state and local tax.) $_____
YOUR TOTAL (Sub-Total, Postage/Handling, Tax) $_____

YOUR ADDRESS (Please print)

Name _____

Street _____

City _____ State_____ Zip _____

Phone (_____) _____ — _____

YOUR PAYMENT
Check one: ☐ Check ☐ Visa ☐ MasterCard ☐ Discover Card
Required credit card information:

Credit Card Number_____

Expiration Date (Month/Year) _____ / _____

Signature Required _____

 Home Planners, A Division of Hanley-Wood, Inc.
3275 W Ina Road, Suite 110, Dept. BK, Tucson, AZ 85741

TB55

ABOUT THE DESIGNERS

The Blue Ribbon Designer Series™ is a collection of books featuring the home plans of a diverse group of outstanding home designers and architects known as the Blue Ribbon Network of Designers. This group of companies is dedicated to creating and marketing the finest possible plans for home construction on a regional and national basis. Each of the companies exhibits superior work and integrity in all phases of the stock-plan business including modern, trendsetting floor planning, a professionally executed blueprint package and a strong sense of service and commitment to the consumer.

Design Basics, Inc.

For nearly a decade, Design Basics, a nationally recognized home design service located in Omaha, has been developing plans for custom home builders. Since 1987, the firm has consistently appeared in *Builder* magazine, the official magazine of the National Association of Home Builders, as the top-selling designer. The company's plans also regularly appear in numerous other shelter magazines such as *Better Homes and Gardens, House Beautiful* and *Home Planner.*

Design Traditions

Design Traditions was established by Stephen S. Fuller with the tenets of innovation, quality, originality and uncompromising architectural techniques in traditional and European homes. Especially popular throughout the Southeast, Design Traditions' plans are known for their extensive detail and thoughtful design. They are widely published in such shelter magazines as *Southern Living* magazine and *Better Homes and Gardens.*

Alan Mascord Design Associates, Inc.

Founded in 1983 as a local supplier to the building community, Mascord Design Associates of Portland, Oregon began to successfully publish plans nationally in 1985. With plans now drawn exclusively on computer, Mascord Design Associates quickly received a reputation for homes that are easy to build yet meet the rigorous demands of the buyers' market, winning local and national awards. The company's trademark is creating floor plans that work well and exhibit excellent traffic patterns. Their motto is: "Drawn to build, designed to sell."

Larry E. Belk Designs

Through the years, Larry E. Belk has worked with individuals and builders alike to provide a quality product. After listening to over 4,000 dreams and watching them become reality all across America, Larry's design philosophy today combines traditional exteriors with upscale interiors designed for contemporary lifestyles. Flowing, open spaces and interesting angles define his interiors. Great emphasis is placed on providing views that showcase the natural environment. Dynamic exteriors reflect Larry's extensive home construction experience, painstaking research and talent as a fine artist.

Home Planners

Headquartered in Tucson, Arizona, with additional offices in Detroit, Home Planners is one of the longest-running and most successful home design firms in the United States. With over 2,500 designs in its portfolio, the company provides a wide range of styles, sizes and types of homes for the residential builder. All of Home Planners' designs are created with the care and professional expertise that fifty years of experience in the home-planning business affords. Their homes are designed to be built, lived in and enjoyed for years to come.

Donald A. Gardner Architects, Inc.

The South Carolina firm of Donald A. Gardner was established in response to a growing demand for residential designs that reflect constantly changing lifestyles. The company's specialty is providing homes with refined, custom-style details and unique features such as passive-solar designs and open floor plans. Computer-aided design and drafting technology resulting in trouble-free construction documents places the firm at the leading edge of the home plan industry.

The Sater Design Collection

The Sater Design Collection has a long established tradition of providing South Florida's most diverse and extraordinary custom designed homes. Their goal is to fulfill each client's particular need for an exciting approach to design by merging creative vision with elements that satisfy a desire for a distinctive lifestyle. This philosophy is proven, as exemplified by over 50 national design awards, numerous magazine features and, most important, satisfied clients. The result is an elegant statement of lasting beauty and value.

Home Design Services, Inc.

For the past fifteen years, Home Design Services of Longwood, Florida, has been formulating plans for the sun-country life-style. At the forefront of design innovation and imagination, the company has developed award-winning designs that are consistently praised for their highly detailed, free-flowing floor plans, imaginative and exciting interior architecture and elevations which have gained international appeal.

Frank Betz Associates, Inc.

Frank Betz Associates, Inc., located in Smyrna, Georgia, is one of the nation's leaders in the design of stock plans. FBA, Inc. has provided builders and developers with home plans since 1977. With their vast knowledge of the speculative home builders business, they specialize in products for a wide variety of locations, price ranges, and markets. Frank Betz Associates, Inc. prides itself in its bi-annual plan magazine, *HOMEPLANS, Designed for Today's Market,* released every February and August featuring the firm's newest and most innovative plans.